ALL CRY
CHAOS

AN HENRI POINCARÉ MYSTERY

ALL CRY
CHAOS

LEONARD ROSEN

The Permanent Press
Sag Harbor, NY 11963

Henri Poincaré, 1854–1912, was a leading mathematician of his day. His great grandson, Interpol agent Henri Poincaré, and all other characters in this novel are creations of the author. No character in this work is intended to resemble a real person, living or dead. Any such resemblance is coincidental.

For information, address:
The Permanent Press
4170 Noyac Road
Sag Harbor, NY 11963
www.thepermanentpress.com

Library of Congress Cataloging-in-Publication Data

Rosen, Leonard J.–
    All cry chaos : an Henri Poincaré mystery / Leonard Rosen.
        p.   cm.
    ISBN 978-1-57962-222-0 (alk. paper)
        1. International Criminal Police Organization—Officials
    and employees—Fiction. 2. International relations—Fiction.
    3. Murder—Investigation—Fiction. I. Title.

PS3618.O83148A79 2011
813'.6—dc22   2010044002

Printed in the United States of America.

For Esther and Sidney—
my foundation; and
for Matthew, Jonathan, and Linda—
my windows and skylight.

ACKNOWLEDGEMENTS

One cannot write about fractals without acknowledging a debt to Benoit Mandelbrot, whose insights into the geometry of Nature have profoundly influenced modern science and, at least in this work, the modern imagination.

I owe a special debt to James D. Jones (U.S. Navy, retired), my math tutor—patient, good-humored, and an expert on fractals and chaos theory; Moshe Waldoks and Meir Sendor, who created a sanctuary in which I could explore the questions that frame this novel; my agent Eve Bridburg, who not only found the project a home but pushed me to revise until a story emerged that was equal to my intention. Without her critical eye, this would have been a very different book. Doug Starr commented on numerous drafts, often seeing possibilities I overlooked. He is a tough and loyal critic, a good friend, and a coach for all seasons. Arthur Golden commented on drafts and has long been generous with his advice. Todd Shuster showered an unknown author with the sort of close editorial attention that has made the Zachary, Shuster, Harmsworth Literary Agency a standout. All these efforts would have come to naught were it not for Marty and Judy Shepard, publishers of The Permanent Press. They have welcomed me and shown extraordinary enthusiasm for *All Cry Chaos*. I cannot imagine having more thoughtful or devoted advocates.

Thanks also to Susan Ahlquist, Beth Keister, Lon Kirschner, Joslyn Pine, Kathy Porter, Graham Orr, Jessica Schwartz, and Jessica Stein for wise counsel in various stages of manuscript development. The following people also read early drafts and offered helpful criticism: Larry Behrens, Martha Brand, Jeffrey Chin, Adam Cohen, Will Cohen, Aaron Cooper, Tina Feingold, Larry Heffernan, Suzanne Heffernan, Kathy Koman, Stuart Koman, Lester Lefton, Mindy Lubber, Emma Marks,

Richard Marks, Bob Morrison, Jenny Morrison, Mark Pevsner, Jeanette Polansky, Rosalie Renbaum, Jed Schwartz, Monica Sidor, Barry Siegel, Jane Siegel, Lois Slade, Frank Sladko, Abe Stein, Norman Stein, and Dean Sudarsky.

I'm a bit gray for a debut; but being an older writer has its advantages, one of which is the pleasure of having adult sons as critics. Jonathan and Matthew Rosen were in-house witnesses to the evolution of this book. They have seen it, and me, through a long process; their support and advice have been invaluable. Robert and Gerald Rosen, my brothers, have offered nothing but encouragement and affection these many years. I celebrate with them the commitment to family on which this novel rests. Most important is Linda Rosen, touchstone for three decades and author of so much that is precious in my life. To Linda, our sons, and the memory of my parents I dedicate this book.

In the Temple, all say "Glory!"
In the streets, all cry "Chaos!"
Who can see the order in the whirlwind?
Who can see the pattern in the wildness?
Who dares cry "Glory" in the midst of chaos?

— R. SHAPIRO, *after Psalm 29*

PROLOGUE

He could not approach the grave all at once. Instead, Henri Poincaré wandered the Cimetière du Montparnasse until the gloom drew him in and down to a place where he could hear spirits scuttling, calling his name.

For thirteen years he had come, circling past monuments to poets, philosophers, artists, and scientists—heroes of the republic all. As a young inspector, he believed that one day he might rest among them, beside his great-grandfather, as a reward for his service to country and love of justice. His ambitions had been that large, driving him not merely to solve cases but to solve them with a fortitude and intelligence that would credit the family name.

What a fool he had been. To restore this one life, he would have given his own a thousand times over. He would have signed away his soul. Yet no devil's bargain, not even suicide, could have canceled his existence. For Poincaré *had* lived and had hurt the ones he loved, the most terrible proof of which lay in a quiet corner of this cemetery.

He walked, therefore, until half shadow himself he stood over the grave.

Clouds churned and trees moaned. He would measure out his life this way: in an overnight train from the Dordogne each week, arriving at noon to clean the granite and exchange new flowers for old. An efficient man would have cleared the debris in minutes; but this man had borrowed a broom from the caretaker's shed and swept for an hour. He plucked a last wind-driven scrap and marveled that it was spring again. He did not understand why the daffodils still bloomed. But they did . . . even here in the cemetery. And the songbirds were back and the trees were leafing out. It should have been a comfort.

He knelt and with his good hand set fresh lilies on the grave. *Dear heart*, he said. *They killed the wrong person. They should have killed me.*

PART I

What is the way to the abode of light?
And where does darkness reside?

— JOB 38:19

CHAPTER 1

When he entered the cellblock, Henri Poincaré braced himself for the clank of steel doors coupling, which produced in him a physical effect not unlike the dysentery he once contracted drinking bad water in Senegal. A long career had made him no stranger to prison corridors; yet the clank of steel on steel still ripped through his insides like a disease bent on killing him, which it did, in its way, with every visit. The extortionists, the counterfeiters and Ponzi schemers, the assassins who for the love of money would take one life at a time and the fanatics who would weep if they killed fewer than fifty: those condemned to these cages thought themselves superior but misunderstood, justified in what they snatched from the world. In Poincaré's estimate, they deserved the daily reminder of these clanging doors, and most of all they deserved each other.

Which is to say, Stipo Banović kept good company.

Cathedral light from high, fixed windows cut through the upper air of the cellblock, though little of the Dutch springtime made its way inside. Here was the prison and this the block reserved for celebrities of a sort, war criminals awaiting trial in The Hague's international court. Four months earlier, at the end of a lengthy search that had taken him to six countries and two continents, Poincaré had found Stipo Banović living in a suburb of Vienna with his young bride and their son and daughter. On the evening men with battering rams knocked through his front door, Banović had been reading bedtime stories to these same children, who sat in his lap in an easy chair by the fire. The very picture of domestic happiness, save for the fact that Banović had in another lifetime personally ordered and participated in the massacre of seventy Muslim men and boys—some younger than the ringleted beauties in his lap that evening. His wife cried bitterly and his children cried as Banović screamed in perfect if heavily accented English: "Can't you see I've started over? I'm leading a *good* life!"

That was not for Poincaré to decide. Before they assigned him the case, his superiors at Interpol-Lyon sent him to the ravine where those bodies lay. It was springtime in the former Yugoslavia, and the snow melt had made traveling to the site a muddy ordeal. But the day was crisp and green shoots were emerging and everywhere the sound of water flowing suggested the possibility of life. Everywhere but in that shadowed ravine, where the stillness of bleached bones and the flapping fragments of cloth dropped him to his knees. No, it was not for Poincaré to decide or to forgive. He had done his job and the courts would do theirs.

He was already busy with another case, supervising security at the ministerial meetings of the World Trade Organization in Amsterdam. This visit was unnecessary, but he had come to face Banović one last time before catching his train, much as he would check to see the fire was off in the kitchen before leaving on a trip. The man, unattended, was dangerous. Poincaré needed to see him in his place, behind bars.

"As I live and breathe," said the prisoner at the approach of footsteps.

"Good news, Stipo. I'm officially off your case. Reassigned. It's enough to make one sentimental . . . all the time I spent hunting you."

Banović turned away. His plaid shirt buttoned to the collar and his wire-rimmed glasses lent the former death squad commander an aspect very like the librarian he was before the Bosnian war: high forehead, small boned, a pianist's fingers. He looked more the scholar than the mass murderer, an impression only strengthened by the fortress of law books he had amassed for his upcoming trial.

His back still turned, Banović said: "It was war time. Ugly things happened. You have your witnesses, those traitorous sons of whores. But the law gives me precedent, Inspector. Battle conditions. Men are beasts, it's true—as even a cursory reading of history will attest. Do you know what Titus's soldiers did to the Jews fleeing Jerusalem?"

"I don't really care," said Poincaré, approaching the bars.

Banović glanced over his shoulder. "They cut living men and women open to look for swallowed gold."

If Poincaré faced him alone in the forests of Bosnia, beyond the reach of law, he knew he would have died and suffered considerably in the process. As it was, standing before this cage was rather like standing in a zoo before a predator high on the food chain. The steel offered some assurance, but even so Banović radiated a danger that backed Poincaré away and made his heart beat erratically. This job had never been easy. Friends predicted that with his fondness for opera and arcane journals he would last all of three weeks. Three decades later, notwithstanding his successes, he wondered if he was truly cut out for this work.

"Years I ran," said the prisoner in a low, rasping voice. "The fight ended. I deserved a life, as combatants do. Now look at me, gagging on law books and reduced to kissing photos of my children. You are responsible, Poincaré. The others Interpol sent showed some common sense, some human concern—an appreciation for my circumstance. I warned them away and they broke off their searches. But you . . ." He reached for a photograph and slowly traced a finger.

How could the man bear to look at those children? If Poincaré lived to be a hundred he would not forget what lay in that ravine, the bones of young ones reaching for fathers, brothers, neighbors—men who, if they reached back, could offer only a willingness to die first. And all of them left to rot until the snows came. "I could have broken off the search," Poincaré agreed. "There was a war. You *were* a combatant."

The prisoner nodded.

"And now that the war is over and you have a new family, you want to go home."

Banović closed his eyes at the thought.

"Like those men and boys wanted to go home. Did they beg for mercy, Stipo? Did they pray?"

The prisoner stared down the corridor, and Poincaré wondered if his words had registered. They had—and the response, when it came, was saw-blade jagged: "Bad things happen in war," said Banović.

"But then you never fought a war. So don't talk to me. Don't you *dare* judge me."

"Not to worry, Stipo. The court will do that."

The cellblock was half the length of a soccer field, the two men the sole representatives of their species on that square of earth.

The prisoner laughed. "Why the visit?"

Poincaré stared at him.

"Come on, now—a clever man like you."

"You disgust me."

"Ah—honesty! There's a start!" Banović held up two fingers, a peace sign, and pointed them at Poincaré's eyes, then his own. "I do declare, Inspector: you came to look in the mirror."

"Go to hell."

"Too late . . . I've been here years already. Admit it—I *fascinate* you!"

"What I admit is a strong desire to see you rot."

"And keep the world safe from bogeymen like me?" Once more he pointed to Poincaré's eyes, then his own. "Take a closer look. . . . You know, you really should have killed me when you had the chance."

Poincaré leaned close to the bars. "I nearly did," he whispered, drawing Banović closer still. "It would have been an easy thing to report that the arrest went bad and we shot you. But that would have been your way. No. I saw what you left in the ravine. You'll stand trial, you'll be convicted, and you'll rot."

Not before he was halfway down the corridor did the wave of bellowing and invective rush past him like effluent from a sewage pipe. "They were animals! You read my file, Poincaré. You knew I had a family! Three children raped and disemboweled—in front of their mother, my Sylvie. Sylvie raped in front of her parents! Then her womb with our unborn child split open and her parents left to stagger through their lives, begging for someone to kill them. You *read* that, Inspector! And still you came. Did you once stop to think why a man becomes a killing machine? I was an ordinary man. A *good* man! I had a family, a job. Then a war I did not make and did not want ruined us. I will put you in my shoes before I die. I swear, you will walk in my shoes!"

I don't let people go, the inspector said to himself, repeating the words like a talisman to get him through the gate at the end of the cellblock, and through another gate, and through another until the final gate closed, steel on steel, and he stood outside the prison walls beyond the reach of Banović's agony. *These are not my decisions.* Poincaré leaned hard against a truck and slipped two pills between his lips.

He felt an attack coming on.

The train from The Hague to Amsterdam ran past acres of fields laid out in rectangles gaudy with color. Against a screen of heavy clouds rumbling off the North Sea, the famous Dutch tulips were an antidote to weariness itself. Poincaré needed the help. More than he cared to admit, Banović had unnerved him. Even now, an hour later, his heart beat erratically—if not from fear exactly then from the knowledge that a prodigious hatred was trained on him. *It's nothing life-threatening*, doctors had assured him. *A nuisance arrhythmia. Too much wine can bring it on. Also cold drinks, and sometimes stress. Do you have a stressful job?*

Soon enough, the pills would kick his heart back into a normal rhythm, and his life would begin to look orderly again. It had all happened before, this confrontation with the blunted, redirected rage of men he had put behind bars. He would set aside Banović's outburst, as he had learned long ago to do.

He flipped open his phone and waited through dead air, hoping she would answer. "It's me," he said finally.

"Ah—Henri! Are you OK? You sound tired."

"Not exactly."

"It's that man in Den Haag. You said you would quit him."

"I know."

"Well, then . . . quit him. Etienne called last night. He and Lucille and the children will join us at the farmhouse after all. You know what an ordeal it is for them to juggle their schedules. Promise—take it easy with work until we're back in Lyon."

"You know I'll be busy through the weekend," he said.

She did not answer. She hardly needed to.

"I'll come straight home from Amsterdam. I promise."

"Enough already. Retire."

A distinct possibility, given the morning. For the thirty years he had worked at Interpol, rising through the ranks, he had taken virtually no holiday that had not been delayed or interrupted by some special request from headquarters. Once, in Patagonia, in a river basin as remote as the Marianas Trench, a local official arrived on horseback to request that on returning to France might Inspector Poincaré first consult with the national police in Buenos Aires on a matter of stolen art. "Interpol-Lyon telex," began the official, hat in hand and so clearly apologetic for interrupting a family on holiday that Poincaré hadn't the heart to object. Claire, by contrast, placed her hands over the young Etienne's ears and, rather than attempting to kill the messenger, turned on her husband. "Could we be any further from civilization, Henri? Should we try for the Arctic next time?"

It would not have mattered. Interpol put Poincaré to strategic use, holiday or no. He had become for many in the security offices of Western Europe and the Americas the agent who had aged with grace. What he had lost physically he gained in intuition. He could anticipate a criminal's moves as if he were the pursued, and his perseverance was legendary—Banović's capture being only the latest example.

Persistence did take its toll, however; on days like this his heart argued for less strenuous work, and he considered retiring to the Dordogne. But he could not, just yet, because the question that had drawn him so improbably to police work—how to hold in one thought the abomination of a Banović in a world that was, in so many ways, sweet beyond description—had not been answered.

There was always the next case.

CHAPTER 2

Paolo Ludovici was a sinewy whip of a man. On loan from Interpol's National Central Bureau in Milan, he met Poincaré at Amsterdam Centraal and handed him a dossier, sparing them both preambles. "Trouble," he said. "While you were in The Hague, an explosion blew the top off a hotel along the Herengracht."

"No rest for the weary," Poincaré said, opening the file.

"We don't know if it was related to the World Trade Organization meetings. But the apparent victim was James Fenster, a tenured mathematician from Harvard who was scheduled to give a talk at the Friday morning session. Graduate and undergraduate degrees from Princeton. No wife, no dependents. Born in New Jersey. Politically agnostic. No debt to speak of."

Ludovici grabbed one of the coffees Poincaré had bought and slipped into an unmarked car borrowed from the Dutch police. "Fenster was the one registered to the room, in any event. What's left of him looks like burnt roast beef."

Poincaré closed his eyes.

"He was thirty. . . . Christ, I'm thirty."

"Tell me something useful, Paolo."

"Alright. Dental records will be faxed from Boston. The Massachusetts police have already secured Fenster's office and apartment. They're collecting samples for a DNA analysis that we'll compare with the results we get off the remains. But there's not much question about *who*, Henri. A hotel clerk confirmed that Fenster picked up the room key to 4-E at the front desk twenty minutes before the explosion. Video cameras in the lobby show him entering the hotel at 9:41. The bomb detonated at 10:03, erasing room 4-E." Ludovici started the car. "And for your information, the bomber used ammonium perchlorate."

"Qu'est-ce que c'est?"

"Rocket fuel."

Paolo revved the engine and pulled the Renault onto Prins-Hendrikkade as if merging onto a Grand Prix course. Just as quickly, he slammed on the brakes to avoid an old man pedaling quarter-time, mid-street, spilling Poincaré's coffee.

He twisted hard off the seat and watched a stain spreading across his lap. "Paolo!"

"It's only coffee, for Christ's sake. Get over it." Ludovici honked and threw the car into gear. "I'll pay for the cleaners."

He was furious, but Ludovici didn't notice or didn't care. Poincaré grabbed a wad of napkins from the glove box. The good news was that the shock had pumped enough adrenaline through his system to snap his heart back into rhythm. He checked his pulse to be sure—ba-bump . . . ba-bump . . . ba-bump, a veritable metronome—then dabbed at the coffee stain with the napkins. Paolo had done him a favor after all, but he would arrive at the crime scene looking like an incontinent schoolboy.

What could be done with Ludovici? Poincaré's sometimes protégé, whom he had requested for this assignment, was a package one accepted completely or not at all. He operated at a single speed, fast forward, his metabolism rivaling that of a hummingbird. He routinely worked eighteen-hour days, boosting the efficiency of anyone who wandered into his orbit. He ate quickly, talked quickly, reached conclusions, generally correct, quickly, and cycled through girlfriends with a speed and callousness that shocked even the open-minded Poincaré.

He was also handsome, not so much magazine pretty as supremely self-confident, which in many creates the same impression. People noticed when he entered a room. He had a fondness for coats slung across his shoulders, Fellini-esque, and more generally a sense of style that Poincaré could tolerate only in Italians. His single worrisome flaw was a habit of taking chances, some foolish, with a near-deluded confidence that nothing could touch him. The day they met, on assignment in Marseille two years earlier, Ludovici had defied direct orders by entering a drug smuggler's hotel room without a protective vest, without a wire, without a weapon, just to "talk." Two dozen special operations police had surrounded the hotel, each positioned behind a protective barrier. The agent and the fugitive had their chat, within full view of snipers' scopes, and an hour later Ludovici emerged alone. "He wants pizza and a bottle of Mas de Gourgonnier 2002," he said when the others pressed him for news. So the command sent out for pizza and found the wine. The fugitive ate and, after profoundly miscalculating the chances of shooting his way out of a tight spot, died by a single sniper shot to the head. When Poincaré went to introduce himself to the young agent who had discovered the smuggling ring in Brindisi and, through Interpol-Lyon, arranged for this welcome party in Marseille, he found Ludovici sitting alone on an upended crate eating the last of the dead man's pizza. "You don't suppose this has any forensic value, do you?" he asked.

Poincaré liked him immediately.

"The title of his talk . . . give me a second." Ludovici wrestled a scrap from his pocket and read while weaving through heavy traffic. He slammed the car to a stop again, this time inches from a teenager who had stepped from a curb, his pommes frites and mayonnaise now scattered on the road. Paolo rolled down the window and threw money at the problem, yelling for the kid to watch where he was going. "The Mathematical Inevitability of a One-World Economy," he said, turning to Poincaré. The teenager banged the hood of the car with a fist before Ludovici sped off. "*Inevitability* of a One-World Economy? Fenster must have been the darling of the WTO. This explains why he was in town, anyway."

They sped through a square with a plump Dutch merchant from the city's Golden Age frozen on a pedestal, clasping a book soiled by generations of pigeons. "Who," asked Poincaré, "kills a mathematician . . . ruling out the usual reasons—debt, failed romance, et cetera?" Traffic slowed several blocks ahead in another square presided over by yet another well-fed burgher. Beneath the statue, in a narrow rectangle defined by police barricades, a knot of protesters stood chanting: "WTO . . . *No*! WTO . . . *No*!" Poincaré noted the sign, a bed sheet painted with a cash register, its drawer open, straddling the earth. Where bills should have been, peasants labeled with Third-World country names were caught wriggling as if in a bear trap.

Ludovici hit the accelerator. "So who kills a mathematician, other than another mathematician? They're supposed to be jealous as hell of each other's success. Maybe the question is who would kill to sabotage the WTO?" He geared down to make a turn and pointed to a knot of emergency vehicles, their lights flashing.

Poincaré looked across the canal to a narrow, cobbled street with brick houses packed as tightly as kernels on an ear of corn. Centuries before, these had been warehouses, and many had fixed hoists used for lifting goods to the upper floors. Most hid their gabled roofs with brickwork in the shape of bells, steps, and spouts. But one building lacked an elaborate façade. Its top was blown off.

Ludovici set his jaw and nodded. "This is as close as we get," he said, parking the car. "We walk from here."

CHAPTER 3

The scene that greeted Poincaré at Herengracht 341, the Ambassade Hotel, defied understanding; for the devastation was confined precisely to one room on the top floor, as if a claw had descended from the clouds and plucked the room with its gabled roof, straight away. The hole left behind was hideous and gaping, in its way a work of art: the rooms on both sides and below the missing room were intact in the way a cake is intact when someone carefully removes a first slice. On the street—intermingled with shattered bricks, roof tiles, and beams thick enough to have framed old merchant ships—were some of the victim's personal effects, each with an evidence number: a sock, a pair of sunglasses with cracked lenses, a tube of American toothpaste, a ripped shirt. Poincaré turned from these remnants of an ordinary life, just as he turned from what lay beneath the blue tarp twenty meters to his left.

All this to kill one man?

The fire crews had left behind a soupy, rank-smelling mess, everything in their wake—cars, street, hotel, debris from the explosion—soaked with the canal water they had pumped to extinguish the blaze. Poincaré watched a man in blue coveralls and latex gloves arguing with one of the firemen.

"Forensics is angry as hell," said a woman. "The fire crews saved the block but drowned the evidence."

Gisele De Vries shook Poincaré's hand, insisting on formalities. As the local agent that Dutch security services had assigned as liaison to Interpol, De Vries was the one member of his team Poincaré had not personally selected. Interpol agents, by charter, held no powers of arrest and were bound in every case to work alongside local or national police of their host country. The flinty De Vries had immediately impressed Poincaré. Give her a data-gathering task and she would finish ahead of deadline, not only collecting information but presenting analyses in multiple views. Her desk was neat; her clothes, carefully pressed; her shoes, square-toed and sensible. Only her long, auburn hair, clasped loosely at her neck and hanging to mid-back, hinted at a rich inner life.

"If you didn't know better," she said, "you'd think someone carved out the room with a laser cannon from over there." She pointed across the canal, where a crowd had gathered.

She handed him a photograph. "Taken ten minutes ago from a police helicopter. The blast patterns are the same on both sides of the building, consistent with a bomb placed *here*, beneath the sink." On a second sheet she showed Poincaré a schematic of the hotel room. "Fenster must have been leaning over it at detonation. Aside from being burned beyond recognition, what's left of the torso is splintered with porcelain. And then there's this." She reached for a piece of wet, charred wood, sniffed, and held out her hand. Poincaré winced.

"Ammonium perchlorate," she said. "Rocket fuel, believe it or not. Burns like a flare and, under specific conditions, will explode. If the bomber had used as much C-4, the entire block would be gone. In fact, it was an elegant job."

Poincaré had seen the effects of all manner of explosives in his career, but this was a first: rocket fuel used for a purpose other than breaking heavy objects loose of Earth's gravity. "Not typical, is it."

"Hardly," said De Vries.

"Well, let's collect some residues." He sniffed the charred wood again. "Send samples to the lab here in Amsterdam for a quick analysis, but I also want the European Space Agency looking into this. And NASA. This could narrow our search."

"To die bent over a sink," said Ludovici. "I suppose there's a moral in that."

Poincaré glanced at the tarpaulin and, again, turned away—an aversion that had nothing to do with squeamishness. He had worked with his share of corpses; but he also lacked the capacity to regard them as pieces of meat once the heart stopped beating. There was this thing called Life—the way Claire would sometimes look up from her work and smile at him—and not Life. Death. Wonder at one entailed wonder at the other, and Poincaré simply could not feel nothing at the sight of a burnt-out corpse. Soon enough, he would shut down certain sensors and approach the remains.

"A moral?" came a booming, sepulchral voice from the hotel entrance, three steps below street grade. Serge Laurent clapped a hand on Ludovici's shoulder. "Young man, the moral here is that cleanliness is next to godliness."

Poincaré's closest friend and confidant in or out of the service checked his watch. "Almost three hours post-explosion and the desk clerk is still shaking. The man needs a new diaper and likely an injection of some sort, but he won't leave his station. Professional pride."

Poincaré watched Laurent note the coffee stain on his trousers and then restrain himself from making a crack about water management and men of a certain age. Both agents had given their careers to Interpol and were so unlike in temperament, so different in their approaches to a case, that no one could have predicted a friendship. If Poincaré faced oncoming force with a kind of mental jujitsu, side-stepping trouble and studying opponents as they tripped from their own momentum, Laurent preferred collisions. If he were a physicist, he would have smashed atoms for a living—precisely the quality that doomed his marriages.

"Forensics just about came to blows with the fire crew for making a mess of the crime scene," said Laurent. "Extracting evidence will be challenging in the extreme, but they've established one salient fact: clean prints off the doorknob to the room and the window cranks match prints on the room key, which match the left thumb and right index fingerprints of the victim—which, since you asked, are the only digits not reduced to jelly or blown into the canal. The torso was lodged in that tree"—he pointed—"and a leg knocked a guy off his bicycle." Laurent closed his notebook. "When I die, for pity's sake let it be in one piece."

Across the Herengracht, a crowd had gathered; some watched from open windows. "Alright, then," said Poincaré. "We've got internally consistent prints, which is not the same as a positive ID. What are we doing to confirm the ID?"

"Data from Boston is due tomorrow morning," said Laurent. "Oh—I nearly forgot." He opened a folder and produced a clear plastic evidence bag with a photograph, which he set, still in its bag, on the hood of a Mercedes half-crushed by a roof beam. "Fenster's— the victim's—prints are all over it." They gathered around the image.

Several moments passed. "Come on, people. It's not a game if no one plays. There's a caption on the back. Two euros to the winner."

Ludovici went first. "The spine of a mountain range. I flew over the Alps last week when I went home. Just like this—central spine fanning out to ridges."

"Gisele?"

"An angiogram. When my mother had a stroke, the doctors showed me a scan that looked something like this. It's a blood vessel, I think. But then again it could be a river with tributaries. Or the roots of a plant."

"Wrong again. Henri?"

"Spare us, Serge."

Laurent flipped the photo and read the caption. "Lightning. Negative image." And then: " 'Series 3, Image A, WTO talk.' Apparently, there are other images we haven't found. Destroyed, I suppose." He surveyed the wreckage. "How did no one else manage to die? Did you hear, there was another explosion today—in Milan. Old-fashioned dynamite."

"Milano?" said Ludovici. "Where?"

"Galleria Vittorio Emanuele."

"No. . . ." It was his birthplace. He dug into his jacket for a cell phone and left them to place a call.

"Six people died in that one," said Laurent. "A man wearing robes called on Jesus to heal the world, then blew himself up. There's nothing remotely religious about our bombing, I suppose."

De Vries thumbed through a sheaf of papers. "Nothing here about anyone wearing robes. I'll check into it. But did you say the reversed image of lightning was related to Fenster's talk? He was speaking on globalization, Serge. What's the connection?"

Laurent smiled. "That's what we call a mystery, my dear."

Chapter 4

Sunlight played across the floor of the bakery where Poincaré had come to gather his thoughts. The shop was quiet, a pair of café tables dominating the tiny space. The window display of fruit tarts and cookies had drawn Poincaré in, but he had chosen poorly. The proprietress, at first a model of Dutch hospitality, by small degrees suffocated him with attention: she cleaned his already spotless table as he began reviewing a long afternoon's case notes; she insisted on straightening a display of chocolates on a shelf by his shoulder; she even swept and mopped the floor, asking him to move. He stayed because this was the only coffee shop in the area and because he needed to sit with a cup of something warm.

"A *third* espresso," she said. "You're certain?"

He should have thanked her for the interruptions. What he had seen made too little sense, and sometimes he found that the straightest course to clarity required that he forget facts altogether and allow his mind to wander. This woman, at least, kept him from stitching one thought to the next.

"One couldn't properly call this a body," he had told the medical examiner not forty minutes earlier. All afternoon—whether he was examining what remained of the apartment, working alongside a firefighter to retrieve the shoe caught high in a tree, or bending over a field microscope to examine a sliver of porcelain—the victim's remains had called to Poincaré. Not until the men in hazard suits were preparing to shovel what was left of the victim into a bag did he steel himself for a look.

"Burn cases can be disturbing," Dr. Günter allowed. As medical examiner, she had taken charge of and controlled all access to the body at the crime scene. Before they met, Poincaré smelled her chewing gum from twenty paces and guessed she was the coroner, many of whom ended up addicted to mints of one sort or another. Something about the sweetness of decaying flesh followed them from the autopsy table, and oil of peppermint proved less complicated and less toxic than gin. "This one didn't suffer," she observed. "A man who knew what was coming would have turned away. He took the full impact here." With her telescoping pointer she touched what used to be the victim's chest, a cavity now blown open to the spinal column. "No lungs, no heart, no viscera: all tissues burned out. Notice that we see no impact wounds on the sides or back. He did not turn away."

Poincaré focused on the tip of the metal rod, trying to hold off his nausea by regarding the corpse as he might an anatomical chart. "He's no less dead for taking it full on," he said.

"True," replied Günter. "Care for a stick of gum?"

He declined.

"Henri, stop by my office on Sunday, and we'll review the case file. By then, I'll have received the DNA report from Boston and we'll have processed our own labs." She dropped the tarpaulin. "Dead is dead," she observed with all the emotion one musters for covering a pile of leaves. "I'll reconstruct the *how*," she said, "and you, my friend, will reconstruct *who* and *why*. These will be the last favors anyone can do for him."

He stared out the shop window to a small, bricked court-yard, contemplating what favors the world owed the dead. He had answered that question once when he spent the better part of two years hunting Banović. He glanced over his case notes and supposed he would be answering it again. "You'll get jittery with all the caffeine," the woman warned, setting down his espresso and yet another plate of cookies. "I use Sumatran beans, roasted in one kilo batches to concentrate potency. Here—you can smell the potency." She inhaled deeply. "Do you smell it? I would eat the cookies for ballast if nothing else. Did you know—"

Poincaré pointed to the two plates, uneaten, already crowding the table. He held up a hand. "Please, no more."

"But you get three with each cup. That's our special on Thursdays. Three cookies, one cup. Three for one. Did you read the sign?" She pointed to the counter.

"My Dutch," he said, "is not very good."

"No matter, I'll wrap them."

"No, thank you. Please."

"I insist. I make them right here." She leaned over to show him her latest batch. "This one I call the Fantine. Do you see the shape— the profile of a young woman wearing a bonnet. She's sweet but was wronged. This is why the lemon, for tartness. She's also angry, which explains the dash of cayenne."

Poincaré stood to leave, and she grabbed his arm.

"Alright, then. I'll just set these down on the counter and go to the kitchen."

She retreated behind a curtain, and he reached for a newspaper folded on the table beside him, opening to the financial pages. Since he and Claire had bought a farm in the Dordogne, Poincaré was in the habit of checking the London and Paris stock exchanges to monitor the health of their investments. Between his salary and the several paintings she sold each year through galleries in Paris and New York, they had paid for their apartment in Lyon and for Etienne's schooling. Eight years earlier, free of debt and anticipating a serene, if not lavish, retirement, they had rejected the advice of two financial consultants and heavily mortgaged themselves to buy a vineyard in the south, complete with a leaky stone farmhouse. It made no sense, this projection of themselves into a bucolic future, for neither of them had farmed much more than harvesting tomatoes from a potted plant or two. Yet while on holiday that year, they amused themselves one afternoon by touring a property that sat on the crest of a hill overlooking working vineyards, a distant river, and an ancient village. It took them no more than fifteen minutes to say yes to an absurdity, and now Poincaré checked the markets daily, his hopes for early retirement waxing and waning with the fortunes of Airbus and Sumitomo Metal Industries Ltd.

As he folded the paper and prepared to leave the coffee shop, he noticed a news brief reporting on the murder of a gang counselor in Barcelona. The young woman, much admired by the police who employed her and beloved by the gangs whose members she counseled, had received citations of merit from the city and been acknowledged at an international conference on the prevention of youth violence. Murdered, then? The news reverberated beyond Barcelona, not the least reason being the circumstance in which the body was found: seated at her desk at the community center, a single gunshot to the back of the head and a note pinned to her blouse quoting Matthew 24: 24.

Notwithstanding all he had seen in his years chasing bad people, Poincaré was still capable of outrage. This morning he had concluded one chapter on a mass murderer; this afternoon he opened another with an assassination. Tomorrow—who knew? On days like this he longed for a more pedestrian life. He made a note to find the passage in Matthew and check the Interpol files on the Milan bombing. Apparently, both involved an appeal to Jesus. While none had been made prior to the Herengracht bombing, Poincaré had seen stranger connections and wanted to confirm that, in Milan, no professors or mathematicians had died. He downed his espresso. *James Fenster*, he thought. What remained of the man was just a few BTU's short of cremation.

He left too large a tip and stepped outside to a day much improved over the past week of steady rain. Sunlight bursting through clouds over that section of the Herengracht gave the famously flat city a towering, vertical dimension. The breeze, freshening from the west, carried a hope of drier days if not clearer thinking. He retraced his steps to the Ambassade, hands deep in his pockets, recalling his less than satisfying conversation with the lead investigator from the Amsterdam police. The bald little man had embarrassed himself in his haste to give the case away. "It's true," Poincaré had allowed. "One doesn't often see a bomb made out of rocket fuel."

"No doubt originating beyond our borders," responded the man, a few inches taller than he was round. "The victim appears not to be Dutch, so on both counts Interpol must lead this case. If we can help in any way, however . . ." Done, then: the case not just handed off but thrown, airmailed, to Poincaré. It was just as well, since Lyon would want to track down the source of the ammonium perchlorate.

The to-do list on Poincaré's notepad was growing. Laurent would speak with Fenster's contacts at the World Trade Organization in the morning to learn more about the scheduled talk. Poincaré would discover what he could about Fenster's research. Ludovici had already begun sorting through the list of protesters presently in Amsterdam and would be recommending several for interviews. And De Vries had made progress. From the hotel's registry she had learned that Fenster, accompanied by a woman named Madeleine Rainier, had stayed at the Ambassade at least three times in the previous eighteen months. On this visit, however, Fenster alone signed the guest register. They would need to find Rainier. The hotel had kept a photocopy of her passport on file.

"You say the manager recognized Fenster?" he had asked De Vries.

"Correct. He makes a habit of learning the names of repeat guests. . . . Here's the Ambassade's guest register for the last two years, with the past two weeks clipped on top." She showed Poincaré the printout. "I'll interview everyone who's currently registered or who checked out within the past several days. This will take some time. I'll also need a day or so to get the names from surrounding hotels." They had spoken two hours earlier, which may as well have been two minutes; for across the canal, De Vries was now waving an arm in his direction and walking briskly. They met mid-bridge. "She's here."

"Who?"

"Madeleine Rainier, the woman who registered with Fenster before, at the Ambassade." She turned and pointed behind her, directly across the canal. "Checked into the Hotel Ravensplein last Wednesday. She's in her room *now*, Henri. The desk clerk handed her a key not more than twenty minutes ago."

CHAPTER 5

The lobby of the Hotel Ravensplein reminded Poincaré of street corners he used to avoid as a teenager. A buzzing soft drink dispenser with a cracked display blocked the emergency exit. Overhead, what might have been a useful, even elegant chandelier in the 1940s threw more shadow than light. The wallpaper was torn, and Poincaré reflexively checked for figures lurking in the corners. At the registration desk, a teenager with purple hair and a pierced lip sat reading a magazine, ignoring him. When he slid his badge across the desk, she rose and backed away.

He took no pleasure in that. However reasonable he thought himself around young people, flanked by Ludovici and De Vries he became imposing by association. The receptionist's eyes darted to the gym bags that Poincaré's associates carried. Paolo shifted his weight, and one could hear a clink of metal.

"This is about the explosion?" she asked.

"That's right, young lady."

De Vries stepped forward. "The clerk who was here before you told me Madeleine Rainier was staying in 4B. Is she still there?" Behind the desk, an empty mail slot for that room answered the question: Rainier had taken the room key on her way upstairs.

"I'd better call my manager," said the girl.

Ludovici started for the stairs, but Poincaré grabbed his coat. "Pardon us," he said. "Make your call, but it would be better if we could go now." Paolo shifted, but Poincaré held tight.

"Will I get in trouble?"

Poincaré released his hold. At the fourth-storey landing, Ludovici slid the safety off the gun he kept holstered beneath his jacket. Gisele stepped to the right of the door, out of harm's way, and banged three times.

They waited, and she banged again.

This time they heard footsteps. A chain slid into place before the door opened, first a crack, then a few inches until the chain pulled taut and Poincaré could see a vertical slice of face. Gray, bloodshot eye set behind a thick lens. Cleft chin. Pale. Tall.

"Yes?"

"Police," said De Vries, thrusting her badge into the opening. "Madeleine Rainier?"

The head bobbed.

"We want to discuss the explosion at the Ambassade Hotel."

Poincaré watched Rainier scan the slice of hallway visible through the opening. "And that requires three of you? Let me see your warrant."

"I appreciate your hesitancy," said Poincaré, stepping forward. He offered his card through the slot. "Please call Interpol in Lyon to confirm our identity. Call them now, or your embassy. We'll wait until you're satisfied—or leave if you're not. We have no warrant."

The door closed, and when a deadbolt slid into place, Ludovici pinned Poincaré with a scowl. An hour earlier he had argued strenuously for arresting Rainier on the grounds that bombers sometimes enjoy watching their handiwork and that this room offered a perfect vantage point. Besides, the fact that Rainier avoided roasting along with Fenster when she was *in* Amsterdam and her residency pattern would have placed her at Fenster's side in the Ambassade raised suspicions. Ludovici lost that battle and settled, barely, for a warrantless interview. Now he made no effort to hide his irritation: "Henri, we should have brought in tea service. That would have refreshed Miss Rainier, and then when we were all feeling happy, we could ask if she killed James Fenster."

"She's a long way from being a suspect, Paolo."

"Give it time."

"I intend to," said Poincaré. "We gain nothing, and might lose a great deal, by intimidating her. In fact—" he looked at De Vries— "I would have knocked on the door gently. But then you both know this."

Ludovici routinely ignored conclusions he found inconvenient, one of the qualities Poincaré admired at their first meeting in Marseille.

Still, the younger man had the habit of pushing a half-step too far. Rather than argue the point, and to keep him occupied while they waited, Poincaré asked him to clear the rooms on that floor of the hotel. De Vries called Laurent to confirm that he and a detective borrowed from the Amsterdam police were in position at the front and rear entrances. Through the closed door Poincaré heard snatches of conversation and, finally, the sound of a phone being set in its cradle. Then footsteps again, a chain sliding off its track, and a deadbolt drawn. The door swung wide.

"I called the American Embassy, and they confirmed your identity, Inspector. They're not happy about an interview without one of their own present. But you're here and they aren't. They instructed me to let you in."

Exhaustion like a bird of prey had settled on this woman. Her skin was pale and waxy, and Poincaré half-wondered if he would find needle marks beneath the sleeve of her loose-fitting sweater. As she leaned against the door jamb for support, she knocked her eyeglasses askew—as if she'd forgotten they were there or was unaccustomed to wearing them. The glasses were not well fitted to the face, and with one lens substantially thicker than the other her gray eyes looked mismatched. A recent surgery, he supposed. Her hair was exactly the color of a wheat field awaiting harvest.

"Please," she offered. "There's a sitting room."

They followed her into a well-lit apartment, better appointed than the hotel lobby would have suggested, with a pair of facing couches, a writing table, a lamp, and an upholstered chair for reading. Poincaré saw no obvious signs of contraband, no bottles of medication. By whatever path she had staggered to her present, spent condition, she appeared to have done so honestly. But something had crushed her. For the moment he resisted the obvious and proceeded with his inquiry: "I assume you heard the explosion this morning?"

"I was out. But one could hardly miss the damage or all the attention now."

"What do you know about it, Miss Rainier?"

"Know? Aside from the fact it was massive . . . and frightening? Was anyone hurt?" Her voice was reed thin, and he strained to hear. She was in her late twenties, though in her present condition looked older.

"A man died," he said. "We believe you knew him."

Poincaré watched closely. When he spoke the name, Rainier groaned as though a foundation in her were cracking. "I must be direct," he continued. "The first hours are critical. On three occasions over the last eighteen months, you and Dr. Fenster stayed together at the Ambassade—directly across the canal from this hotel. This is true?"

She stared past De Vries and Ludovici, to the casement windows and a tangle of tree limbs just days from leafing out. The same breeze that floated curtains into the room carried music from a nearby street fair. Poincaré heard snatches of laughter and the pipes of a carousel. The evening might have been called lovely had they come on other business.

"Miss Rainier?"

"We stayed together. . . . Yes."

"Yet for this visit you registered here, with Dr. Fenster across the canal."

She wrapped her arms around herself and began to sway.

"Miss Rainier?"

"We were engaged to be married then," she whispered.

"Then?"

"Not now."

"You saw him in Amsterdam?"

"Dead. You're certain he's dead?"

Poincaré spared her his impression that nothing could be more dead than those charred bones. "He didn't suffer," he assured her. "The coroner reports that death was instantaneous and caught the victim completely unaware."

She sat on a yellow chintz couch, a mirror behind, a scuffed, coffee-stained table before her. De Vries and Ludovici stood off to the side, heavy roof beams angling above them. Poincaré sat opposite. Nothing moved save the sweep hand of a cheap windmill clock and the curtains lifting at the window. "Miss Rainier: did you see Dr. Fenster in Amsterdam?"

"We met for dinner when I arrived."

"And since?"

She shook her head.

"You're here because . . . ?"

"I buy and sell antiques, and Amsterdam is my base in Europe. James joined me the other times. The neighborhood is convenient for my work. This time when I was scheduled to visit, he said he'd booked the Ambassade for a conference. I decided to stay here. . . . The explosion—so much damage, Inspector. Only the one death?"

The effort to sit upright taxed her, and Poincaré considered detaining Rainier if only to send her to a hospital. "At that hour, the hotel was largely empty," he explained. "People had gone about their business, thank goodness. But much of the credit goes to the bomber's precise placement of explosives. There can be no doubt, Miss Rainier, that the bomber was a professional and that this was murder. Who might have wanted Dr. Fenster dead?"

She stared at the coffee table.

De Vries pulled aside a curtain for a better look at the canal in the lamplight. "Is it a coincidence that you visited Amsterdam the same time as Dr. Fenster?" she asked. "And that you had such a perfect angle from which to observe the explosion?"

Rainier continued staring.

"Miss Rainier?"

And then, with sudden violence: "*Perfect* angle? How *dare* you!"

"But you don't find any of this—what's the word in English?" De Vries searched the air as if the answer would appear in a bubble. "*Achterdochtig*. Suspicious—that's it. For me, at least, it raises the question why he died and you didn't. After all that time you spent together at the Ambassade . . . I'm thinking you should have died with him. Who broke the engagement, Miss Rainier?"

The brutality of that question jolted Poincaré. The answer mattered, but he would have found his way to it later, more gently. Rainier wept at the suggestion she was a bitter, jilted lover bent on revenge. When she finally composed herself enough to speak, she ignored De Vries and addressed Poincaré: "You saw his body?"

"I did."

"Perhaps you need me to iden—"

Poincaré declined. "There can be no mistake."

He did not have the heart to add that only a forensics lab could at this point pin a name to that disaster. He leaned forward, hands clasped, and regarded the woman. It was time for another, patient foray; but Paolo was restless for answers and Poincaré could not maneuver to block a blundering question: "Have you ever worked with explosives, Miss Rainier?"

The interview, barely begun, was over; but still Paolo continued: "We're searching for chemical residues," he said over a fresh paroxysm of tears. "We need your permission. So if there's nothing to hide . . ."

Rainier waved a hand between sobs, as if to say *Get on with your damned business and get out*, then signed a document that De Vries placed before her. De Vries snapped on latex gloves and pulled metal tongs from her gym bag, along with a supply of thin cotton discs. Using the tongs, she took a succession of discs and wiped each across a different surface in the room, including Rainier's handbag and luggage. She then dropped the discs into separate evidence bags, carefully labeling each. Paolo, meanwhile, explored the apartment, stepping into and out of view as he searched the bedroom and bathroom.

For the ten minutes they were occupied, Rainier had settled into a state of quiescent despair. Poincaré had seen some killers weep with remorse and some with relief at having finally done the deed. Others wept for not having killed sooner. At this point, he did not understand Rainier's grief, but it was real enough that he fought an urge to comfort her, an absurdity given the circumstance. If she had killed for love, as Paolo and Gisele suspected, then welcome, he thought, to the tangled history of the human heart. But Poincaré doubted the bombing could be explained so easily.

"I'm done," De Vries announced. Ludovici emerged from the bedroom at the same moment, sliding an evidence bag into his jacket. As Poincaré stood to leave, he turned to Rainier, who looked at him from across the coffee table as if across a freshly dug grave.

"I'm sorry to have delivered this news, Miss Rainier."

Five seconds, ten, would have been a decent enough interval before a final, necessary question. De Vries did not grant even that courtesy because for her the jugular was simply another vein. "How long will you be in Amsterdam, Miss Rainier?"

The woman's eyes wandered back to the curtains.

"Your schedule," insisted Ludovici.

"Tomorrow. I leave for Brussels tomorrow."

"Stay the weekend," Paolo suggested, scribbling something into a notebook as casually as if he were writing a parking ticket. "We might have additional questions. If you have other plans, cancel them—with all due respect, of course."

"What he means," Poincaré added quickly, "is that questions are all we have at this point, and we'd like to know where you—or anyone remotely connected to the case—can be found. It would be helpful."

"I did not kill James."

"No doubt the tests will confirm this. But someone did. We must do our job."

Unexpectedly, she reached for a large leather bag at the end of the couch, prompting Ludovici to slide a hand inside his jacket. Poincaré saw these movements unfold as if the two moved across a dance floor toward the other, in slow motion. He prayed Rainier would not be so foolish. If Paolo was rash in many respects, in the matter of firearms he practiced the strictest discipline. From close quarters to a thousand meters, he was the finest marksman Poincaré knew. Paolo kept his hand hidden and watched closely. If she emerged with a gun, he would shoot and Rainier would lose a finger or a hand.

She produced a calendar.

"I can stay," she announced. "I'll rearrange a meeting. I want to help."

Poincaré exhaled. Then, without explanation, Rainier turned to him and asked a question with her eyes as if she had lost something that only he could help her find. So frank, so unexpected was the query that she altogether froze him for an instant—one eye, behind those glasses, oddly larger than the other. Rainier studied him, and he studied her: the oval face and gray, almond eyes; the long, subtly sloping nose; the thin lips; the wisps of wheat-colored hair that framed so much turbulence. She was a slender ghost annihilated by exhaustion and some unspoken loss. She would not avert her gaze, and he looked more deeply.

Poincaré did not see a killer, but he did wonder how Rainier had managed to talk with them at all. No one could speak to another's grief; but Fenster had once been her fiancé, the emotional pivot of her life. If her grief was real at the news of his death, her shock that he had been murdered was not. That shock had registered earlier, Poincaré sensed, before their arrival—which explained why, when she first opened the door, he felt as if he had stumbled into the closing act of a largely completed tragedy. Before Gisele had banged on that hotel door, before he had broached sad news and studied her reaction, the explosion at the Ambassade had already desolated this woman.

In a moment it was over, this silent, puzzling interview of the interviewer. Rainier stood to see them leave, apparently having settled something for herself and having asked something of Poincaré—though what that might be he hadn't a clue.

CHAPTER 6

"Paolo," he said, reaching for a splinter of brick that had blown across the canal. Dozens of windows on the Ravensplein side of the Herengracht had shattered in the explosion, and property damage would be in the millions—a nightmare of insurance claims. "A scissors sometimes works better than a hand grenade."

Ludovici was just then tucking away his cell phone. "What's that, Henri?"

Poincaré reconsidered. With the WTO conference beginning the next day, lessons on subtlety could wait. He did not suppose he would be working with De Vries again, so correcting her for laying open Rainier's throat made little sense. But Paolo would need to learn. This time his protégé's rush to judgment had merely compromised an interview. One day it might get him killed. "I said the residues will come back negative. She didn't kill Fenster."

They approached a stone bridge that would deposit them a short distance from the Ambassade. Not one to mince words, Ludovici regarded the tree limbs swaying in the evening breeze and said, evenly: "And you deduced all this from her eyes? What brand of science went on back there?"

"It wasn't science, Paolo."

"Then tell me where to sign up for the course on reading souls. Jesus Christ, Henri—the woman knows more than she's saying. You deny that?"

"I don't. But this doesn't make her a murderer."

"We should arrest her."

"If the tests come back positive, we will. Gisele, can we get the results tonight?"

Across the canal, generators powered a bank of lamps positioned around the Ambassade, where workers swarmed over the remaining debris like beetles over a carcass. Poincaré watched them shovel shattered brick and glass onto a barge that would be floated down the canal and dumped in the North Sea. Tow trucks had already hauled away ruined cars, and the street would be cleared by the morning rush.

"If the lab bumps our evidence to the head of the line, we'll get the results. A big *if*," she added.

Ludovici produced two plastic bags from a pocket, one with a toothbrush and the other with strands of hair the color of ripened wheat. "While you're at it, ask them to run these."

Poincaré stopped.

"What?" said Paolo.

"When did you start working for Joseph Stalin?"

Paolo spun on his heels. "You're joking."

"I'm not."

"Did you see the woman?" With an exaggerated motion, he re-created the sweep of Rainier's arm that gave them permission to proceed with their search. "She clearly meant *search it all*, Henri, every room. She signed the paper."

"Under duress."

"Like hell. We could have ransacked the place and been legal."

"The document limited our search to chemical residues, not DNA. Toss it."

"*What?*"

"I said toss it."

Ludovici appealed to De Vries, who took a moment to unclip her hair before answering. "Settle it with pistols," she suggested. And then, to Ludovici: "He's right, you know. Rainier signed for a residue check. Your evidence won't stand in a Dutch court. Maybe North Korean. Why don't we petition for a change of venue?"

Ludovici walked a short distance, bellowing to no one in particular: "Frigging literalists!" To Poincaré he said: "You know, this is the reason bad guys win—because scrupulous pricks like you play by the rules."

Poincaré was having none of it. "This is not difficult, Paolo. You searched beneath her bed. And when you didn't see a box labeled ammonium perchlorate, big surprise, you collected her DNA. You went fishing."

"Correct. I fish, then eat. Do you know of a better way to survive?"

"I'm in the habit of establishing facts before arresting people. Or is this too old school for your tastes?"

Ludovici grinned.

"Very funny. Did you ever hear of Dmitri Kouric—maybe three or four years ago? He killed a dozen people in four countries with his bare hands, then ripped apart their bodies. A sociopath of the most twisted sort. Fingers, bits of intestines, what have you were showing up in random mailboxes. We built an airtight case and then watched him walk free because of tainted evidence. Because of an overzealous agent. *That*," said Poincaré, pointing, "is tainted evidence."

"I remember the man. A month later a truck ran him down in Budapest. What a coincidence, Henri. I don't believe they ever found the driver."

Poincaré said nothing.

"I thought so. We . . . what's the word I want, we *improvise* to satisfy the demands of common sense. This is common sense. The woman knows something, and her DNA will prove useful later. Don't worry," he added. "I won't hesitate to say *I told you so*."

"If you want her DNA, get a warrant."

"Which takes *time*."

"Which is why we agreed, you included, to interview her tonight. We went through this before we ever left for the Ravensplein. Remember—pros and cons, warrant, no warrant? We talked it through, Paolo, and still you went your own way. You pushed her too hard and blew the interview. Not even dogs piss where they sleep."

"Fine!" Ludovici approached a trash barrel, holding the plastic bags away from his body in a grand gesture. He might as well have been carrying radioactive waste. "You're still angry about the coffee stain, aren't you? I said I'd pay for the dry cleaning."

At the Ambassade, Poincaré looked up at what used to be a room, now ripped from the building as if with a pair of pliers. At his feet, an oblong tracing of chalk marked where one of Fenster's legs had landed. He saw that outline and knew he would take the case—a decision that had less to do with receiving an official assignment from Interpol than with certain tumblers clicking into place, privately. The formal requirements would have to be met, of course: a crime the commission of which and the solution to which crossed national frontiers. But no case began for Poincaré until its details moved him. He recalled his meeting with Banović that morning and, two years earlier, his visit to a killing field in Bosnia where the tumblers had also clicked. The burnt shell of a man met that standard, the murder an assault on decency itself.

No one deserved to die bent over a sink.

Chapter 7

In the three days post-explosion, neither the Dutch police nor Poincaré's team had linked Fenster's death to the WTO meetings, reason enough for the Dutch to declare the conference a success. The trade ministers met behind closed doors without incident and emerged with policy initiatives wrapped in grand statements, the preamble to which made its way into a press release:

> The economic health of farmers in the Sudan is tied to the fate of weavers in Colombia, to computer programmers in India and the United States, and to consumers everywhere. Today the speed of communications, travel, and transport has created a single economic tide that will lift all or inundate all. With or without our guidance, the world economy is converging; and we, the representatives of both developed and developing nations, resolve to direct this convergence to our mutual benefit.

Fenster merited no mention in the conference proceedings, his spot on the program taken at the last minute, unannounced, by a speaker from a local university who lectured on the impact of global warming on corporate profits. Almost before his eyes, Poincaré watched public memory of the bombing erased. The Ambassade received speedy satisfaction on an insurance claim and was opened for business after two intensive days of cleanup and a repair to its major systems. By the end of the conference, workmen had repainted the facade and begun building out the demolished room beneath a cover of heavy industrial sheeting. News coverage of the bombing quickly slipped from the front page to a middle section of the Amsterdam daily, by Sunday vanishing altogether. Within twenty-four hours the "bombing" had become, less ominously, an "explosion." For their part, the Dutch police had come to regard Fenster's death as an isolated case fomented by outside interests. An attack made on an obscure mathematician did not threaten the Netherlands proper, relieving the security services of any need to mount a serious inquiry. Poincaré understood. Fenster's killing worried local authorities less than would a purse-snatching ring that disrupted the tourist trade.

By Sunday afternoon, the medical examiner had confirmed that the deceased was, indeed, the mathematician from Harvard. Annette Günter slid a pair of x-rays onto a wall screen and pointed. "Without question we're looking at the same mouth, Henri. Do you see the fillings at numbers 3, 11, and 14? And this root canal?" She used a grease pencil to mark areas of interest. "Notice also the boney protuberances on both sides of the mandibular jaw. Very distinctive. The image on the left was e-mailed to us by Fenster's dentists in Boston—I believe it was the school of dentistry at Harvard. Digital records. The whole field is moving in this direction, you know. These fillings were done by different people, some with finer technique than others. This second image I developed myself yesterday afternoon. I trust you appreciate the match."

It was the first time Poincaré had met with the medical examiner away from the crime scene. Annette Günter was a matronly woman his age, built for endurance on a stocky, double-chinned and squarish frame that suggested Winston Churchill with curls. Had he not known her profession and met her at the counter of a cheese shop, or at a party, he would never have guessed she spent the better part of each day elbow deep in viscera. She was naturally too pleasant to have turned world-weary, a malady common to coroners. Günter impressed him as a sort of diligently pleasant neighbor who organizes blood drives and knits booties at birth announcements. By day she just happened to keep the company of corpses. "There can be no doubt about identification," she concluded. "Look at these." She held before him two images, a pairing of dark, vertical columns interrupted by bands of bright, horizontal strips.

Even to Poincaré's untrained eye, the match was perfect.

"The state crime lab in Massachusetts ran an analysis of dried urine from the rim of the commode in Fenster's apartment and an unwashed coffee cup from his office. Hair from a comb, with some follicles intact, rounded out the sample. Those three specimens had a single DNA signature, and as a unit they're identical to the analysis we ran off a sample of the victim's thigh bone. And then we have the fingerprints from Fenster's office and apartment in Boston, which match the prints we developed at the crime scene. He's your man," she said, pointing to a cardboard box in the corner of her office. The box was large enough to hold a soccer ball and was lined with heavy plastic sheeting folded over its top edges and covered firmly with a lid.

It took Poincaré a moment to register her meaning. "You cremated him?"

"He was three-quarters there anyway. We're shipping the remains tomorrow. And I'm going home because I promised my husband a pot roast. If I don't get started within the hour . . ." She checked her watch, then reached into a desk drawer for a tin of peppermints.

"By whose authority?"

His question edged toward accusation, a mistake. Günter carefully placed two mints on the tip of her tongue and then slid the tin across her desk, where they sat untouched. "A woman named Madeleine Rainier."

Poincaré adjusted his tie, the depths of his miscalculation clear. "She's a possible suspect," he said.

Günter was not impressed. "You know, I once had a case in which three different parties made a claim on a suicide. One insisted on cremation. One demanded embalming. The other said, 'Let the bastard rot.' Which is to say it's a waste of my precious time standing between a corpse and people fighting over it. No one told me not to proceed as usual. This isn't a cemetery, you know. When I complete my work, I move the bodies out like that." She snapped her fingers. "But I see you're upset, so . . ." She grabbed a file from a stack on her desk and flipped through papers and photographs until she found a page and paused over it. She slid the entire file across the desk. "Fairly straightforward, I'd say. It's not as if we did anything *illegal*, Henri."

In fact, the memo before him could not have been clearer. According to Fenster's attorney in Boston, a fully executed will dated thirteen months earlier stipulated that Madeleine Rainier would serve as executor of Fenster's estate. If the memo was authentic, which Poincaré saw no reason to doubt, Rainier would have been within her rights to run Fenster's remains up a flagpole in Dam Square.

"They were engaged to be married when he agreed to this," he said.

"Lovely. What's that to me?"

"When did she order the cremation?"

"Last night, sitting where you are now. My assistant reached the provost's office at Harvard, which was able to locate the attorney, who contacted Miss Rainier. She arrived rather quickly, I must say."

"She was already in Amsterdam."

Günter retrieved her tin of peppermints. "Well, then. There's a coincidence."

He closed the file and returned it, aware that Günter was now watching him with the same detached interest she showed her cadavers. His bile rose at how thoroughly he had misread Rainier. Three days earlier, the woman was barely capable of breathing unassisted. And now a move to destroy evidence? "Annette," he said, "you didn't find it odd that a thirty-year-old man with no dependents, in perfectly good health, would write a will?"

"Apparently I lack your talent for doubting every possible fact." She straightened her desk blotter and squared a felt-lined box that held an elaborate fountain pen. Günter's office suite suddenly oppressed him with its smell of disinfectant and gurneys awaiting fresh customers.

"Would you mind?" he said, pointing to the tin. "You wouldn't happen to know who the beneficiary was?"

"Why would I? Look. The man's parents were dead. He had no relations. Do you think he wanted some paralegal at a law office in Boston choosing his casket? Under the circumstances, thirty is a reasonable age to write a will. I wrote mine at twenty-two."

"You're a coroner, for God's sake."

Over her shoulder, a cut-through to the autopsy room gave Poincaré a clear view of an assistant lifting the organ set from a recent arrival. He slopped the whole mess into a steel pan. *And this is what makes a life?* Poincaré thought. He needed air.

"You want me to apologize," Günter said. "For the cremation."

"It's done. Forget it."

"Well, I won't. The attorney's instructions were clear, as were Rainier's. Now if you'll excuse me, I've got a pot roast to make." She retrieved her coat and turned to him with a consoling smile. "Cheer up, friend. You would have lost the remains to burial in a few days, anyway. Did I tell you she asked to see the body? I've been at this nearly forty years, and I've yet to see anything so affecting. These were gruesome remains, even by my standards, and I advised Miss Rainier against looking. When I pulled the drape, she smiled so sadly, then ran a hand over the bones as if she were bathing a child. I welled up at that, I'm not ashamed to say. She put her forehead to what remained of Dr. Fenster's and whispered something. She loved that man, what was left of him. How does one forget this?"

POINCARÉ STEPPED into the street, a cell phone pressed to his ear. "Gisele, for pity's sake tell me you have the lab results." Not only had the residue screenings not been conducted the night of the bombing; Amsterdam's police lab, busy analyzing its own long list of physical evidence from other cases, could not be cajoled, bribed, or threatened into faster service. Poincaré had waited thirty-six hours, until he could wait no longer, and dispatched De Vries to The Hague, to a different lab. Without a positive test, he could not detain Rainier. In fact, understaffed and preoccupied with the WTO meeting, he could not even monitor her movements properly. He had approached the Dutch police for surveillance help, but they ignored him. The detective who had so happily washed his hands of the affair, the one who promised full cooperation, waited twelve hours to return his call and said: *Why would we undertake the expense?*

Poincaré resorted to the one option left him, calling Rainier at her hotel at regular intervals on the pretext of posing follow-up questions. If he could hear her voice at least, if he knew she hadn't fled Amsterdam, he could detain her at a moment's notice. They had last spoken that morning, and he was beginning to relax his guard. Still, he needed those results and, at last, Gisele had them: "Positive for ammonium perchlorate," she reported. "Inside her suitcase and on the front of a pair of jeans and a blouse. I called the moment I heard, thirty minutes ago—and then every five minutes. I'm on the train from Den Hague right now. Shall we meet at the hotel?"

He hailed a cab. "No—get an arrest warrant, and we'll hold her until you come." Poincaré made a second call and, twenty minutes later, arrived at the Ravensplein just as Ludovici and Laurent stepped clear of a car. They converged on the lobby to find the same clerk, her hair now jade green, working the reception desk. This time as Poincaré jerked open the door, the young woman stepped around the desk.

"I called," she said, pleading her case. "I did. Both numbers you left me. The lady checked out ninety minutes ago. I called. I couldn't get through. I'm not in trouble, am I?"

"Did she take a cab? Did someone pick her up?"

"Just walked away, I think."

"She paid in cash, I suppose."

"It was a large bill. How did you know?"

Two levels below street grade, the medical examiner's suite turned out to be a graveyard for cellular signals. Poincaré had told no one of his appointment, assuming he could be reached by mobile phone and resolved, after the botched interview with Rainier, to work alone. Interpol had not yet assigned him the Fenster case, and so he had made no "errors" as such; still, he knew he had blundered monumentally. Outside the Ravensplein he faced Ludovici to take his medicine full-on, Laurent present as witness.

"Excellent work, Henri. She lied in the interview, she destroyed evidence—cremated it, then fled the scene of a crime. But at least you went by the book. Well done!"

Guilty as charged. The one course left him was a protocol so automatic, so pointless, that he despaired of ever catching Rainier.

He alerted rail-station and airport security on the chance she would be foolish enough to leave the country in plain view of the authorities. De Vries posted an alert to the Dutch border crossings. He also had Interpol issue a Red Notice—an international arrest warrant, which would permit local authorities to arrest her on sight in 188 member nations. But Rainier would remain in Holland for weeks, he figured—perhaps make a holiday of it in the Dutch countryside, then slip away unnoticed.

Later that afternoon he reached Fenster's attorney in Boston, a friendly man who had no interest in sharing information. "I suggest you get a subpoena and then we can talk," said the man. "She's not exactly my client. But I still may invoke attorney-client privilege since I know her only through Dr. Fenster." So Poincaré arranged for the subpoena, aware that any information he pried loose would be dated: for Rainier had already discarded the phone numbers and addresses the attorney had used to locate her. With her usual efficiency, De Vries learned that Rainier had recently shuttered her antiques business, sold her condominium, canceled her credit cards, and closed her savings and checking accounts after wiring all funds to a bank in the Bahamas—an account she subsequently closed within days. With each inquiry De Vries asked if Rainier had left a forwarding address. The answer surprised no one.

Both a priest and a legal scholar would have praised Poincaré for not arresting the woman on Thursday: the priest for his willingness to risk compassion and give Rainier every benefit of the doubt; the jurist for his guarding the outcome of a later trial by respecting due process. Better to let one criminal go free than to abuse the law and jeopardize the rights of many. A fine theory, though now Poincaré would live with the consequences. He would find her eventually; but the world in which he would search seemed, at present, very large.

Chapter 8

Rainier's escape stuck in his throat like a bone he could neither swallow nor cough up. By temperament, Poincaré trained a careful, brutal eye on his failures because failure woke him up to himself. When his son was old enough to understand how papa earned a living, the child asked: "Do you know Sherlock Holmes?" Poincaré could only smile and say *yes*—the great detective was a close, personal friend. But the penetrating, unpleasant truth was that, unlike Conan Doyle's savant, Poincaré—more successful than most—could nonetheless point to real, live failures in his case files, and these failures offended him mightily, personally.

He stretched, tipping back in a chair he had glued twice to keep from collapsing. The Dutch security services had done Interpol the supposed favor of engaging a short-term lease for the grand ballroom of an eighteenth-century palace near Dam Square. Without a hint of irony, Poincaré's hosts called the disintegrating cavern prime office space in the heart of Old Amsterdam. *Old*, at least, was accurate: every plastered surface was cracked and flaking. What cornice moldings remained suggested a drunk with blasted teeth. The parquet split and creaked underfoot, and the faded curtains elicited from Poincaré an actual groan when he first saw them. For no color moved him like the rich velvet crimson of an opera house, with Claire or Etienne at his side; and no color depressed him more than a beautiful red left to fade. He once knew a man much like this room, a sixth-generation baron who was cash poor but ego rich, a poseur who waxed the ends of his mustache.

The door squealed open and Laurent, back from one of their final tasks in Amsterdam, called to Poincaré: "Four more photos . . . The administrator who booked speakers for the conference didn't know where to send these after Fenster *canceled*." He held a folder aloft. "Her actual word, the harpy. He'd sent them ahead so they could make copies for distribution at his talk. No doubt now—the image we found at the crime scene was part of the presentation."

Poincaré reached the conference table just as Laurent set his briefcase down and frisked himself for a cigarette. A match flared.

"Serge, please."

Laurent had already lost a lobe of one lung to cancer and had since tried quitting, twice. He sucked hard and aimed a blue-white plume over the table. "It's confirmed," he said, pointing to the folder. "We've got a certified enigma in James Fenster. Let's trade assignments, Henri."

Interpol had just that morning assigned Poincaré the Fenster case. After identifying the body, Dutch authorities contacted the American Embassy, which reserved its right to call in the FBI but asked that Interpol take the lead, with two provisos: that the Americans be kept informed at all stages of the investigation and that special attention be paid to sourcing the ammonium perchlorate. They wanted no more rocket fuel bombings. Fenster, apparently, was an afterthought.

"So your new posting came through, Serge?"

"By e-mail. Lyon gave me the Soldiers of Rapture, a miserable goddamned business." Laurent cleared his throat and spit into a handkerchief. "Also known as Rapturians—a fundamentalist, evangelical cult preaching an End-Time theology. They form themselves into autonomous cells, like al-Qaeda, with no central authority other than the New Testament, no church per se, each cell led by a self-anointed prophet who derives instruction through his own interpretation of the Word. They're Bible-thumping terrorists. They've committed at least two dozen murders, each time leaving a passage of Scripture as justification. They're also setting off bombs for Jesus—the Milan event was one of theirs. Henri, they want to make the world *more* miserable in order to hasten the Second Coming. Apparently, Christ will only reappear at a time of absolute chaos, so a devoted Christian should not only *not* repair the world but should work actively to tear it down. Hence bullets, bombs, and murder for

Christ. Just when you thought people had exhausted the possibilities for stupidity . . ."

Poincaré would not have believed it but for the Barcelona killing. He located Matthew 24:24 on his computer:

> For false Christs and false prophets will appear and will perform great signs and miracles to deceive even the elect.

"It's got to be the same people," he said. He logged onto an Interpol database and read enough to confirm a connection. "The police report says the shooter clipped the note to the victim's hair, above the entry wound, so blood wouldn't obscure any words."

Laurent dropped his cigarette into an open can of soda. "Detail oriented," he said. "Don't you just love that in a killer? It makes them so . . . *human.*" He lit another Gauloise and expelled a lungful of smoke. "Only the religiously inspired could be so twisted. As for the Milan bombing, I don't even have the words. The guy exploded himself next to an ice cream parlor. Five of the six victims were children." Laurent coughed, his chest rattling ominously. "We've worked together a long time, Henri. You know I've never run from a case. But I actively detest these people, and it's no good beginning a job this way. Let me take the Fenster bombing. I'll make it right with Lyon."

Poincaré considered the offer. True, investigating the Soldiers of Rapture would be an unpleasant business, but then so was every assignment. Neither of them had signed on to repair hiking trails or deliver warm meals to shut-ins. Tomorrow, Poincaré knew, Laurent would have in place the beginnings of a plan. "I can't," said Poincaré. "But I'll help if I can. How do I know a Rapturian when I see one?"

Laurent spit into a handkerchief. "Look for people straight out of a Hollywood Bible epic, wearing robes and quoting Scripture. All ages, some as old as seventy. Twenty countries have reported active cells, and they want Interpol to coordinate a response. And, no, it won't do to arrest everyone wearing a robe. Not all of them are maniacs, and you can't tell for the looking. I'll likely go to the States for this one—I'm thinking Las Vegas." He coughed again and opened a file. "Thank God for the merely puzzling," he said, pointing to four photographs.

SERIES 2: A

SERIES 2: B

SERIES 2: C

SERIES 2: D

"I'm supposed to guess?" said Poincaré.

Laurent nodded.

"Alright, then. The first one is a snowflake—though it's a strange color for a snowflake. But image A also looks like image B, which is clearly an island or a peninsula. Image A could be an x-ray of B—the boney structure of mountains. Put some flesh on the skeleton and you've got a land mass. C is possibly another snowflake or could be a slice of pine tree viewed from above. D, obviously, is a branch with leaves. You play with the scale a bit and you could place it in any of the other photos. I couldn't tell you what any of it has to do with globalization."

Laurent flipped each photograph in turn and read the captions: "Two out of four, Henri. You fail. Image A—I can barely pronounce this, is an example of something called 'epitaxial islanding.' It says here that 'these are individual atoms of gold attaching themselves to a layer of silicon with characteristic dendritic branches.'" Laurent looked up. "It's gold, not snow." He flipped image B and read: "'Christchurch, New Zealand, as seen from space. Note the dendritic extension of mountain ridges—central ridgelines fanning out to finger-like sub-ridges and sub-sub-ridges down to the water's edge.' Image C: 'Bacterial growth, Petri dish . . . dendritic branching.' And image D," Laurent concluded, realigning the images, "is a fern leaf."

"Let me guess, Serge. Showing dendrites."

Poincaré studied the images, registering two examples of the biological world, two of the geological. One was so small as to be invisible to the naked eye; another, so massive that its structure could be appreciated only from earth orbit. One was a plant on a forest floor; the other, a colony of living organisms gorging on laboratory agar—a pinwheel galaxy in a Petri dish. Poincaré sat quietly.

"Look at the leading edge of each image," said Laurent. "They're cousins. Each is at some level a version of the other." He twirled a massive ring as he spoke, a present from his third wife prior to his final, failed effort to quit smoking. It was less a ring than a nugget of raw silver with a hole bored through the middle. During his six months of fighting insomnia and night sweats, the hope was he would reach for the ring instead of a cigarette. "Better than prayer beads," he said at the time. "Ella wanted those, but I decided to leave God out of the equation."

The silver worked no magic, unfortunately, and all Laurent could show for the effort was a new habit to accompany the old: he now smoked three packs of filterless cigarettes each day *and* twirled the ring. "I made copies for you," he said of the photos. "I'd give my left testicle to know how Fenster was going to work these into a talk on globalization."

The ballroom door squealed open, and in walked Ludovici and De Vries on either side of the last protester to be interviewed in connection with the bombing. Poincaré resisted settling on single suspects early in a case. He had set a worldwide net for Rainier through electronic postings, but he was also looking to others—in this case the anti-globalists. One of them, he reasoned—possibly in league with Rainier—may have targeted Fenster, whose promised talk on a one-world economy might have made him a target. Yet no one Poincaré interviewed thus far had any plausible link to the mathematician. None even admitted to having heard of him, let alone knowing his work well enough to plan and execute a murder. Last on the list, Eduardo Quito, was a former academic and their likeliest prospect. Poincaré looked forward to this meeting both because Quito was famous in his own right and because the interview was all that stood between another night in Amsterdam and a flight home to Lyon. Claire had left to prepare the farmhouse and welcome the children, but still it would be good to drink familiar wine and sleep in his own bed. The photos, he figured, could wait.

Chapter 9

Peru's Ministry of Tourism would have done well to paste Eduardo Quito's likeness on brochures meant to separate rich North Americans from their hard-earned vacation dollars. He walked into the temporary Interpol headquarters every bit a son of the Andes, wearing the clothes of an alpaca herder—his job and the job of his father and grandfather before him. With a calico shirt, bandanna knotted at his throat, waxed-cotton jacket, and fedora over silver-flecked hair, Quito looked more the herdsman than the scholar or political gadfly. Improbably, he was all three. With equal ease he could argue before the International Monetary Fund, lead street protests, and navigate remote mountain trails. One week might find him in Paris speaking, in fluent French, at a forum on indigenous rights; the next, in Berlin shouting down G-8 ministers in flawless German. And then a flight home to the Andes like a condor returning to its nest. He was compact and powerfully built, with piercing black eyes.

Poincaré had turned the matter over in his mind but was still not sure how to engage Quito, who would have remained a herder save for an alert priest who recognized a talent for numbers in the child. This led to a series of schools and, eventually, an endowed chair at the University of Lima where he specialized in the economics of colonialism. At least one European country had put Quito on a terrorist watch list; several others, calling him a provocateur, routinely denied him entry. And then there were the whispered conversations among academics that he was Nobel material. The problem, detractors claimed, was that he allowed a stunningly original mind to be corrupted by politics. Quito's supporters celebrated that same influence. At the height of his powers, he abruptly quit his academic post, returned to Pisac, the village of his birth, and launched what he called the Indigenous Liberation Front, or ILF. Using the Internet, a tool appropriated from the Enemy, Quito reached 300 million indigenous peoples worldwide and became the voice of a surging political and human rights movement. Poincaré had read the profiles in *Le Monde*, the *Guardian* and the *New York Times*; he had studied Quito's now classic papers on the systematic economic destruction of native peoples; and he fully doubted anyone could be so prolific or instantly charismatic—until, that is, the man stepped into the room. Without removing his pack, Quito walked directly to his host as if arriving for a long-sought audience.

"Your reputation precedes you, Inspector."

Bright, probing eyes met Poincaré's, followed by a firm handshake and a kind of preemptive friendliness that put one simultaneously on alert and at ease. The man had an undeniable force.

"*My* reputation?" Poincaré responded.

"No one who knows Interpol can afford not to know you."

The spell broke the instant Quito closed two hands over Poincaré's outstretched hand, a touch that recalled bricks thrown in Seattle and cars burned in Rotterdam. At the WTO riots in Paris, a policeman lost sight in one eye—all protests directed by the man who greeted Poincaré so warmly now. Yet Quito had never once been named in a complaint. He was that clever.

"Yours is the reputation," said Poincaré.

"I'll take that as a compliment," he said laughing. He dropped his pack and followed his host to the conference table. "Nearly every major security service in the world has found a reason to interview me, save Interpol. This meeting was inevitable, Inspector, so I prepared—just as you have. When this young man"—Quito pointed to Ludovici—"asked me to stop by to talk, I agreed. I also made additional inquiries and came across the name Poincaré time and again."

"The Internet?" asked Poincaré.

"Obviously. And other sources. Three decades at Interpol. Twelve different commendations for heroism. Invitations to London, Washington, and Moscow to speak on transborder crime. Success where others failed. And more than once, I understand, you rejected promotions so that you might remain in the field. Bravo!"

"I don't read my press clippings, Professor."

"And modest! The quality that fascinates me most is that you're said to be like these English dogs that bite and never let go. I once read of a dog that needed to be hit in the head with an iron bar to release its grip. The animal died not letting go."

Poincaré watched his guest slap at the table, enjoying himself as if among friends at one of Amsterdam's brown cafes. "We must have a common ancestor because my wife calls me the most stubborn donkey alive. In our village this is known as *tenaz*." He laughed again but stopped short upon noticing the photographs Laurent had cleared to one end of the table. "Lovely. What are these?"

"Just some pictures, Professor."

"No, I don't think just some pictures. Fractals, yes?"

At that instant Poincaré had been studying Quito's hands—which, in fact, confirmed that he earned his living, at least part of the year, working outdoors. "We've been puzzling over these," he said. "Could you shed some light?"

"I'm no expert, Inspector." But it was a false show of modesty because Quito was soon positioning the images for a closer inspection. After a few minutes, his interest clearly piqued, he looked up: "With fractals, you can't determine scale—that is, the size of an object. Take this one." He was holding before them the photograph of Christchurch, New Zealand. "If I photocopied the edge of this peninsula as you see it from space, then took a close-up photograph of, say, one meter of the same coast—and if I resized both photos, you would not be able to tell the 300 kilometer image from the one-meter strip. With a fractal, the geometries of part and whole are the same. The whole is visible, as it were, in the part. Do you eat cauliflower, Inspector?"

"Excuse me?"

"Cauliflower—also broccoli. Do you eat them?"

"Yes."

"Both fractal. A single floret of either looks like the whole. Do you see?"

Poincaré did. "The world in a grain of sand," he said. "You knew Fenster."

Quito nodded. "I'm an economist, and he was a mathematician. Sometimes odd ducks will dance."

Nearly a minute passed, not a word spoken. When it occurred to Poincaré that his guest thought he was done with explanations, he opened his hands as if shortchanged at the market. "That's all? I'm conducting a murder investigation. I need something more than ducks."

"What can I say?" answered Quito. "It wasn't a happy period. James and I collaborated for a time and very nearly published a paper, but then—" He paused to align the photographs. "I'll try to explain. Mathematicians write equations; they play with numbers and symbols that do not, necessarily, attach themselves to things in the world. They love the purity of that. Economists model real events, and reality—it's such a mess."

Poincaré was thinking of the blue tarp flapping over the remains of James Fenster—of that and the jewel box of shattered glass around the Ambassade. "I've noticed. What were you working on?"

In all seriousness, Quito folded his hands and said: "A mathematical model of love."

Laurent erupted as if someone had set a torch under him. His laughter set off a spasm of coughing that turned his face bright red.

"Go on," said Quito. "Have your fun. We were developing a concept—a notion that mathematics could model the most unruly, unpredictable of human behaviors. If we could model love, we could model anything. We tried representing lovers' affections symbolically, and then we set out to graph outputs that might predict behavior in famous literary relationships. Our first paper was to be an analysis of *Romeo and Juliet.*"

"Finally," Laurent gasped, struggling to catch his breath, "I know why my marriages failed. I never understood nonlinear equations!" He began coughing again and excused himself to find a cup of water.

This time Quito joined the laughter at his own expense. "I've endured worse. So few people take this seriously, I'm afraid. But there *is* a mathematics of the heart. My parents understood it, yet they were illiterate."

"And what's that?" said Ludovici, who until this point was content to watch.

"Among those who love, one plus one rarely equals two."

"Amen to *that*!"

"For better *and* worse, young man."

Quito turned to Poincaré: "The premise is not as absurd as it sounds—although I admit it was calculated to get people's attention. James and I were attempting to make a larger point. How to illustrate it?" Poincaré followed his glance out a window, to the square. A truck horn blared, and Quito snapped to attention. "Fine," he said. "A typical example. Traffic. Imagine traffic in a city of your choice during the summer on a Friday afternoon at five o'clock. Describe what you see, Inspector."

"Gridlock," answered Poincaré. "A parking lot."

"Exactly. It's a human system: humans at the wheel, humans in cars that other humans built, humans on highways that other humans laid. Will you grant me this—the cars and the gridlock are a purely *human* system?"

Poincaré nodded.

"Good. Traffic engineers use mathematics—principles of fluid dynamics—to study traffic flow. Tell me why, Inspector, an equation that describes the speed, volume, and flow of a river should also describe the flow of traffic during rush hour? One is a human system, one is natural. In one we have minds at work—humans controlling every vehicle—in the other only laws of gravity. And yet humans behave enough like water for traffic engineers to use fluid dynamics in designing highways. Why should the two be related—at all? It makes no sense, but they are."

Poincaré could only shrug. "I've never considered these things."

"Well, James and I did. We set out to show that human behavior can be modeled mathematically, just as any complex, dynamic system in nature can be modeled—a weather system, for instance. We intended to push the thesis and suggest that the same rules that describe complex systems in nature can also describe complex human behavior."

"I doubt that," said Poincaré. "Maybe fluid dynamics describes traffic flow. What kind of mathematics describes love?"

Quito shifted in his seat. "We never got that far."

Ludovici snorted and, under his breath, said *little wonder.*

Quito's eyes flashed.

"He's offended you. Paolo, apologize."

"Don't patronize me, Inspector. The idea was sound. We worked for several months before James lost interest and the collaboration ended. I had no idea he was scheduled to deliver a paper at the WTO conference, but I see from his title that he didn't lose his interest in mathematical modeling. So perhaps I had an effect on him after all. I'd like to think so."

A mathematics of globalization. Poincaré did not think it likely. But then, from what he had gathered, Fenster was a special breed of brilliant. As was Quito. Who could guess what might come of their collaboration? "I imagine," he said, "that you came to Boston to study the behavior of markets, not love."

"Of course," said his guest. "James was an intuitive with equations. He could watch a fly buzzing around a room, write an equation to describe its movement, graph that equation—and the graph, rendered in three dimensions, would reproduce the fly's movements. He had an astonishing, first-order mind—quite evident in his papers—so I sought him out. This was three and a half years ago."

"A disappointment, I'm sure."

Poincaré reached for the photograph of the bacteria growing in a Petri dish. Speaking to it, not to the president of the Indigenous Liberation Front, he asked whether in a single part of the economy one could find the whole. "Like the floret of cauliflower," he suggested. "I bought a cup of coffee this morning. In that exchange, could you see the entire global economy, Professor?"

Quito quietly applauded. "That *would* be the holy grail. If you're asking whether or not the global economy can be described using fractal mathematics, I've never given it much thought."

Absurd! Poincaré did not believe it for an instant and could tell that Quito *knew*—which apparently made no difference. Calm, as composed and affable as the moment he entered the ballroom, he pointed to the photos and said: "It's clear from these and from his paper's title that James was set to argue the global economy is related, at the deepest level, to the geometry of nature. He was pushing our thesis. He must have made progress since our split."

Quito arranged the images into a neat pile. "I assume we're done, Inspector. I've told you everything I know. I'm sorry James died, though I'm glad we've met. I can't say I care much for your choice of venue, however. This place disturbs me. I really do need to leave."

Poincaré had no plans for Quito to leave just yet. But rather than push the point, he tried coaxing his guest into further conversation. He had learned long ago to keep his subjects talking because talking was better than not talking and sometimes talking, even idle talking, led to a fragment of a hunch that might take months to formulate and months more to prove. Quito was pointing to a chandelier. "Built in the early 1700s, I should think. The timing's about right. You've heard of the Dutch East India Company, I assume?"

"Traders," said De Vries. Poincaré could see her fascination with the man, even with his transparent effort to end the interview. She played along. "The architects of Amsterdam's Golden Age," she said. "Dutch children can't finish grade school without learning all about it."

"Architects would be one description," said Quito. "There are others. Have you any idea of what made all this possible?" He opened his arms to the room. "This ridiculous place and all the Rembrandts and Vermeers and those paintings of plump Dutch burghers in the Rijksmuseum? Dutch wealth and Dutch tolerance were built on the backs of slaves in the Atlantic and Indian oceans, from Curaçao to Madagascar. This ballroom exists because of a carefully planned program of state-sponsored rape. The Spanish, the Dutch, British, French, Belgians, Germans, and Americans: one after the other, they unbuckled their pants and robbed the Indigene of everything sweet and worthy. You summon me here, Inspector, and I see suffering. I hear whip cracks and screams. James saw numbers."

Poincaré had found his fragment, sooner than he expected. "And this is why your collaboration failed," he said.

Quito studied him, the gay mask gone: "The Indigene is done asking nicely. What is it that you people *want*? An advertisement in Angkor Wat for iPods? The times are too subtle for rape, but nothing else has changed in 500 years. Now you pay us two dollars a day to build your cell phones and televisions. I'm done here. This room disgusts me." He reached for his backpack.

"Please, another moment," said Poincaré. "Did you and Dr. Fenster discuss your political views?"

"Why? Our paper was to be an analysis of *Romeo and Juliet*."

"You mean to say that your philosophical differences never—"

Quito looked to the corners of the room; when he turned back to Poincaré, he had mastered his emotions: "The Indigene will be equal partners now, with our own cultures, or we will make your lives miserable until we are. Don't misunderstand," he added pleasantly. "I hold dear the Western love of learning, your willingness to question, to challenge received wisdom. But I really have taken too much of your time. James and I worked together, then we didn't. Our schedules overlapped in Amsterdam, true. He was killed. But unless the rules of logic and evidence have totally abandoned me, you cannot connect one to the other. It's been a pleasure just the same." Quito stood to leave.

The phone rang. De Vries crossed the room to answer and then motioned Poincaré to his desk. He excused himself to take the call and asked Quito to stay one last moment. There were no private offices in the ballroom, just four desks and a conference table spread across the huge expanse. The only privacy one could hope for was a turned back.

"Please hold for the director of the Scheveningen prison," a voice said. Odd, Poincaré thought. He believed he had seen the last of that place with his visit to Banović. Possibly he might be called back to The Hague for the trial, but that would not be for months.

"Inspector Poincaré?"

By reputation, Roman Skiversky was a humorless administrator for whom a good day meant the prison cages remained locked and no inmate enjoyed himself too thoroughly.

"I'll be direct," Skiversky said. "Intelligence we cannot acknowledge suggests that prisoner Stipo Banović, whom you visited last Thursday morning and placed in our custody this past January, has put the lives of your family at risk. It's a serious matter, Inspector. Our people just translated a conversation surreptitiously recorded between the prisoner and his so-called attorney, and Banović has ordered the . . . elimination of your wife, your son, and his wife and children." A pause. "This is an unusual development, to be sure. Banović said that you were not to be harmed."

A sudden heat rose through Poincaré's chest. His breath caught in his throat, his grip on the phone tightening. "How do you know this? He's locked in the most secure prison in the world. What harm can Banović do?"

"Several of his lieutenants remain at large, as you know. His death squad was disbanded, but their money was never found. With those men and those millions, Banović can reach anyone he pleases—even from prison. Understand that our facility cannot acknowledge tape recording a privileged conversation between a client and his attorney, even if that meeting turns out to be a ruse. That would only confirm our violation of international agreements. But given the extreme circumstance, I am alerting you—off the record. Ask your questions, Sir. This is the last I can speak of the matter."

"Banović would go after *my family*?" Poincaré yelled, forgetting where he was. He spun, dazed, and saw Ludovici, De Vries, and Laurent staring, their faces slack. Quito studied the photographs.

"Who knows what this man will do?" answered the director. "His contact is Aleksandr Borislav. From what we can gather, he flew to The Hague for this one visit, arriving three nights ago, and returned to Bosnia just after the interview with Banović. Borislav's so-called law offices were located in Mostar. We have since discovered that this address is a cafeteria. We surmise that Borislav knew Banović from the war. My own view is that since we photographed and fingerprinted him, as we do everyone who enters this facility, and since Banović knows as much, Borislav is not himself the contractor but rather the agent who will procure contractors. I suggest that you begin with him. We will fax you his photograph, his prints, and a transcript of the conversation. You know where to find Banović and can have access to him at any time—quietly, of course. As for Borislav, we can be sure this is not his real name. He left The Netherlands on a flight to Bosnia; beyond that, we don't know where he is. I'll leave it to you to bring this information to Interpol. They will shield you."

Poincaré stared into the dead space below the ballroom's chandeliers. All his life he had labored to keep the brutality of his work from Claire and Etienne. And now a threat not of his making, that he could not control, had intruded. What had Banović to lose? Adding a few more murders to scores already committed, heaping new agonies on old, would mean little at his sentencing. The most severe punishment the International Court could pronounce was life in prison, and Banović was already assured that. As long as his life was forfeit anyway, Banović must have reasoned, why not have his fun?

"This interview is over," said Poincaré.

Quito looked up from the photographs. "Some unpleasantness? I couldn't help but overhear, Inspector. Only the worst sort of man would threaten innocents."

"Forget what you heard."

"Consider it forgotten. But let me say that Indigenes have endured centuries of brutality. Our great mistake was not meeting force with force. How else could Pizarro and 180 soldiers have conquered an empire of millions?" Quito shouldered his backpack. "Protect your innocents, Inspector. Meet this threat with force. It's all the barbarian understands."

Poincaré walked to the door and opened it. The contract would take weeks, possibly months, to put in place. He had time, but not much time. He reached to meet Quito's outstretched hand and heard a voice that sounded like his own say, "Thank you for your visit."

Quito took a long, last survey of the room and of Poincaré. "Meet force with force," he said. "Brutality only understands itself."

CHAPTER 10

Car horns breaking pitch, an onrush of lights. Pounding Afro-pop and Poincaré's heart revving to speeds fearful to contemplate. *Not dangerous* he told himself. *Not dangerous.* But the beast clawing to burst free of his chest would not listen. The dream had come fast and hard. He could only have been asleep in the taxi for seconds; but that brief span returned him in vomitous detail to the killing fields of Bosnia. His eyes rolled to resist the vision. He moaned. His heart protested with such violence that he bit his lip to keep from passing out.

He was sitting in the rear of a UN truck, with a driver and guard. In the lead truck, two more peacekeepers well-armed and guided by maps and GPS systems negotiated a firebreak through deep forests south of Banja Luka. Rain earlier that week had muddied the trail. Wheels spun, mud flew. The truck bounced and slid sideways, lurched and stalled. Pine trees to either side of the firebreak stood thick enough on a cloudless day to reduce the sunlight to dusky shadows on the forest floor. The rear window of the lead vehicle bobbed before them, festooned with clots of mud that obscured the blue UN logo.

At any point on their journey, rogue militias could have attacked. Though the war was over, disaffected young men continued to prowl the area and, based on alliances that shifted daily, decided for themselves whom to kill or kidnap and hold for ransom, including representatives of the UN. One entered these forests reliant on the goodwill of known murderers. Five hours into the mountains, the lead vehicle stopped. Three observers—Nigerian, Japanese, and Canadian—wearing identical fatigues and berets stepped from their trucks and consulted a topographical map. As Poincaré and his driver exited their vehicle, the Nigerian pointed into the forest. "Less than a kilometer," he said. "Due east. Banović marched them through here."

Under intense questioning and backroom methods no one cared to discuss, a captured lieutenant from Banović's death squad described how, the previous October, with the ground frozen hard but the snows still weeks away, they had rounded up the men and boys of a village to the south, tied them one to the next like slaves meant for market, and piled them into open air trucks. Some had died of exposure from the trip. At this spot, according to UN intelligence, the dead were cut from the line and their bodies dumped several meters into the forest. The Canadian peacekeeper consulted a map and walked twenty or so paces off the firebreak. "Here we are," he called, his voice as alien in that wilderness as the ticking truck engines and the squawk of military radios. "I count the remains of four bodies. Bring bags."

A week of mild weather had broken the back of a hard winter, and the air smelled sweet. Poincaré approached the skeletal remains. Exposure and gnawing animals had stripped the bodies, leaving a few tendons and wisps of hair. No one spoke. Tarps were laid in an effort at posthumous dignity, as the officers marked positions on their maps. One of the peacekeepers consulted a compass and pointed: "This way."

They walked single file, Poincaré last in line. Aside from the sound of boots sucking in ankle-deep mud and the men's labored breathing, there was nothing to be heard in the false twilight of the forest floor. Where were the birds, Poincaré wondered. High above, the wind tousled the treetops. He stared at his boots to distract himself from the effort, one muddy step at a time, with no thought but a dark anticipation of what lay ahead.

Nothing could have prepared Poincaré. Breathing hard, eyes focused on his boots, he bumped the man in front of him, who had stopped abruptly. Before them opened a ravine, at the bottom of which lay an open grave with too many bones to count. Old bones and young ones, some poking through a few remaining patches of snow like tree limbs broken in a storm. The forensic anthropologist who would later map the scene explained how the positioning of bodies suggested that the men had tried shielding the boys from the gunfire. DNA analysis confirmed what the villagers had said: every victim was male. Their crime? Nothing but a potential to threaten Serbian purity by fathering a new generation. Every man and boy, Muslim.

At Poincaré's feet, shell casings from automatic weapons glittered like precious metal on a blanket of pine needles. Nearby, a series of rocks formed a ledge, a table of sorts, where Banović's commandoes had left the remains of their lunch: sardine tins, trash, and balled up aluminum foil that suggested the sandwiches had been prepared elsewhere, with forethought. Poincaré dropped to his knees. He closed his eyes against a screaming that rose from the ravine in a language the killers did not understand. Husbands called for wives, boys for mothers, old men to heaven, as all went dark in a hail of gunfire, smoke, and steaming blood. Poincaré rocked forward, his forehead touching the cool earth. He had seen the worst of man's depravity, but never this. He retched, moaning *God, dear God, God, God, not this, tell me it isn't so.* But it was so, and he retched until his stomach emptied and the bile rose in his throat.

The peacekeepers turned away, leaving Poincaré to his grief. After a few minutes, when his heart had hardened sufficiently to stand and resume his role as witness, he noted how the yellow, nylon ropes binding the victims waist-to-waist lay slack and snaking through the bone pile. Photographs were taken and signs posted in four languages: *International Criminal Court. Evidence. No Trespassing. No Tampering.* And so it was decided: Poincaré would search for Stipo Banović and would not rest until the man stood to answer for his crimes.

He woke from this dream at the point he often did, as the Nigerian peacekeeper was pounding a sign into the earth above the ravine. This particular evening, each hammer blow struck at his chest until he lurched in the rear seat of the taxi thinking he might die from the building pressure. He woke, music pounding in his ears. Not in Bosnia then but here, on his way home from Saint Exupéry airport. Lyon. Home. He reached as calmly as shaking hands would allow into his suit pocket for his pill case. Two multi-coloreds, two when things got bad. A sip of water, always at hand. And then the waiting, who knew how long, for the beast in his chest to stop.

The driver exited the highway and wended his way to the Presqu'île peninsula, where Poincaré directed him through a maze of streets and paid him to carry his bags five flights to the apartment. An hour later, as he lay in bed, he turned on his side and wished he could have held Claire and been permitted to say nothing. It would have saved him that night to know she was safe. Poincaré drifted away, words bobbing to a darkening surface: *brutality only understands itself.* Was it true, he wondered. He feared he was about to find out.

THE NEXT morning, the newspaper lay unread at the breakfast table. Poincaré sipped his coffee, staring across the Rhône as if he might find answers to his predicament in the broad, troubled sky. Just as he reached for the phone to dial the director of Interpol, having earlier faxed the transcript of Banović's interview and the photograph of Borislav, the phone rang. It was Albert Montforte himself.

"Henri, this is an outrage! We will hunt down this Borislav."

"Yes, Albert."

"It can't be you, Henri. Someone else . . . Ludovici, I think. We just assigned him to a drug case in Spain, but I'll pull him this morning and he'll be in Bosnia tonight. If Banović has targeted your entire family, there would have to be more than one contractor involved, and they would need to strike simultaneously. I don't think that kind of coordination is possible without a substantial network in place. Our biggest advantage is that they do not know we know. Let Paolo find Borislav and extract information. Meanwhile, your grandchildren, your son, his wife, and Claire will get twenty-four-hour coverage, with a desk agent in Lyon to coordinate—indefinitely, until we have settled this business. This Banović strikes at the very heart of civil order. I'm putting every resource I have on the line."

Poincaré said nothing.

"Henri, you will give my assistant photographs and addresses of your family. We will handle the rest. Where is everyone now?"

He told him. "Give me a few days, Albert. Nothing will happen that quickly. Borislav will need some time to recruit."

"Acceptable. And what about you? When you're with Claire, you'll be protected. But not when you're on assignment. We should have someone shadow you, I think."

Poincaré had not considered the possibility of working while under this cloud. But the timeline for any attempts on Claire and the others was indefinite. Would they forfeit their lives for a month? A year? Would they go into hiding or assume new identities? "Banović wants me to suffer," he said. "He has every intention of keeping me alive so that I can witness the destruction of my family. Maybe, after that, he'll dispatch someone to end my misery."

"Assuming he can be believed."

"Believe him," said Poincaré. "My death would take the fun out of his little divertissement." He could find no way to be hopeful, notwithstanding the director's forceful response. Opposed even by all of Interpol's resources, an experienced killer would simply wait for an inevitable opening. Unless he moved his family to a fortress or entered a program that gave them new lives elsewhere, they were not safe and could never be safe.

Nothing to do but walk. He turned his collar up, hands thrust deep into his jacket, and roamed the streets of the old city. He was hours at it. He walked through the old Saint Just and Saint Irénée quarters, the former necropolis. He sought out the old places, the traboules, the narrow, covered passageways built so many centuries ago, which Claire adored. He walked through neighborhoods that layered Renaissance palaces upon medieval bulwarks upon Roman baths, past the fountains and shuttered markets, up the cobbled streets and familiar alleys until he stopped, finally, before the Cathedral of Saint Jean.

When Etienne and his family visited from Paris, Poincaré would take the twins and Chloe on walks that would often as not end in the nave of Saint Jean, where they would sit as quietly as children could, contemplating the vast empty spaces and stained glass until the sun set. At six, Émile and Georges were young for religious sentiment; but like their grandfather they were drawn to the vaulted darkness of cathedrals. Chloe, by contrast, sat listening as if she heard spirits conversing in the shadows. The four would sit on simple caned chairs and, by unspoken agreement, not stir until the red of the apostles' robes winked and went dark—at which point the squeals of *Papi, ice cream!* would coax from Poincaré what no house of worship, on its own, ever had: a prayer.

He walked inside. Though he had tried over the years, he never understood Claire's faith. He attended church occasionally because she asked and because he was comforted, for her, as she slipped a hand into his when the priest, in defiance of orders from Rome, reverted to the Latin mass. She had insisted Etienne be baptized, and he agreed though he thought the ceremony little more than voodoo. How surprised he was, then, at the emotions rising in him when the priest offered a blessing and sprinkled holy water on the forehead of his son. That some could consider water holy; that Etienne, who *was* holy in Poincaré's sight, would be blessed by another in the name of mysteries larger than them all; that this sacrament could take place in a cathedral built when oxcarts plied the muddy streets of Lyon; that his wife and her family, without embarrassment, could welcome Etienne into a fellowship two thousand years old; that he, Poincaré, a rank non-believer, could be moved so nearly to tears at the ceremony that he forced himself to turn away, sharply, in search of control—all this stood as evidence to a single fact: that Henri Poincaré was a man who longed to believe, a man who was moved by mystery and beauty but a man for whom belief was impossible. He was too much a scientist, ever the investigator in a world bound up in webs of cause and effect that had served him well in every regard save one: that at the hour between dusk and darkness, when the sky slid from deepest cobalt into night, he suspected something large, momentous even, was out there just beyond his reach, the shape of which flashed into his awareness now and again but vanished whenever he tried to grasp it.

He stood and nodded to a priest, whose footsteps clicked in the great silence. He had time enough to return home and shower before catching a train south. There was time, yet, before he would face the ones he loved to explain the chaos that he, in an effort to do a difficult job well, had heaped upon their innocent heads. What would he say? He thought of the man in the old story who had wept himself dry and, in the process, filled a lake with his tears. A child of the district woke the next morning and approached the man: "Monsieur," she said, "this is a wonder. Why are you sad?"

Seeing the goodness in her, he told the truth: "Because life is so sweet."

The child tugged at his sleeve. "Monsieur, I don't understand."

And the man, weeping anew, said: "Neither do I."

Chapter 11

$\mathbf{H}$e arrived in Fonroque after everyone had gone to bed. Half-roused from sleep, Claire opened her arms. For several hours he lay awake and, finally giving up, checked on the children before stepping outside to lose himself in the mists that gathered over the vineyards before sunrise. Poincaré was in trouble, and he knew it. The transcripts from Banović's interview with his so-called attorney were both explicit and chilling. "Lay not a finger on Poincaré," Banović had instructed his lieutenant with the diction of an eighteenth-century divine. "But touch the others. Touch them all."

The moon lingered above the horizon like a condemned man above a gallows door. Poincaré began to walk: one row down, the next row up. Down and back he walked, casting a long shadow in the spectral light until he ran out of rows at a stone wall that marked the ancient property line. An hour had passed and as the moon died, birds woke. Jacques, their mean-spirited but fertile rooster, shattered the morning with his cockle-do, and pheasants answered from a nearby copse. Down valley, undulating fields lay beneath a mist so thick that a stranger might have mistaken this corner of the Dordogne for lake country.

Behind him, smoke rose from the chimney at the farmhouse. Claire so enjoyed the pleasure he took in poking embers in the massive hearth that she likely woke, found him gone, and made a fire for his return. There would be fresh eggs and bacon from Laval's farm—and, with the children visiting, morning buns. Everyone he loved was rousing in that old, rough house with its leaky roof. He fought the urge to leave Fonroque without a word and race to The Hague, where he might kill Banović outright. But that would not protect his family; for the librarian had spoken and somewhere that morning, safe in the comfort of a warm bed, Borislav would wake to a breakfast of toast and poached eggs. He would consult his Rolodex and arrange meetings with men who longed for the good old days, when civil strife made the world safe for murder. They would be professionals: ex-military, versatile, and beyond remorse.

Poincaré had once trusted Paolo Ludovici with his life, and he had returned the favor. But to save an entire family—hope was not this elastic. And so Poincaré, the one to whom others turned for answers, despaired. He would have hunted down Borislav himself, but to leave Claire or Etienne was unthinkable. He stood in the vineyard, the countryside waking around him, and resolved never to leave. He would build a walled city; he would triple Montforte's security detail. He would . . . do no such thing, for to shut them away would give Banović his victory. *Ponder this*, the former librarian was calling across the continent: *Reduce a man to dirt. Destroy all that he loves, and watch what he becomes.*

CLAIRE STOOD over the stove with Etienne at her side, the two reunited as a culinary team. Their son's single passion beyond architecture was food—and, happily, he had the metabolism to eat everything he cooked without gaining a gram. For years he and Claire had collaborated on elaborate dinners. Etienne's specialties were sauces and then plating completed meals as if they were submissions to a design exhibit. And why not? At eight, Etienne was constructing buildings from kitchen pans and utensils, with cantilevers and weight-bearing arches. By ten, he was stockpiling construction materials for model skyscrapers he would build deep into the night. At sixteen, he had turned his bedroom into a studio in which he might one week build models of urban villages that honored France's rural past, and in the next build lunar colonies. During those years, Etienne slept beneath the plywood platform he used as the foundation for his projects. In the blink of an eye he had completed graduate school and become the youngest partner in a Paris-based architectural firm with commissions stretching from Dubai to San Francisco.

"Papa—up early, then?"

"You'd think he'd be able to sleep here, of all places," said Claire. "Look at the bags under those eyes." She handed him his coffee. He reached for a piece of cauliflower, but she rapped his knuckles with a wooden spoon. "It's for soup, Henri. Lunch."

Poincaré put a hand to Etienne's cheek and kissed his wife. "Where are the children?"

Claire nodded toward the sitting room, her hands thick in a yeasted dough for morning buns. "They insist you see their project. Lucille calls it 'butter art.'" She shrugged. "From some magazine. It's easier if you go look than my explaining." So he walked to the parlor where he found Émile, Georges, and Chloe seated at the table before the fireplace, Lucille opposite with a bowl of softened butter, watching the children at work. For the first four years of their lives, Poincaré could not tell the twins apart. For a time he depended on Chloe to name her brothers without losing patience, no matter how often he asked. But when the boys discovered his weakness, they exploited it without mercy. Émile and Georges would answer randomly to their grandfather's calls. Poincaré asked Lucille to tie name-tags on strings, which the boys wore necklace style—dutifully at first. But then they switched tags, which sent Chloe into fits of laughter when either one of them entered a room. In the end, the Lord provided when on the back of his left hand Georges developed a cyst that had to be surgically removed. The scar revealed what the boys would not, and Poincaré never shared the source of his sudden knowledge.

"What's this?" he said, leaning over the children.

"Butter art, Papi."

"See here," said Émile. "You take two plates of glass. You spread butter on one. You press the pieces together, pull them open—and look!" He was just separating the plates and proudly presented the result, which looked precisely like the veins of a leaf or the tributaries of a river. *Dendrites*, he said to himself. He searched the room for Fenster's ghost.

"I've got two unused glass plates, Henri. Give it a try."

"If you don't mind, I'll watch," he answered.

Lucille handed him a magazine, *Teaching Science at Home.* "Suit yourself. You may as well know that the children have become proxies in a fight Etienne and I are having. He builds blocks with them and reads stories. I do math with them and science projects. And I don't see anyone complaining!" She was right. Fully absorbed, Georges and Émile ignored their mother and grandfather as they smeared butter on glass. Chloe stood by the window, inspecting her most recent effort.

Lucille left Poincaré to sit by the hearth with the magazine. He was not supposed to have a favorite, he knew. But Chloe was his living treasure. She returned to the table to wipe her glass plates. "Papi," she said. "Look—if you change the amount of butter, you change the pattern." The boys had begun kicking each other beneath the table and finally abandoned their efforts and ran outside. Chloe gathered her brothers' glass, cleaned them, laid all out neatly, and with care measured out increasing amounts of butter across the set. "Do you like shapes, Papi?" She had Claire's round face and blonde hair; but the eyes were Etienne's and the budding scientist pure Lucille.

"Yes," he answered. "I like shapes. I want to see every shape that you make. No tricks! Show me each one."

It had happened before in his career but never with quite such intensity, this confluence of finding like information in every direction he turned. He began to read the article Lucille had left on attuning children to patterns in nature. The boys were outside chasing chickens from the sound of things. Etienne called a ten-minute warning for breakfast, and Poincaré felt a tapping at his knee. Chloe stood before him, hand extended, a yellow barrette hanging by a strand. He unfastened the clip and curled the hair away from her eyes.

"Alright, then," he said, rising to follow. She carried her most recent sample of butter art in one hand and with the other led her grandfather through the kitchen, silently, past an admiring Etienne and Lucille. Poincaré paused to examine two pieces of cauliflower on the countertop—the small floret a miniature of the larger and both, versions of the whole. Chloe tugged at him to continue, and they were soon standing before a door to the barn, where inside the boys were attempting to corner Jacques. Poincaré warned them away from the rooster, and they buzzed past, back into the house. Chloe moved no further, so Poincaré knelt to his granddaughter's height and stared at the door, which had accumulated layer upon cracked layer of paint over a long history. The child pointed.

"Alright, then," said Poincaré. "What do we have?"

"*Look*," she said.

"I see a door, Chloe. I'm looking."

She held her butter art beside the paint. "The patterns are the same. Why, Papi?"

They were the same.

"Why?"

"I don't know, dear."

His mind was racing.

"It's very pretty."

"It is!"

"Do you know what I think, Papi? I think that God is tiny and also very large. I think God lives in the butter and the paint. He lives in shapes, Papi."

Poincaré heard the boys rumbling around the corner, Georges calling: "I found a new toy in Papa's briefcase! Come on!" And they were gone, leaving Poincaré to wonder how an eight-year-old had seen what Fenster saw. Or perhaps Fenster's gift had been to see what children saw and attach a mathematics to that.

They returned to the farmhouse, where Chloe resumed her project and Poincaré continued with his reading. Astonishment had become a new, steady state in all matters relating to James Fenster as Poincaré began to grasp the reach of the man's mind. The geometries Fenster studied were hiding everywhere in plain sight: cracks spread across plaster walls like lightning bolts frozen in time, like mountain ridges photographed from space, like the veins of Laurent's perpetually bloodshot eyes. Poincaré looked down and saw a forearm branching to a peninsula—a hand with five digits, and in that saw the fan of a river delta. He set the magazine aside and closed his eyes, willing enough to see rivers in lightning and lightning in mountain ranges. But he could not follow Fenster to the movement of goods and services across national boundaries. A *mathematics* of globalization? His purchase of a train ticket yesterday afternoon did not obey the same laws that governed the growth of the oak tree on his terrace.

He could not make that leap.

What happened when Poincaré opened his eyes came so quickly that he was able to reconstruct the event only moments later, as he lay on the floor with Chloe sobbing in his arms, everyone bent over him as if he had suffered a seizure. He had been sitting in his chair by the fireplace. Etienne, Lucille, and Claire were just finishing their preparations for a grand breakfast as the boys dodged in and out of the house with their game. When Poincaré looked up from his magazine, he saw Chloe bent over her project, a narrow red beam trained on her forehead. Before he could speak or think, he dove across the room, snatched the child, placing his body between her and the windows, then rolled behind the table. Chloe shrieked. Still holding her, he edged the two of them into the hallway, beyond view of the windows. Utensils dropped and in the next instant Poincaré was staring up at them all. "Laser," he stammered. "Targeting laser. Chloe's head." The child squirmed from his arms and ran to her mother.

Claire, a hand to her own forehead, leaned against the fireplace for support. Etienne knelt beside his father and put a hand to his cheek.

"Chloe—she's alright?"

"The boys were playing, Papa. They found a laser pointer in my bag. Just before we came down, I gave a presentation in Paris. They were *playing*." Etienne sat him up. "Lucille. Please, some water."

"Chloe?"

The child turned and sniffled. Etienne nudged her into his father's arms. "She's fine—see?"

"Papi, you scared me." Chloe put a hand to his cheek.

Poincaré pulled her close and waited for Lucille's return. "I'm sorry. I'm so sorry," he said over and over, fighting for composure.

They must see him strong. "I have something to tell you," he said as Claire knelt beside him. "I have difficult news."

In their room that night, the window open to a hint of summer, Poincaré lay waiting for Claire, who had gone to check on the children. The bedroom door creaked open and she went to a bureau to comb out her hair before climbing into bed. No one could say how old the bed was—possibly older than the farmhouse itself, the documents for which could be traced back three hundred years. It had come to them along with every other well-used furnishing as part of the sale. Claire gave everything to the parish church save the farm table by the hearth and the bed, which had seen who knew how many births and deaths. Poincaré watched her tie a scarf through her hair before turning off the light.

She drew close beneath the duvet. Her head rose and fell with his breathing. "Henri," she said. "How bad is this?"

"Bad," he answered.

"Will that man hurt us?"

"I'm afraid he'll try."

"We can't hide. I won't do that, you know."

He listened for unusual sounds in the night and relaxed only on realizing that if professionals came, Claire and the others would be dead before anyone heard a thing. He could say none of this. He hardly knew how to speak of Banović to himself.

"We'll do what we have to," she said. "Interpol will protect us. It's you I'm worried about. You're already a challenge to live with. You're about to become impossible."

He stroked her hair.

"We'll be alright," she said. "You know, Etienne laughed at me just now."

"Why?"

"Because when he came to check on the children, I was already checking on them. We stood there a moment, watching them sleep."

"Then he's no better than you."

"And Lucille. With her schedule—everyday, it's another project with them. Yesterday morning she asked Marc Laval if the children could gather the eggs. You should have seen the chaos! The chickens flying, Chloe and the boys screaming. Marc stood in the doorway, arms crossed. He wasn't angry exactly, but I could tell he wasn't pleased, either. . . . Do you know Georges and Émile set up a table at the end of the driveway to sell the eggs. For three hours they tried, but not a single car came down the road! Finally Laval bought the eggs himself."

"He didn't."

"He did!"

"But the man collects them every day for us. He has his own chickens!"

Claire propped her arm on a pillow. "What do the children know of that? They have a little money in their pockets and think they're rich. Lucille will have them up in the morning working on some new project. She's wonderful with them, Henri. Better than I ever was."

"That's not true."

"I didn't have her energy, and God knows I don't, now."

"You did." He kissed her hand. "You're just too senile to remember."

She poked him. "I've finished a painting—did I tell you? I'm in the middle of crating it for an exhibition in June. New York this time."

"What of?"

"You mean *who.*"

"Alright. Who?"

"You, my dear."

Poincaré sat up.

"Relax. It's abstract, even for me. Not even Etienne will see you in it. But it's you just the same."

"And this is going to hang in some stranger's house?"

"We'll decide that after the exhibition."

"I'll buy it. Don't send it off."

"I've made a commitment. And I'm not selling—to you, anyway. Possibly to Etienne for a euro or two."

"Claire, please. . . . Have you titled it?"

"I'm considering 'A Serious Man.' Or just your initials, above mine. When we're back in Lyon, you'll come for a look." She slipped a hand beneath his shirt. "Did you see Etienne trying to be stern with them at bedtime? It's an impossibility, same as it was for you." She laughed, and Poincaré listened to her breathing and to the creaking of the farmhouse. Through the open window came a scent of honeysuckle and a fluttering of leaves. Claire turned, and he drew her to him and they kissed. Their lips parted, barely enough to let a secret slip through, and they lay like that for a time, breathing one another's air as moonlight slanted across the bed. Claire opened her gown. "I'm just a country girl," she said, "but I know some things." And with that, for a time, Poincaré forgot Bosnia and Amsterdam and every damned place that had ever claimed a piece of him. He was with Claire, and the world was right.

Chapter 12

Interpol had laid the thickest of blankets over Poincaré's family. Short of moving two households in two cities into a single fortress, the plan could not have been more thorough—with armed guards standing four-hour shifts around the clock; electronic surveillance of perimeters; and coordination with local police, with increased patrols. But Poincaré felt he could do more and took an indefinite leave of absence to coordinate his family's security. Well into that effort, with no end in sight to projects that were turning his apartment in Lyon and Etienne's in Paris into mini-police states, Claire's mood darkened. She warned against destroying villages in order to save them. She advised, gently, that he return to work. He ignored her complaints even though they triggered a painful memory of the time she took Etienne on a month-long holiday, alone. "Love us first," she insisted. "Love your family first, then your job." In time, they compromised: while his assignments might take him away for weeks on end, when he returned he would do so in body *and* mind. He would shield his family from the business of police work. For three decades, the agreement held—until Banović voided it.

In a corner of their kitchen one morning, she took his hand and pressed it to her cheek. "I'm suffocating," she said. "Etienne called to say he doesn't want you visiting anymore. You're scaring the children." She leaned into him. "The agents watch us every second. Please. Let us breathe."

"Those men are out there," he insisted. "You have no idea—"

"You're right," she said. "I don't."

In the living room, he poured himself a tall glass of Rémy Martin and collapsed onto a seat overlooking Lyon. When they had found this apartment just before their wedding, with only a bed and a single pot to their names, they drank too much wine one evening and, standing naked before these same windows, watched the remnants of a storm break apart and sail away. They toasted the future, drank more wine, and made love until their exhausted bodies cried for sleep. All these years later, the lights of Lyon had not changed much—this ancient city, ever young. But Poincaré had changed. In recent weeks he had felt the pull of gravity. His bones ached and his head throbbed. He drank his cognac, then another. Claire joined him and laid her head on his shoulder.

"Banović will win if you don't go to work," she said. "He's winning now."

"I can't. Not with you and Etienne exposed like this."

"Go to work, Henri. We're protected, and you're driving us mad."

"No."

She reached her arms around him. "My love, I'm not asking."

Poincaré knew she was right. "The case I'm working on will take me to the U.S. I'll work again if we can talk each day," he said. "Then, if you need me, I could get back to Lyon within hours."

"That would be fine. Go."

"Promise me you'll be OK."

She promised, but that changed nothing.

THE MAIN lecture hall in the Science Center of Harvard University was a concrete bunker set into a building as chilly and bare as a mine shaft. After he cleared customs at Logan airport, Poincaré had time enough to hail a taxi and catch the last twenty minutes of Dana Chambi's final class of the term. As Fenster's senior graduate student, she had taken on his "Mathematics of Nature" when he did not return from Amsterdam. Poincaré wanted to see Chambi at work before interviewing her.

The steeply pitched amphitheater funneled to a platform with a lab bench, a demonstration table, and a lectern. Chambi stood by the bench and a computer as some two hundred students looked on. She must have succeeded at a difficult task, he reasoned; for though Fenster was gone, having taught just two classes of his perennially oversubscribed course for non-majors, the students remained. Poincaré took a seat.

"So, then," she said. "Which three brave souls will share their answers to the final exam question? You were to write an equation, run it 100,000 times on your computers, graph each data point—and model this:

"A common fern. From the number of you who sought help this past week, you probably don't care to see another one ever again."

The students laughed.

"But consider. Stroll through a forest and you'll find millions of ferns, yet no two are identical—even if you can't distinguish them genetically. They will be similar, but not identical. Just like oak trees, Macaque monkeys, snowflakes, and people." Poincaré thought of the twins. This was true. "How does a fern decide, if I can use that word, where to place its branches, how long they should extend, in which direction? It's as though nature has a rough model called 'fern' to which individual ferns are attracted, but which leaves room for individual variations. Your job was to write, then graph, an equation that could serve as a model for this fern. Volunteers, please. Let's share the wealth—and perhaps end the semester with some entertainment."

The room buzzed as students anticipated who would risk a public hanging. Chambi leaned against the lab desk and made an exaggerated show of impatience, tapping her foot and folding and refolding her arms. She said: "If I announced that the first volunteer would receive an A for the term, would that change anyone's mind?"

Twelve students stood.

"Excellent," she said. "I haven't said that. But as long as you're standing, you—" She pointed to a slender young woman. "Ms. Cheng, I believe? Please. And you—" She pointed to a heavily tattooed man seated two rows before Poincaré. He thought she registered his presence before moving to her third choice. The students made their way to the pit of the amphitheater.

"Don't worry," said Chambi. "The first time I tried modeling a fern—" *How long ago?* he wondered. She was in her late twenties, at most. "I produced something that looked like a porcupine on a stick. So be patient. Our math majors—all four of them in this class—will get other chances. No one else need bother. But the next time you read a weather forecast or a prediction about climate change, you'll know that mathematical modeling is involved. I wrote this exam to offer a hint of how difficult the job can be—and modeling those systems, I can assure you, is infinitely more complicated than modeling a fern."

The first student, the tattooed one who also wore metal rings in his lips, attached a flash drive to Chambi's computer and pulled up the image of a fern on hallucinogens.

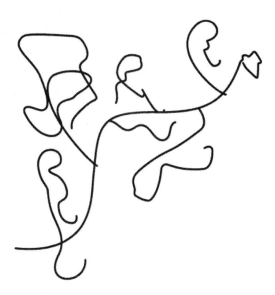

The class erupted as the young man deadpanned: "People think only dogs look like their owners." Even Chambi was laughing. "My initial values were clearly wrong for x and y, and I couldn't find a way to properly represent the function of chance in the equation. If I saw this thing in a dream, I'd wake up screaming." He left the lectern to applause, with students congratulating him all the way to his seat. The second young man looked as though he stepped directly off a yacht into the lecture hall. He wore salmon-colored shorts, a white polo shirt with an upturned collar, and an expression not quite sardonic enough to mask his terror. "Mr.?"

"Henley," the young man said. "Wendell."

"Well, Mr. Henley. What do we have?"

The student pulled up his work. Again, the class howled.

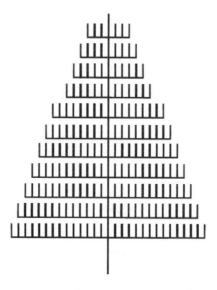

"I tried," he said. "It looks like a telephone pole with too many cross pieces and toothpicks for leaves. I went at this hard for a solid week, changing one value after another, trying to build a curve into the form. I should have locked my fern in a room with that dude's fern. Their children might have had a chance." His tattooed classmate raised a fist in salute. "It was all good through about 20,000 iterations. Then everything stiffened up, no matter how many times I changed the equation. Brute force usually works for me. Not this time."

The students in the lecture hall were enjoying themselves, and so was Poincaré. The pressure was indeed off, they realized, because no professor would risk failing an entire class. The relief was palpable, until the young Asian woman stepped to the lectern. Poincaré knew what was coming. The student wore a thin, pale green sweater and a pleated skirt—much like a grade-school uniform. She stood with hands folded neatly before her, looking down, as the others presented their images. When she stepped forward, her straight black hair shining in the spotlights, the room went silent.

"Here is the graph and here is the equation I used to create my fern," she said, her voice difficult to hear though she spoke into a microphone. She was a flower, marveled Poincaré, with a prodigious mind. She said: "I iterated this function just over 100,000 times. Thank you very much."

$$\begin{pmatrix} x_{n+1} \\ y_{n+1} \end{pmatrix} = \begin{pmatrix} a & b \\ c & d \end{pmatrix} \begin{pmatrix} x_n \\ y_n \end{pmatrix} + \begin{pmatrix} e \\ f \end{pmatrix}$$

She returned to her seat, and a few students rose to congratulate her. The majority sat quietly, stunned.

"Cheer up," said Chambi. "Ms. Cheng is fifteen and ran out of math classes to take in her native Taiwan. Many of us believe she has a promising career. What will count for the rest of you is your explanation of how you approached the problem. As you may have discovered along with Mr. Henley, brute force does not work with mathematical modeling. One must use the math—must be intuitive, even."

A hand shot up. "Professor Chambi. Poets are intuitive."

"So I've heard," she said.

"This is a math class."

"Good mathematicians are poets, too," she answered. "They use a different symbol system."

Another hand went up.

"Yes? Mr.—"

"Groupman. I'm confused on a point. Ms. Cheng's equation—of the fern. Would you call it a description?"

Chambi shuffled her notes into a neat pile. "Please rephrase. I'm not quite clear on what you mean by *description*."

The student stood. "Say I start with a fern in the forest. I could write a paragraph describing it, I could paint it, or I might take a picture. No one would confuse these with the fern itself." As Poincaré watched Chambi listen, he thought he glimpsed a smile curling her lips. She allowed the student to finish. "The equation of the fern is more of a blueprint than the painting or the paragraph would be. I'm saying that the mathematics is, or could be, the thing—the fern—itself. It's like DNA, but it's not DNA. You could add a little dirt and water to the equation, and there you go. Dr. Fenster and you have convinced me that every process in nature can be modeled with an equation. Is the point that these equations are not just descriptions of reality but reality itself?"

Chambi crossed the amphitheater stage, trailing a hand along the lab bench. "Mr. Groupman," she said. "By *reality itself*, what do you mean?"

He stamped on the concrete floor. "This." He picked up his knapsack. "And this. All of it."

"I see." She adjusted the microphone. "Allow me to answer this way. For us to even consider what you suggest, the mathematics has to be good—so good that for this fern, when you run a 3-D graphing program, you think you're seeing an actual fern in an actual forest. We're talking about a model elegant enough to anticipate the way wind moves along the forest floor and the way dew settles on their fronds in the early morning. If the equation succeeds at that level, and if you're a mathematician, you would use the word *describe*. You would say that the equation *describes* what you see. But if you're a theologian, you might use a different word."

She posed the question without posing it and let the room go quiet. If Poincaré had shut his eyes and did not know better, he would have guessed there were only a few students in the cavernous hall. The seconds passed until, from a far corner, a student called out: "*Govern.* A theologian might say that equations govern what we see."

"Possibly," answered Chambi.

"But that would raise the question of a *governor*," called another student.

"Yes," said Chambi. "Governor. Architect. What have you. Who would write the equations of nature?"

Again, silence.

The young man who had spoken earlier stood. "According to the catalog, this class fulfills a *math* requirement."

Chambi grinned. "Never mind that. What are you, Mr. Groupman, a mathematician or a theologian? Or perhaps that's something one doesn't decide."

The student shrugged. "I can't really say. Neither. Both. Depends what time of the morning you ask."

"An honest man! If you need a second opinion, the Divinity School is around the corner, on Francis Avenue."

The students laughed, and Chambi glanced at her watch. "That's it, then. I'll review your work and send along your grades via e-mail. A final word, if you'll indulge me. I stepped in for Professor Fenster when he died unexpectedly in Amsterdam. I want you all to remember him, not me, as your instructor for this course, though he was with you for a few weeks only. These were his materials and his notes. The idea for this exam assignment was his. Dr. Fenster was a great man, and mathematics for him was not just a job but life itself. He found exquisite beauty in equations—and, yes, he was regarded around the world as an intuitive with them, a poet. As for your confusion, Mr. Groupman . . . it is the best possible confusion. Keep at it. Good day to you all, and enjoy the summer. It has been a privilege."

Applause, then a commotion of books closing and backpacks being zippered. Two dozen students descended from the amphitheater to surround Chambi. For twenty minutes Poincaré watched this animated, dynamic woman engage her students, who continued taking notes as they spoke informally. His cell phone buzzed and a text message came through from Gisele De Vries:

> Analysis at European Space Agency agrees with Dutch forensics: Amsterdam explosive = ammonium perchlorate with additives. NASA says sample = military grade fuel not available on open market + additives to boost explosion. More later. GDV

Poincaré typed a return message:

> Bomber had access to or knowledge of military grade rocket fuel. Send request to NASA, European Space Agency + Russian + Chinese agencies. Ask: On staff, who had knowledge to doctor AP? If Russians or Chinese balk, ask American Intel for listing of personnel at those agencies. HP

Chambi dispatched her final student with a handshake and a wave. She climbed the stairs along the far side of the theater, then crossed a long row of seats to Poincaré. She was of medium build with a round face, broad nose, and a rope-like braid of jet-black hair—Ecuadorian according to Poincaré's notes, in the country on a student visa to study the modeling of complex systems. From a biography posted on the math department's Web page, he had learned that her particular interest was the spread of drug-resistant tuberculosis. Her intention was to model the spread mathematically; then she could return home and join the Ministry of Health to combat the disease, which disproportionately affected the country's indigenous poor.

"If you're the Immigration and Naturalization Service," she said, "my visa's in order."

He laughed. "Is it that obvious? You have a gift, you know. Henri Poincaré." He extended a hand. "Excuse my not asking permission to attend, first. I hope I wasn't a distraction."

"You are now. You said *Poincaré?*"

And then he remembered. "My father's grandfather."

"Jules Henri Poincaré was your great-grandfather?"

"One doesn't choose, you know."

She walked him to a concrete alcove by the main entrance to the Science Center. "A remarkable man. Truly a giant of mathematics."

"Which I'm not, unfortunately. My parents hoped I would have the family's math gene, but I disappointed them, Dr. Chambi. I tried for a time but gave it up—turns out I wasn't a poet with equations." He smiled.

"And I'm no Doctor of Philosophy—yet. James was my thesis advisor, and when he died no one else in the department would take me on because no one understood his work, or mine. So I'm left with three-quarters of a dissertation and only a few possible mentors in the world, none of them very good. Now if your great-grandfather were around . . . Meanwhile, Harvard's forcing me out."

"Impossible. You're too good."

She wore a scarf at her neck, and Poincaré could see the edges of a large port-wine stain that discolored her otherwise smooth, honey-nut skin. She adjusted the scarf when she saw him looking. "I'm expendable. The math department's chock full of grad students, and the dean's not feeling particularly loyal to me at the moment—never mind that I took over James's class with absolutely no warning. But enough," she said. "The blood of Jules Henri runs in you! You never met him?"

Poincaré laughed. "I'm old, Ms. Chambi. Not that old."

The sudden veneration bordering on awe: it was the same whenever he met a mathematician or physicist. As a young man, Poincaré felt so burdened by the family name that he considered changing it. These days he simply accepted posthumous compliments and moved on. "About all I inherited was a fondness for puzzles," he confessed. "Useful for someone in my trade. But between you and me, I can't tell a derivative from a derriere."

Chambi laughed easily and set her computer bag on a ledge. "I somehow doubt that. Your great-grandfather's talent comes along once in a generation. In fact, he was James's personal hero. He kept quotations of Poincaré's around the office, taped to his computers. I'm serious: these were words to live by for James. Einstein should have referenced Jules Henri, you know. At the very least, your great-grandfather anticipated the general theory of relativity, if he didn't get there first. Not to mention chaos theory."

Poincaré the younger pointed across a corridor, to a small cafeteria. "I'm here on business, Ms. Chambi. I want to learn more about Dr. Fenster. I'm investigating his death." He handed her a business card.

Chambi studied it. "Interpol?"

"That's right."

"The whole subject upsets me."

"Yes, I know. It upsets me, too. A terrible loss."

"I'm sorry, Inspector. I can't talk about it." She jerked a hand in front of her face to read a wristwatch, then adjusted her scarf. "I forgot. I have to be somewhere."

"Just five minutes," he said. "Then a follow-up tomorrow, perhaps. I'll be in Boston through Saturday."

"I can't."

He produced a photo of Madeleine Rainier. "Do you know this woman?"

Chambi held up her hands. "I can't. Really."

"Tomorrow, then. We'll meet during office hours. I believe you're in all morning."

"You checked? I won't talk about this. It makes me too sad. The answer is *no*."

"And you won't talk because you're sad? Or is it that you're busy?"

"Busy. Sad. Both. I have to go."

"This is an official investigation," he reminded her. "I could learn something that will help us find out what happened. I know you want to help. Talk to me."

"I *must* go."

"Tomorrow, then."

"I'm seeing students."

"All day? You have to eat. How about 12:30 in that café, tomorrow?" He quickly considered possibilities: a broken affair, rage that Fenster had somehow stalled her dissertation. Or perhaps precisely what she said: sadness. "How's Thursday?"

"I'm busy."

"Ms. Chambi, I must insist."

She shouldered her bag and collected her notes. "Mid-morning, Friday. Check the department's Web site for my office hours." With that Dana Chambi crossed the corridor, negotiated a revolving door, and made her escape.

At his hotel that afternoon, Poincaré called Lyon.

"Henri! You had a good flight? You're well?"

Everything was fine, he assured her. "What's happening there?" In fact, she had answered his question by answering the phone. He relaxed.

"Nothing's changed. I told you we'd be OK, and we are."

"Etienne and the family . . . you've checked?"

"They're also fine. Really. Come, kiss me goodnight. I was just turning in. Call earlier tomorrow."

Poincaré made a sound with his lips. When he flipped his phone shut, he imagined lying beside his wife in their bed at Fonroque, listening to the crickets and to the field mice rooting around the foundation of the house, looking for a morsel and a warm bed of their own. Perhaps this arrangement could work, he thought. He would call, she would answer, and all would be well.

CHAPTER 13

Poincaré groped for his phone, unsure of what continent he was on. "What?" he mumbled, knocking over a glass of water. He sat up and shielded his eyes against a sunburst at the edges of a hotel curtain.

"Henri, news."

"Paolo?"

"Borislav's real name is Christof Mladic, and he was Banović's number two in Patriots for Greater Serbia. Interpol issued a Red Notice for his arrest two years ago, but the Dutch border police missed him both coming and going. I found him in Banja Luka, living above a laundromat." A delay, clicks and static, then a reconstituted voice: "It's true, I'm afraid. Banović bought four contracts: on Claire, Etienne, Lucille, and the children—he counted them as one. He may or may not have taken a contract on you. I've alerted Albert."

"Their identities, Paolo. *Who?*"

More data would not change grim facts; but he listened for some detail, some overlooked nuance that might suggest a defense or, better still, an angle of attack. He swung his legs to the edge of the bed.

"That's a problem. Mladic didn't know the contractors. He worked through a middleman to add a layer of security. At Banović's instruction, he passed names, addresses, and money to the middleman, who then made the arrangements."

"Made?"

"I was three days too late. The contractors are likely solo operators from formerly Eastern bloc countries, ex-Stasi types. I'm in the process of locating the middleman now. He's Hungarian, and I'm in Budapest looking for him. Mladic was able to give me that much before his accident."

Poincaré did not ask.

"This information is solid, Henri. I'll call with news as it develops, but I thought you should know."

Poincaré dropped his head into his hands, for nothing he could do on this side of the Atlantic or that could alter Banović's decree. He dialed Monforte, who assured him that the news merely confirmed the wisdom of arrangements already in place. "Ludovici's report changes nothing," the director told him. "Ambassadors don't get the kind of coverage we're giving your family. Trust the system, Henri."

Poincaré had entrusted his life to that system; but he demanded something better for his family, a guarantee that did not exist. If prime ministers and presidents could not evade determined assassins, how much easier a target, then, a child on the swings at a park or Etienne, stepping into his car on a run for milk? He showered, found a quick cup of coffee, and read enough of the *Boston Globe* to confirm that his personal world was not the only one in collapse. Ethiopian separatists were executing Chinese oil riggers; Sunnis had drilled holes into Shiites, calling it God's work; Shiites were decapitating Sunnis in the name of that same God and dumping bodies in alleyways; and in a spot of local color, a college student in Massachusetts had murdered thirteen classmates. Just because.

Poincaré left the hotel. The day was clear, and a bright sun had turned the Charles into a reflecting pool on the surface of which rowers glided in pairs and foursomes, nimble as water spiders. He climbed a footbridge and positioned himself mid-river, the cities of Cambridge to one side and Boston to the other waking around him. Cyclists and joggers plied the footpaths; traffic buzzed along the boulevards. He watched and he waited, until he could wait no longer.

"Claire?"

He could see her smile on the hammered surface of the water. *Talk*, he instructed himself. She had begun a new canvas? Excellent. The children were learning to swim. And Etienne—he won a commission to design a new wing for a museum in Brussels. That they were living ordinary lives reassured him not at all. He scrubbed the anxiety from his voice. Face-to-face, he would have given it away. He could hear her breathing.

"Claire?"

"Yes, Henri?"

A rower emerged from beneath the bridge in a long glide. The oars dipped, the back straightened. A surge of power. With reasonable connections, he could be home by dinner.

"Nothing," he said. "I just wanted to hear your voice."

NOTWITHSTANDING THE uncertainties in France, Poincaré had come to the States with a full agenda: to learn more about Fenster and his work; pin a history to Madeleine Rainier; discuss rocket fuel and its off-label use as an explosive with a propulsions expert. Before Ludovici's call, it had all seemed manageable in a three-week visit that began in Boston and ended at the Jet Propulsion Laboratory in Pasadena. Now, just arrived, he wanted to cross the Atlantic and erect steel barriers around his family.

Barely a mile out of Harvard Square, he compared the address on a slip of paper with the less-than-promising match before him, a badly weathered door sandwiched between *The Bombay Bistro* and *Mike's True Tattoo*. He pressed a buzzer and listened to a receptionist mangle his name over a call box wired sometime before the Eisenhower administration.

"Ponky—*who*?"

"Raaay," he said, leaning closer. "Pwon – Ka – Raaay."

"Inter-*what*?"

After too many minutes of this, he must have uttered the right combination of syllables, for a lock on the door buzzed and he stepped inside to find Peter Roy at the third-floor landing, ready with an apology. "My wife's mother," he shrugged. "If I fire her, I'll have to find another bed to sleep in."

Roy could have been one of the rowers Poincaré had seen. Lanky and graceful, he showed his visitor into a modest reception area appointed with a worn leather couch and a few folding chairs. Across the room, Roy's mother-in-law sat behind a government surplus desk ready to leap at his throat or bake him cookies, he couldn't tell which. Skin hung in heavy folds from her neck and upper arms, and even from a distance Poincaré could smell the powder she had dusted herself with that morning.

Roy shouted his introduction. When she cupped a hand to her ear, Poincaré understood their tussle at the call box.

"He's French?" she said, brightening. "I went to France thirty-seven years ago with my first husband. We saw the Eif—"

"Gladys, I'm sure the inspector is interested but he's very busy right now. Maybe later." He nudged his guest towards the conference room, but not before Poincaré reached for the old woman's hand and kissed it. She was just the age to have fallen for Maurice Chevalier in *Gigi*.

"Think of her as the mother of the woman you love," he said moments later, taking a seat.

"In theory," answered Roy.

The conference room had at some point in its recent history been an oversized closet. Poincaré could see poorly patched screw holes for coat hooks and brackets, still attached, to hold poles. At the plastic table before him, he counted five folding chairs. The walls were bare, save for two diplomas in gilded frames—one from Princeton and the other from Columbia Law School. The room's single window opened to a brick wall across a narrow ventilation shaft.

"I've got nothing more to offer than when we spoke by phone," said Roy.

This was not a problem, Poincaré assured him. He had come to learn about James Fenster from people who actually knew the man, even if slightly. "One can't investigate a name," he said, reaching for a notepad.

"I'll try to help, then. . . . I met Dr. Fenster only once," he began. "For about ninety minutes—but that was enough to form an impression. He arrived one day, without an appointment, for help completing a will he had printed off the Internet. I never paid much attention to math, so I hadn't exactly heard of him. But he made such an impact that after he left I looked him up and confirmed what was fairly obvious: the man was the kind of brilliant that has to slow itself down to interact with the world. Fenster was altogether friendly, but as you spoke with him you got the sense he was downshifting to a speed you might have a hope of understanding. He had this way of taking fifteen or twenty seconds to frame a simple sentence, like—*Yes, I printed this document off the Internet.* You heard it and thought *you* were the one who had missed something obvious. There were galaxies spinning in his head. I knew as much even before I read the bio and discovered all the papers and awards.

"Don't misunderstand," Roy continued. "The man wasn't patronizing. You could see him trying to communicate, but at some level he simply couldn't. Put him in a computer lab or a library, stand him in front of a lecture hall, but heaven forbid you should invite him to a cocktail party. He was a rail thin six feet with a halo of blondish, curly hair—at twenty-nine still boyish looking. Meek socially, ferocious intellectually. The very last person on earth someone would kill out of malice."

"So people say, Mr. Roy. Your only business with him was the will?"

"Peter, please. That's right." The attorney rolled his sleeves and folded heavily calloused hands. In fact, Poincaré noted, he may have been a rower.

"Who was the beneficiary?"

"The estate's settled, so there's no harm in telling. A $60,000 term life policy became seed money for an after-school Math League in the City of Cambridge. Dr. Fenster said he didn't believe in insurance. The money came from a university policy that he couldn't have disclaimed if he wanted to. He needed merely to fill in a beneficiary."

"No family, then?"

Poincaré knew the answer but waited for confirmation.

"None that I could find. Fenster didn't list anyone with Harvard's human resources department or with any office at Princeton. In its admissions files, Princeton had a mailing address for him in Ohio, so I tried that. Nothing. So I engaged a private investigator in Cleveland who discovered that he had been a ward of the state—bounced through five foster homes over eleven years. The investigator contacted each provider and heard more or less the same story. Fenster was not considered adoptable—apparently not the son fathers want to play ball with or take on fishing trips. The Department of Youth Services wouldn't release his birth records without a court order, and I decided to drop the inquiry since the sums involved were not large. I would have needed to hire a local attorney and in the process eat up half of his estate filing papers, so I let it go and just last week issued checks to the Math League, once the will cleared probate.

"But a certificate of birth exists?"

"The denial was automatic, so I doubt anyone checked. In some adoption cases, not even the adoptee can access the records. I don't know if that's the case here. We never got that far."

"Well, presumably he was born. I'll have Interpol request the file as part of my investigation." Poincaré made a note to himself.

"It would make no difference," said Roy. "You'll need a court order. Of course I'll e-mail you the full investigator's report, but I can tell you now it makes for some pretty grim reading. I don't doubt the foster families' hearts were in the right place, but they didn't know what to do with that kind of intelligence. School was Fenster's one anchor, and even there teachers didn't know how to handle him. I'd say that between the ages of four and fifteen, he suffered from benign neglect until Princeton rescued him with a full scholarship. He completed his doctorate at twenty, went to teach at Harvard the next year, and was tenured three years after that. Not only did Fenster have no family or siblings, he almost certainly had no social life here in Cambridge. As a first-year professor, he couldn't very well socialize with undergraduates—people his own age. And as a young twenty-something he wasn't going to be accepted as a social equal by his colleagues, regardless of his gifts. He was an adult to the undergraduates and a child to his faculty colleagues. He never fit."

"Was James Fenster his birth name?"

"That much I know. The first family—the one that planned to adopt him—gave him the name James, or 'Jimmy' Fenster. They actually gave him back after a six-month trial, citing incompatibility. There had been some glitch in the paperwork, and when the time came to make the adoption official, the family balked. Then it was off to four more homes. The name stuck, though. Getting admitted to Princeton was the best thing that happened to Fenster. Altogether rescued him."

Poincaré reasoned that at some point Fenster must have turned a corner socially. The engagement to Madeleine Rainier, though broken, proved that much. "Was he nervous around you?" Poincaré asked. "Did you sense that he thought himself in danger of any sort?"

"No. He seemed calm enough."

"Medical issues, then. Why make a will at so young an age? Was there any indication of sickness?"

Roy shrugged. "He looked healthy in a sunken-chest sort of way. After the bombing, the police reviewed his medical records— apparently, he used the university's medical and dental schools for routine visits. All that looked fine, I was told. As for his state of mind, he seemed perfectly at ease about making a will. Absolutely no hint of crisis. Fenster sat where you're sitting and said he found me in the yellow pages and now that he was here, he appreciated—what did he call it—my *austerity*. You may have noticed all the mahogany and framed art in my office. My clients regard my services the way they do pizza. One slice is as good as the next, so you buy where you live. I'm the neighborhood attorney. I keep my overhead low and my prices low. Dr. Fenster said that this was just the way he liked things. Simple."

"What do you charge per slice?" Poincaré was pointing to the diplomas.

The attorney laughed. "When I was younger, quite a bit. Princeton and Columbia were useful at my last job at a downtown firm— former partner, large salary, larger ulcers. When the practice of law became too much of a business, I left to get back to a scale I understood. Here no one cares where I went to school as long as I can help renegotiate a mortgage or make peace with the immigration police. My services aren't free, Inspector—there are public agencies for that. But I don't charge $500 an hour, either. And if you happen to be short on cash, I'll negotiate. One client paid with a year's worth of homemade jam. So it all works out. Fenster paid by check. He had another $60,000 saved in a bank account, and that went to the Math League, too. He didn't own a car. He rented his apartment.

I'm not sure when the investigators are going to release that back to the landlord."

"His belongings—what will you do with those?"

"Donate them, eventually. In my disposition of the estate, I've sorted through all his finances, which didn't take much time. He paid most of his bills by check and maintained a credit card only to make occasional purchases online. There was no outstanding debt. Nothing at all remarkable about his estate—except his laptop computer, the one he used at home. Harvard claims it holds Fenster's intellectual property and therefore belongs to the university. One of Fenster's funding sources, Charles Bell, says that it was his foundation's money Fenster used to buy the computer and that, therefore, it belongs to him. Strangely enough, the dispute is headed to court. At the moment, the state is holding the hard drive as evidence."

"What's on it?"

"That's just it," said Roy. "No one knows because no one can crack the password. The forensics lab hired a cryptologist, but Fenster apparently invented his own digital lock on the hard drive, so you can imagine how difficult this is going to be. Still, Bell and Harvard have already sued each other and the Commonwealth to release the drive."

"What are the sums involved? How much did Bell give Fenster?"

"I've heard the figure $8 million in conversation. Bell insists he's entitled to some return on his investment—return on a hard drive that's likely worth $400. Harvard calls the millions a tax-deductible donation to the university, not an investment. The fight could take years to resolve."

Poincaré wrote down Bell's contact information as Peter Roy looked on, smiling.

"What?" said Poincaré .

"Judge the man for yourself. Let's just say he has a personality consistent with his success."

Poincaré liked Roy. He liked the idea of accepting homemade jam as payment. He liked the bare walls and the outline of coat hooks under a rough splash of paint. He liked the plastic tables and the care Roy took in knotting his bow tie. He especially liked his mother-in-law. "So what does your lawyerly instinct tell you about

Madeleine Rainier?" he asked. "Did you get any sense that she was after Fenster's money? A hundred twenty thousand dollars is not insignificant."

"Ms. Rainier? I hardly think she was after money. She asked me to fax a letter to the Dutch authorities authorizing her as executor and then immediately hired me to dispose of the estate as quickly as possible, according to the will—in which she had no financial interest whatsoever. After a series of phone calls just after the bombing, I lost contact. The phone numbers I had used went dead, and my e-mails started bouncing back to me. I did get this, though." Roy produced a postcard with a "Welcome to Switzerland" arched in block letters above a photo of mountains and a cow grazing on a steeply angled meadow. On the reverse, in a script the authenticity of which Poincaré had no reason to doubt, was a simple note: *Thank you for your help in a difficult time. M. Rainier.*

Postmarked Zurich, two weeks after the bombing. So she had slipped out of the Netherlands after all. "I understand the money went to the Math League," said Poincaré, "and that Rainier saw none of it. Still, I'm never surprised when money sits at the bottom of a case. Would you mind if I reviewed Fenster's financial records? Perhaps you could copy his bank statements and canceled checks. Anything along these lines could prove useful."

"It's pretty sleepy stuff," said the attorney. "But help yourself. He maintained all his finances online with a single bank here in town. I've got the past five years of his savings, checking, and credit card accounts on a flash drive. You're welcome to it."

Poincaré rose to shake the attorney's hand. "I'll be direct," he said. "I consider Madeleine Rainier a suspect in James Fenster's murder. Interpol has issued a warrant, so at present she's a fugitive from justice. This means that if you hear from her again—"

"Of course," said Roy. "I didn't share her contact information before—"

"You were perfectly within your rights, and hers. She wasn't a suspect then. It's just that attorney-client privilege often complicates my work."

"A necessary complication, Inspector."

"I know, I know," Poincaré sniffed. "Rule of law."

Roy walked him to the tiny receiving area. "Give me a moment to copy Fenster's financial records. In the meantime, take a seat. You can watch Gladys abusing my next client."

MASSACHUSETTS AVENUE was alive with the bustle of city life in fine weather. Poincaré consulted his map and determined that he could take a Red Line train across the river and then walk to a building near Government Center where the state police kept the contents of Fenster's Harvard office. At the entrance to the subway, he folded his map to music drifting from below—a disembodied saxophone playing "My Favorite Things" in a sad quarter-time. *Raindrops on roses . . .* He paused as people hurried up and down the subway stairs; to his left, a line formed for *arepas* at a food cart; across the street, a piano moving company attracted a crowd as large men lowered a baby grand from a third-storey window. City life hummed around him, set to a melancholic tune. *When the dog bites, when the bee stings, when I'm feeling sad . . .* The musician turned that last note into a plea that shook loose from Poincaré memories of his own favorite things: of Etienne, at six, on his lap explaining the intricacies of a new tower he had designed; of Claire's discovering him at a gallery, each there secretly to buy the other the same gift; of Chloe leading him to a barn door, saying: *Papi, look!* What would he not do for them? If the doors of a jet bound for Paris opened before him that instant, he would have boarded.

A car horn shook Poincaré back to the moment and he descended the stairs, prepared to thank the saxophonist. Instead, he nearly stumbled into a strange young man with a soft beard, wearing sandals and a robe—and holding a placard. Just as if Poincaré had dropped a coin into the slot of a mechanical fortuneteller, the Soldier of Rapture—for that's who he must be, Poincaré decided—raised a hand and broke into a recitation of the words on his placard, delivered with righteous anger:

> . . . the sun will be darkened and the moon will not give its light, and the stars will be falling from heaven, and the

powers that are in the heavens will be shaken. Then they will see the Son of Man coming in clouds with great power and glory. And then He will send forth the angels and will gather together His elect from the four winds, from the farthest end of the earth to the farthest end of heaven.

— MARK 13: 24-27

"The Rapture?" asked Poincaré.

"Verily."

He stifled a laugh. But then there was nothing funny about the social worker in Barcelona or mutilated children beside an ice cream shop in Milan.

"Tell me," said Poincaré, "how much time is left?"

"Enough to save yourself, Brother! Signs and portents are everywhere around us. Armies on the move. Husbands beating wives. Mothers aborting children. Children shooting other children in our streets. Hurricanes, tsunamis, AIDS. Tell me: have the times ever been so twisted? The end draws near!"

He said it with conviction, at least. Behind him, decades of grime sloughed off metal girders. The platform smelled of machine grease and urine. An approaching trolley on the far tracks screamed against the rails.

"The Rapture," said Poincaré. "Days away or months?"

"Look to your faith, not the calendar!"

"That's hard."

"Of course, it's hard! Only one question matters anymore: Do you *know* God in your heart?"

"I try to make things right, if that counts."

"Don't we all!"

On this point Poincaré was perfectly clear. "No, we don't. Not everyone."

"True, praise God! Yes! Fall on your knees and pray for those who reject His path. Conquer pride. Embrace the redemption that is right here, right now—waiting. God is waiting! Pray for the fallen! Join us!"

Poincaré did not envy Laurent's making sense of this rant. Instead of bending a knee, he said: "I want to learn more." He leaned close. "What's your name, son?"

"Simon."

"Simon, tell me how to learn more. I want to be redeemed. I do!"

Poincaré expected a phone number scribbled on a piece of paper, but the Soldier surprised him with a brochure dedicated to New Testament proofs of the Second Coming. On a reverse panel was a toll-free number, the addresses of Rapturian welcome centers in New York and Los Angeles, and the URL of a Web site. Laurent would want to see this.

He pocketed the brochure and stepped through a turnstile onto the subway platform, where he found the saxophone player—a man his same age still singing for his supper. On another day, Poincaré would have taken him to lunch and learned his story. Instead, he dropped a few dollars into an open case. At the approach of a train, a gust blew from the tunnel and lifted the front page of that morning's paper from a trash heap. It spiraled, dipped, then stalled before Poincaré's face long enough for him to read the headline: "Earthquake Shakes Pacific Rim!" The train stopped and he boarded. When he turned, the shepherd smiled and raised a hand in benediction.

Chapter 14

That evening Poincaré confirmed that the life of James Fenster, as told by a scrupulously balanced checkbook, was both orderly and unremarkable. A credit report showed that he used a single credit card once or twice a month for internet or phone purchases and to guarantee car rentals when he traveled to conferences. Over the course of two years, on the income side, Poincaré noted automatic deposits of Fenster's Harvard salary; on the debit side, he found checks written at weekly intervals for groceries, two or three checks a year to clothing stores, and monthly rent checks. On Mondays he would withdraw $140 from an automatic teller for the week. The man was an anachronism: he rarely used plastic money, carried no debt, and saved most of what he earned. An Internal Revenue summary of Fenster's tax history and the absence of a criminal record or traffic violations showed James Fenster, private citizen, to be exactly what Peter Roy claimed: modest, quiet, and unexceptional.

By 2 AM Poincaré had all but concluded this inquiry when, scrolling through the last of the cancelled checks, he found an anomaly. For two years, the man had either cleaned his own apartment or paid someone, perhaps an undocumented worker, in cash to do so. But Poincaré doubted the expense, inasmuch as Fenster gave himself an allowance of only $20 per day—too little to accommodate even a modest man's needs let alone extra for paying a cleaner. Yet during the course of a single week before departing for Amsterdam, he had written three large checks: one for $1,500; another for $2,025; and the last for $2,750—all to local cleaning companies. Poincaré saw no notes written in the memo lines of these checks, so after a few hours of sleep he located the companies and made inquiries. On successive days, it turned out, Fenster had hired professional cleaning crews to work on his apartment—the last specializing in "laboratory and surgical clean room standards" according to its Web site.

"Strange but not unprecedented," said the owner of MicroScrub. "Usually, local biotech companies or the universities hire us to maintain their clean rooms. You know, for biomedical work or manufacturing computer chips. Every once in awhile we'll get a call from a civilian, so to speak."

"What did you do for Dr. Fenster?"

As the man consulted his paperwork, Poincaré checked his cell phone for text messages. Nothing from Claire or Etienne. "Standard mopping and disinfecting. At the client's request, we wiped every surface with a mild bleach solution, including books, dishes, utensils, walls, door knobs and drawer pulls."

Poincaré removed his reading glasses and looked out the hotel window, across the Charles. On a footpath, a lone runner paralleled the river. "It was the apartment's third cleaning in three days," he said, reviewing the checks once more. "Did you know this?" The owner of MicroScrub did not but added that the crew chief's notes indicated the apartment was already clean. *Spotless* was the word in the report. "Why would someone clean an apartment that was already clean?" Poincaré asked. "You say you've done this before for individuals."

"Medical reasons usually," the man answered. "Earlier this year we did a similar wipe-down of a house in Lexington. The owner was just coming home from one of those cancer treatments where they knock out your immune system. For the first month he had to avoid infections at all costs, so the family hired us. I'll sometimes get similar calls during allergy season—though for these people we're cleaning pollen, not germs. So we do get requests of this sort. But for the most part it's biotech and the universities."

"Did the customer explain his reasons?"

"Mr. Fenster wasn't home," said the man. "The notes show that a Mr. Silva let us into the unit and locked up behind us. The caretaker. We were paid by check in advance."

Poincaré leaned back in his chair, working through the possibilities. He had read the state police report. The investigators had full access to Fenster's medical records and certainly would have noted a health crisis. True, it had been allergy season, but a single cleaning would have managed that problem and, in any event, during the previous spring Poincaré found no similar expenses. Fenster did not hire three cleaning services to rid the apartment of ragweed.

The building was a three-storey brick box that blighted a neighborhood of century-old Victorians. Poincaré made his way down a tree-lined street along brick sidewalks that bucked and heaved. Two men stood at the entry of the apartment building, one young and slender, dressed in a suit plain enough to be a mechanic's uniform; the other, thickset with lacquered gray hair and a forest of eyebrows. From what Poincaré could see, the older man was unhappy in the extreme at being forced into polite conversation with a kindergartner who also happened to be an FBI agent. Eric Hurley was howling mad as he read, then signed, a sheet of paper. At Poincaré's approach, the veteran cop said: "I suppose you're Interpol . . . another burr in my ass. This case was closed."

Poincaré shook the detective's hand, then Agent Johnson's.

"I've heard the stories, Inspector. It's an honor. Truly."

"Well, don't start pissing yourself with excitement," said Hurley. "I'll unseal the room—" he looked at his watch—"and you'll call me when you're done and stay put until I get back. I've got things to do. And for the record, we had our best forensics teams out here after the murder. They produced IDs that confirmed all your findings in Amsterdam—so I don't mind saying that my opening this apartment so you can validate my work offends me. Just so we understand each other."

The man was perspiring and smelled of buttermilk. "I understand," said Poincaré.

"I don't care if you do or don't understand. Let me see that warrant again." When Agent Johnson produced the document, Hurley jerked open the vestibule door and climbed to the second landing, quickly for someone his size. He was just starting down the hall when he nearly knocked over a custodian who was vacuuming a carpet. In another moment, he stopped at a door where Poincaré saw adhesive labels set across the jamb at four spots, making entry impossible without breaking a seal. Hurley noted the time, initialed each label, then sliced them with a penknife. He unlocked the door and pocketed the key. "Knock yourselves out," he said. "And don't leave until I get back. Here's my number." He flipped a business card to the carpet.

Rumbling down the hall, Hurley looked like a truck driver negotiating a narrow street. The custodian pinned himself against a door to let him pass, and Agent Johnson said: "I'm betting the only two people who ever loved this guy were his mother and his football coach."

Poincaré laughed. "He's right, you know. Everything they found confirmed the forensics report in Amsterdam. As far as their end of the investigation is concerned, this case *is* closed." He had motioned to the custodian, who shut off his vacuum and approached. Poincaré explained their business.

"Finally," said the man.

"You knew Dr. Fenster?"

"Well enough."

"How well was that?" asked Poincaré.

"We'd watch the Red Sox together some nights. He'd bring pizza over to my place, maybe carry-out Chinese. I live in the basement unit, next to the heating plant."

Jorge Silva was a fragile-looking seventy-five or eighty with papery skin, sloped shoulders, and a preference for talking to the floor in the presence of strangers. He pulled at his hands to mask a tremor. "I thought the police gave up."

"We haven't," said Poincaré.

"Good. Because Jimmy Fenster deserved better. People here say *good morning* and make noises like they care. Only Jimmy cared. One time I got sick, and he came by twice a day for a week to bring soup and bread. Who else noticed? I got no family anymore. No kids to take care of me." Silva looked ready to spit. "When I think of him blown up . . ."

Finally, Poincaré thought. "So you were friends?"

"Yes."

"And you'd see him how often?"

"In baseball season, at least twice a week. Otherwise, maybe once. Sometimes we'd sit outside, on the bench. Just chatting, looking at things. He liked to look at tree limbs, clouds. We'd walk down the block sometimes and get ice cream."

"What about clouds?"

Poincaré was not even sure why he asked.

"The white, puffy ones," Silva began. "He said on his very first airplane trip, to some kind of math competition, he was flying across the Midwest in summer. Just a kid at the time, maybe eight years old, and he saw the shadow of the clouds on the fields—he said they were islands and coastlines, the shadows. I said, They reminded you? And he said no, they were the same, clouds and coastlines. I don't know," said Silva. "We just enjoyed each other's company. With some people you do, with some you don't."

"Before he left for Europe," said Poincaré, "before the bombing, he hired a cleaning crew. You let them in and out. Is that right?"

"He left instructions. Three companies over three days."

"How clean does an apartment need to be, Mr. Silva?"

"It's strange. That's true."

"Did you ask?"

"No. Why should I?"

"Was Dr. Fenster sick? Did he have to keep the place that clean to avoid germs?"

"Not sick, no. He could have used twenty more pounds, but he was healthy."

"Did he have a regular cleaner?"

"No—he cleaned himself. It's a small place. You'll see."

"And the last cleaning crew," said Poincaré, his hand now on the apartment door. "Tell me about them."

Silva scratched his head. "They came with their own vacuums, detergents, dusters and a couple of machines I didn't know what. Three or four people, with gloves and paper socks over their shoes. I saw them wiping everything clean. I know somebody who does work like that down at Mass General."

"When did you see Dr. Fenster last?"

"It was a Wednesday because that night was the last game of the opening series with Tampa Bay. The Red Sox won. Jimmy stopped over with pizza. He was all packed and brought his bag with him to my place. He had just come from another trip out West, I think—gone a couple of weeks."

Poincaré knew that Fenster had spoken at conferences in Tokyo and Seattle on topics unrelated to globalization—and that he had flown into Boston for an eight-hour layover before his flight to Amsterdam. "Go on," he said.

"I think he must have come straight from the airport to have pizza with me. I'm not even sure he went back to his apartment because he told me he just came from his office and the pizza parlor, then straight here. He loved baseball. After about the fifth inning he called a cab to Logan from my place and I walked him out to the street. He said he was glad we were friends. He held up his hand and smiled."

"You shook hands."

"No." Silva raised his right hand as if he were swearing on a Bible. "He did this."

Johnson opened his forensics kit. "Mr. Silva, did the cleaners wear socks over their shoes?" He held up a blue bootie, standard issue for forensics personnel at crime scenes.

"Different color, but that's right."

"And you said they were wiping things."

"Books, glasses in the kitchen. Everything."

Poincaré pulled a photograph from his briefcase. "Do you recognize her?"

The caretaker, hands shaking, opened a hard shell case at his belt for a pair of glasses. "Sure—that's Madeleine. His fiancée. She stayed over some nights."

"And you know this because—?"

"Because no one comes or goes I don't know about." Silva shifted his weight. "I walk people's dogs, I sign for deliveries. I let workmen in, guests. I know what goes on here."

"When was it you last saw her?"

Poincaré waited for Silva to remove his glasses and snap the case shut. "Awhile ago—months, anyway. She stopped coming. And don't ask me why because I never asked."

So strong was Fenster's presence when Poincaré opened the door that Fenster himself may as well have greeted them. What Poincaré saw was more gallery than efficiency apartment. A single line of photographs, in pairs and also groupings of three or more, extended in a horizontal line at eye level across every vertical surface—windows and kitchen cabinets included. Poincaré had seen some of these, or ones very like them, in Amsterdam: photos of trees in full leaf and in winter, lightning strikes, mountain ranges. Each image was trimmed to an identical dimension and was set in an identical black frame with cream matting against stark white walls. Fenster had moved what few pieces of furniture he owned toward the center of the room to create a perimeter space for his gallery, a layout that forced the observer to regard images in their groupings and from a set distance. Nothing had prepared Poincaré for the beauty and strangeness of this display.

"Not your average genius," remarked Johnson.

Poincaré scanned the room.

"With the place wiped down by three different crews, Inspector, I'm wondering how the state police found *any* prints or DNA, let alone samples that corroborated your results in Amsterdam. Back in Virginia we'd call that a puzzle."

Poincaré took a quick inventory: wooden table, boney chair, thin mattress on an iron spring frame, single bookcase, galley kitchen with a frying pan, pot, and tea kettle. No radio, no television. No phone. No crosses on the walls or Buddhas on altars. Only Fenster's monkish belongings in a room that, photos aside, was as spare as a prison cell. A large box held dozens of additional photos, which Fenster must have rotated through the gallery.

Johnson approached a grouping of six images that had rattled Poincaré the moment he entered the room. When the agent reached for the first in the series, Poincaré said: "Vive la France. It's the national boundary."

"The next image shows the borders of my country's twenty-two regions. Next, the one hundred departments. Then the three-hundred forty-two arrondissements."

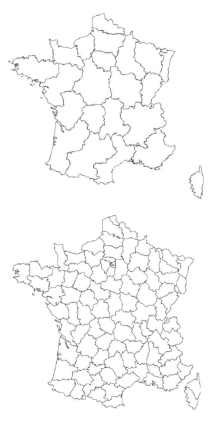

"And finally, the country's smallest administrative units, the communes. There are some thirty-five thousand. From the looks of the coastline, these are the communes for Bretagne, Normandie, Nord-pas-de-Calais, and Picardie."

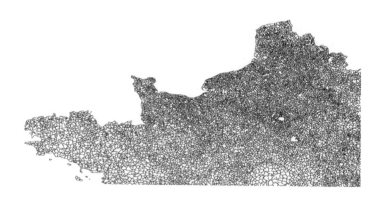

Johnson found a magnifying glass in his forensics kit and paused over the communes. He moved the glass to the preceding images in the series and returned to the communes. "Each is a smaller version of the one before," he said. "The units repeat—though not exactly. They're related—"

"Geometrically."

"That's right. Let's see about this last one. It looks like a magnification of several communes. Fenster was thorough in laying out his sequences, in any event. Large to small to smallest." Johnson lifted the sixth and final image of the set off the wall and read the caption.

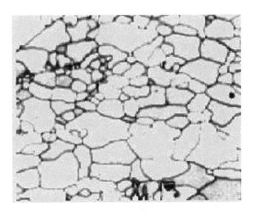

"A close-up?" asked Poincaré. "I wasn't aware of a smaller administrative unit than the communes. But it's the same geometry, no doubt." Johnson handed over the frame. On the reverse side was the following:

Grain boundaries, alloy of Al-Mg-Mn

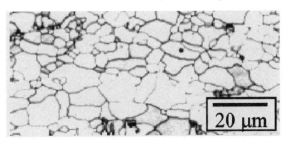

$$n = 1 + \log_2 N = 1 + 3.32 \log N$$

Poincaré sat hard into Fenster's chair and waved off Johnson, who was about to caution him against contaminating potential evidence. "What?" said Johnson.

"It's not a magnification of the communes or of any other map of France."

"So then?"

Poincaré looked to the wall, then back to the image in his hands. "The line in the box at the lower right shows a scale of 20 one-millionths of a meter in length. This is a photograph of a piece of metal under high-powered magnification. These are the crystal boundaries in an alloy of aluminum, magnesium, and manganese. The equation is a mathematical description of the alloy."

Johnson stepped around a chair. "Why," he asked, "should the crystal structure of a metal look like the communes or regions of France? Or the national boundary, for that matter?"

Poincaré was staring into the dead space at the center of the room. *That would be the right question*, he thought. Fenster was bending his mind in two directions to make a single point. First, the outlines of France's communes reproduced the fractal shape of the country's successively larger administrative units and then, improbably, the national boundary itself. It was not conceivable that eighteenth-century bureaucrats in Paris set the borders of 35,000 communes with an eye to reproducing the geometry of France's coastlines and mountain borders. Second, a photograph of a piece of metal under intense magnification showed the identical geometry. With colleagues Fenster would have used mathematics to make these comparisons. For lay people he had assembled this gallery, which was just as much an argument—the same argument he was set to make in Amsterdam in his talk on globalization.

Above the caption on the rear of the last image, Poincaré read three words: *The same name*. Curious, he thought. He returned the frame to its hook and flipped the preceding image. Above its caption: *The same name*. He moved down the line and found that each image on Fenster's walls had both an explanatory caption and, above that, the three words. Fenster had paired a cauliflower leaf with a river delta photographed from space. He had paired aerial photos of mountain ranges with lightning strikes and the root structures of plants. Most improbably, he had paired Ireland, as photographed from a NASA shuttle, with a thumbnail sized piece of lichen and the shadows of cumulous clouds on summer farmland. Each was a version of the others.

"What's the point?" asked Johnson.

Poincaré was sure he didn't know. But one thing was certain: the waters in which he swam had gotten very deep, very quickly.

CHAPTER 15

"So explain this," said Johnson. "How could the state police have lifted such perfect prints from an apartment wiped down by three successive cleaning crews over three successive days? If I'm recalling the forensics report, they also found Fenster's DNA in dried urine. Am I to believe the man hired all this help and someone forgot to scrub his toilet?" Johnson removed tools from his forensics kit. "Give me thirty minutes," he said. "This Fenster-man's got my attention now."

At the bookcase, Poincaré reached for a volume at random: *Mahābhārata, Epic of Ancient India.* A second: *The Aeneid.* Another, well known to him: *La Chanson de Roland.* On his haunches, he ran his fingers across the spines of some forty books: poetry, history, philosophy—not a volume of mathematics. Nor did Poincaré find translations. Only books composed in English were printed in English. The others, with Fenster's handwritten notes in the margins, were printed in their language of origin: Sanskrit, Latin, French, and Greek. Across the room, Johnson was standing on a kitchen chair, shoes covered with booties, to dust a light bulb.

"Have you ever tried screwing in a bulb without leaving prints?" he asked.

Poincaré had not. He returned to Fenster's reading chair to examine a cigar box left on the book shelf, which turned out to be a time capsule of sorts. Fenster had divided the contents into three neat sections: photos tied with string; a small plastic case with baby teeth; and a stack of medals with faded ribbons. He began with the photographs. Each showed Fenster between the ages of eight and fourteen, according to the date stamps, shaking the hand of a different adult beneath more or less the same banner: *Geometer of the Year, Advanced Calculus Champion, Albert Einstein Young Scholar Award.* He counted some two dozen photos in all, twenty-four awards distributed across seven years. Poincaré laid out the photographs chronologically and studied the progress of an awkward, lanky child growing before his eyes. In each image the boy looked pleased enough with his award, but also posed and uncomfortable in the extreme, his smile forced. The clothes fit poorly. Could the foster parents have pocketed the money provided by the state and kept the child in hand-me-downs? Across this entire span of years, the young Fenster looked pale beneath his halo of blond curls—even though he had won at least four of his awards during the height of summer. Poincaré held up one of the photos. "Agent Johnson," he said. "Could you take prints off this?"

Johnson had climbed down off the chair and was now bent over Fenster's laptop. "Bring it over." he said.

"Who keeps your memories," asked Poincaré.

Johnson looked at him.

"Your memories of childhood—until you went off to college. Who keeps a record of your childhood, besides you?"

"My parents and brothers, I suppose. They have pictures—but mostly stories. Like the one of my brothers and me in a three-way boxing match. Instead of gloves, we used paintbrushes—we were painting an iron porch railing at the time. We each dipped two brushes in red Rust-Oleum and started jabbing. The one with the most paint on his face lost. That was me." Johnson chuckled at the thought. "My mother came tearing around the corner, screaming—but she had the good sense to take a picture, at least. She swore she was going to blackmail us when we got married."

"And has she?"

Johnson made a thumbs-up sign. "The funny part is, I was only five or six at the time and I don't actually remember getting painted. But I'm in the picture and my mother and brothers tell the story—so it happened, I suppose. . . . What are we talking about?"

Poincaré handed him the photo. "Fenster lived in five foster homes between the ages of four and fifteen. We have no idea about the circumstances of his birth, but he was apparently abandoned and then handed along until Princeton rescued him with a scholarship. The only proof he had of a childhood is in this cigar box. Besides the box, he had nothing—no stories, no boxing matches. Imagine a child that young knowing that if he didn't collect these things, no one would."

Poincaré returned the cigar box to the bookshelf, but Johnson called him back. "I need you to look at something," he said. "Fenster's laptop obviously won't boot because the state police took the hard drive. They left an evidence tag, so it's all kosher. Here's the thing—the slip of paper he taped along the side of the monitor. Are you related?" Using tweezers, Agent Johnson held before Poincaré a strip of clear tape laid over a narrower strip of paper on which Fenster, likely, had printed twelve words and a name:

Mathematics is the art of giving the same name to different things. — Jules Henri Poincaré

"My father's father's father," he said. The explosion in Amsterdam, on his watch; the death of a mathematician who happened to venerate his great-grandfather: the case, it seemed, had chosen him. "And no, I never met him."

"True?"

"It is. Jules was a mathematician—apparently a hero to Fenster."

"Well, this is strange."

Agent Johnson could not begin to guess.

"One more trick of the trade," Johnson said. "I dusted the outside of the tape for prints. This was likely wiped along with everything else. But there's no way to wipe the sticky *inside* of a piece of tape. Unless you're using tweezers or wearing gloves, you're going to leave prints on the adhesive when you lay it down."

"When will you have results?"

"Several weeks."

Poincaré returned to the cigar box, this time for Fenster's baby teeth. "I'm assuming you can extract DNA from these?"

"Pearly whites? There's likely some soft tissue dried up in there. And even if there isn't . . . We'll likely find something."

Poincaré only half heard him, concentrating as he was on words floating in the ether: *different, name, things, same.* What language was this? Jules Henri had seen what Fenster saw, but they were both too dead to tell.

Poincaré left Johnson to wait for Hurley and close the apartment, for he had seen too much. The room was too small. At the front of the building, on his knees with a spade and claw hammer, Jorge Silva sat working a slab of cracked concrete. "The builders poured this when it was cold," he said. "Concrete won't set well if you pour below thirty-two degrees. Sure, it'll look pretty for ten years. Then, after the contractor's long gone, you've got this mess." The caretaker pointed. "Who takes the long view anymore?"

Poincaré saw the cracks and walked away.

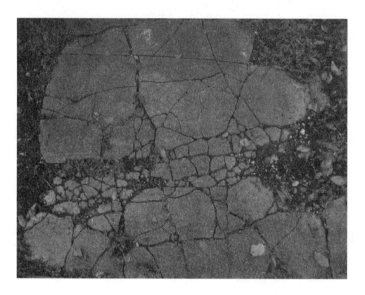

CHAPTER 16

From his perch high above the financial district, Charles Bell ran the most successful mutual fund to have emerged in a dozen years. In just under eighteen months, the fund's holdings had ballooned to $24 billion, money following money until Bell became the young lion of the investment world. His portfolio consistently beat major stock indexes in up markets and, in down, offered the stability of municipal bonds. Unlike the blackguards who ran investment frauds, Bell opened his books to major accounting firms that confirmed his successes were legitimate, although no one outside the company could explain that success. The combination of high yields and low risk proved irresistible, and Bell was soon straddling a mountain of gold that impressed individual investors as well as the portfolio managers of universities, pension funds, and insurance companies.

The man himself was famously philanthropic, with a Texas-sized personality transplanted in staid Boston. He sat on the boards of schools and hospitals, museums, and assorted defense funds for the indigent, all of which enjoyed his largesse. Charles Bell was also James Fenster's benefactor. According to a grants officer at Harvard, Bell's funding paid for Fenster's supercomputers, graduate student stipends, reduced teaching loads, and leaves of absence for research. Bell was to Fenster what Lorenzo Medici was to Michelangelo. *Why* was the question. More typically, foundations and corporations funded university research, not individuals.

Poincaré's stomach churned as the express elevator shot him skyward, into precincts reserved for the rich and politically connected. The elevator glided to a stop, and he stepped uncertainly into a reception area set on an open ledge above Boston Harbor. The walls opposite the elevator were glass, floor to ceiling. One lived in the clouds at this altitude, among peregrine falcons.

As he paused to acclimate himself, a voice boomed down a corridor. "Inspector Poincaré, I presume! It takes some getting used to, but it's a grand view!" It was Bell himself, recognizable from the fund's promotional materials, with a greeting that hit Poincaré like a blast wave. As he strode down the corridor, Bell rattled off instructions to an assistant who took notes and peeled off down a side corridor. He continued without breaking stride into the reception area, smiling broadly. "I am *so* pleased!"

"Magnificent," said Poincaré, gesturing to the conference room and the harbor beyond. "Who can work with such a view? I'd get nothing accomplished. Congratulations on all your success, Mr. Bell."

The man laughed like a horse whinnied. Clearly, he cared nothing for what anyone thought of him. "I'll tell you my secret," Bell confided, loud enough for anyone standing within twenty paces to hear. "If you work for me and don't produce, you lose the view. You're downgraded to a basement cubicle in our satellite office in Watertown. And if you still don't produce, you're out! Same rule for everyone—me included."

"Effective," said Poincaré. "But given what I've read of your funds, I doubt anyone's in danger of losing the view. The performance is . . . historic."

"Yes, well. We've been fortunate." Bell showed Poincaré into a glass-walled conference room, to the very edge of a cliff. "Sandwich, coffee? Pastries? Mineral water? Without waiting for an answer, Bell called: "Eleanor, mineral water."

They sat at one end of a thirty-seat rosewood table, at each place a leather captain's chair. At the far end of the room hung a screen for video conferencing. Bell, all Armani, settled into his chair. His fingernails, Poincaré noticed, were manicured.

"We're scheduled for fifteen minutes, Mr. Bell."

"Please call me Charles."

"Charles. Since I have only a few moments of your time, let's begin."

"Play on, Inspector. You already know that James Fenster was a dear, dear friend, and I want to help any way I can."

"How did you know him?"

"Through his work."

"You sponsored him, I understand."

"I did. James and I agreed on a number that would be useful to him, and I wrote a large check—only to discover that Harvard adds sixty percent for something they call overhead—which is another word for thievery. So I wrote a larger check. It's outrageous. But yes, I believed in his work."

"Because it related to your own?

"Peripherally."

"How so?"

Bell laughed. "I appreciate the question, but this is like asking Coca-Cola for its secret formula." The quarter-smile might have been mocking Poincaré.

"In general terms, Charles. Could you say?"

"Alright. Algorithms. Fenster modeled nonlinear dynamic systems. Water boiling. Air flow. Processes of nature."

"And the stock market . . . is that a process of nature?"

Over Bell's left shoulder, a plane touched down at Logan. Over his right, tugs guided container ships to unloading docks and triangles of sail leaned into an onshore breeze. Bell commanded it all. "I don't see how it could be, Inspector. What would the behavior of a thunderstorm have to do with the stock market? Of course, James had some interesting ideas for modeling the markets. We use proprietary algorithms at the Bell Funds. It's called a quantified approach to investing. Some analysts read sheep entrails to guide their stock picks. We model the markets." He tugged at the corners of a French cuff until they aligned.

"Do you know last week I invested 200 euros in your fund and today that 200 is worth 223? Over ten percent in a week. And in this economy! I'm considering a larger investment."

"Good for us and good for you, Inspector. Though the Security and Exchange Commission forbids me to say so, in our case past performance *is* a guarantee of future success. But I'll deny it if you quote me!" He whinnied again, and the receptionist seated beyond the conference room door looked up. Bell's face settled into a smiling mask once more. "The way we work is as follows," he said, looking suddenly earnest. A woman opened the door, carrying a tray of bottled water and two glasses. "Not now!" he snapped.

The door closed.

"I subscribe to former President Reagan's view. You hire good people, set them loose to do good work, then take a nap. No, seriously, Ronald Reagan had a vision, he hired smart people to carry it out, and then was clever enough to get out of the way. I call that leadership. This corridor is lined with the very best minds, and I give them enormous incentives to succeed. I get out of their way, and they create a product that I can sell. That sells itself."

"Was Dr. Fenster one of your very best?"

"Yes and no. When I was thinking of starting this company, I searched for promising mathematicians who might lend a hand. I had this idea that a certain sort of mathematics could help analysts anticipate trends in the markets. I offered ridiculous salaries to lure them away from whatever they were doing—and most came. They couldn't run fast enough from their academic appointments. And we're talking Ivy brains, Inspector. But not James Fenster. The man was the purist expression of a mathematical mind I have ever seen. He had his job. He did not want another job at roughly seven times the salary and the promise of even larger bonuses. 'But I admire your work,' I told him. 'Well, then,' he says, 'fund it.' 'Why should I?' I asked. 'Because it's important,' he answered. It was, so I did!" Bell clapped his hands. "I'm a rich man, Inspector Poincaré, which has certain advantages. I believe it was Thornton Wilder who said that money is like manure; it's not worth a thing unless you spread it around. So I spread some in James's direction."

"And in return?"

"Roses grew."

"More particularly?"

"Ah—I see. I financed James's work for the pure admiration of it. You can believe that or not. In any event, even if I were inclined to answer, which I'm not, this is a Coca-Cola question. *Go fish*, as we say in America."

Poincaré did not understand the expression.

"Never mind," said Bell. "What I will say is that on occasion James offered some scribbles, more or less, on the backs of napkins.

And he gave me the satisfaction of encouraging one of the finest minds of his generation. Nothing I could say or do would pull him away from the massively parallel processors I donated to his efforts. He threw me bones, I'm afraid."

"Nothing to build a company on?"

Bell's quarter-smile broadened. "Not hardly! Nothing nearly so comprehensive as that. James was no more interested in the mutual fund business than I am in—" he searched the sky above downtown Boston for comparisons, his eyes finally settling on the bowl of fruit on his own rosewood table. "In becoming a vegetarian. I like my steak. James did not care about this business or about making a personal fortune. He cared about his equations, God love the man."

"No quid pro quo, your money for his—"

"What I received in return were too few conversations over expensive coffee in that hulk of a building they call the Science Center. Sometimes, as I said, he would share his musings on napkins or the backs of register receipts. He tolerated our chats as a necessary tradeoff for my funding his research. I built him his playground . . . and now he's gone. I can hardly believe it." Bell's face darkened. "Bastards. Total, complete bastards. James was such a gentle man. To kill someone like this?"

Poincaré searched Bell's mask for surface cracks and found none. The outrage sounded real enough. But so, too, did the relief that Fenster would never share his napkin musings with another fund manager.

"Do you in any way credit Dr. Fenster with your success?" Poincaré asked.

"How many ways can you ask the same question, Inspector? He was more conceptual than a mathematician in this industry can afford to be. He flew at 35,000 feet all day long. A mutual fund company must operate at ground level."

Another plane touched down at Logan. "And also at twenty-nine floors up, sometimes."

"All this," said Bell, "is for show. I grew up in the real estate business, and my father once told me never to drive clients to a property in a junker. A Cadillac or Mercedes is the better choice because if you present yourself as successful, people will see you as successful and will want to do business." Bell pointed down the corridor. "My employees are responsible for our success, not James. Funding James was like paying a monk in the Middle Ages to pray for me and store up points in heaven. You'd have to have met him to understand. How else can I say it? He *deserved* those computers and graduate students. He was pure in a way I could never be."

Bell spun his chair to the glass wall, showing Poincaré his back. He said: "I want to help you find whoever committed this atrocity. It hurts, Inspector. James's murder *hurts* me. Is there anything I can do? Do you lack for funding in this investigation?" Bell spun back to face the room.

With that, Poincaré finally found his bearings with Charles Bell. Bribes were usually handled more coarsely, but then one had to account for the fine view and the gold cufflinks. "I appreciate your offer," he said. "But Interpol is well funded."

"Perhaps you need money *personally* for your investigation?"

"That's very generous, Charles. Here's what you can do."

Bell was listening.

"Write your congressman to pressure your government into paying its dues on time to Interpol. One hundred eighty-eight countries, and America—the richest—won't meet its obligations."

Bell checked his watch some thirteen minutes into the conversation, which was fine with Poincaré. He had got what he came for. They shook hands and exchanged wary smiles. By the time Poincaré arrived at street level after a more or less controlled free fall in the elevator, he wondered what, exactly, Fenster had scribbled on the backs of those napkins.

When he landed in the lobby, Poincaré felt the familiar buzzing of his cell phone and discovered an update from Gisele De Vries:

```
NASA's Jet Propulsion Lab says bomber
most likely worked at some point for
them or equivalent lab in France,
Russia, possibly China. Amsterdam APCP
too specialized and mix too unstable to
```

```
produce anywhere else. All academic labs
capable of mix affiliated with space
programs. GDV
```

The news was not unexpected.

All mirrors and marble, the lobby confused Poincaré enough that he lost his bearings and exited onto an unfamiliar street. Opposite the office tower and behind a police barricade, he saw a dozen protesters walking an orderly circle, holding signs, their chants led by a bull-horned man dressed—what was it, Poincaré wondered—like a Trobriand Islander: woven grass skirt, shoeless on the sidewalk, shirtless, copper skinned and heavily tattooed with concentric circles and geometric patterns, his hair jet black and thickly braided, falling to mid-back. The scene was so incongruous in a district otherwise populated by men and women in business suits that Poincaré half thought he had stepped onto a movie set. The tattooed man yelled into the bull horn: "IMF, INTERNATIONAL MOTHER FUCKERS. THE FIRST WORLD SMILES WHILE THE THIRD WORLD WEEPS!" Then a call: "GLOBALIZATION!" And response: "KILLS!" "GLOBALIZATION . . . KILLS."

Again and again.

Stationed nearby, a police detail looked thoroughly bored. The protesters attracted little attention despite their noise; still, Poincaré found himself interested enough to approach an officer: "How often do they march?" he asked.

"This particular group?"

Poincaré noticed a chocolate stain on her collar.

"Every month or so they try to make the walls of Jericho come tumbling down. Major financial centers are getting picketed. New York, daily. London, Hong Kong. They call themselves natives restless for something or other. Who knows."

He looked again at the man with the bullhorn.

"The Indigenous Liberation Front?"

"That's the one," said the officer, yawning. "They're everywhere. But I say if they're so damned clever, why didn't they just beat us back with their sticks five hundred years ago? We defeated them fair and square, so why all the whining now? Buck up and get on with it. Compete like the rest of us. No one's giving *me* anything, for damned sure."

Poincaré walked on and felt a buzzing in his breast pocket, then heard a familiar chime. The LCD glowed—a call from France. Not Claire. The Interpol exchange. He pressed the cell phone to his ear and used his free hand to block out the street noise.

"Henri."

"Bonjour, Albert."

A pause.

"Henri. They've struck. Come home."

⟶ PART II ⟵

Have the gates of death been shown to you?
Have you seen the gates of the shadow of death?

— JOB 38:17

Chapter 17

Eva Laval cleared her throat before entering the room, carrying a tray with coffee, a poached egg, and a crust of last night's baguette with a smear of jam. She set the tray on a rough wooden table, and Poincaré looked up from his book.

"Thank your grandfather for taking those chickens off my hands. I know you end up feeding them and cleaning up. I'm sorry for that."

"It's no bother, Monsieur."

"You'll be back at noon?"

Laval's granddaughter wiped her hands on an apron. Besides himself, Eva and her mother were the only ones Claire let touch her. With other attendants she would curl into a ball and groan—just as she had with Eva until Laval's granddaughter, barely fourteen, took Claire's hand with the tenderness that comes so easily to children and put it to her face, holding it there until the groaning stopped. *It's Eva, Madame. Remember—you're teaching me to paint.* She had prepared breakfast and lunch daily for the Poincarés. With school in recess, she would stay nights when Poincaré went up to visit Etienne and his family in the hospitals in Paris.

He set aside his reading and placed a napkin across Claire's lap. "Coffee," he said, putting the cup to his lips to test the temperature. "Laval says the harvest will be decent this year. Do you remember our first harvest, Claire—the Everest of grapes and our not knowing if the wine would be drinkable? But then it's never a brilliant vintage from Chateau Poincaré—is it? We drink it, though. We drink it. . . . Claire?"

She did not answer. For six weeks she had not answered. The doctors assured him the problem was psychological and that there was no actual physical reason she did not speak or open her eyes. But since the attack, or more precisely three hours after the attack when she learned the fates of the children, the Claire he knew had departed. As a forensics team combed the Lyon apartment and the medical examiner's staff removed two bodies—her attacker's and the Interpol agent he had killed, Claire frantically called Paris to check on Etienne and the children. When news finally came, she screamed, tore her hair, and collapsed. A physician sedated her, and it was in this diminished state Poincaré found his wife when he finally reached the hospital.

She progressed to a certain point, then no further. She would allow herself to be bathed and fed, and she would lift an arm through a sleeve as he prepared her for bed. She would startle at a loud noise but never made a sound, even in her sleep. "In cases of severe catatonia," one specialist advised, "the outcome isn't assured. If the trauma is great enough, the refusal to engage can last years. I recall one patient—" But Poincaré did not want to hear about other patients. Early on, he put as great a distance between the doctors and Claire as he could in order to pursue his own cure, which began each morning with an embrace and whispered assurances they were all alive.

Barely. In a synchronized attack, Banović's contractors had moved on Claire, Etienne, Lucille, and the children. Only the Lyon assassin's eagerness to begin a brutal business averted the worst in Paris; for when Luc, the agent on duty in Lyon, failed to call a coordinator's desk at an appointed time that changed daily as a security precaution, the desk agent at Interpol-Lyon immediately alerted two colleagues in perimeter positions to move on the apartment. They found Luc dead at his station and Claire bound hands and feet to a bed frame, naked, her mouth duck-taped, her attacker standing over a roll of surgical instruments laid flat on a bureau. They shot him from behind as he was stepping out of his pants. Blood from the exit wound sprayed across Claire's face and torso.

The alert went simultaneously to Paris, and it was only the premature move in Lyon that gave the perimeter agents protecting Etienne and his family time to spot and take down the attackers—but not before they detonated well-concealed bombs stuffed with nails and ball bearings. Instead of killing the Poincarés, as planned, the blasts merely maimed them. Georges lost his right leg below the knee and would not have survived had one of the agents not cinched a belt above the wound. Émile, eardrums shattered, was blown so violently against a tree that two vertebrae splintered. In separate blasts, Etienne suffered a crushed hip and collapsed lung and Lucille, third-degree burns on her back and arm. Chloe, burned over seventy percent of her body, lay in a coma breathing with the aid of a ventilator.

Banović's men had breached Interpol's protective net. "They planned to strike within the same minute," Albert Monforte explained, "so that one attack would not alert us to the others." Poincaré had flown all night from Boston and, after rushing from one horror to the next in Paris, boarded the TGV to Lyon where Monforte met him at the station. The director was pale as he delivered news. "She's alive," he said. "Not a mark on her. But she's in trouble, Henri. The worst was about to happen."

"She was conscious through it all?"

"Conscious? Claire must have heard Luc fall and gone to investigate. The contractor dragged her to the bedroom, and there were gouges on his face and neck, and several bites that drew blood on his arm. We've already run IDs, and Paolo was correct: every one of them former state security, East Germany. They traveled on Italian passports and had been in the country for two weeks, watching the family." Monforte's famously steady right hand was shaking.

With Claire in the hospital in Lyon and Etienne and the others spread across three hospitals in Paris, Poincaré shuttled between cities, sleeping two or three hours a day, determined to sit by their beds even if they could not register his presence. One of Claire's doctors advised him to moderate his pace or risk a breakdown. Poincaré ignored that. He pushed past exhaustion as he raced to their sides only to watch in silence, as if manic energy alone could undo the damage. He moved Etienne, Lucille, and the boys from three hospitals to a private ward in Etienne's hospital, where—he hoped—they might somehow comfort one another and heal that much sooner.

At two weeks, Georges was conscious though he had not been told he lost a leg. Lucille, burned severely, swam in a delirium of morphine. Émile floated in a strange, quasi-coma and would respond to pinpricks one day but not the next. And Chloe—Chloe, who at the worst possible moment ran from her bodyguard to catch a grasshopper for an insect zoo she was assembling for her brothers, grazed her legs against the very backpack that all but took her life. She lost an arm outright and suffered shrapnel wounds and third-degree burns along her entire right side. The doctors conferred in hushed tones along the corridors of the burn unit and spoke in less than optimistic tones about her prospects. Her breaths were so shallow and irregular that without a ventilator they doubted she could live.

To visit with Chloe in an isolation room meant scrubbing and gowning as if preparing for surgery. Poincaré would weep at her bedside, his tears steaming the goggles he wore as a precaution against infection. To clear the goggles meant stepping outside and scrubbing once more, which wasted precious visiting time. So he forced himself to sit quietly and look not at Chloe but at the wall calendar or at the grain patterns on the faux wood cabinet—anything to hammer down his grief. Where she had taken the force of the blast, the child's hair was burnt to a blonde thatch on a blistered skull. Her eyebrows and eyelashes were singed clean; the skin of her right cheek was crusty and festering; a tent protected the raw skin of her abdomen and legs.

Sometimes he would recollect family outings, speaking aloud in the hope she might hear him and be soothed. *Do you remember, dearest, last summer at the beach? You and your brothers decided to enter a sand castle contest and build a miniature Giza Plateau. Always such a grand project with you three. The boys ran off—don't they always!— leaving just the two of us to do all the work. But we won a red ribbon, Chloe! Your brothers insisted it was their ribbon, too, and you agreed. I was proud of you for that, but your father was prouder still. He talked about your Sphinx for days and how soon you'd be working alongside him. There will be more good days, Chloe. I promise.*

WHEN THE car pulled up to the farmhouse, tires crunching on gravel, Poincaré had just finished feeding Claire lunch and was helping her to a chair by the window, where he planned to read aloud or work a crossword puzzle, asking for her help. He might say, "What's a nine-letter word related to *seasonal* that begins with *d*?" She would not answer, but he would continue in this fashion for as long as an hour. Because she had a fondness for historical novels, he resurrected a copy of *Les Misérables* from his college days and read to her in thirty-minute intervals. Sometimes he would switch on the radio and search for a changed expression, perhaps the shadow of a memory passing across her brow. Try what he may, Claire would not return.

The vehicle on the drive could only be Laval's ancient truck, the old man arriving with news of migrant workers expected for the fall harvest. But when the door opened and closed without the usual protest of rusting metal, Poincaré walked outside to discover Paolo Ludovici, with suitcase, about to knock on the jamb. They stood on either side of the threshold for a moment, Poincaré reading in Paolo's face all he needed to know of his own slide into oblivion.

"Christ, Henri—leave it to you to find a spot in the middle of nowhere."

Poincaré did not invite him in just then. He stepped onto the terrace and walked Paolo through the vineyards, grateful they knew each other well enough to say nothing. It surprised Poincaré that he took comfort in his visitor. After six weeks without a single medical report that could be called hopeful, he thought all comfort gone from the world and that, in any event, he did not deserve comfort while his family suffered.

At dusk, the three of them sat on the terrace beneath the ancient oak, overlooking the vineyard and the valley. Poincaré had grilled chops from a hog Laval had butchered, and Eva had picked greens from the garden for a salad. Ludovici regarded the contents of his glass, then the unlabelled bottle Poincaré had set on the table. "It's drinkable," he said. "Barely. I'll leave this evening if you want. I didn't call because you would have said *no*."

"Stay the evening," he answered. "Eva will make up a bed."

Ludovici stayed the week. He rose early to take on jobs that Poincaré, in better times, would have tackled with pleasure. One morning found him on the roof with a bucket of pitch, hunting leaks. Rain the evening before had left the floor of the house in puddles, and Poincaré settled for placing buckets and hoping for the best. Another morning, Poincaré woke to the sound of a truck dumping a load of firewood, Ludovici having conferred with Laval and contracted with a supplier down valley. Each day saw another chore crossed off a list Poincaré had neglected to make. It was as if he could no longer project himself into a future in which he might appreciate a roof in good repair or a warm hearth in December. Poincaré, in fact, had no future because the attacks had reduced his life to a series of endless, blasted moments. Ludovici responded with work. The repair of a stone wall, the replacement of broken windows in the barn, the re-pointing of a foundation: every new project was a hand extended that Poincaré chose not to grasp.

Paolo did ask Poincaré's permission once—and Laval's. The hard shell case he had brought with him was a sniper's rifle he had mastered during his service in the Italian army. He worked at keeping his skills sharp but had found too few places to practice at 1,000 meters. "I can't very well shoot targets in Milan, can I?" he said. "If I miss, I kill some old lady's Pekingese." Poincaré agreed, so long as the noise did not upset Claire. Laval fought in the resistance as a teenager and could not say *yes* quickly enough. He joined Paolo in these daily outings and reported faithfully to Poincaré each evening. The usually taciturn old man could barely believe Ludovici's skill at hitting targets Laval had trouble seeing with binoculars. Laval followed at Ludovici's heels with questions about the latest telescopic sights that compensated for bullet drop and wind drift. Ludovici worked with two scopes of Swiss manufacture, one for level terrain and one for sloping. What used to be simple cross hairs in Laval's time were now carefully engineered instruments for determining distance to target. The bolt action gun itself was made in Germany and broke down to a briefcase. "A thing of beauty," Laval declared. "With my rifle I couldn't hit a mountain at 1,000 meters. He set out ten targets the size of my thumb at 100-meter intervals, at various elevations, and hit the center of each! I approve your friend, Henri."

A week passed. One afternoon as the men followed a stone wall that marked the property line Poincaré shared with Laval, Paolo announced his departure as casually as he had arrived. "I'm expected in Lyon tomorrow," he said.

They continued for a time. At the south vineyard, Ludovici inspected the arbors that Laval, in Poincaré's somnambulance, was now maintaining. He was tying up a vine, facing away from Poincaré, when he said: "I found the middleman. Albert told you?"

"Yes," said Poincaré.

"In Dresden."

Dresden? The syllables meant nothing.

"Did he also tell you they've completely isolated Banović? He's permitted Dutch representation, only. No more contact with anyone not cleared by the International Court. They've assigned a defense attorney even though he insists on representing himself. They've completely shut him down, Henri. The trial will begin soon. They're reading the charges in open court next week."

Poincaré secured a vine to a post.

"Henri, are you understanding me? Banović's people are dead." Poincaré began walking again. Paolo caught up to him. "Eva's good with Claire. She's a sweet kid."

Poincaré nodded.

"Stop and look at me."

Poincaré stopped.

"I did everything I could. I barely slept."

Poincaré opened a knife and worked dirt from his fingernails.

"I tracked him to Dresden and found a fleshy, middle-aged snot living in an apartment with his wife and grown son. They sold vegetables in a stall at the market, and to pass him on the street you wouldn't think twice. Except he was former Stasi and confessed that since the Wall came down times had been hard for people with his talents. 'No hard feelings,' he kept saying. I assured him I didn't have any either as I threw him off the roof of his building. They're dead, Henri. All of them."

Poincaré cut a cluster of grapes. He held it at arm's length and thought the fruit was progressing nicely. "Paolo," he said. "It's been six weeks. Etienne has two metal plates in his hip and tubes still draining his chest. They get him out of bed with a walker each day until he collapses in pain. He screams . . . and he curses me, and they sedate him. Lucille's had five skin grafts for her burns, but that's nothing compared to what she's going through with the children. She's inconsolable. She can't even visit Chloe because of the risk of infection to them both. Georges is being fitted with a prosthetic leg and cries because of the blisters and because he misses his brother and sister. Émile is in some strange sort of dream state, unresponsive one moment, rousing the next, then falling off again." Poincaré turned toward the farmhouse. "So you see, it's a little late in the day to hear that the contractors are dead. You tried. It wasn't your fault. It was my fault. It was up to me to protect my family. I didn't. I should have quit Interpol years ago. Claire told me to quit. I should have quit."

The color rose in Ludovici's face. "You should have killed Banović in Vienna is what you should have done. You knew he deserved it. In six months the judges in The Hague will find him guilty, and then what—all this grief to satisfy some sacred code of yours about the rule of law? Would you once, just once, call the world what it is! Curse God and get on with it, Henri. *Use* your anger. Come back to us."

"Did Albert send you?"

"*No!* This was my vacation, for what it's worth."

"I'm done with Interpol."

"You're not!"

Poincaré was tired. Even if he still believed in the mission of a war crimes tribunal—that what separated the Banovićs of the world from the jurists who would try them was the trial itself, an insistence on conscience and law—he had neither the energy nor will to speak. Ludovici lived by a different code and would not understand in any event. "Paolo," he said. "If you find any miracles on the road to Lyon, send one this way."

Ludovici grabbed his arm. "You're a principled, scrupulous prick!" Was Paolo weeping? Poincaré did not care. The very earth was weeping. "Do you mean you wouldn't kill him if you had the chance, not even now—if he were standing right here? *I* would kill him!"

"Paolo, don't."

"I could find a way. I still could. They're bringing him to open court late next week. A head shot at 1,500 meters when they transfer him from the prison van—I know the Criminal Court. I know the surrounding area. This could never be traced."

"Enough," said Poincaré.

"Come back to us, Henri. Leave Claire with the girl. You're dying here."

Poincaré buried his hands deep into the pockets of a favorite jacket that, of late, had grown large in the shoulders and chest. He stared down the valley, struggling to recall what had drawn Claire and him to this place. Here was the same broad sky; the same acacia and cypress, the same tang of manure and the neat vineyards and the narrow road that led to a world now devoid of everything he loved. "Paolo, you're wrong," he said, turning up the hill to the terrace where Claire sat alone, a pillar of salt. "I'm not dying. I'm dead."

CHAPTER 18

But that was not quite true. If death meant a long night insensible to pain, then Poincaré was not finished suffering. The day after Ludovici left for Lyon, he resumed his usual schedule and traveled to Paris to sit with Etienne and the family as they slept, against Etienne's wishes, and then by day to sit with Chloe. The cost for a private ward with round-the-clock nursing was ruinous, but Poincaré did not care. He sold the apartment in Lyon, and within a month the profit was gone. He tapped his savings. The bleeding was profuse. It did not matter.

At the sound of double doors opening at the end of a long corridor, the evening nurse, Marian Berrenger, checked several charts and looked up into the eyes of a wraith. "No change," she reported. "Your son took a few more steps with his walker, but they've given him morphine again. There's some concern he's growing dependent, and not so much because of the physical pain. The doctors are meeting tomorrow to find another drug. Georges"—she checked a chart—"he's developed some oozing where they're fitting him with a prosthesis. The child continues to ask for his brother and sister, and a psychologist has been called. Your daughter-in-law has largely fought off the infections from her burns, but Dr. Kempf is continuing an intravenous antibiotic, and I see here a prescription for a new anti-depressant. Lucille is scheduled for her sixth and perhaps final skin graft at the end of the week . . . this one on her arm, I believe. Thank goodness she wasn't burned on the face." Berrenger apologized immediately. "That was thoughtless, Inspector."

Poincaré steadied himself against the desk. "My granddaughter is receiving the very best care," he said, clearing his throat.

Why the pretense? The child would become the object of playground derision. As a young woman applying foundation cream to scars she could never hide, Chloe would run from mirrors her whole life, wondering what man could ever look past the ugliness and ask her to dance. But Poincaré could not think Marian Berrenger cruel. It was she, after all, who had saved *his* life that first day when Etienne, staggering to awareness, saw his father and screamed: *Get out! You've ruined us!* She took his hand and said: "I've seen it before, Monsieur. It's the morphine talking. Your son doesn't mean it."

Still, Etienne's grief had knocked Poincaré backwards down a tunnel, and he recalled the sensation of falling when from somewhere a hand grabbed him and a firm voice called: "He doesn't know what he's saying. Don't lose heart, Monsieur. You mustn't!"

He did not believe her, but he let himself be comforted that first, terrible day as she walked him to a side corridor, out of Etienne's sight but still within range of his cries. Poincaré was falling, but Berrenger would not let go. She sat him down in a chair wedged between a soiled clothes hamper and a gurney. When she returned with a cup of water, she held his trembling hands and knelt so that he might see her. She looked into his eyes. "I read the papers, Inspector. You did your job. Your *job*! The world can be such an awful place."

He left the hospital that day and began visiting by night, as Berrenger suggested, while Etienne and the others slept—until such time Etienne was ready for a more reasoned meeting with his father. Six weeks into the ordeal, Poincaré had already settled into something of a routine: up before sunrise at the farm, a thirty-minute drive to the station, then a series of trains that deposited him at gare d'Austerlitz more or less around midnight. There would be a taxi ride and then the long walk to a remote wing of the hospital, where he would sit for five hours by their beds. At first light, he would leave for the burn clinic across town to keep his daytime vigil at Chloe's bedside.

"What of Émile?" he asked.

The nurse checked another chart. "He's developed an infection in his lungs. We're treating that with intravenous cefuroxime. Please, go in. I've set a chair by the door. And I don't need to remind you that if anyone wakes—"

In his life Poincaré had been shot and beaten so severely he was left for dead. He had buried a child with Claire, Etienne's sister, when she was weeks old, and he had mourned three miscarriages with his wife. On a daylong trip with his father into the Rhône Alps, many kilometers along a remote trail, his father died of exertion, his heart seizing with the finality of snapped twig. Poincaré carried him out. Years later, he had prayed over a ravine filled with the bones of children, and he had sat across a table from his mother, whose dementia was so profound that she did not recognize her only child. But none of that pain could touch this pain—of watching a feeding tube run to Émile's stomach, or watching Georges sleep beneath a sheet tented over his amputated leg, or seeing Lucille propped on her side, her arm held above and away from her by a complicated trapeze. None of that pain could touch the loss of Etienne's affections.

Poincaré gripped the arms of a metal chair, lost in his son's jagged breathing. He heard a child's voice: "Papa, look! If you place weights against the columns just so—" He could see a young Etienne piling blocks along the outward edges of two columns and feel his joy at discovering the flying buttress: "If you set the weights just so, you can build an arch and the columns won't give way. And on top of the arch you can place more blocks!"

For her birthday that year, Etienne built Claire a gingerbread cathedral, a replica of St. Jean of Lyon. For a month or more his room had been declared off limits to both parents. When the work was complete, for the grand presentation Etienne set candles inside the cathedral and switched off lights throughout the apartment. The effect was startling; but that did not keep the Poincarés from eating gargoyles that night or nibbling the cathedral's grand façade. What had they done to deserve such a child?

The only lights along the ward were LED readouts of machines that monitored blood pressure and respiration. At 4 AM, Etienne stirred. Before Poincaré could slip from the room, his son saw him in the half-light and croaked: "Get out!"

Poincaré rocked forward, opening his hands.

His son stared him down: "You didn't push the buttons. But the bombs exploded just the same, Papa. Because of you—of what you do. Leave. We're ruined." Etienne spoke calmly; it was no longer morphine talking.

So Poincaré rose. He loved his son enough to say nothing, enough to turn and walk away.

LATER THAT same morning, as he prepared to enter the sterile environment of Chloe's burn unit, a nurse approached and informed him that the child's father, now well enough to reassert his parental rights, had called to cancel Poincaré's visitation privileges.

"That can't be!" Poincaré protested.

The nurse produced a piece of paper.

"I won't!"

"Monsieur, what you want makes no difference. I have a document."

"But you know me," he said. "I've been coming for weeks. You yourself said no one else visits. All I do is sit and talk—where's the harm?"

The nurse listened with bland, professional concern. "I'm sorry," she said. She was not sorry and Poincaré told her so. She said, "The rules are clear." He produced his Interpol credentials to trump the rules. She said: "Forgive me, but there's been no crime committed here."

"Get your superior," he snapped.

Her exit gave Poincaré the opening he needed. He recognized Etienne's signature on the facsimile and knew that he was within his rights to bar him from Chloe's room. He quickly scrubbed, pulled on a pair of gloves and a gown, adjusted his goggles and then secured his mask and hat. On entering the room, he understood that he would have perhaps five minutes with his granddaughter before others could properly scrub and gown themselves. When they came for him, he would leave quietly.

He stood just inside the door, watching her chest rise and fall with the whirr of the ventilator. Then he stepped to the bedside and drew the curtain so that they would be alone. The sheets were white and the curtains, which ran in a track from the ceiling, were white and Poincaré's hospital scrubs and mask were white for once, not hospital blue, such that he could imagine the two of them cushioned by clouds well above the world and its troubles. He heard a commotion and knew time was short.

"Chloe," he said. "It's Papi."

There was no part of the child he could touch without risking infection, so he held his arms above his granddaughter as if to cradle her. Which he did in a fashion—recalling the newborn Chloe in his arms, in a corner of her nursery as Claire and Etienne and Lucille laughed and wept and pointed because Poincaré could not face them, holding his first grandchild, without losing his composure. He had turned his back to them that day to be alone with her, as he was alone with her now with the curtain drawn in room 2C of the burn unit. He began to rock back and forth, and a melody rose of its own from some quiet, peaceful place. Poincaré sang low and sweetly, cradling the empty air with such tenderness that when the security staff finally pulled the curtains wide they stared for a moment and listened. "She understands," he said as they led him away. "She heard me."

POINCARÉ SAT on a bench before the hospital, struggling to absorb the fact that he could no longer visit Etienne or the children, not even as they slept. The late June sun punished the people in the plaza. Heat rose in waves off the pavement. From his bench, Poincaré had a good view of the second floor windows but could not see Chloe's room because the isolation units were situated along an inside corridor. Still, he had a clear enough image of the ward and its layout to know the rough position of her bed. If need be, he would keep his vigil in the plaza and project himself to her side. Etienne could not prevent that.

Poincaré had not slept in close to fifty hours. A bad case of nerves at the farm had kept him awake the night before his departure for Paris, and he had remained awake on the trip north and through the evening with Etienne and the children. Now, in the heat, he let himself doze with the knowledge there were some hours yet before his scheduled return to Fonroque. He closed his eyes and, whether five minutes had passed or twenty, he woke with a start to the sound of an alarm ringing as people streamed from the main entrance. When he looked for evidence of a fire, he was horrified to see smoke billowing from a second-floor window, very near Chloe's room. He sprinted toward the open doors but was stopped by a security guard.

"Interpol," he said, flashing his badge.

"I'm getting people *out*," the man yelled.

Poincaré backed away as firefighters in full gear ran past. He sprinted the length of the hospital and, turning a corner, found an emergency exit—its stairwell packed with staff and visitors moving in the opposite direction. He edged sideways, fighting current and curses, and overheard one man say, "It's a trashcan fire in the burn unit—somebody's sick joke. If it were real trouble, we'd be evacuating patients. I think they've already handled it with a fire extinguisher."

As if on cue, the alarm stopped and the river of evacuees reversed itself, carrying Poincaré to the second-floor landing. He calmly walked through an emergency door that had been propped open and smelled the smoke, which was being exhausted through a window facing the plaza. He was relieved by the sight of hospital security standing casually around a charred trashcan, mid-corridor. Aside from scorch marks along the wall, Poincaré could see no damage. A prank then, or carelessness. He was turning to leave when a nurse exiting a utility room ran past him clutching a tube in sterile plastic sheathing. The tube, he thought, looked very much like part of the ventilator system that kept Chloe alive. He followed the nurse, quickening his pace, and this time when he showed his badge he was motioned through. The nurse who had given him such difficulty was seated atop a gurney, dazed. On turning the corner, Poincaré saw the doors to his granddaughter's room thrown wide and at least six staff in white coats standing over her bed.

"What!" he yelled, entering the room.

A woman probing Chloe's chest with a stethoscope turned on him savagely. "Out!"

Chloe's ventilator tube had been cut and the power cord ripped from the machine. A doctor on the far side of the bed was inserting another tube that was attached on one end to a blue plastic ball, which an attendant began pumping as soon as she heard the words *I'm in*. Chloe's chest began to rise and fall once more as a third doctor with a stethoscope abruptly stopped her probing and said: "No pulse." She interlocked her hands over the child's breastbone and rocked forward and back in a rapid motion. "Paddles!"

They worked on her for thirty minutes.

The doctor who had called for security found Poincaré in the visitor's lounge, head slumped in his hands.

"I'm so sorry," she said.

He opened his eyes, he closed them. He opened them. No difference. "We don't fully understand what happened," the woman continued. "Someone set a fire along the ward, and in the commotion your granddaughter's ventilator tube . . . was sliced. We didn't get to her for eight minutes." The woman's voice broke. "The police are investigating. I'm so very sorry, Monsieur—" she looked down at a card—"Poincaré."

Chloe's room was now a crime scene, and he would be denied entry. He asked the doctor to leave and close the door behind her. Staring out the window across a plaza shimmering in the heat, he thought of the child—hand extended, leading him to the barn and an old door with cracked paint. *Look, Papi!* He looked, not at the paint but at his granddaughter. He kissed her eyes and offered her up to the clouds. Then, all business, he called Etienne's hospital and Albert Monforte to advise the posting of extra security. He left the building, for the first time in weeks with a purposeful step. He would mourn her later. For now at least one of Banović's men remained, and Poincaré would find him—after, that is, he concluded a bit of business in The Hague.

CHAPTER 19

Poincaré did not wear the turmoil of his life on the outside like a new jacket or wristwatch. To pass him on the street by a flower stall in The Hague, one would think the man merely exhausted—or possibly ill. But beyond the wrecked exterior—to see him as he saw himself, as Claire would have instantly seen him were she well enough to open her eyes and yell *Stop!*—was a man reduced to raw nerves and a scream. He had come with murder on his mind, and he had planned with care.

If, that is, one who had not eaten or slept in a week could be called careful. Closing his eyes meant seeing the child, so Poincaré did not sleep. Food was for the living and, inasmuch as something essential in him had died—not just his dreams for Chloe but some fundamental belief that life is fair and that people are decent—he did not eat. Palpitations racked him. He ate pill after pill, attempting to silence the beast clawing in his chest. His hand shook as he attempted to shave. He cut himself and when the blood ran, he flew into a rage for more. Banović would pay. Banović's wife and children would pay. Poincaré would kill them all, curse God, and die. He cleaned and oiled his gun a third time. Then he stepped from his hotel room to plan the final act of a wretched life.

"A STRAIGHTFORWARD assignment, Monsieur Depaul," said the man, handing Poincaré a folder. "You'll find everything you requested on a disk—a summary document with a daily timeline, a separate folder of photographs, and a spreadsheet integrating the two. You can open any cell, locate where Madame Banović and her children are likely to be at a given time on a typical day, and then click to see them *in situ*—with pertinent photos, addresses, and phone numbers. It's all here." He patted the folder. "She's an unusually punctual woman. Sundays to church, a tram to the prison, then to a park by the sea with the children. Weekdays she walks them to and from school. I don't exaggerate: she does not let go of their hands, not for a moment, until they reach the schoolhouse door. Then it's to the stationer's where she works as a clerk. Market day is Tuesday, after picking up her son and daughter. I've listed her typical purchases in the spreadsheet—mostly pasta, beans, potatoes, and milk powder. At the butcher she'll buy bones or fatty scraps for soup. Her margin is rather thin, I must say. I've checked with the government agencies, and she has not applied for assistance. They live in a one-room apartment with a shared bath in the hallway. It's all in the file."

"You broke into their apartment," Poincaré said matter-of-factly.

The man sniffed. "I was repairing the lock when the door opened."

Using an assumed name and a bogus e-mail account accessed from a cash-only Internet café in Paris, Poincaré had hired Dominicus Groot sight unseen, without references, from an online registry of private detectives in the Netherlands. At the Groot Investigative Services Web site, he found an ad that boasted: "Infidelity Our Specialty!" and "We find persons gone missing in The Netherlands!" The man himself made an unlikely investigator, hardly someone who could blend easily into a crowd. He was a head taller than Poincaré, with long legs, a thatch of gray hair, and thin enough that a puff of wind might have lifted him away like the bird he appeared to be. Groot was also strangely robust for someone so brittle-looking, with the ruddy face and the strong, chapped hands of a man who worked outdoors for a living. To see Dominicus Groot once was memorable; to see him more than that would arouse suspicion. He must have been good, however, because his report about Banović's family had required steady surveillance. Apparently, the wife had no idea she was being followed.

The private investigator opened a package of hulled sunflower seeds and popped a handful into his mouth, throwing another handful to the pigeons in the square—which prompted a commotion of cooing and pecking. "A straightforward assignment," he repeated.

"As for your e-mail inquiry last night, this would not be a typical Thursday because Monsieur Banović, of course, will appear in court this afternoon. The wife did not take the children to school today, so I would expect them in court. From what I could tell, they were walking, which would be unfortunate because the ICC would be far for the little ones. Public transportation from their part of the city won't be of much use. And a taxi for someone on her budget is out of the question. No, they'll walk twelve kilometers—and for not much gain, I'm afraid. The reading of charges won't last an hour, including the statement of the accused. The trial begins next month, and I can't imagine Madame Banović would take the children each day." When Groot paused to eat another handful of seeds, the pigeons gathered at his feet. "Altogether an unusual circumstance," he continued, "hardly in line with my typical assignment. There's nothing *wrong* here, Monsieur Depaul, unless you object to a young mother and her children living in poverty. Perhaps you are a philanthropist?"

Poincaré handed him an envelope. "There's no need to count it," he said.

The man opened the envelope and began counting. "In my line of work—"

"In your line of work," said Poincaré, "you should know better than to ask clients why they hire you." He collected his things and placed the folder, with its disk, in his briefcase. "But to satisfy your curiosity—yes, I'm a philanthropist."

As THE agent of record in Stipo Banović's arrest, Poincaré was granted entry to the courtroom and was allowed to carry his firearm into the gallery. He had called ahead to inform court security of his attendance, and the staff had reserved a seat for him in the second row, as it turned out directly behind a woman flanked by two curly-haired children wearing their Sunday best. Poincaré smiled grimly. By design, he arrived late so that he could take his seat unnoticed by either Banović or his wife, who would be directing their attention toward the three judges on the dais. At a table to Poincaré's left, the chief prosecutor's assistants sat attentively, ready to produce any of a hundred tabbed files on demand. Banović sat alone at the defendant's table, a single yellow legal pad and a pencil before him. The court had granted his request for self-representation, with the understanding that an appointed defense team would be waiting in the wings to assume the case should his efforts fall short of standards required to ensure a just verdict.

Poincaré recalled the ravine in Bosnia—for that alone he should have shot Banović instead of arresting him; and with the blood of his family now crying for relief, he considered jumping the gallery barrier and putting a gun to Banović's head. Why had he not killed the man months ago? Poincaré made no move just yet, because in this case the demands of justice and revenge conflicted. Justice demanded death; revenge demanded that Banović witness the murder of his wife and children before he himself died. Poincaré wanted revenge, so he forced his attention to the chief prosecutor, who was just now completing his reading of the charges:

> . . . In sum, the accused stands before this Court for the crime of killing seventy-three men and boys of Muslim descent, the torture and inhumane treatment of said victims in transport to the ravine in a forest south of Banja Luka, the destruction of property prior to said transport and murder, the rape of women and girls, some as young as six years, in the presence of family members prior to said transport, and the intentional launching of an attack against a civilian population in village dwellings. Under Article 8 of the Rome Statute, Stipo Javor Banović, as leader in name and in fact of the paramilitary group known as Patriots for a Greater Serbia, stands accused of Crimes Against Humanity. With respect, the Prosecution will seek a sentence of seventy-three consecutive terms of life imprisonment.

The prosecutor returned to his seat. Banović, appearing much the same as when Poincaré saw him last, in a plaid shirt and wire-rimmed glasses, rose to address the court. The former librarian made no gesture to his wife or children. From the rear, one could see him slowly scanning the room from prosecutor, to judges, to clerks and guards. Here was Stipo Banović the commander: supremely self-possessed with a bearing that showed contempt for anyone's law but his own. His voice rang strong and clear:

> This Court does not sit to adjudicate so-called acts of genocide, Crimes Against Humanity, or War Crimes but rather cases that are politically useful to the signatories of the Rome Statute. I therefore reject the Court's jurisdiction. The Chief Prosecutor has never charged China for Tiananmen Square or the United States for Guantanamo Bay. Yet you devour freedom fighters like me, men elected by God to cleanse the world of filth! The United Nations sits idly by as Yugoslavia implodes, then you create The Tribunal for the Former Yugoslavia to salvage a guilty conscience. I spit on your empty gestures. I spit on charges spun from thin air. I spit on a verdict that was sealed before this trial ever began!

Banović stood long enough to let his brief statement echo and die in the corners of the room. Poincaré eased himself into a crouch and reached beneath his jacket. *Shout his name, wait for him to see you, then squeeze off three quick rounds. Grin. Make sure he sees you grin.* Here was the plan, finalized even as he walked into court. In normal times, poised on the balls of his feet, to think for Poincaré was to act. But with his body on the verge of collapse, he lost his balance and tipped a knee against the chair before him. Banović's daughter turned and stared at him and at the bulge of his hand beneath his jacket. Rich, auburn curls. Dimples. Large brown eyes. Was she even six years old? The child smiled, her cheeks flush from a long walk. Could she understand the doom he had pronounced?

She's someone's Chloe, he realized in a whip crack of clarity. *A perfect, beautiful child.* His hand slipped from the gun as he groaned and slumped forward, jostling the mother, who turned and recognized him: "You!" she screamed at the author of her sorrows—the man who had read charges against her husband, in their home, in a language she did not understand, and who led him away in shackles. "You!"

Two hundred people flinched.

He had seconds before a rush of guards ruined his firing angle. He crouched once more and watched Banović turn and lunge in a single predatory motion. But the guards tackled him midair, and the prisoner let loose a howl at once so vicious and heartsick that for an instant the very earth stalled on its axis. Poincaré *knew* that sound—a howling that called to him from across the vineyards when he touched Claire and found stone where once there was flesh. It was the howling that knotted his gut when Etienne cried: *Get out,* the roar that rose from his own breast at Chloe's death.

Had he actually tracked a blameless woman and her children in order to kill them—for what? To restore Chloe? To restore his family, as if grief heaped upon grief could yield anything but grief. For an instant, Poincaré's own howling mingled with Banović's over a wasteland so far from human settlement there could be no return— that is, if he pulled the trigger. He saw Banović's son in his sailor suit; the girl, in her pinafore starched and ironed that morning; the woman, wearing a brooch, her one treasure, desperate at the prospect of raising a son and daughter fatherless, in poverty.

The brooch—a little turtle, gold with bits of colored glass. There had been another turtle . . . Lucien running from the woods by the soccer field, crying "Look!" as Poincaré and his mates crowded their friend saying *What, show us!* A common box turtle was all, its shell a miracle of diamonds, yellow and orange, its scaly head and legs retracted for safety. "Watch!" cried Luc as he held the turtle aloft then slammed it against a rock, its diamonds shattering as the children held their breath. There was life yet, a wriggling and oozing. The boys drew closer and Luc said, "It's pink!"

Poincaré's hand fell from the gun once more. He could not kill this way—not even Banović. Not if he wanted to live in the world of men. He dropped to his knees as the defendant's wife set upon him with her fists and as Banović himself screamed and kicked at the guards who carried him from the courtroom. "Irina! Casimir! Nora! I love you!" Other guards detained the wife and children. But Poincaré, wearing his credentials on a lanyard, was left alone. *The end,* he thought, *the absolute end.* He rested his forehead against the seat before him, whatever strength he had summoned for this work spent. His family was gone, revenge useless. Through it all, the gun never left its holster.

He heard footsteps and felt a hand at his shoulder.

"Henri."

He opened his eyes and saw a pair of expensive Italian loafers.

"What just happened?"

"Go away."

"The moment I heard about Chloe, I rushed to Paris. When I couldn't find you, I tried Etienne's ward. I called Fonroque. And then I gambled you were here. The man deserves to die, Henri, but his people didn't kill your granddaughter. Look at me." Poincaré did not lift his head, not even as Paolo thrust a photograph before him. "The hospital's surveillance system caught everything. We have an image—a woman impersonating a doctor. We've got her entering the unit, pouring an accelerant into the trashcan, and then striking a match before walking down the corridor towards Chloe's room. We haven't put a name to the face yet, but I'm certain she's not one of Banović's agents. She's Mesoamerican—about as far from ex-Stasi as you can get. Henri, look at me!"

Slowly, Poincaré lifted his head and saw a hand come into view. It held a photograph. "What," he said, his eyes rolling in the direction of Ludovici.

"Christ! You need a doctor!"

"What surveillance? A photo?"

"We're leaving—now." When Ludovici reached under Poincaré's arm to hoist him up, he bumped the shoulder holster—and jerked Poincaré to his feet. "You brought a gun—*here*? You were going to shoot him in open court? My God, Henri—who's going to save you from yourself?"

Poincaré tore the photo from Ludovici's hand, enraged that he had no reading glasses. The image would not focus, and he extended his arm far enough to see someone in a white hospital jacket standing along a familiar corridor. A woman. Squinting, he thought she looked familiar: medium height, honey-nut skin, dark hair braided in a thick cord. He wiped his eyes on a sleeve and looked more closely at her neck, at a port-wine stain. It was Dana Chambi.

CHAPTER 20

"Claire? . . . Dearest, can you hear me?"

Silence.

"Claire, I'm leaving on a trip. Business. I'll be home soon." He imagined he could hear her breathing across the phone lines. That would have to do for now.

"Alright, then. I'll call. I'll call every day."

And with that Poincaré emerged, as if from a crypt, to find his granddaughter's killer. For ten weeks he had read no newspapers, watched no television, and listened only occasionally to the radio in a futile search for music that might calm his nerves. His shuttling between Fonroque and Paris took no account of a world that continued to turn, indifferent to the catastrophe of his life. It came as something of a surprise, then, that media of every sort had seized on August 15th as the day on which Christ was to redeem His faithful. Improbably, in two short months the Soldiers of Rapture had so focused attention on their prophesy of the Second Coming that whatever one thought of End Times theology it was now impossible to regard August 15th as just another day on the calendar. Somehow, the Soldiers had become modern-day Isaiahs sent to prepare the world for a New Day, and there was simply no avoiding their battle cry that "God is Near!" They shouted hosannas across twenty-four time zones, on highway billboards and city streets as if repeating August 15th loudly enough, and often enough, could itself bring about the hoped-for deliverance.

By the time Poincaré stumbled back into the world, the Rapture had become news for being news, which guaranteed media coverage that would build to a crescendo on the appointed day at 11:38 AM. Rapture parties were planned for public venues in Tokyo, London,

New York, and Amsterdam, and already one could find calendars and clocks counting down the days and seconds. In Poincaré's absence, the Rapture had gone viral—a pandemic transmitted via broadcast news, e-mail, and word of mouth. He could only stare and wonder, not the least reason being that the assassinations Laurent was investigating had intensified, following the model of the murdered social worker in Barcelona: a bullet to the back of the head, a passage of Scripture pinned to the clothing, and the clear message that doers of good works were no longer welcome because their virtue delayed the Tribulation and, therefore, the Second Coming. As if this logic weren't strained enough, Christian-inspired suicide bombers, following the example set in Milan, had continued detonating themselves for Christ in hopes of actually hastening the Rapture. Since Redemption would come only amidst great troubles, they reasoned, more troubles would lead to Redemption sooner.

Poincaré blinked hard at all this, as if he had walked into a collective hallucination. Facts that were essentially the case two months earlier—the same civil strife, the same global warming, the same famine and disease—were now called definitive signs of the End Times. Millions believed the Rapture was near because millions of others believed. Millions more, agnostic on the question of Christ's return, still wondered if they should be concerned for the disposition of their souls. And most everyone else had grown wary of people wearing white robes in public and possibly concealing bombs. Serge Laurent would know more, Poincaré decided. Laurent had been investigating this madness and would have something useful to say.

AFTER LUDOVICI delivered the surveillance video to Monforte, Interpol worked to identify the woman in the lab coat on Chloe's hospital ward. Poincaré watched the analysts scramble but offered nothing, for he had decided that finding Chambi would be his concern, alone—and resuming the Fenster investigation would provide suitable cover. Given all that had happened, he had no interest in pursuing Fenster's killer and even less in tracing the source of the ammonium perchlorate. But with Chambi at large, Poincaré needed

Interpol's tactical and financial resources to locate her. So he called Albert Monforte one morning to announce his renewed interest in Fenster. "I'm rotting in Fonroque," he said. "I need to work again." He lied so convincingly that his superior summoned him to Lyon for a meeting.

"I'll be frank," said Monforte. "I don't want you going anywhere before you spend another few weeks recuperating. You look like hell."

"And a very good morning to you, Albert," said Poincaré.

"Not really. The directorate has advised me to retire. . . . Forty years at Interpol is enough, they said. And thirty should be for you, Henri. Let this Fenster business go. Claire and the children need you."

On this point Poincaré was very clear. "In fact, they don't. Not at the moment."

"I can't believe that."

"Suit yourself. I leave this afternoon." He handed Monforte an itinerary.

"I won't stand in your way—although the next director might unless you wrap this up quickly. There's talk of moving old timber out the door. Take my advice and quit on your terms."

Poincaré said nothing.

"Alright, then . . . for the moment. You'll be searching for rocket fuel?"

"What else? That's what this case is all about."

"NASA, then—begin with the Jet Propulsion Lab. While you were in Fonroque these several weeks, I started a file of reports directed to you from the JPL and Lieutenant De Vries—assuming someone else would take over the case." Monforte pulled a folder from a stack on his desk. "It appears you're looking for someone who's got a background in chemistry, who can grow specialized crystals called HMX that were used to doctor the ammonium perchlorate, and who works with propellants. We're talking a few thousand people in the world who meet the criteria—a relatively small set. But your job's made easier because the precision placement of the explosive charge suggests someone with a background in mining. Think about it. The pictures of that hotel in Amsterdam show a room more or less sliced whole out of the top floor. This takes skill. So you can narrow your set of about three thousand down to a few hundred. Of that subset, you want to know who was away from their lab bench in mid-April—from NASA, the European Space Agency, Russia, and China. And of *that* sub-set, who traveled to the European Union? There can't be more than eight people on the planet who meet all the criteria. You'll find names here, and some of the candidates are from JPL. One who looked promising on paper died three weeks before the Amsterdam bombing."

Poincaré took the file and turned to leave, but Monforte was not finished.

"I've got nothing new on Rainier."

"I understand," said Poincaré.

The director stared across a parking lot to a stand of trees on the edge of the Interpol campus. "You know, I could actually be fine with leaving—but not like this. The executive committee demanded explanations for how Banović's men got into the country and attacked your family—and later got to Chloe. I couldn't tell them because I don't understand myself. Banović's men were dead. Ludovici thinks this last attack came from a different direction."

Monforte looked like a man resigned to being hanged in the morning. The tremor in his hand had worsened. "All I could tell them was that we're investigating our system breakdowns and will report back. The directors don't want reports, and I don't blame them."

The men faced each other.

"I failed you, Henri."

They had been friends once.

At the door, Monforte said, "Forty years, and the worst mistake of my career . . . I can't even bring myself to ask forgiveness. Chloe."

Poincaré said nothing.

"Very well. About this woman at the burn clinic, I've put every—"

"We are *not* discussing my granddaughter's death."

"The woman appears nowhere in our databases. If she had so much as stolen a candy bar, we'd have found something. Why anyone would attack a child in that condition . . ."

Poincaré opened the door.

"Bonne chance, Henri. Let's hope the JPL will give you answers. Otherwise, the search could turn difficult."

"I wouldn't worry," said Poincaré. "I'm feeling motivated."

He took a last meal in Lyon before returning to America—at the Café du Soleil, near his former apartment. He could not walk in that district without thinking of Claire. In the early years, she would take him out on Saturday mornings simply to run the cobbles beneath their feet and feel the press of crowds in narrow spaces. *Close your eyes*, she'd tell him—waiting for Poincaré to actually close his eyes so that she could lead him by the hand. With Claire his senses blossomed. He would smell the baguettes and croissants at the boulangerie and hear the cries of the fruit monger and the fish man. *You feel human here*, she said. *Connected*. With her, he had been.

"Henri!"

The café's owner clasped him warmly. Like everyone else, Samuel Ackart knew of Poincaré's troubles. The two were old enough friends that what needed saying Ackart said with his eyes and a squeeze of the hand.

"Do you suppose," said Ackart, "I could get rid of that?" He was pointing over Poincaré's shoulder across the alley. Poincaré turned and saw a large number thirty-nine pasted onto the side of a building. "Countdown to the end of the world. It's all anyone talks about, and frankly I've had a belly full. Christ should come or not and let's be done with it. I've got a business to run."

Poincaré turned back to the table. "I'd figure the Second Coming would be good for business, Samuel. If the world ends, who'll need money? May as well spend it on your food and wine."

Ackart spit into a cup. "As a matter of fact, receipts are down."

"Then you only have thirty-nine days left to suffer."

"Just put me out of my pain now. I tear them down, the countdown numbers, and they sprout right back up like some evil weed. I don't want to be reminded!"

Poincaré missed the change in Ackart's tone. Talking had become a chore for him; but because Ackart was a friend, he tried—conversing as if painting by numbers, out of habit: "Your menu's the problem," he said, "not Christ. I've been telling you for at least a decade to use a better grade of cognac in your coq au vin—and to get more fresh vegetables onto your plates."

Ackart struck a match and let it burn to his fingertips. He struck another and lit a cigarette. "Did I mention these Soldiers of God or whatever they call themselves have got hold of Alain?"

Poincaré set his glass down.

"Two months ago he quit his job. Last month he shows up wearing robes. We can't talk to him now that there's a published date for the Second Coming. It's insane. I have no idea if he might turn into one of these lunatics blowing themselves up for Christ. He's devoted his life to saving others. Now this? If he had wanted to be a priest, fine. But this End Time craziness . . . it's vulgar. Cheap."

The news hit Poincaré hard. Growing up, Alain and Etienne had spent as much time in each other's home as in their own. Their families had shared meals and vacations, the boys constant companions. When Poincaré saw Alain last, two years earlier in Paris, he was a successful public defense attorney in a silk suit who still, across a luncheon table, addressed Poincaré as *uncle*. "So he went to Los Angeles," continued Ackart, "because Los Angeles, he said, is the city most in need of saving. The new Sodom and Gomorrah. Cecile and I are terrified we'll read about him in the morning papers—that he'll set off a bomb on Rodeo Drive, shouting *Jesus Lives* before pushing a button. I've gone out there twice trying to talk sense into him. All he did was point me to the daily headlines. 'What more proof do you need of the End Times?' he said. 'The world's flying apart. Read all about it!'"

To this point, the Soldiers of Rapture had been little more than a very dangerous comic book to Poincaré. On the one hand, there was the youngster with his *verily*s in the subway in Cambridge, playing prophet with robes from central casting—a lad barely alert to his own theology. On the other, there were bombers and assassins on the loose intent on sowing fear to hasten the Second Coming. Before Samuel Ackart's news, Poincaré had dismissed the one as a joke and treated the other for what it was: terrorism plain and simple. But Alain? He was no Scripture-squawking parrot, no killer of innocents. He was a thoughtful, gentle man whose choice of profession, law, suited him for the same soul-sustaining reasons that architecture suited Etienne.

"How did this happen?" said Poincaré.

Ackart's face was a study in the shifting grays of depression. His eyes were puffy, their luster gone. Poincaré stared out the window with him, both men lost in an unspoken conversation with the number thirty-nine.

"You know he was a sensitive child," Ackart said after a time. "Arguments upset him. If Cecile and I raised our voices over dinner, he'd run crying. When he was seven, we had to stop delivery of the newspaper because the articles turned him morose. I asked why all the sadness, and he pointed to a photo of a child in Somalia with rickets. . . . At some point the rest of us let it go. Alain couldn't. He hasn't."

The smoke from Ackart's cigarette settled about their heads like bad weather. Poincaré shifted in his seat but could not get comfortable. "Civil wars, murders, riots," said Ackart. "The suffering of others broke him down. He chose law to repair the world—and it was beautiful to see. But after six or seven years, he turned sullen again. Two months ago, he decided we were in the Tribulation and he would leave the whole mess for Christ to set right. 'All the suffering's got to be a sign,' he said. 'Because if it isn't, life is not worth living.' That's where it ended," said Ackart. "With those words, which scare the hell out of me. Then he left for Los Angeles. Cecile and I are desperate. We've lost a son. This End Time madness is ruining our business. Worse, I couldn't say that Alain won't become a bomber for Christ. I'm at my wit's end."

Ackart looked out through the cigarette haze, his eyes moist. Poincaré's own grief was immense, but Ackart's grief had moved him. "I'm leaving for the States in the morning," he said. "One of my stops is Los Angeles. I could grab Alain and ship him home for deprogramming."

"Deprogramming . . . so that he can wake up to the same head-lines? The world *is* going to shit, Henri. How does one take it in and live a life?" Ackart shook his head. "Look. You've got your own troubles, and I have no right . . . But I can't go on like this." He scribbled an address. "Find him. If you think he's dangerous, get him off the streets before something bad happens."

Chapter 21

"**M**r. Punky-ray. You come right up!"

Poincaré recalled Peter Roy's mother-in-law with affection, though in all honesty he had forgotten about the old woman until he tried negotiating, once again, the grimy call box on Massachusetts Avenue. She buzzed him into the building and greeted him at the office door with a smile and the same heavy-jowled crankiness he found so endearing on his first visit. This time, she extended her arm in the dim hallway light, palm downward—waiting. Poincaré bowed slightly and kissed the back of her hand. "Enchanté," she said. "Rachel's husband is expecting you."

"Rachel's husband?"

"Peter, my son-in-law."

Roy appeared behind her. "Browbeating our clients again, Gladys?"

She patted his shoulder on her way into the office. "You're the father of my grandchildren and you pay my salary—so I won't say anything unkind. But Mr. Punky-ray could teach you a thing or two about manners. You could start with a kiss each morning. Here, for instance." She put a finger to her cheek.

Roy cleared his throat. "Welcome to America, Henri."

Poincaré had also forgotten the appeal of Peter Roy, who reminded him of country lawyers he read about as a young man. Here were the suspenders, the bow tie, and the wire rims behind which dark eyes suggested principles that would not bend. Yet this country lawyer had hung his shingle above a tattoo parlor in an East Coast city.

"Gladys heard you were visiting and baked muffins," he said.

"Stop that! It's a surprise!" She rounded a corner with a tin of poppy-seed muffins, reminding Poincaré of Felice Laval introducing herself the morning Claire and he took possession of the farm. Overwhelmed by its ramshackle condition and suffering a brutal case of buyer's remorse, Poincaré was just working his hand through a hole in the foundation that he had somehow failed to notice before the sale when Felice arrived, croissants in a basket, a thermos of coffee, three paper cups and the reassuring news that field mice were a problem only ten months a year.

"With you being so far from home," said Roy's mother-in-law, "I thought you might appreciate some American hospitality. Does your wife bake muffins?"

"At the moment no, Madame."

She hobbled from view in search of coffee. Walking to the conference room, Poincaré said: "I suppose you understand how fortunate you are."

"To have Gladys? Half my clients bring her chocolates or flowers. The other half wonder how I haven't lost my mind. . . . What can I do for you, Henri? I seem always to be in a rush these days. When I was a partner at a downtown firm charging $500 an hour, I kept my meter running in ten-minute increments to make my billable quota each month. Now that I've set a rate my new clients can afford— $40 an hour, not even half of what a competent massage therapist makes—I run the meter at two-minute intervals just to keep the lights on. My time wasn't my own downtown, and it's not here. My wife says I've traded one prison uniform for another."

"And I'm not a paying customer," Poincaré offered. "Or am I?"

Roy smiled. "Sit, Henri. I imagine you want updates. I haven't heard from Madeleine Rainer again. And Fenster's estate is settled— all the legal matters are tucked away, save one. The battle over the hard drive has heated up. Eric Hurley, the Commonwealth's lead investigator on the case, contacted me two weeks ago asking if Fenster had left any indication in his will about the disposition of his laptop computer. My strong presumption, though no one has asked for my opinion, is that because James left everything to the Math League Trust he established to benefit the Cambridge school system, the burden will be on others to prove why his computer and whatever's on it shouldn't go to the Trust as well. In fact, no one knows what's on the hard drive—but the interest, shall we say, is high."

"I'll call Hurley," said Poincaré. "We've met."

"You should. The State has finally released Fenster's apartment back to the landlord, who sued so he could rent the unit again. The investigation has tied the place up for—what has it been, now—four months? The man deserves his rent."

"Of course. What about Fenster's belongings?"

"Donated, I believe. The landlord put the caretaker in charge of that."

Poincaré slid three photographs of the same person across the table. Honey-nut skin. Jet black hair. Round face. One photo came off the Harvard Math Department's home page months ago. The Massachusetts Registry of Motor Vehicles mailed Poincaré the second. The last was a passport photo, provided by the Counsel General of Ecuador. Roy studied the images.

"She's fond of scarves," he said. "Beyond that, never met her."

"Dana Chambi," said Poincaré.

"Fenster's graduate student? She and I spoke by phone several times after the bombing, mostly about the Math League and how that could become an important part of Fenster's legacy. We never met in person, but from what I can tell she's bright and agreeable. What do you want with Dana Chambi?"

"She's a person of interest in my investigation."

Roy folded his hands. "I shouldn't think so—not the woman I met by phone. She was nothing but helpful, conscientious. You saying she's a murderer?"

"I'm saying she's a person of interest."

Roy nodded. "Well, then. I can tell you how to find her, but not where—if that makes any sense. She's the 'Resident Expert' at the Math League Web site. When students log on, they find study sets, puzzles, mazes, and so forth. There's also a message thread that she monitors, providing free tutorial services. She said it would be a way of staying connected to Fenster's mission. She built the entire Web site and is running everything for the summer on a trial basis, until other tutors take over. Fenster's fund pays for advertising here in Cambridge—small money. Ms. Chambi takes care of the rest, gratis. It's an impressive site by any standard, an entire math curriculum to supplement what goes on in the classroom. She consulted teachers system-wide on its development, and apparently there's support for introducing it into the curriculum. I believe summer enrichment classes are already using it. So you can find her on the Web. Where she happens to be seated physically, of course, is anyone's guess."

"Who hosts the site? Where does she rent server space?"

Roy opened a second file. "The Math League Trust pays all expenses. The domain registry, the site hosting . . ." He flipped through several pages. "Yes, here it is." He pointed to copies of invoices establishing the Trust as the purchaser of services. "Gladys wrote the initial checks to launch the site. It's a yearly fee, not much. I'm custodian of the Trust, temporarily at least. Following Ms. Chambi's instructions, we bought the domain name and paid for server space. The company we dealt with is located in Philadelphia, but the actual servers could be located anywhere. Chambi could be on a world tour at the moment and still maintain the site without disruption to end users. So there's nothing in any of this that establishes a location for her. You could subpoena the company in Pennsylvania, but they would only point you back here, since we're the only ones who really exist for them."

"But she must log into their server with a unique IP address."

"No. All she needs is a username and password, and she's in. Same as it would be for you sitting down to another person's computer anywhere in the world and accessing your email. If you wanted to find her, and she didn't want to be found, all she would need to do is not use the same computer twice. I don't know your business, Henri. But from my dealings with Ms. Chambi, I found her to be forthright and personable. There's no doubt she's dedicated herself to Dr. Fenster's legacy. See for yourself." Roy scribbled a Web address on a sheet of paper.

Poincaré stood and folded the URL into a pocket.

"Later this year, the Math League will sponsor free tutoring classes at every school in the Cambridge system—with real, live tutors. Dr. Fenster inspired it all. . . . By the way, did you ever find his birth certificate?"

In fact, the day following their meeting in April Poincaré instructed Interpol's legal staff to secure a court order. Not unexpectedly, the process had taken nearly three months to complete, and he came across the correspondence when reviewing the file Monforte had assembled in his absence. "It's odd," said Poincaré. "The Ohio adoption office found a long paper trail documenting Fenster's passage through their system, but they couldn't locate his birth records. Misplaced, they said. There's nothing before his change of names by the first foster family. Apparently, he was never born."

Roy smiled. "Bureaucracies . . . I deal with this every day." He stood and extended a hand. "One last thing, Henri. A favor."

"Of course."

"On the way out, don't kiss my mother-in-law."

WHAT HAD struck Poincaré as diffidence at their first meeting—Jorge Silva's refusal to meet his eyes, the nervous tugging at his hands—seemed now an act of heroism. Well into his eighth decade, the man rose each day and maintained this hideous brick box of a building as if it were Windsor Castle. The mulched beds of impatiens, the painted rails, the trimmed grass, the pointed brickwork: all told a story that Poincaré had missed on his first visit. He found the caretaker sweeping the walkway in front of the apartment.

"I'll just finish up," he said at Poincaré's approach.

Silva had swept grass clippings into a neat pile, which he then deposited into a bag instead of pushing them back into the lawn. He leaned heavily on his broom and reached for a candy wrapper. "The kids on this street," he said, turning the wrapper in his hand. "Half go to Harvard, half to MIT and not one of them thinks twice about fouling up this neighborhood. What are they teaching, anyway?"

Poincaré produced a card and was about to reintroduce himself when Silva said: "There's nothing wrong with my memory, Inspector. Did you catch the people who killed Jimmy?"

"Not yet," said Poincaré.

"What are you waiting for?"

"It takes time, Mr. Silva."

"You know, I may not have a lot of time. Get me news." Silva dropped the wrapper into his bag. "They rented his apartment last week."

"I heard," said Poincaré. "Did the state police leave much?"

The caretaker nodded. "They told me to keep it all, sell it all, donate it, burn it—they didn't care. And that was it. I had Goodwill come for the furniture. The clothes—perfectly good, but I had to throw them away. I couldn't stand the thought of someone else wearing them. I kept his books, not that I can read any. Only a few in English. None in Portuguese. Maybe the university wants them."

"And his photographs?" said Poincaré.

"Those I've got. I'm keeping two. You're welcome to the rest. They should go to a museum, I was thinking. I'll show you."

Silva's apartment would have appealed to Fenster. Poincaré was visiting unannounced, yet he found the simple, unadorned space as clean and tidy as if it were being shown to a prospective buyer. Silva checked a pocket watch. "The Red Sox just started a day game over at Fenway. I could switch it on and show you how Jimmy and I worked the scorekeeper's book."

Poincaré had called Hurley's office and set up an appointment for the following morning at the Cambridge Police Station. His search for Dana Chambi—the 'Resident Expert'—could proceed online, at any hour; so he removed his suit jacket and draped it over one of the two chairs at Silva's kitchen table. "I remember your saying you would listen to the games and eat pizza. Let me buy us some," said Poincaré.

Silva made the call and switched on the radio.

"Jimmy didn't watch television," he said. "He told me listening reminded him of when he was a kid. He had four, maybe five, foster parents, and he said they were strict about bedtime. So he'd sneak a radio under the sheets and listen, with an earpiece. When he came down to visit, we'd switch on the radio, which I liked just fine." He checked his watch again. "We've got maybe twenty minutes before the pizza arrives. Come on back here."

Poincaré followed him to a small bedroom, bare except for a crucifix on one powder blue wall and, opposite, a triptych that hung originally in Fenster's apartment: photos of lichen from the Alaskan tundra, a single-celled sea creature magnified ten thousand times, and human lung tissue. Without the captions on the reverse of the frames, one had no hope of telling them apart.

Poincaré heard a loud click beyond the wall, followed by a low thrumming—the boiler firing up to heat the building's water. "Here," said Silva, pointing to a pair of boxes. "The books and the rest of his pictures. Help yourself."

Silva left to meet the delivery boy and Poincaré to flip through the collection with the reluctance of a tourist forced to sprint through the Louvre. He had minutes, and one could spend days. From the next room, he heard the game. With runners on first and third, no outs, the announcer breathless with what David Ortiz could do if he only relaxed at the plate and rediscovered his swing, Poincaré worked through Fenster's gallery. The photo marked *Erosion patterns, stream bed*, shared a striking resemblance to the photo marked *Graph, cotton futures, 100 years ending 1934*. Here were the images of France, again, and tree limbs juxtaposed with veins of the human eye. On the reverse of each frame, above each caption within each set of images, Poincaré found a word or phrase—in the case of erosion patterns and cotton the word *Difference* with an exclamation point. He flipped through the collection a final time to record everything Fenster had written.

The apartment door opened and closed, and Silva returned to find two photos propped on his sitting room couch. "Those!" he said. "I was thinking about those for myself. . . ."

They sat eating pizza, listening to the Red Sox throttle the Yankees. "Here's how Jimmy and I would work it," said Silva. "First, the scorebook. You list the players for one team on this page and the players for the other team here—in their batting order." Silva worked through the particulars of scoring a baseball game, and what struck Poincaré was the complexity of the recordkeeping and the potential to generate mountains of data.

"I'd keep score," said Silva, "and after each inning Jimmy would repeat to me every play up to that point, from memory, without looking at what I wrote. It'd be easy for the first few innings—who got a hit, who got out, who caught fly balls. As the game got longer, he'd still be able to do it. All the way through the ninth, he'd replay the game, hit by hit, from the first inning. I'd check against my scorekeeper's book for accuracy. What was scary is that he could do this for every game he ever heard. I'd test him on the ones we listened to together. Some, a year or two old. And he'd get it right! You French don't know baseball. But do you have any idea that people just don't do this?"

"I have some idea," said Poincaré.

"It gets better, Inspector. He'd bring his computer and open it to a baseball statistics site. When a guy comes up to hit, Jimmy gives me his batting average, his on-base percentage, and his slugging numbers. I'd check the computer, and he'd be right! He'd memorize the opposing team's statistics before each game. He'd say things like 'So-and-so hits .270 with two outs and a man in scoring position.' I asked how he did it, and he gave me one of these who-knows looks—that that was the way it always was for him, from the time he was a kid. He said it was how he made friends, moving from one family to the next. Because everybody likes baseball, he said."

Poincaré finished a second slice of mushroom with sausage, and though the game had hours yet to be played, he thanked the caretaker and gathered his things—including the photos. At the door, pointing to them, Silva said, "I see these and I think of Jimmy. Now we'll both think of him, Inspector. But after us, there'll be no one. Some people deserve to live," he said. "Some people should never die."

CHAPTER 22

```
>Hi. I'm Antoine.
>I'm your tutor today.
>What's your name?
>Call me Tutor, OK? You go to Cambridge
Rindge and Latin?
>Yup. 10th grade summer enrichment program.
>Great. What's up?
>Got a word problem today. "In 4 years Jon
will be twice as old as Matt. Two years
ago Matt was 1/4 as old as Jon. How old
are the brothers now?" I can figure out the
answer if I start with age 1 year for Matt
and then keep trying with different years.
Matt is 5 and Jon is 14. But that's not the
point, my teacher says.
>Correct. Don't use brute force. Use your
brain. Let the math do the work for you.
```

Poincaré had worked through the problem in advance and spent ten minutes recreating the fumblings of a tenth grader, so that—taking direction from Chambi—he produced the following:

```
>2M = 10. M = 5. Matt is 5 years old.
>Which means Jon is how old? Use Matt's age
in the equation for Jon.
>J = 4M-6. J = 4(5)-6 J = 14. Jon is 14
years old.
>Excellent, Antoine!
>Thanks. I've got one more question,
though.
```

```
>What's that?
>The math is all on paper or in my head.
What if Jon and Matt are real people? How
does math connect with real things?
>A mathematician's question! Good for you.
But it's too late for me to get into this
right now. I'm sleepy. Write me tomorrow
or the next day with another word problem.
When do your classes end each day?
>I can usually get to a computer in the
library by 3.
>Good. 3 PM two days from now. I'll be sure
to be online.
```

Poincaré checked his watch.

```
>It's only 7 o'clock. You're sleepy??
>Long day, Antoine.
>OK. Thanks. You're not in Cambridge, I
guess.
>Good night.
```

For her, Poincaré thought. But the sun had yet to set in Cambridge, Massachusetts. He logged off the Math League Web site and e-mailed a colleague in Lyon, Hubert Levenger, who headed a recently commissioned office responsible for tracking cybercrime. In an earlier conversation, Levenger offered to infiltrate the Math League Web site and track the IP address of the person chatting with Poincaré—provided she did not use any of several tricks to mask the address. "If we can get her IP," said Levenger, "we can identify the service she used to connect to the Internet. That will give us a country of origin, at least. Depending on the service, we can get a location to within fifty miles, possibly closer."

Poincaré waited for a return e-mail. When it arrived, the answer was not what he hoped for. "The person chatting with you used a proxy server positioned between her computer and the Math League to log onto that server as an authenticated user. She could be anywhere,

Henri. Give me another shot when you chat next. I'm tired. See you later."

Levenger had done him the favor of staying up until 1 AM in Lyon. It occurred to Poincaré that if Chambi was tired, too, she was not in the Americas. Seven PM in Boston was only 8 PM in Brasilia and Buenos Aires. Taking her at her word, it was *late* wherever she sat. At thirteen hours later than Boston, Hong Kong was not likely. He ruled out the Far East. It was Europe, he concluded, or Africa—chatting with him between midnight, Lisbon time, and 1 AM in Johannesburg.

He logged into his Interpol account to confirm that a Blue Notice had been issued for Chambi. Immediately before leaving for the States, he had mastered his rage sufficiently to tie Interpol into his search. Monforte had poisoned everything he touched in Poincaré's life. Still, if Interpol could not guarantee personal safety, what it did well was track and arrest fugitives who crossed international borders. Because Chambi was not yet indicted and could not be held against her will, Poincaré issued an Interpol Blue Notice that, without detaining her, would yield information on her whereabouts and activities. Rainier's Red Notice listing, by contrast, would lead to her arrest. But with both women well out of sight, the system of Notices had yielded nothing. Eventually, he expected, one or both would make a mistake and when that happened the chase would be on. Monforte had seen to the details, and Poincaré updated Chambi's profile regarding her likely location. Before walking into Harvard Square for dinner, he sent a text message to Gisele De Vries:

```
Dana Chambi. Ecuadorian national. Was she
on hotel list compiled in Amsterdam?
```

He pushed *send*, confident that De Vries would answer him within the hour.

"You missed the worst of the storm," said Eric Hurley, standing at the door of the Cambridge Police Station and surveying the sky. "Can you stand American coffee? Just up the street. Come on."

He didn't wait for an answer, and Poincaré followed him to a shop called the Busy Bee, where the detective greeted the woman behind the counter and wedged his stevedore frame into a booth. "The Fenster case got more interesting," he said. "Annie—coffee and a corn muffin. Grilled. Same for my friend."

"What is it with Americans and muffins?" asked Poincaré.

"Look, Inspector. It's been a couple of months since you were here. You must have been out of touch because Agent . . . what's his name—the kid . . . Johnson—contacted me. Said you dropped off the radar. I never knew Fenster had his apartment cleaned three times before he left for Amsterdam."

"Did you speak with the custodian?"

"No." Hurley adjusted the knot of a hideous paisley tie, his neck bulging over a yellowed collar. "If the place was cleaned, the last time by a crew that wiped everything down, then how did our forensics people find *anything*? My report shows dozens of fingerprints matching the ones you pulled off the body in Amsterdam. Also a direct DNA match from two samples—urine on the toilet rim and hair with some intact follicles from a brush. No way, not with the place wiped."

"Is that the report?" said Poincaré.

Hurley slid an envelope across the table. "Your copy. Johnson turned out to be better than I figured. He pulled one set of prints from the computer keyboard, the kitchen glasses, the picture frames, and the covers of Fenster's books. Those matched the prints we found. So far, no surprises. He even pulled prints off the goddamned light bulbs. All perfect matches. But then there was this." Hurley opened his own copy of the report. "We missed a second set of prints that he pulled from the sticky side of a piece of tape on Fenster's computer. These matched the prints Johnson pulled off the *inside* of Fenster's books. There were some glossy pages that yielded perfect prints. So we have two coherent sets of prints in that apartment. Tell me, Inspector. What cleaning crew that you ever heard of would wipe down the individual pages of every book on a shelf?"

"None," said Poincaré.

"Correct. I called them, the companies, and they said they *did* wipe the covers. But not the inside. Why would they?"

"What about the teeth—in the cigar box," said Poincaré. "I asked Johnson to run those."

Hurley made room for their coffee and muffins. "The DNA from the baby teeth matched DNA from the urine and hair samples—which matched your results in Amsterdam. So we're to conclude what," said Hurley. "That Fenster handled the covers of his books but didn't read a page of any? Or that someone else read his books but didn't touch the covers? And that same someone wrote all those notes in the margins, in five languages, in the same hand, and attached a piece of tape with a few words to Fenster's computer? Inspector, I assume you examined an actual body in Amsterdam."

Poincaré tried rescuing his coffee with sugar. "I did," he said. "What was left of it."

"Then we've got a puzzle. And there's this." He produced a second set of envelopes and handed one to Poincaré. "Copies of complaints in Middlesex County Superior Court filed several weeks ago to establish ownership of Fenster's hard drive, which is now being held as evidence by the state. Harvard and a man named Charles Bell have retained downtown law firms that bill at $600 an hour."

"What's on the drives?"

"Wouldn't everyone like to know. I put our best people on this, but they couldn't access a damn thing after months of trying. Apparently, Fenster created a password that mere mortals can't touch. They've gotten this far: the password consists of sixty-seven characters. Inspector, there's not a word in the dictionary for the number of combinations in a sixty-seven character password. I've run out of resources. Officially, this case is closed on our end. We did our work, our results confirmed yours, and we're not the agency of record investigating the murder. Which means I won't be getting any more money for data analysis. The state budget's too tight, and we've got an eight-month backlog as it is at the forensics lab. Officially, we're done. But from where I sit, this case is not nearly closed—for you, anyway. The FBI report complicates things. And then there's the hard drive."

"What will you do with it?" Poincaré asked.

"That depends."

Poincaré sipped his coffee.

Hurley leaned close enough for him to count the pores on his nose. Too close. "Everyone knows the crime lab in this state has its problems. We've got a habit of losing things. In fact, at the moment this is sitting on an evidence shelf at the lab in Sudbury, Mass." From the side pocket of his sport coat, Hurley produced a sealed Tyvek envelope. It was smaller than the other envelopes, with their documents. This one looked to have some weight to it. "To think the Commonwealth is closing this case down just when it's gotten interesting. . . . I've seen too much," said Hurley. "My work is all about budgets now, not like the old days when the boss said *Just go find me the bastards*. Next February will be thirty years, and I'm outta here. Probably time, anyway—with how forgetful I've been getting. Every now and then I'll go out for coffee and actually leave things—keys, cell phone. So I've decided to retire with dignity before they wheel me out. You be in touch, OK . . . and pay that check, as long as you're sitting here."

Hurley slid from the booth and exited the Busy Bee without a backwards glance. When Poincaré stood, he saw that the detective had left the Tyvek envelope on his seat. Poincaré sat once more. He did not know Hurley, who had shown him nothing but contempt ten weeks earlier. If the man, playing nice, now wore a wire and was setting him up to receive stolen evidence, then his career was over, stained for good. But that hardly mattered anymore. He lifted the envelope, feeling its heft, and slipped it into his briefcase.

Outside the coffee shop, Poincaré could almost hear Ludovici laughing about the virtues of tainted evidence; and when his phone rang he half expected it to be Paolo with a hearty *It took you long enough. Welcome to the world, Henri!* But the screen blinked with an incoming text message from the ever-efficient De Vries:

```
Chambi stayed at pension 2 blks from
Ambassade. Checked in 1 week b4 bombing,
left day of. GDV
```

Chambi was *in* Amsterdam and *in* Paris with no apparent reason to kill either Fenster or Chloe. Yet there she was and they were dead—with Poincaré, Poincaré alone, the link. If he found her, he would kill her. His heart lurched and he took another pill.

CHAPTER 23

The view had not changed from the twenty-ninth floor of the State Street office tower, nor had Poincaré's fleeting but intense vertigo as he stepped from the elevator into the glass-walled offices of Charles Bell. A receptionist showed him to the same conference room where, months earlier, Bell had made such a lasting, unpleasant impression. Poincaré was sweating, though the ventilated air of the conference room was a pleasant seventy degrees. He felt ill and asked for water.

"Inspector! It's been months—terrific to see you again!"

Like the view of Boston harbor from these offices, the man striding into the conference room was unchanged: his smile as broad as a continent and not a millimeter deep. Poincaré had met less polished versions of Charles Bell in markets from New York to Marrakech. The smile was the thing. If the rug happened to have fewer knots per square unit than advertised, where's the harm? A wink and a special discount reserved for our very *best* customers.

"Mr. Bell," he said. "Thank you for seeing me on short notice."

"Charles, remember? Why are Europeans always so formal? I'm hoping you've brought news of progress, Inspector."

"We're working . . . Charles. That's all I can say for the moment. But while I was in town this time investigating the murder, a few questions occurred to me. Do you mind?" He produced his photos of Chambi and Rainier and watched for cracks in the mask.

"Ah, Dana! Very talented. I tried hiring her—giving her a stipend until she completed her degree. I would have paid her whole overpriced ticket to Harvard, but she said someone was already doing that—and that she was returning to Ecuador once she completed her degree. Fenster and his altruists. She couldn't be involved in any of this."

"The other one?" asked Poincaré.

"Never seen her, Inspector."

"When did you last see Ms. Chambi?"

"Two months ago, at least. After James died, I contacted her. She said *no* again—pleasantly, as always, then left Boston without a forwarding address. Up to that point, for perhaps a year, I kept her on a retainer. You know, a few hundred dollars a month to come down every so often and talk with my people."

"In order to—"

"To entice her to stay. What else? One of my personal marketing schemes that failed."

"She and your staff would talk?"

"That was the point. We'd catch up on new trends in mathematical modeling. There's nothing like a grad student to keep you connected to what's hot in a field. She'd learn about our operations, but as I say she didn't bite. I've tried a half-dozen ways to find her, starting with the Ecuadoran Embassy. Let me know if she turns up, OK?"

Poincaré worked himself into a chair and unbuttoned his collar. In his briefcase was the hard drive, in Hurley's envelope, which Bell would have ripped open with his teeth if he only knew. "Dr. Fenster had a laptop computer, Charles. Apparently, you and the university can't agree on who owns it."

"You might call it a difference of opinion. That's right."

"More like a war is what I heard."

Poincaré loosened his tie.

"I hate a bully, Inspector. Harvard has no right to the hardware I bought for Fenster. It wasn't enough I paid the university close to $8 million for the computers they linked into a massive array somewhere in the Science Center basement? It's madness. Those machines cost at most $5 million and the university pocketed the other $3 million for overhead. A total scam—James knew it and I knew it. So I also paid him on the side, for incidentals. He used that money to buy the laptop—he told me so directly. I only want what's mine. The only thing a bully understands is a punch in the nose."

"So you filed suit."

"Which is how people with money fight in America. I've spent $20,000 on lawyers already, and I'm prepared to spend ten times that. It's galling, the way the university grabs whatever it wants. Not this time." His face flushed, and he looked and sounded just like a man driven by principle.

Poincaré did not believe a word of it. "You know, I was talking with Peter Roy the other day, Fenster's attorney, and I learned that in his will Fenster left everything to the Math League of Cambridge. If he didn't leave you his laptop specifically, wouldn't the Math League have the strongest claim? But I see they're not involved in this suit just yet. I've read the filings."

"This is your idea of entertainment—to read court filings?"

Poincaré felt too sick to parry.

"Not to worry, Inspector. I've already reached an understanding with the faculty advisor at the high school. If my suit fails, I'll back the Math League's claim to the hard drive. They will prevail, and for a consideration I've already paid they'll give me the drive. Or, rather, loan it to me for a time. It's a win-win: Harvard gets spanked and the Math League won't have to worry about funding for the next 200 years. And I get to support a cause dear to James's heart."

"Excellent," said Poincaré. "I heard you were generous. Now I know you're clever and generous."

Bell caught his reflection in the glass and aligned his cuffs.

"It's admirable," Poincaré continued, "that you would help the Math League this way. But it's difficult to imagine that the contents of Fenster's hard drive have nothing to do with your generosity. What do you suppose is on the drive?"

Bell watched an Aer Lingus flight land at Logan. "Let's settle this," he said. "I've told you about Fenster's relation to the work we do, about our occasional chats. What we've accomplished with our modeling of the markets goes well beyond anything he and I discussed over stale biscuits and coffee. I want the hard drive because I want it. Because Harvard pisses me off. They own his mainframes, which I paid for, and everything on them. And now they want a $400 hard drive as some sort of cherry to crown their $25 billion endowment—which has sunk like a stone because they didn't invest in my funds? Like hell! I'm going to bloody their nose, and I don't care what it costs. And I hope you came with another question because this one's exhausted. What's the French word for that—*exhaustion*?" Bell turned back to the room. "Inspector?"

Poincaré heard the question but could not answer. He had slumped sideways across the table, clutching his chest.

⇥ PART III ⇤

Who cuts a channel for the torrents of rain,
and a path for the thunderstorm?

— JOB 38:25

CHAPTER 24

He woke with no tags on his toes or coins on his eyes. He could see monitors blinking and hear the squeak of rubber-soled shoes along a corridor. If Poincaré needed further proof he was alive, every part of him ached as though he'd been pistol-whipped. Alive, then; but hardly well: a tube ran from under the sheets to a bag he chose not to examine too closely; IV lines ran into veins at both arms and at the back of each hand; a sensor clamped on his finger monitored levels of oxygen in his blood; wires ran from leads on his chest; and at his bicep a cuff inflated every ten minutes, waking him each time he managed to doze. A bona fide hospital had got hold of him.

"I imagine you've had better days," said a doctor, stepping around a curtain. He flipped through the pages of a chart and checked the monitors. "The first thing to do is change your medications. Your heart responded well to intravenous dosing with an anti-arrhythmic, so we'll continue that approach in pill form. Your heart's now in normal sinus rhythm, Mr. . . ." He consulted the chart. "Inspector . . . Poincaré. That's the good news."

The embroidery on the man's jacket read *Maxwell Beck, Director of Clinical Cardiology*. Poincaré had been rushed to the emergency room of one of Boston's teaching hospitals; later, as he drifted in a medicated sleep, he was transferred to the Cardiac Care Unit, where he now lay tethered to his bed like a dog to a fence post. Aside from the births of his son and grandchildren, he had not a single positive memory of hospitals. He fought a strong impulse to pull out the tubing and run.

"If I'm in a normal rhythm," he said, "I can leave."

Beck worked a stethoscope across his chest, then felt the pulses at his wrists and ankles. "Your normal rhythm was the good news, Inspector. Do you realize how dehydrated you were? That sent your atrial fibrillation into overdrive. You may be on the mend, but the truth is you should do nothing more than sleep and eat for a month. I mean it. You are perilously close to a total collapse."

The advancing hands on the wall clock would not permit a collapse. "I'll compromise," Poincaré offered.

"You're hardly in a position—"

"Discharge me this afternoon—by 4 o'clock. I have a flight to Québec City at 9, and I have to get back to my hotel first and collect my things." He shifted his weight, which pulled at the tube beneath the sheets. "I feel fine," he said.

"Compared to what? Death?"

"Remove the tubes. That would be a start."

Poincaré looked beyond the partially drawn curtain in an effort to be anywhere else and saw an orderly wheeling a fully dressed man down the corridor. The woman following the gurney might as well have been trailing a hearse.

"Before I can release you," said Beck, "I need the results of a cardiac enzyme test. Assuming that's fine, 4 o'clock it is. My job is to get you back in sinus rhythm. Beyond that, you're free to dig your own grave. People do. We can fix your atrial fibrillation," continued the doctor. "What are your triggers? It's caffeine for some people. It could be a cold drink on a hot day or a large meal late at night. Sometimes, heavy drinking. Do you have any obvious triggers? You'll want to avoid them."

"I couldn't really pin it down,' said Poincaré, who was thinking that his whole life must be a trigger—and that someone had already dug his grave. "The attacks come of their own accord," he said. "They leave just as suddenly. I try to ignore them."

"Which is difficult, I imagine."

Poincaré nodded.

"What about your latest onset—tell me what was happening."

The question recalled his visit to Charles Bell and a large problem, potentially. Poincaré scanned the room, then asked the doctor to open the closet door. He saw only his suit and shoes. "Is there a briefcase beneath my bed?"

Beck looked. "I don't see one."

"Does your emergency room log personal effects when someone's admitted?"

"Your valuables are in the hospital safe. I wouldn't worry." The doctor glanced at Poincaré's chart. "I see the ER called your headquarters in Lyon. It was the only contact number they could find in your wallet, and when someone arrives presenting with cardiac symptoms they look for next of kin. The note here says they left a message on a machine."

Poincaré tried lifting himself off the bed. With Monforte in midexit, he would have to leave the hospital before the new director could locate and then recall him from the field for health reasons. Beck, meanwhile, was leaning against the window sill and watching his patient closely. "Take your new medication on schedule and promise to stay hydrated. Eight glasses a day."

"Including wine?"

"No. But if you're drinking wine, make it red. Do you sleep well?"

"Not particularly."

Poincaré looked at the wall clock. "Could you arrange for me to use a computer? I need to meet someone online at 3 o'clock."

Beck folded his arms. "Did you hear the part about total collapse?"

It was not a fair fight. Poincaré had tubes running into and out of him. He wore a thin hospital gown over a body that smelled of stale sweat. He made a calculation. "Let me explain," he said. "The person I'm after cut the breathing tube of a six-year-old, killing her. This same person very likely assassinated or assisted in the assassination of a once-in-a generation talent, using a modified explosive that any of a dozen terrorist organizations would be eager to use. I've got to be on a computer at 3 o'clock and I've got to leave here by 4 o'clock. I appreciate that I'm not the one to be making demands, Dr. Beck. But I need to leave here."

"What happens when you crumble?" said the doctor.

A fair question. Poincaré assumed that nothing would happen. Interpol would drop the case and the Americans, attending to more pressing needs, would forget about Fenster. Etienne had disowned him; Claire might never wake up. All he could do was face his jailer and lie: "If I go down, someone takes my place."

Beck approached the bed. "I won't call your superiors and insist they recall you because I don't know what it means to hunt a killer, let alone a child killer. But you had better rest. Once you're strong again, we can repair your heart." He took a pad of paper and sketched a diagram of the heart's chambers, then drew lines—catheters, he called them—that could be threaded through the femoral artery north to the heart where, guided by imaging technology, surgeons could shoot radio-frequency pulses to destroy the cells that triggered his arrhythmia. "Lately," said Beck, "the technique is becoming more science than art. You ought to consider it."

"You could restore a normal rhythm?"

"If we agree on how to define *normal*, yes." Beck flipped through Poincaré's file for a pamphlet that the nursing staff left with each patient admitted for atrial fibrillation. "Usually you'd get this on discharge, but since you asked—" He turned to a page with several graphs.

Self-Similar Dynamics

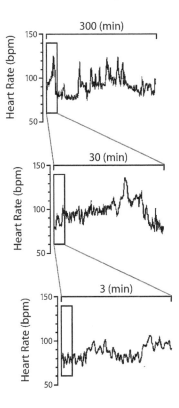

"You're probably thinking when you say *normal* that a healthy human heart beats like a metronome. Not so. These graphs show you electrocardiograms of a healthy heart over three minutes, thirty minutes, and three hundred minutes. Notice that the rates go up and down: they're somewhat erratic but erratic within known, healthy parameters. At any interval we choose to measure, the normal heart might beat two beats at a rate of seventy per minute—if it was sustained over a full minute, then for the next four beats run at ninety, then eighty then up to eighty-five. A normal rhythm has a variability that we can't predict because in every dynamic system—and the beating human heart is a dynamic system—the details of the motion are buried in such complexity that they are, even in principle, unknowable."

"Because?"

"Because the possibility of disorder is always present in an orderly system."

Poincaré recognized something in these graphs. "They have the same shape over different scales," he said.

"That's right. To look at one you might as well be looking at the others. The part contains the whole."

Fractal. Poincaré turned the word over in his mind. He felt himself slipping down a chute. He said the word.

"Right again, Inspector. Cardiologists have begun talking to mathematicians, believe it or not. I've always thought these tracings look like the day's stock market returns. Or the Alps. Here's a compressed, fifteen-minute strip of your heartbeat when you were admitted with A-Fib," said Beck, pulling a page from Poincaré's chart. "Look how the beats range from fifty to one hundred twenty, then drop down again—dominated by chaos.

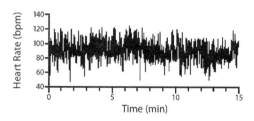

"There's no discernable pattern here, the hallmark of A-Fib. Now let's print a compressed strip of your last fifteen minutes in sinus rhythm." He tapped several keys on a console and presented the printout.

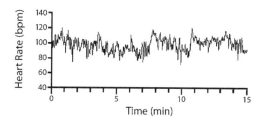

"Look how your normal rate's variable but orderly—not a metronome, but orderly within a bounded range and rate. What's particularly telling are the intervals *between* beats, which in normal sinus rhythm are also orderly. In A-Fib, chaos rules the intervals. You'll get a slow beat, wait three seconds for four rapid beats, wait another two for a run of slow beats and then speed up to 120. And so on. In the EP lab we measure intervals with a mathematical tool called a Poincaré Plot." Beck looked up. "Any relation? It's not a common name."

"My great-grandfather," said Poincaré, "pulling strings from beyond the grave."

"A coincidence!"

Poincaré hoped so, because otherwise this case was finding him.

"Look, Inspector. It comes down to this: we have a ninety percent chance of permanently restoring your sinus rhythm by destroying the cells responsible for flipping your otherwise healthy heart into the exaggerated chaos of A-Fib. No errant cells, no cascade into chaos. You'd be a good candidate for the surgery."

Beck checked the time. "My advice is to catch this person you're after, rest a few months, and do the surgery. There's a good group in Bordeaux if you want to pursue this in France. Or come see us here in Boston. In the meantime, you should get some relief with the new medication." Beck inspected the IV bags and flicked at a line. "I'll write the discharge papers for 4 PM. And I mean what I said about hydration. It will get back to me if you die from exhaustion, and that would be inconvenient for both of us."

Chapter 25

The nurse who had removed his IV lines and urine bag sent for his belongings while he showered, and Poincaré emerged from the tiny bathroom to unpleasant news: the plastic bag on his bed held a wallet, watch, wedding band, satellite phone, and hotel key—but no briefcase. The ER nurse who admitted him the previous day did not recall seeing it, nor did the orderly who wheeled him to the cardiac unit. All Poincaré could do was to leave one message for Charles Bell and another for the dispatcher at the ambulance company. At 3 PM, dressed and ready to leave, he logged onto the Math League Website. Hubert Levenger had instructed him to keep Chambi online, chatting, for the fifteen minutes his tracing software needed to establish her location.

>Hey there, Tutor.
>Antoine, is that you? How are the word problems going?
>Got a new one today: A commuter train leaves the station at 7 AM, traveling at a speed of 80 mph. An express train leaves the station at 8 AM traveling at 100 mph. At what distance and at what time will the express train meet the commuter train?
>A classic. What's your approach so far?
>I've worked it out by drawing two lines with 1 hour blocks, but this is an algebra class.
>That's right. Use x's and y's. Use your head, not your fingers. How many equations do you need?

```
>One,  I  think.  You  still  sleepy?
>Silly  question!  It's  only  dinnertime."
```

Poincaré's watch read 3:12 PM. She was still east of him. He checked a second window open on the computer. Dinner at 9 PM could place her as far east as Sofia or Jerusalem. But he doubted that. She was seated before a computer somewhere between 10° West and 15° East longitude. That left a large slice of the globe to search, but it was not the entire globe. He checked his watch and began working through the problem with her, feigning confusion at every turn to stall for time. After ten minutes, he produced the solution:

```
>100t  =  80t  +  80.  20t  =  80.  t  =  4.  The
commuter  train  travels  (t  +  1)  hours  =  5
hours  at  80  mph  and  goes  400  miles.  The
commuter  train  left  at  7  AM  +  5  hours  =  12
noon.  The  express  train  travels  4  hours  at
100  mph  and  goes  400  miles.  The  express
train  left  at  8  AM  +  4  hours  =  12  noon.
>Well  done,  Antoine!  What's  hard  about
this  type  of  problem  for  you?
>Nothing,  as  long  as  you're  helping  me!
I  want  to  study  math  in  college.  I  like
how  everything  in  math  has  an  answer--
everything  works  out.  Not  much  else  does
in  my  life.
>Go  to  college,  Antoine.  Always  a  good
plan.
>I  want  to  study  with  you--in  Europe!
>Who  said  I  was  in  Europe?
>You  said  it  was  dinnertime.  That's
Boston  plus  4  or  5  hours,  right?  This
spring  we  studied  time  zones  in  geography
and  I  learned  that  at  any  one  time
somewhere  on  the  planet,  in  a  narrow
band  running  north  and  south,  people  are
```

eating dinner. So right now it's 3:15 PM
along the east coast of the U.S. 3:15 +
4 or 5 hours = dinner time = Europe!
>Or Scandinavia or Africa. But good work.
How old did you say you were?
>Fifteen.
>Going on 35! You can study with me
anytime, online. But I'm not teaching in
a school at the moment. There are good
math teachers everywhere, though. Email
me when it's time to set up another
session. Got DINNER plans! Ciao.

Poincaré checked his watch again. He needed another three
minutes.

>But we haven't talked about my question
yet from last time!
>Which was?
>Math and real things. How do the x's
and y's of math that I write on a piece
of paper connect to real trains?

A visitor, this time without a stethoscope, stepped around the
curtain into Poincaré's room with a smile and an ID badge that identified her as a chaplain. Poincaré greeted the woman half-heartedly,
hoping that would turn her around.

"Mr. Poincaré? I'm Rita Collins, pastor at—"

"Thank you for stopping by Miss Collins, but I'm busy just
now."

"We like to check with everyone in the unit, you know. I see
you're scheduled for discharge. Feeling better?"

"It's kind of you. . . . But I'm in the middle of—"

"That's fine. I wanted to wish you well and leave you with a little
something. You know, people who land in the cardiac unit often
have questions. At a time like this, it's natural to feel depressed or
wonder what you're doing with your life. You may think you've had

a trauma only to your body, but the hurt often runs deeper." She laid a pamphlet on the table by his bed. "There's a phone number if you need to talk," she said, stepping back around the curtain.

```
>Now I remember! In math you use
equations to represent--to stand for--
something in the world. The x's and y's
of math are like words, but a different
symbol system. When you have a question
about how things in the world behave,
if you have a good equation you can
use math to find answers without a lot
of bother. Imagine if the only way to
answer the train problem was to buy a
ticket for a commuter train, wait for
the express train to catch up (if you
could find one going the same direction
on a parallel track), and then look at
your watch! That's a lot of effort, but
doable for trains. For most problems, you
can't buy a train ticket.
>Like what?
>Like if you need to know the reentry
angle for a spacecraft so it won't burn
up or skip off into space. You want to
figure these things out ahead of time and
not put people's lives at risk. Got to
run, Antoine. Ciao!"
```

He placed a call to Lyon.

The satellite link from Europe was clear enough that Poincaré heard an announcer on a radio in Levenger's office reading the evening news.

"Hubert, did you get a trace?"

"I did, Henri. Trouble is, your subject used two proxy servers to log onto the Web site for this session. She doesn't want to be found, and she's being clever about it. We hacked the log file of the second server, the one that connected to the Math League site. That server's in Belgium—likely Brussels or Antwerp. We traced the first server to Italy, but that's as close as we could get because the log file was shielded. Of course, she could have logged onto that server from South America or Asia."

"It's not dinnertime in South America or Asia."

"What's that?"

"Never mind. I haven't scheduled the next chat, but I'll let you know."

"Try getting her to write an e-mail, Henri. An e-mail has to be sent from somewhere definite, and I can find definite."

"With or without a subpoena?"

There was a pause. "I couldn't quite hear you. You're breaking up."

"That was a hypothetical, Hubert."

"I thought so. Happy hunting."

Poincaré set down his phone and typed an e-mail to Ludovici.

```
Chambi's likely in Italy. Contact Lyon
and refocus Blue Notice alert to Italy,
Austria, Switzerland, and France. Still
on for tomorrow in Québec. Breakfast at
8 AM, hotel.
```

He stretched and closed his eyes. At 3:30, he had nothing to do but wait for the results of a final blood test. Careless though he was with his own health, Poincaré did want to know if he had suffered a heart attack because that information would determine how hard he could push in the coming days. He needed time, and he did not want to collapse again before finding Chambi. So he waited, instead of walking out. With his briefcase missing and no files to review, he pointed a remote to a television bolted high on the wall, flipping through channels until he found a news station. He let that drone in the background as he reached for the pamphlet the chaplain had left: a single glossy sheet, folded once on itself and printed on four sides. From the title "Revelation Now!" he guessed its contents and read the first of eight passages, each a proof text that a day of reckoning approached:

> Then I saw another angel flying in midair, and he had the eternal gospel to proclaim to those who live on the earth—to every nation, tribe, language and people. He said in a loud voice, "Fear God and give him glory, because the hour of his judgment has come. Worship him who made the heavens, the earth, the sea and the springs of water. A second angel followed and said, "Fallen! Fallen is Babylon the Great, which made all the nations drink the maddening wine of her adulteries."

In a critical care unit? he marveled. Poincaré turned back to the television news. A woman with bobbed blonde hair who looked like every other newscaster with bobbed blonde hair was reading the day's headlines.

> The latest bombing in Baghdad killed 128 people, mostly children on a school trip to a local market. Police are bracing for a retaliatory strike. In the Caribbean, the hurricane season is well underway. Category four storm Elsa has already left 10,000 people homeless and another 200,000 without power in the Dominican Republic and is now bearing down on Florida. Elsewhere—

He turned it off when a nurse entered with a piece of paper for him to sign. "You're discharged," she said. "The tests are negative for heart attack. Dr. Beck's instructions are here." The woman touched his shoulder. "Rest, Inspector. You'll find a taxi outside the main entrance. Good luck."

When she left, Poincaré bent over to tie his shoes and fought off a wave of nausea. Someone new stepped around the curtain.

"Damn but you gave me a good scare!"

It was Charles Bell himself, with a smile Poincaré would be pleased to forget one day. In his right hand, he offered a bouquet of irises. In his left, a mere hatchet stroke away from the object of his desire, was the briefcase. Before rising to thank the last man he wanted calling on him in a hospital or anywhere else, Poincaré checked the locks of the briefcase. Neither showed signs of tampering. More reassuring still, the wheeled tumblers—both right and left—were set as Poincaré had left them the morning before. In a ritual as routine as brushing his teeth, he had for decades changed the combination to his briefcase every week; and for the first time in a quarter-century that simple precaution returned the favor. He would need to check, for Bell was a clever and determined man; but Fenster's hard drive was likely safe. "Charles," he said, standing to receive the flowers. "I suppose I owe you my life."

CHAPTER 26

Bell had overheard the nurse's advice and insisted on driving Poincaré to his hotel. He accepted, then abruptly declined when Bell steered the conversation to their last meeting. "Inspector, I'm hoping I've settled your concerns. I don't like loose ends."

A car roared from an underground garage, and Bell peeled a ten-dollar bill from a clip for an attendant. Poincaré faced him and said, "You're prepared to spend hundreds of thousands in legal fees for a hard drive that's meaningless? And Harvard would do the same? I somehow doubt either of you would go to war over a principle."

"I'm spending the company's money, not mine."

"So much the worse," said Poincaré.

The attendant opened the passenger's door, and Poincaré promptly shut it. "You know, Mr. Bell. The more you talk, the more confused I get. I'm going to sleep, and then I'm traveling for a few days. But I'll be calling again. If business takes you out of town, tell your assistant where I can find you." He left the man slack-jawed at the curbside and walked to the head of a taxi queue without a backwards glance. *Let him twist in the wind*, thought Poincaré. Minutes later he opened his briefcase and found Hurley's envelope, untouched. *Well, then*, he thought. If Bell were a killer, at least he was honest.

Poincaré postponed his flight until the morning and stopped at an electronics store for a cable that would let him connect his computer to Fenster's hard drive. He showered, ordered in food, and devoted hours to untangling what a team of data analysts, with powerful computers, could not achieve in months. But Poincaré had an advantage, he believed: the analysts had worked in a lab, running random numbers—brute force, Chambi would call it; Poincaré had seen Fenster's apartment and interviewed Roy and Silva and had a feel for the man himself. The odds of accessing the drive were still long, but he set to work and offered up an amateur's best.

First, he typed Fenster's home address, manipulating abbreviations and spacing until he counted sixty-seven characters. Nothing. In dozens of combinations, he typed the names of the foster families that had taken him in. He typed the names of courses Fenster had taught and their numerical IDs, and versions of his name and Madeleine Rainier's. Nothing worked. Exhausted, he shut down his computer and slipped the hard drive beneath his pillow—the way he had done once with a book in a failed high-school experiment the evening before an exam. This time, who knew? The information on that disk might somehow work its way into his slumbering brain.

In the darkness, Poincaré thought of Claire. There was no point calling to say he was ill. Instead, he thought of better times when a word was enough to bring her to his side, where he wished her to be now. He had sent a telex on his return from an assignment in Lebanon: *Air France. 10 AM tomorrow. Flight 2113. Ticket bought. Dress for five days on wine dark sea. HP.* He sent nothing more, confident she would rearrange her life on impossibly short notice and step from the plane in Athens. She arrived wearing a sun hat and carrying her foldaway easel, a bathing suit, and little else. On the ferry from Piraeus, they retched in heavy seas. But no sooner had they landed and bathed then Claire handed him a pair of swim trunks and hailed a taxi from their balcony. "Perivolos," she told the driver, Poincaré having no idea who or what *Perivolos* might be. Thirty minutes later they lay on a stretch of black volcanic beach, Claire curled to his side as Poincaré contemplated the drift of clouds and a distinct impression that he was floating in time.

That evening, she sat across from him over a checkerboard tablecloth, not just the café but the town itself perched on a cliff above the sea-swamped caldera. For three days they drank too much wine and dozed, entangling themselves in a bed by a window that opened to the sea—both old enough to know it could not last. Life, or death, would intervene and their moment would be gone. But it was not gone then, nor was it now. Yet.

QUÉBEC IS the only walled city in North America. As the taxi approached one of its fortified gates, Poincaré imagined that the brief flight from Boston had somehow veered east and deposited him in medieval France.

"Où voulez-vous aller?" asked the driver.

"Chateau Frontenac."

The Chateau was several blocks from his hotel, and he wanted to see it again and walk. The morning was bright, and with the new medication taking hold, he felt his energy returning.

"C'est impossible, Monsieur."

Poincaré soon understood why. The first sign he saw read "G-8 Criminals Out of Québec!" Initially, he thought the number thirty-two posted on trees and nearby buildings had something to do with the summit; but then he recalled the Soldiers of Rapture. The newspaper folded in his lap was dated July 14th, which meant that Jesus, provided He did not get delayed by traffic, was due to redeem the world in one month. "A security cordon at the Frontenac?" he asked.

The driver nodded. Soon enough, Poincaré saw the show of force for himself. Six blocks out, Canadian military police with automatic weapons patrolled the streets. Closer to the hotel, army units had established command posts. In addition, Poincaré knew, national security services from each of the G-8 countries would provide their own protection for heads of state. The Old City was in lockdown, and not even Poincaré's Interpol credentials could get him within strolling distance of the hotel.

The summit of the Indigenous Liberation Front was a different matter. Quito and company wanted to attract as many people and as much press attention as possible. For three years the ILF had mounted a counter-summit to the G-8, enjoying the reflected glare of press lights on the world leaders whose economies dominated global trade. ILF spokesmen would make their case against trans-global power while conferees attended sessions on topics ranging from sustainable farming to preserving indigenous languages.

By 8:30, Poincaré had checked into his room at Hotel Sainte-Anne and found Paolo sitting in the breakfast room with a plate piled high with cheeses, smoked meats, and pastries, reading *Le Soleil de Québec*. Poincaré sat and Paolo said: "So you've given up on sleep entirely? You're a medical wonder."

"It's good to see you, too." Poincaré pointed to the newspaper. "Anything interesting?"

"Same old mayhem. The ILF issued a report last night accusing the G-8 nations of promoting a new colonialism. The phrase is getting some play." Ludovici cut into a particularly ripe goat cheese and smeared it on a crust of bread. "Aside from that, the usual wars and famine. How was Boston?"

"Useful."

Ludovici arched an eyebrow. "I heard you had an adventure. Stay here, and I'll get you some food."

"I'm not a patient anymore. I'll get it myself."

"Sit!"

Poincaré unfolded a napkin and contemplated their day ahead as Ludovici worked his way through the buffet line. Quito was scheduled to speak at a rally across a park from the Frontenac. After that, they would meet and Poincaré would ask him about Chambi.

"Two of everything," Ludovici said, returning with a plate piled as high as his own. "Eat, so you don't faint with the news I'm about to tell you. And remember: it's poor form to kill a messenger."

Poincaré worked a spoon into a poached egg.

"Well, don't you want to know?"

Poincaré set down the spoon. "I can guess."

"You've been promoted, Henri. Congratulations. Out of the field, to an administrative spot being created just for you. You're off the ammonium perchlorate case."

"Last I checked, the file name read *Fenster*."

"Come on, Henri. Since when did Interpol care about the death of a single person—even someone with Fenster's résumé? We're not equipped for that. Our interest begins and ends with keeping a recipe for souped-up rocket fuel from the marketplace. Those are my instructions. I'm your replacement, by the way."

"A man died in that hotel room."

"True—and that's going to go unsolved unless the Americans invest some resources. But whatever they do, we will find the source of that explosive. What part of this surprises you?"

"None of it," he said. "Nothing. You're right."

As Poincaré ate, Ludovici explained how the axe finally fell on Albert Monforte and how the new director—an American from their Bureau of Alcohol, Tobacco, Firearms and Explosives—was instituting a policy to retire all field agents older than fifty, effective immediately. In Poincaré's case, an offer was being made to fill a newly created post: "Something like Senior Mentor to Field Operatives," said Ludovici. "You'll be the Uber-Op. The director texted me this morning and asked me to ask you how your heart is holding up. They received a message from a hospital in Boston, and he's pissed he can't get hold of you. Have you tried turning your phone on?"

"It's on."

"And you didn't take his calls?"

"I'm busy when he calls," said Poincaré. "And my heart is fine."

"Except that it puts you in the hospital. This new guy—Felix Robinson—isn't taking chances. He knows what happened to your family. He heard how you took a beating from Banović's wife in The Hague and wondered what the hell you were doing there in the first place, which I defended as proof of your professionalism—some bullshit about your commitment to justice. As if that could explain your sitting in the gallery with a gun—which, by the way, Robinson doesn't know about. Maybe I *should* have told him you intended to kill Banović. And now a heart attack? You're falling apart—and you had better quit before you embarrass yourself or this agency. His words, not mine."

"It wasn't a heart attack."

"He doesn't care if it was a hemorrhoid. You're gone in a week. He wants you in Lyon on the 23rd to turn over your credentials and firearms. He wants you home with your family, and he's willing to set you up with a secure line to Fonroque where you can be a resource to reckless people like me. This will be perfect—you sipping bad wine, dispensing wisdom."

Poincaré had to admire the new director. Termination by promotion was clever. "So I'm to think of this as my final assignment."

"I'd say the winding down of your final assignment, because if you haven't cracked this case in three months, you're not going to crack it in a week. Maybe it's for the best, Henri. Maybe it's time to stop."

"You think so?"

"I don't know."

"I'll stop when I catch Chambi," he said.

"You'll stop on the 23rd. I'm to meet you in Lyon, and you're to hand over everything you have."

Poincaré set down his fork and knife. "She was in Amsterdam, Paolo. Gisele confirmed that Chambi left the day of the bombing. She was too nervous to discuss Fenster's murder when I questioned her in Boston. Now she's dropped out of sight."

Ludovici rolled a slice of ham. "Not enough," he said, stuffing his mouth. "You want to find her because of Chloe, not Fenster or the rocket fuel. The new director agreed with Monforte on that point, at least. He's made finding Chambi a priority—but that's an altogether separate case. Interpol *will* find her. Let it go. It's clouding your judgment."

"The cases are connected."

"*How?*"

"I don't know yet."

"Well, there you go."

"It's called an *investigation*, Paolo. You begin with questions, not answers."

"So *that's* how this job works? Now you tell me . . ."

"She's implicated. Of all the people to attack Chloe, it was James Fenster's assistant? *I'm* the link. I was investigating Fenster. Somebody wanted me off the case because I was too close to something, and I don't know what that is."

"And I'm supposed to chase this woman's shadow around the world based on your intuition? When the case is mine, I'll start at the Jet Propulsion Laboratory and run down the chemical signature of that bomb, then I'll figure out how Madeleine Rainier, an antiques dealer, managed to dust her clothes with ammonium perchlorate. If you're going to search for anyone, search for her."

"I'm already on that," said Poincaré. "I'll be at the Jet Propulsion Lab in two days, and tonight I'm on my way to Minneapolis, where Rainier was born. I'll leave my notes in the file."

"Go back to France, Henri. Take the week off. Relax for once in your life."

"No, thank you."

"Suit yourself. I'll be at Fort Benning in the meantime."

"Georgia? Doing what?"

"The International Sniper Competition, at the army base. I'm thrilled."

"Give it a *rest*. You use your brains in this job, not guns."

A waiter filled their water glasses. "What's it to you? I'm taking a week's vacation, and I have the honor of being the only non-military member on the Italian team. Look, I was never any good at soccer. But this? I can make Italy number one in the world."

"Doing what, exactly?"

"Aerial shooting, convoy live fire, night shooting, anti-sniper ops, and who knows what else—shooting the fuzz off peaches at three hundred meters. Thirty marksmanship teams compete, including the US military, and the winner gets bragging rights for a year. The individual points leader wins a pair of snakeskin cowboy boots. I intend for the Italians to win, and I intend to wear those boots."

"Excellent," said Poincaré.

Ludovici snapped a breadstick. "Spare me. You make bad wine. I've got this—" He held up the trigger finger on his right hand. "Which is a God-given talent."

"I mean it," said Poincaré. "Go win the competition. You're the best marksman I know. As for handing over this case, I'm glad it will be to you." He set a fork on the rim of his water glass, and they both watched it teeter, then balance. "I'm also glad you're here today. You're the only one I could have called."

Ludovici put a napkin to his lips.

"It's OK, Paolo."

"I'm not going to let you die out here, Henri. Go back to France."

"No one's dying. Not yet."

"Then finish your damned breakfast. The ILF Summit concludes with the rally near the Frontenac. Twelve hundred delegates flown in from around the world—with what, for money, I couldn't tell you. But they're here and they've been protesting the G-8 non-stop. I saw Quito yesterday at a smaller rally near the Parliament Building and passed him a note, just as you asked. He told me he was looking forward to the meeting."

"He said that—those words?"

"He wants to express his condolences personally." Ludovici tapped the table to get the waiter's attention, looking in every direction but Poincaré's. He took another sip of coffee. "What's next for you?" he finally asked. "After Interpol, I mean. What will you do?"

"That depends."

"On what?"

"On whether or not I find Dana Chambi this week."

CHAPTER 27

When Poincaré arrived at the rally site, he found rented propane cook stoves, portable sanitation stalls, and gas-powered generators for a sound system and lights—the cables for which had been carefully laid and secured. He also saw a first-aid tent and a raised platform that offered the press corps good angles across the crowd to the speaker's dais and the Chateau Frontenac beyond. It was an impressive show of logistics. Drummers were in place, pounding out rhythms unheard in Québec since the time of Champlain.

The delegates mingled, the mood festive but also tense; for on the far side of a barricade stood a police line in full riot gear. Between the police and the Chateau, army regulars patrolled a small park with automatic weapons slung across their shoulders. A helicopter hovered nearby; men in sunglasses and bulky jackets worked the edges of the crowd, speaking into their lapels. The Canadians would allow freedom of assembly because not to would make them look like Soviet-era thugs in full view of the international press. But the freedom would extend to speech, not movement: no one from the ILF side of the barricades would be allowed to approach the Chateau.

Apart from Quito, in a fashion. Poincaré watched the president of the Indigenous Liberation Front, this once-modest herder turned economist, ascend a portable platform erected as a kind of forward battlement. The moment he stepped to the microphone, one eye cocked on the cameras, Poincaré understood: Quito would use the technology of the West against itself, just as he had appropriated the Internet to assemble a virtual nation from across the globe. He spoke simply and briefly. He was addressing the world.

> My name is Eduardo Quito. I am the son, the grandson, and the great-grandson of herders extending back before

the Spanish invasion. Originally, my people were farmers. The ones that Spanish axes and pikes did not kill, measles infected and killed. My fathers and mothers fled to the mountains, but the soldiers pursued us. We suffered and died. Hundreds of us live now, where once there were hundreds of thousands. I struggle to teach my young ones the old ways, but I weep because I know so few of them myself. My name is Eduardo Quito.

He reached into a large earthenware bowl and produced what looked to be a pebble, the size one shakes from a shoe. He held the pea-stone aloft for all to see, turned, and heaved it over the barricades at the police line. It clinked off the riot shield of an officer who could not have been more than a year out of the academy. Quito turned and helped an old woman to the stage. She was dressed in leather leggings and a leather parka lined with white fur that fluttered in an updraft off the river. "Mother," he said. "Speak." She did. And so did man after woman after man. A reindeer herder from Lapland; a bushman from the Kalahari; a Lakota Sioux; a Kaiapo shaman from the Amazon. Slowly and without direction, hundreds of men and women formed a queue that snaked through the rally grounds to the makeshift stage. Each, in turn, told a story of a world undone, then held a pebble to the crowd and hurled it at the police. Many wept; now and again, someone raised a keening cry. All the while, drummers kept their rhythm.

Poincaré's cell phone rang. The number showed Lyon, and he ignored it. The phone rang again and he turned it off. By 3 PM, he sensed agitation among the police, who endured one pebble after the next clinking off their riot shields. Mounted security had begun to restrain skittish horses. Not only had Quito outmaneuvered the Canadians, he was baiting them. The vigil was now being broadcast to the world, bounced off satellites and doubtless across the park to the presidents and prime ministers who sat, so well guarded, in the Chateau.

Evening fell. Organizers had set up food stations, but local vendors from within and without the walls of Old Québec had begun arriving with sandwiches and encouragement, shouting *Viva la mani-festation!* A crowd of onlookers swelled and began jeering the police. Poincaré had not anticipated such a long rally, but Quito had: cooks began dispensing soup and coffee; chairs were being set out for the elders; marshals with signs kept orderly queues. One speaker followed the next when Poincaré noted a short man with a broad face and chocolate skin stepping to the microphone. The gesture is what caught Poincaré's eye. Before speaking, the man raised his arms. "Brothers and Sisters!" he cried:

> I am of the Pitjantjatjara people from the Western Desert of the land invaders call Australia. When I was six, agents of the occupying government stole me and a whole generation from our homes to be raised in mission settlements. To civilize us. To make us serve them. I ran at the age eight, and they caught me and beat me. I ran two years later. I ran for good at the age of twelve to drink whiskey and wander. The old ways are lost. The new ways are empty. My parents died not knowing what became of their children. I am a Pitjantjatjara from the Western Desert of the land invaders call Australia.

The man stepped from the microphone, opened a penknife, held his free hand aloft, and ran the blade across his palm. Blood flowed, and into the blood he ground a pebble. *Don't do this*, thought Poincaré. *You're winning. Don't.* But the man turned and whipped the pebble across the barricade, letting the penknife fall harmlessly to the platform. The stone clinked off a riot shield and left a red dot. It was in a strange quarter-time that Poincaré observed the stunned silence that followed. He watched as if in slow motion an earthquake opened a fissure at his feet. The equilibrium that had held all day cracked. He heard a whistle, and the melee was on.

ILF delegates rushed the barricades, throwing anything they could find at the police, who responded with tear gas and rubber bullets. Men and women fell, putting hands to bloody heads, screaming. A cookstove overturned and a grease fire started. Delegates who had pressed forward on the attack began stampeding to Poincaré's right, separating him from Ludovici. The police broke through the barricade, advancing with riot clubs. To his left and behind, rows of shops cut off all escape, and Poincaré was caught in a pincer. The truncheons fell first across the drummers, who held their positions and suffered the blows as if they were standard-bearers in battle. They dropped in place. Tear gas boiled from canisters. Some delegates, on their knees with arms raised, prayed; others wrapped shirts around their faces and threw cobblestones. The cameras caught it all.

A policeman bludgeoned a man standing to Poincaré's left, then turned and raised his club. As Poincaré crouched to shield himself, he heard a jolt—the sound of a strong electric current as the policeman fell, breathing but twitching. Then a gong went off in his head and his body went limp. But before losing consciousness, he felt a pair of strong hands lifting beneath his arms and carrying him off.

How MANY hours later he was not sure, but Poincaré woke to bright lights in a room with sofas, a coffee table, and a wet bar. "Paolo?" He blinked and put a hand to his throbbing forehead. "How did you—" Ludovici was nowhere to be seen. When Poincaré attempted to stand, a hand at his shoulder restrained him.

"You took a nasty blow," said a familiar voice. "Lucky for you our people were in place. Now you know what life is like on our side of the barricades!"

"Quito?"

"At your service, Inspector." He stepped into Poincaré's field view, joined by a man who looked a good deal like him, though younger and even more powerfully built. "You have my assistant Juan to thank for your . . . how do you people say it? Your *extraction*."

Poincaré sat up and realized he was well clear of the riot, in the calm of a hotel suite. Quito began pacing before him on a carpet. "Believe it or not, Inspector, I did not want violence. We were gaining the world's sympathy. I felt it!"

Poincaré agreed. "It was brilliant theater. But as for not expecting a riot—every moment of that rally was planned. I suppose you put the Aborigine up there to incite the crowd?"

"That's an offensive word."

"The man who cut himself. Did you stage that, too?"

Quito stopped his pacing. "What can I say? I create sculpture gardens that people inhabit. I'm an artist, Inspector, and these actions are my art. You saw how these events bring out passions. I didn't put him up to it. I wish he hadn't cut himself—but then, what did he do wrong? It was only a pebble, no different than the rest. I assure you that spilt blood, in itself, is not the problem. The problem is that for 500 years it's been our blood, never yours."

"For what it's worth, you won my sympathy out there."

"It's too late for that," said Quito, who resumed his pacing. "I told you in Amsterdam: we will no longer wait quietly for others to rescue us."

"You'll be crushed."

"We are already crushed."

Poincaré felt a bandage on his forehead. "What happened?"

"What happened is that one of Canada's finest knocked you across the head with a truncheon. I'd been watching for you in the crowd since your assistant told me you were coming. I must say you weren't hard to miss with your pale skin and suit!" Quito laughed. "When my security hurried me from the trouble, I had Juan go back and bring you to a car—but he was a bit late. At the moment, you're outside the city in a secure location.

"I took the liberty of having my physician sew you up while you were unconscious. Not your first battle scars, I think!" Again, Poincaré ran fingers along the bandage and, indeed, felt a ridge of stitches. Quito seemed to read his mind. "Consider it a memento, Inspector. Something to remember me by every time you pass a mirror. And don't worry. We Indigenes believe in germ theory. My physician used sterile needles and antiseptics and left these for you—" He fished in his pocket for a pill bottle. "A few days worth of Bactrim, I believe, just to make certain no nasty bugs invaded your system."

"Your physician?"

"Don't look so surprised. The potentates in the Chateau have theirs. As I get older, my wife insists I travel with one. What did you expect from a poor Andean herder—a poultice of chewed tobacco? Ha!"

"What happened to my partner?"

"The young man was arrested with everyone else. But the police released people this evening before ever charging them—under orders from a magistrate who watched the event on television. She said she was moved to tears. Mr. Ludovici is likely back at your hotel, worrying about you."

Poincaré tried to stand. "Should he be?"

"You dishonor me. Juan will drive you to the hotel when we're done here. You know, I liked you from the first time we met. It's our *tenaz*—our bull-doggedness. You're still here, on your case, even after all your sorrow. I was stricken to learn of your family's misfortune and the death of your granddaughter. Who would do such a thing—that man I overheard you talking about in Amsterdam?"

Poincaré stared at him.

"Bad news travels, I'm afraid."

"I came on business, Professor."

"I'm sure you did. But I've told you everything I know about Fenster's murder. You have new questions for me, perhaps. It would be a shame to have come all this way and taken seven stitches for nothing." Quito nodded to his assistant, who stepped into an adjacent room and closed the door. "Inspector, what can I do for you?"

Poincaré pushed himself to his feet and walked unsteadily to a table. He set out three photographs of Dana Chambi.

Quito reached immediately for one. "Dana!"

"So you know her?"

"Of course. The ILF sponsored her studies at Harvard. She could never have afforded the airfare to Boston, let alone tuition. She'd already been accepted into the doctoral program, but the university had no money to offer. So she applied for an ILF scholarship and we—the committee responsible for these things—reviewed her application and sponsored her. A terrifically bright woman, but a bit erratic recently."

Poincaré lowered himself into a chair. "She just happened to work for Fenster."

"Why not? She found him, then found me. There were no hard feelings between James and me when our collaboration ended."

"You're telling me that of all the mathematicians in the world for Dana Chambi to study with, she found James Fenster—who just happened to have collaborated with you? Did Fenster know of the connection?"

"I never asked. Should I have?"

"You're calling it a coincidence?"

"Purely."

"In what way had she been erratic, Professor?"

"She would file reports, updating us on her progress. When we heard nothing last May, after the spring term, and June passed, we tried contacting her. Nothing. Now we're worried and have been looking. She's left Harvard, you know."

"Yes, I know."

"She's one of us, Inspector. I want to help her find a new position so she can complete her studies. We Indigenes need all our Dana Chambis if we're to improve our lives. She thought she was studying disease prevention, but I've been grooming her for a leadership position in the ILF. I won't live forever."

Poincaré's neck was stiff and he wanted a drink. But not here.

"So you must have been impressed with Dana. Everyone is. She could not possibly be connected to Fenster's murder. You don't honestly believe this?"

"I don't believe anything just yet," said Poincaré. Which was true. On the one hand, she had been in Paris and Amsterdam. On the other, by all accounts—Roy's, Bell's, Quito's, and even his own based on a ten-minute interview—she was no killer. "Did you see Ms. Chambi in Amsterdam?" he asked. "She was there on the days leading up to the bombing."

Quito looked genuinely surprised by the news. "Impossible," he said. "She would have known about the Amsterdam action against the WTO. She would have found me. I was not exactly hiding. This is hard to believe."

"I have hotel records and an authenticated signature. Believe it."

"Assisting Fenster?"

"Or not."

"She had no reason to harm him."

"Then who set that bomb?"

Quito walked to the window and lifted a curtain. "We went through this. There's nothing I can add, except to remind you that proximity does not make a murderer of me—or her. Dana could not have done this."

Poincaré had to turn his entire body to see Quito. "She was in Amsterdam. I saw her once after that, in Cambridge. Now she's gone and does not, apparently, wish to be found by me, you, or anyone."

Quito crossed the room and held out his hand. "Let's make a pact, you and I. If I find Dana, I'll ring you up. If you find her, you can return the favor. Good evening . . . and take care."

"But another question," said Poincaré.

"I don't think so, Inspector. Go rest. You are looking very, very tired."

CHAPTER 28

"I checked every hospital," said Ludovici when Poincaré entered the hotel lobby at 2 AM. "I called walk-in clinics. I called the morgue. Christ, Henri, you don't look much better than a corpse."

Poincaré explained what he could remember, which left him unable to account for roughly two hours. The policeman with the truncheon had gone down, tasered. Someone else had clubbed him—possibly Quito's own man. But there was no reconstructing that now, and in either case the pounding in his head made speculation pointless. He had been clubbed, and he felt unsteady and nauseated. "I don't believe Quito," he said. "He's not telling what he knows about Chambi."

Ludovici rolled his eyes. "Don't start with this again." An ugly bruise colored his cheekbone, and he walked with a limp.

"Paolo, I've got a week to do this my way. See you in Lyon." Poincaré started for the elevator.

"Alright. Fine. How about we don't talk shop and both take something to kill the pain. You know that I actually knocked one cop cold. He didn't give a fuck when I flashed a badge in his face. The man was a lunatic once he crossed the barricades. What kind of training do they give their people out here?" Ludovici pointed to an alcove: "I ordered two glasses and a bottle, figuring you'd show up sooner or later. Come on, you can tell me about all the other riots you've been in, and I can tell you about the suit I'm going to bring against the Canadians for police brutality."

That night, Poincaré did not sleep. He drank with Ludovici until 4 AM. Then, sending him off to his sniper competition, he wandered to his room, using the walls for support. After examining his wound—Quito's physician had laid down a neat row of stitches—he opened Fenster's case folders on the bed and set Rainier's and Chambi's photos beside them. He thumbed through the images from Fenster's gallery but could not attach a story to any of it, though with an instinct approaching certainty he knew that pertinent pieces of paper were arrayed before him. He reconsidered the photo of a single leaf—an image that for months, even while away from the case in Fonroque, had fascinated him. Fenster's cropping of the image invited a close inspection of the extraordinary in the absolutely mundane. A leaf.

This time, the image caused Poincaré discomfort in the extreme, for when he saw it he thought of maps: streets and neighborhoods and house plots. On visiting a city, he was in the habit of printing maps from the Internet—aerial views that would give him a broad sense of distances and direction. He retrieved his map of Québec, then folded it into quadrants and laid that on the bed, beside the leaf.

This was no metaphor. Cities were not *like* leaves but rather *were* leaves in some essential way: a single principle that was deeper than biology, prior to biology, organized both. Poincaré studied the shared structures—the avenues for fuel, waste removal, and communication. No cell existed without a route back to a main line; cells were contiguous until a sharp border was reached; vital operations within cells kept the larger organism functioning. Cities, leaves. What else? Poincaré saw it, what Fenster had seen; but still he resisted Fenster's move from things one could touch—leaves and cracks in asphalt—to entities as abstract as the global economy and the districts of France. He took pen to paper and sketched the flow of letters of credit, trade agreements, and tariffs as if they were components of an organism that grew routes for transport to and from centers of production. He could see it; he could not accept it.

When the sun rose, Poincaré knew he had walked half a road with James Fenster over a very long night; but there would be no going the full distance just now. He collected his materials, closed the curtain in his hotel room, and slept all day—waking for dinner at five and an evening flight to Minneapolis. He showered and dressed with care, which refreshed him on the inside, at least. On the outside, he did not cut much of a figure. Mirrors do not lie, and neither had Quito or Ludovici. Still, his heart was behaving. He had eaten an actual meal, and he had slept.

Outside the fuselage window, Poincaré watched the Aurora twisting in broad, green sheets. He had seen other such displays. Once he had tracked a child pornographer to the upper reaches of Norway where, in a village lost to the sun several months each year, a desk clerk amassed the most execrable digitized photo library of abuse to minors—some as young as a year—as could be imagined and then distributed it for profit across the Internet. The wonders of technology. As this thin, mousy father of three walked to a police car—the only one in a cluster of a tiny villages that far north, agents carried computers and filing cabinets to a waiting van. Poincaré leaned against a post and stared at a sky much like the one outside the airplane. If at that moment someone had tapped his shoulder and said: "It's dinosaurs fighting—this is what causes the Northern Lights," he might have answered *Why not?* With a book knowledge that explained nothing, he watched particles streaming from the sun and exploding high in the atmosphere while down below, with as much astonishment, he watched a pornographer's wife struck dumb as authorities led away a stranger she had called husband. How did one understand either?

And how he had lived fifty-seven years, altogether missing the beauty of what Fenster saw and what Chloe observed that day in Fonroque: symmetries upon symmetries invisible to him and yet as near as his next heartbeat? In his electrocardiogram lived a patterning common to lightning strikes, trees, and the incremental growth of cities. He did not dare ask where or with what it all ended because to ask was to invite inquiries he was not willing to make. But of this much he was sure: to Fenster, the very world—above *and* below— shimmered like the Aurora, and in that shimmering lay the key to his murder.

Poincaré turned away from the window.

The Minnesota Department of Health building on Robert Street was a long, low-slung structure of stone and tall glass panels that wore part of its steel skeleton, insect-like, on the outside. Poincaré was greeted by an office manager who, with the barest of preliminaries, steered him to a room piled high with storage boxes. *One cigarette*, he thought, and 15,000 people would cease to exist on paper. "They're only health advisories and internal memos," the woman said, reading his concern. "Vital records are digitized and backed up both on our mainframe and on computers out of state. Follow me. I believe I have what you're looking for."

He was old enough to remember sorting through vital records in shoe boxes. "I won't take much of your time, Mrs. Reynolds."

"Good," she said. "Because I don't have much time."

They reached a solitary, windowless office that had been used for janitorial supplies in an earlier life. Along one wall was a sanitary sink filled with discarded paper. Pamphlets, neatly stacked in boxes, lined shelves; on the door, oddly enough, was her nameplate. She worked in a storage room inside a storage room.

They sat at a desk, and Poincaré produced his copy of Madeleine Rainier's birth certificate, which he had requested. "November 8, 1980. Hennepin County Medical Center. May I see an original—or your digitized copy?"

She examined Poincaré's version of the certificate. "Two things," she began. "First, the paper originals are kept in a vault somewhere up in the Iron Range. The best we offer here is a digital facsimile. Second, you have a certified copy—do you see this mark here? It's legitimate but may be missing some information. Give me a moment." She entered Rainier's name into a database; when the screen refreshed, she reached for glasses that hung on a chain around her neck.

"Parents—the same; the addresses match. Same file. You're working with an authentic record," she said, looking up. Reynolds swung the monitor to Poincaré's side of the desk, and he began comparing the paper in his hand against the information on the screen. "What's this mark on the original?" he asked. "It's not on my copy."

The woman swung the monitor back. "As I said, certified copies omit information that's not pertinent to establishing proof of citizenship or date of birth. This mark indicates that Madeleine Rainier had a twin." She clicked on a link and a second record appeared. "A brother, Marcus . . . three pounds, seven ounces. Born eight minutes after." She checked Madeleine Rainier's record. "And runt of the litter. The sister was six pounds, three ounces."

Poincaré backed his chair away from her. "Curious."

"Inspector, *this* is the difference between certified and uncertified. Weren't you listening? Some people don't care if others know they're a twin, which is their right. But we assume most people want their privacy, so all certified birth certificates mailed from this office list a single name only."

She reminded him of a teacher he had been saddled with for a year in primary school. She fixed him with a stare. "Do you understand?"

"I understand," he said. He asked for copies of Rainier's full certificate and her brother's, then pointed to the address common to each. "They lived in Minneapolis. Is this street nearby?"

She turned off the monitor. "You say you're visiting from France?"

"That's right."

"Then it's nearby. Forty minutes in traffic."

Poincaré had tracked serial killers from large, extended families at whose trials siblings and parents wrung their hands and said: *We never saw it coming!* Banović had brothers. France's own Jack the Ripper, Joseph Vacher, had a sister. Still, Poincaré never quite expected that anyone damaged enough to land on his case list could be other than a lone, unhappy child.

So Rainier had a brother. Poincaré doubted the news would materially affect the case, and he doubted that after nearly three decades he would find anything useful at her childhood home. Still, he handed his driver an address and sat back, reviewing what information he had on Madeleine Rainier. Forty-four minutes later—he expected no less from Mrs. Reynolds—he approached the neighborhood on a street not much wider than a bike path that followed the shoreline of several connected lakes. The homes were stucco and brick, stately with well-tended lawns and picture windows through which he could see thick curtains and chandeliers. The driver stopped before one of the larger homes, and Poincaré followed a terraced walkway to a portico supported by four large columns. He knocked and admired the view across the lake, to the towers of Minneapolis.

The man who answered the door was so stooped at the shoulders that he had to strain his neck to receive his visitor. "May I help you?" The strong voice surprised Poincaré. He showed his badge, which the man studied as if it were a relic. He looked from the badge to Poincaré, and back again. "I was a federal judge in a former life," he said. "Is one of my cases coming back to bite me?"

From down the hallway, someone called: "Who is it, Nate?"

"One moment, dear . . . What's this about?"

"Mr. Rainier?"

The man looked perplexed. "No. Nathan Jorgenson."

Poincaré showed him the birth certificates, pointing out the address on each. Then the names. "Have I come to the wrong place, Monsieur?"

The man studied the certificates and, after a moment, craned his neck once more. "I haven't seen this name or thought of these people in a long time. Please come in, Inspector. My wife should hear this."

Poincaré followed him down a hallway off of which he saw a parlor, a music room, a staircase, a dining room, and a kitchen. At the back of the house he turned right into the smallest of the rooms, with a window that looked over an herb garden. Mrs. Jorgenson, seated in a wheelchair beside a space heater, set aside her needlepoint and smiled as her husband introduced their visitor. Poincaré noted examples of framed lace on the walls and said: "You did these? I never saw finer work in Bruges. Where do you find the patience?"

Mrs. Jorgenson laughed and patted her legs. "Right here. It's my specialty, sitting. And even if the rest of me is falling apart, my hands and my eyes are still good enough to sew. What can we do for you, Inspector?"

"He came asking about the Rainier children, Anna."

Her husband sat beside her.

Poincaré stated his business and, in the moment it took Anna and Nathan Jorgenson to work through difficult emotions, he wondered if Claire and he would have the chance to grow old together. Did he even want to live long enough to see her in a wheelchair?

"It's a terribly sad story," Mrs. Jorgenson began. "We never met the children. There were three of them."

"*Three*? I understood Madeleine had a fraternal twin."

"She did. And also an older brother. She was two and the older one was four, I believe, at the time of the accident. We bought the house about a year after. . . . From what we learned, the Rainiers were a young, professional family. I believe the father was an attorney and the mother taught at the university. The children were home one Friday evening with a sitter. The parents had gone to the theater, and on their way back a drunk ran a stop sign and killed them. They had no relations. And remarkably, there was no will. I never understood that—except, possibly, I heard the family had moved to the Twin Cities after some failed business venture back east. I believe the twins were born here. The older child was born in Massachusetts, I think. Or Connecticut. That was it. They came from New Haven. The mother taught at Yale."

"But this house," said Poincaré. "How could they have afforded it?"

"Apparently the woman was a brilliant chemist, and to lure her the university bought the house and paid the mortgage. The Rainiers didn't own it. They had tied up everything in that business, and they were starting over."

"They had even cashed out their life insurance policies," said the husband, "to pay off debts. It was an honorable thing to do. They avoided bankruptcy, but it ruined them. A sad affair. The children were left penniless."

"And with no family to take them in!" said the wife. "They stayed with neighbors until arrangements could be made. There was plenty of talk about what should be done, but in the end, no one in the neighborhood was willing to take on three orphans without a nickel to their name. The state put them up for adoption. I know they were separated, but I don't know what became of them after."

Anna Jorgenson's white hair was thinner than her husband's. A plaid, wool blanket hid her legs. "Nate," she said. "I know this business was settled before we ever moved into the house. But I wish we had taken them. We came from out of state," she said to Poincaré. "We hadn't heard about the accident. But I wonder sometimes what if the timing had been different. We could have taken them and they would at least have had each other and this house and their neighborhood." She put a handkerchief to her nose. "We had five, Inspector. What's three more? . . . You know, the heart breaks. It does."

CHAPTER 29

Poincaré woke to news of a suicide bombing in Piccadilly Circus, near the Shaftesbury Memorial. The morning broadcasts showed nothing but demolished shops and sobbing witnesses describing how a man shouted *Jesus is the Lord!* moments before detonating himself. And then the flash and body parts mingling with sundresses and tank tops. The toll: twelve dead, including a pregnant mother of three.

This particular bombing for Christ was the first of its kind on British soil. Six other countries in the EU had been hit, as had the United States at Rockefeller Center and Fisherman's Wharf. Previous bombers had worn vests stuffed with explosives, ball bearings, and nails beneath loose-fitting white robes—a signature obvious enough for Soldiers of Rapture everywhere to come under increased scrutiny. The London bomber avoided detection by placing his vest beneath a turquoise Hawaiian shirt accented with palm trees and pineapples. In a video mailed to the *Times*, he spoke of the Tribulation in a calm, well-schooled British accent that was notable mainly because early suspicion had centered on American evangelicals. "The Troubles are upon us," he declared, standing before his Webcam in robes. "And I am compelled to contribute. I sincerely hope my martyrdom will hurry the Second Coming and bring blessings to all." He stated his sincere belief that, upon killing himself, he would rise to Paradise. He also offered thanks for the privilege of escorting those who died with him to the Master's right hand. Poincaré could only think how ordinary he looked, like any neighbor anywhere setting out for a stroll with his family to a park. If this man could blow himself up, everyone was suspect.

Swiftly and predictably, in the harshest language, spokesmen for the Roman Catholic and Greek Orthodox churches, the Anglicans, and mainline Protestants condemned all violence in the name of

Christ. But their outrage had done nothing to stop previous Christian-inspired bombings, so no one listened now. Nor were many consoled by public figures who advised against creating monsters from unlikely threats. According to statisticians, the risk of dying at the hand of a Rapturian bomber was roughly that of dying from a direct asteroid hit. Nonetheless, a new class of Bogeyman was born: the Caucasian Christian fundamentalist male bent on destruction for the greater good. Jihadist suicide bombers in Kabul now had cousins: self-detonating Joneses and Bellinghams in Piccadilly Circus. A teenager who survived the London bombing summed up the mood this way: "If I can't run to the store for a pair of socks without risking my life, what's the bloody point?"

In the lobby of the Elmer L. Andersen Human Services Building in downtown St. Paul, Poincaré consulted a directory listing and soon found the State of Minnesota Adoption Office, where a courteous clerk told him, in effect, to go away. "Sir, I can't release personal information without a court order." The man held his ground, politely, no matter how many ways Poincaré angled to see Rainier's file. Finally the clerk explained that if Poincaré was determined he could go to the state police, who would establish his *bona fides* and point him to an administrative judge for an order to release the file. "Look," said the man. "I don't know your business, but I've seen all kinds of unhappiness caused by mishandling confidential records. I've seen information released that the adoptees don't know themselves—about birth parents, for instance, and financial records. I'm sure you have your reasons, but we've got ours. If you want to see anything, you'll need a judge's order."

Poincaré devoted the rest of the morning to meeting with the state police. It was just early enough in St. Paul that the Interpol offices in Lyon were still open and could verify his credentials. The police, who were also able to view and download the Red Notice on Rainier, were helpful—but not helpful enough to spare Poincaré several hours filling out forms. Eventually, an aide walked him to a nearby courthouse and, spotting the judge they were seeking, dashed ahead to make an introduction. Before Poincaré could say a word, he was given to understand that whatever his business, the judge's was more important. In recess from a trial, she looked at her watch and said: "I understand the request, Inspector. What's the compelling interest in releasing information on Marcus and Theodore Rainier when it's the sister you're after? You've got ninety seconds."

"She might be seeking refuge with either, your Honor."

The judge arched her eyebrows. "The file indicates they last saw each other twenty-six years ago. You'll have to do better than that. What, I repeat, is the compelling interest? . . . You've now got sixty seconds."

"They may know her whereabouts."

"That assumes she's located them. In any event, I'm not moved by *may*. Denied. I'll sign for Madeleine Rainier's file—no one else's." She stepped inside her chambers and closed the door in his face before he could say *thank you*.

He lost no time returning to the adoption office, where the clerk was waiting with Rainier's file already called up on a microfiche reader. "The state police gave me a heads-up, and I located the file. Here we are." He pulled a second chair to the reader, and the first thing that struck Poincaré was the photograph of Rainier, age two years, four months: straight blonde hair, oval face, dimpled chin, the same gray eyes—unmistakably the person who a quarter century later would appear too fragile to place in custody. He read the file closely, taking notes, and asked the clerk for a hard copy. "How would I find out if she attempted to contact her brothers?" he asked. "Wouldn't you expect a child who learns she's adopted and has siblings to want to find them? You must keep those records."

"We do," the clerk answered, checking the administrative order. "But you have no access." The man shrugged. "It's frustrating, I know. But imagine you're Marcus or Theodore Rainier—or whatever their names are now. You're twenty-eight and," he checked the file, "thirty years old. And out of the blue an Interpol agent knocks on your door with questions about a sister you never knew about. You have no problem with this?"

"I'm investigating a murder," said Poincaré.

"And both of these men have the right to lives that don't get turned upside down. But we could debate this until the cows come home. The judge said *no*." The clerk reached behind his desk for a phone directory and found the name listed on Rainier's adoption record. He circled it, then turned the directory around for Poincaré to see. "Same address. They're still here, as of a year ago when this directory was printed. Good luck."

THE HOUSE sat on the western edge of St. Paul, on a corner lot enclosed by a rusting fence. An aluminum pool, its sides caved in and filled with leaves, occupied most of a large concrete slab set in what passed for a yard. Along the rear edge of the property, the bones of an upended swing set rose from a weedy sand pit. No one answered when Poincaré knocked, and he thought the house abandoned. He circled to the back, knocked on another door. Again, nothing. He knocked at the front door a final time, prepared to leave when, unexpectedly, a hall light flashed on. A man opened the door and shielded his eyes. He wore a stained, sleeveless undershirt and nothing else. Poincaré introduced himself.

"What is it?"

"Are you Richard Scott?"

"I paid my taxes and the utility bills this month."

Poincaré planted a shoe across the threshold. When Scott slammed the door, it bounced in his face.

"That hurt!"

"Madeleine Rainier."

"You said *what?*"

"I'm looking for Madeleine Rainier. Or Madeleine Scott."

"How do you know her? Who are you?" He ran a hand through filthy hair and blinked hard in the afternoon light.

"Mr. Scott," said Poincaré. "Pull on a pair of pants, and we'll talk."

"You heard from Maddy?"

"Get dressed, Mr. Scott."

The man looked older than his sixty-three years. Unsteady on his feet, he sat in a wingback chair the same color as his cadaverous face. Hard use had knocked the stuffing out of both. The house reeked of garbage.

"Happy times," said Scott. "What do you want?"

He had worked as a maintenance man at one of the General Mills plants in town. Like everyone else in the Twin Cities twenty-five years earlier, he and his wife Irma, a schoolteacher, had followed the sad fortunes of the Rainier children. "One couldn't avoid the news," he recalled. "For days the papers ran weepers, and Irma finally broke down. We were in our thirties and didn't have kids. We tried. A year before, we got approved to adopt and we were just waiting for the right situation. Then came the accident, and Irma couldn't get those children off her mind. Maybe you've seen the pictures. We contacted the Department of Human Services right off. They took their sweet time, then called one day and said everything had to be completed right away. They said we could adopt one of the children, not all three.

"But we wanted all of them. We applied for three. For years we had saved and built this house for a family. You should have seen it back then, everything new and painted. I built it myself. We could have managed," he said. "We weren't rich but we could have managed with public schools and the State U. We begged them. But some case manager in a bow tie and a string of initials after his name said *no*—that it was in the best interests of the children to be separated. Best interests? You don't *do* that to kids—two of them twins, no less. That man had all those degrees, but where was the common sense of it? Better those kids had been dogs in a kennel. At least if they were mutts, I could have brought three home."

Scott moved Poincaré into a narrow galley kitchen for coffee. Unwashed dishes and half-eaten TV dinners overran the sink and counters. There were bugs, and Poincaré figured he was at risk even breathing the air. But Scott was talking, and Poincaré said he would love a cup.

"So they made us choose," he continued. "I was boiling mad, but then you can't go yelling at caseworkers because they'd call you unfit to raise children! Irma took my hand and said these people were professionals, that they knew what was best and that she wanted a daughter. She had always wanted a daughter. I told her it wasn't natural separating them and I wanted no part of it—that they would suffer even if they didn't remember each other. Irma just kept saying she wanted a daughter and this was our best chance. It was like they were selling cars: Buy now or the offer's off the table."

Scott excused himself, and from the next room Poincaré heard a clinking of glass. The wife had died some years ago from the look of things, and Scott himself was on schedule to follow soon. Every horizontal surface not covered by used dishes was piled high with dust-covered magazines. Boxes with broken kitchen appliances and books on duck hunting and cabinetmaking were stacked three deep along every wall.

"Want a drink?" he asked from the doorway.

Poincaré declined.

"What are you doing here?"

"I'm looking for your daughter."

"*We* wanted to find her!"

Scott chiseled another teaspoon of instant coffee from a jar and offered to freshen his guest's cup. He excused himself again, and this time Poincaré heard a stream of water through an open door.

"Maddy's leaving killed Irma," he called from the bathroom. "It took nine years, but it killed her." No flush, no running water. He rejoined Poincaré at the table. "She was a difficult child. God, how we tried to make her happy. I built a playground out back. Irma knew all about children on account of her work, and she said, 'Give it time, Richie. She'll come around.' Was sixteen years enough time? I could never get out of my head what the state did to those children. It haunted Maddy. . . .

"But our Maddy was smart! The child was born for school— exactly the way I wasn't. Good for her, I thought. I saved all those years, and what were we going to do with the money? We gave her the best we could. We gave her our *name*. But she was never happy, and I don't think it was us, either. It was destroying Irma.

"So I took Maddy to breakfast one morning, in her senior year. She was eighteen and had been accepted to a school out east—full scholarship. She applied only to colleges in other states. It was time she knew her past, I decided. Irma told me not to, that she might never come back to us . . . and she was right. Maddy just sat across the table, very quiet. She knew she was adopted—we'd told her that her parents had been killed in a wreck out in California. We wanted to spare her going back through those newspaper stories. I told her about her brothers, and the next day she was gone. She kissed Irma and me goodbye, like she always did in the morning. We left for work, but then she circled back and collected some things, and that was it. We never saw her again. She never enrolled in that college, either. The last we heard, just a year later, was that she had changed her name back to Rainier. The state sent us a notice. That's when Irma began dying."

"You haven't heard anything since, Mr. Scott?"

"Not for ten years. Then two weeks ago, out of the blue, I get a letter. Maddy writing like she left yesterday. No return address. Stamps from Europe, I think. She said she had to leave when she did, the way she did, and that she was sorry for hurting us. She knew about Irma because she checked on us from a distance, and that she still loved us—but that not to know for her entire childhood about her brothers was too terrible. She said she suffered every day as a child from half-remembering people who were important to her. She had dreams of playing with the same two boys but could never see their faces. She knew it wasn't our decision to split them up, but it was just too hard to come back to this house."

Scott opened a cupboard and produced an envelope.

Poincaré snapped on a pair of gloves and read the letter. It looked like Rainier's handwriting. To be as certain as he could be outside of a lab, he opened his file from Amsterdam and found a photocopy of her registration at the Hotel Ravensplein.

"Is she in some sort of trouble?" asked Scott.

"Possibly. I saw her last in Amsterdam just over three months ago. I need to find her. Could I take a picture of this letter? And the actual envelope would help—I'd like to conduct some tests."

"I suppose . . . under one condition."

"What's that?" asked Poincaré.

Richard Scott turned toward a window. "If you find Maddy, ask her to visit."

When he said that, the space in the narrow, filthy kitchen grew very small; for the man had driven home a distressing truth: if Claire, Etienne, Lucille, and the boys did not return to Poincaré, this kitchen would one day be his kitchen. Scott stared at him as if from some future mirror: rheumy-eyed, unshaven, bitter coffee in one hand and a half-glass of toxic whiskey in the other. Poincaré said nothing. One could not sit in the presence of such destruction and say a word.

"What kind of trouble, Inspector. What happened to her?"

"Someone died. There was a bombing."

The man set his whiskey aside, then his coffee cup. "You're saying Madeleine was involved?"

Poincaré nodded.

"It's not possible," he said. "Even if my daughter disowned us, I know her heart. She was kind. She *is* kind. Once she came home from school without her winter coat. And it gets *cold* in Minnesota. Irma asked what happened, and Maddy said that there was a child at the bus stop in a sweater, and that she gave him her coat because he didn't own one. No," said Scott, "she didn't kill anyone."

"And if the facts suggest otherwise?" asked Poincaré.

"Then you had better check your facts."

Somewhere over St. Louis, Poincaré attempted to sleep. Wedged into a window seat, he tried maneuvering into a comfortable position but could find none. The woman ahead of him had reclined her seat; the young man to Poincaré's right dozed with his mouth open, snoring softly, his book—*How You Can Profit from the Rapture*—open on his lap. The lad had body piercings to rival St. Sebastian's: tiny steel swords in both ears, a safety pin in one nostril, and rings in his eyebrows, lower lip, and who knew where else beneath a ripped T-shirt and jeans. All he needed was a good cause and an untimely death: someone might have named a chapel after him.

The plane tracked south, following the Mississippi before making a hard right to Los Angeles. Several rows ahead, a young woman extricated herself from a middle seat and made her way to a restroom. Poincaré had noticed her while boarding—confident, with her hair tied back and a shoulder bag brimming with books. He saw her and mourned the adult Chloe would never be; the pearls he would never buy her; the bottle they would never share in a café, late into the evening, in Paris, as she—lost in the enthusiasm of new studies or a new young man or her first job—would talk without realizing he listened not so much to her words as to the music of her voice. Was she truly gone? Was it not possible she would greet him when his plane landed in Los Angeles? Poincaré ached with an ache that would not mend. Had he the skill of prayer, and had he read his Bible, he might have asked for the strength to accept what the Psalmist long ago had accepted: that the child would never again come to him but rather he, howsoever long it took, must wait and one day go to her.

Chapter 30

The Jet Propulsion Laboratory looked to Poincaré like an aging industrial park spread across seventy scrubby acres—at first glance, hardly a place one would expect cosmologists to be analyzing the structure of solar wind or searching for Earth-like planets orbiting distant stars. But among JPL's dozens of buildings could be found a spacecraft assembly plant and a mission control center. In the late 1930s when a Cal Tech professor used the site to test early rocket designs, the area was relatively remote. Over time, the expansion of Pasadena gradually bumped homes and then a freeway up against the sprawling campus, leaving Poincaré to wonder at the weird proximity of hamburger joints to clean rooms where errant flecks of dust could doom $80 million space missions.

The grounds were pleasant, with mature trees and, oddly, small herds of deer that wandered down from the San Gabriel Mountains. Poincaré had arranged to meet Dr. Alfonse Meyer, who worked on propulsion systems for each of the unmanned space vehicles NASA had launched in the previous decade, including the Mars Rovers and the long-range bullet, Deep Impact, shot into the heart of a comet 268 million miles from Earth. Escorted from Visitor Control by an officer through a maze of numbered buildings, Poincaré was shown into a nondescript mid-rise office complex and up a stairwell into a large laboratory.

Just inside an open double door sat Meyer with his high-topped sneakers propped on a chaotic desk, blue-jeaned, bearded, and with a ponytail that barely corralled his graying brown hair. He was holding a phone the way cartoon bullies do victims, by the scruff of the neck, yelling: "And another thing, you Bozo—It'll be your ass if you don't get me a sample of that new ceramic by Friday!" He ended the call making arrangements for beer and something called a "canyon run" later that week. Turning at the security officer's polite knock, Meyer took one look at Poincaré and another at his watch: "As I live and breathe—an actual Interpol agent! My official position, Inspector, is that murder by rocket fuel has got to be a first."

He rose to shake Poincaré's hand vigorously, opened a refrigerator stacked with soft drinks, and offered his visitor his pick of six different diet colas. On his desk sat an empty pint of ice cream.

"Any relation to Jules Henri?"

"Slightly. Yes," said Poincaré.

"Really, now! Do you know the last problem he was working on? The stability of the universe—using nothing but a pencil, paper and that remarkable brain of his. . . . The news is good, by the way." Meyer laughed his belly laugh. "Is that your business, too—proving the universe won't unravel while we're eating dinner?"

Poincaré hadn't been sure what to expect from someone who held doctorates in chemical and mechanical engineering, owned a pilot's license, and sang in a Methodist choir. At the very least, he could now see, Meyer would make an excellent drinking companion. The tables in his lab were chockablock with motor parts, containers with long chemical names, centrifuges, and mixing chambers. At three separate stations, large ventilation hoods rose through the ceiling. Poincaré counted eight computers and four refrigerators, one marked with a radiation warning. At the rear of the lab, a technician worked beneath a large red and yellow sign that read: "DANGER: Discharge Static Electricity Before Entering Area."

Poincaré had known scientists who wanted nothing more in life than to buy expensive toys and be left alone. Meyer looked to be one of them. His lab was a slice of adolescent heaven in which aging boys got to build things that went *boom*. He insisted on giving Poincaré a tour and a brief lecture on the evolution of propulsion systems. As they edged around burn chambers and simulators, Poincaré saw miniature thrusters and solar arrays, lasers and at one station hydroponic grass growing beneath heat lamps—for a study of energy gain, he learned. Twenty minutes later, he found himself contemplating a poster-sized photo at Meyer's desk.

"That's a good one. My personal favorite."

Poincaré considered the image from different angles. "I'm at a NASA facility, which means that whatever I'm looking at has got to be far away. But if you told me it was a slice of pancreas under a microscope, I wouldn't be surprised."

Meyer laughed. "It's further away than your pancreas."

"How far?"

"Eight billion light years, more or less. It's a computer simulation of galaxy clusters in a particularly dense part of the universe. The inset is an x-ray image of an actual cluster. What's interesting is that large clusters look essentially the same as small ones, and distant ones look essentially the same as near ones—provided you make an allowance for red shift. That is, galaxy clusters scale just like nested Russian dolls. Take a smaller one and a larger one, resize them: you can't tell the difference. The inset image was taken by the Chandra X-ray Observatory. I worked on the thrusters for that. . . . But you didn't come to talk about scaling phenomena in the cosmos. Tell me, Inspector. Who died?"

Poincaré made sure he had heard correctly. "Galaxies scale, too?"

"That's right—in size and distance. What do you mean by *too*?"

"Forgive me," he said. "A mathematician, James Fenster. Perhaps you knew him, or of him?"

"Mathematical modeling?"

"That's right. He was killed for something he knew—exactly what, I'm not sure. So your answers here matter, Dr. Meyer. I read your report. Very thorough on the additives to the rocket fuel. I would have come earlier, but there were . . . some developments at home."

Poincaré's host shifted uncomfortably.

"When they start coming for mathematicians, Inspector, no one's safe. The Dutch chemists largely got it right in naming the propellant, but you were smart to send post-burn samples. What you're dealing with is a more powerful, less stable cousin of ammonium perchlorate—double base ammonium perchlorate cyclotetramethylene tetranitramine aluminum, to be exact. Your bomber mixed in nitroglycerine and solid crystals of the explosive HMX. Which is good for you because if this were your grandma's rocket fuel, you'd be shit out of luck. Every space program, every military ordnance program, and every amateur rocket jock and fireworks manufacturer in the world uses straight-up APCP. You'd be hunting for a needle in an impossibly large haystack. But your Amsterdam propellant has these two distinctive signatures. That's a thread to hang onto, anyway."

"Some questions, then, if you don't mind."

Meyer kicked back in his chair and locked his hands behind his head. "Take your time, Inspector. The meter's running."

"Excuse me?"

"Lost in translation. Continue."

Poincaré opened a notebook. "First, I know nitroglycerin is difficult to handle. What about HMX crystals?"

"Also difficult. It's a delicate substance that has to be grown under strictly controlled conditions—not an easy material to handle, even for us. It's also expensive."

"Why use HMX?"

"Because it makes regular APCP a higher energy composite, with a shock propagation of about 9,000 meters per second. HMX is used with TNT in high explosives and shaped charges in the military. Second point: the problem with DB/HMX is that it has a pressure exponent of only .49 and burns at a rate of only one centimeter per second, more or less, so it's not as unstable as the bomber might have liked. The tests I ran indicate the addition of TNT to the mix, which brings the pressure exponent above one. The double base APCP would slow down the shock wave from the HMX considerably, but would also provide very hot gases for an intense burn."

"Suggesting?"

"Suggesting that your bomber was a damned fine chemist and an equally good rocket jock."

Poincaré followed Meyer into the lab and stopped before a bin labeled *Ammonium Perchlorate (AP)*. He opened the lid and scooped a white granular substance into Poincaré's open palm. "Notice that AP is whiter than table salt. It's an oxidizer—it supports combustion. You add powdered aluminum for fuel and bind it with hydroxyl-terminated polybutadiene, and in an hour or so you've got solid rocket fuel—which feels rubbery, like a bicycle tire. The HTPB binder also acts as a stabilizing agent, burn-rate inhibitor, and fuel for the APCP. NASA uses approximately two-and-a-half million pounds of APCP for each shuttle launch."

Poincaré brushed the ammonium perchlorate back into its container and rolled a few grains between his fingers. "Could the bomber have purchased this anywhere—in Europe?"

"Absolutely—or made it himself. In my report, I wrote that your guy worked or used to work for us or for an equivalent lab in France, Russia, or possibly China. The mix is simply too unstable in production to achieve anywhere but in a lab, under controlled conditions. Just about all the academic labs capable of this work are affiliated with space programs."

"So you could have made this explosive?" said Poincaré.

"That's right."

"And where were you the first two weeks of April?"

Meyer hesitated, then caught the edges of Poincaré's grin. "OK, so the French have a sense of humor."

"But I will be checking your alibi. I'll have to."

Meyer grabbed a pencil and a slip of paper off a shelf. "I knew someone would be the moment I found HMX in the mix. My wife's family owns a cabin on a trout stream in Idaho. The town store and local gas station will have credit card receipts, with dates— a trail about as long as my stomach is round. No problem establishing that."

"I don't doubt you," said Poincaré.

"But you should, Inspector."

"Because?"

"Because your bomber looks a lot like me. Minus the ponytail and high-tops, maybe. But I'm the type you're looking for."

"More about that in a minute," said Poincaré. "Why did the bomber go to the trouble? Why use nitroglycerin and HMX crystals when ready-made plastic explosives or TNT would have killed Fenster just as thoroughly? For that matter, a bullet would have done the job."

Meyer walked Poincaré back to his desk. "The remains," he said. "I imagine they were fairly crisp?"

"Burnt beyond recognition. That's right."

"Your bomber didn't want the body identified. Not visually, anyway."

Poincaré had long thought so. His only remaining business was to determine who at the Jet Propulsion Laboratory, beside Meyer, had the knowledge to grow HMX crystals of exceptional quality, smuggle them out of the lab, and mix a batch of enhanced APCP in Europe. That had to be the scenario, Poincaré reasoned. The eight or ten pounds of composite fuel needed to blow apart a hotel room could not have passed through airport baggage screening undetected. But a container of table salt might have. Meyer offered the information without hesitating.

"Anyone in this lab could have grown the HMX. But all four of my guys stay here when I'm on vacation. Again, you'll have no trouble verifying this." Meyer reached into his mini-fridge in search of another drink. "This must be a rotten business. You have to catch the guy who did this and possibly dodge bullets in the process." He pulled a tab and took a long swallow. "You couldn't pay me enough."

Poincaré checked his notes. "What about Randal Young? I reviewed the bios of more than a hundred people at this facility, and he stands out."

Meyer sat on the corner of his desk. "I figured this would get around to him."

"Because?"

"Because he was a damned fine chemist and rocket jock with a degree from the Colorado School of Mines. Look, Inspector. A bomber can't be driving around with an HMX plus nitroglycerin mix in the trunk of his car. It's simply too volatile, which means whoever grew the crystals also mixed the fuel either onsite or close to onsite just prior to detonation. Your Dutch analysts were right to observe that the bomber used reflectors of some sort to concentrate and focus the blast. That would have been key. There's only one person I ever knew who fit the profile—Randy Young, and I thought of him immediately. But A, he died sometime in March; and B, he was a sweetheart of a man. Not a malicious bone in his body. So my considered opinion is that you'll have to look elsewhere."

Poincaré left Meyer in his lab and was escorted to the offices of Valerie Steinholz, Director of Human Resources. Because his investigation involved a potential breach of JPL security, she released the names and addresses of six people without any of the privacy concerns that had frustrated Poincaré in Minnesota. The six were Meyer himself, his staff of four, and Randal Young on the off chance the dead can reach from beyond the grave. But it was the lab assistants Poincaré wanted to know more about. Young was interesting but unlikely. The timing was wrong.

If it happened that neither Meyer nor anyone in his lab had left the United States in April, then Poincaré would soon be interviewing their counterparts at national space facilities around the globe. Nothing about that would be easy, but he would not know one way or another for twelve hours. All he could do was wait.

CHAPTER 31

In the meantime, Poincaré set out to find Alain Ackart and handed his driver the address Samuel had given him in Lyon. The ride took only thirty minutes but slid Poincaré hand over fist down links in an unfortunate chain, from the pleasant hills of Pasadena with its palms and watered lawns to the gritty, asphalt-ringed heart of Los Angeles. Not far off the Freeway, men on street corners sipped pint bottles from paper bags. He saw broken glass on the sidewalks and trash in the gutters. The July sun baked the streets, and the heat rose in waves such that as he approached the All Souls People's Ministry, a store-front in an otherwise abandoned strip mall, the sign strung between the arches of a defunct McDonald's shimmered as if Poincaré had approached from across a great expanse of sand.

He stood at a large window. A geologist might have called the crack that bisected the plate glass, with localized zigs and zags, a San Andreas fault in miniature; and in fact, it resembled the line drawn on maps of California that Poincaré had seen. It was also a near-duplicate of a run of weeds poking through the sidewalk at his feet, a connection by now so familiar he took scant notice. On opening the door, he found eight robed men and women ranging in age from twenty or so to well past seventy seated at a row of folding tables before computers, blinking phones, and credit-card verification machines. Each Soldier wore an operator's headset and was busy recording donations, the mood bright and cheery however odd the juxtaposition of first and twenty-first centuries.

"God bless!" One of the operators ended a call.

On the far wall hung an enormous twenty-seven; on another, a large map of Los Angeles with more than a hundred flagged, numbered pins—one of which, Poincaré hoped, pointed to Alain Ackart. But for the robes, the All Souls command center might have been the headquarters of a politician seeking reelection.

A woman with gray pigtails and yellowed teeth rose to greet him. She smiled as Poincaré held out a photograph. "Alain Ackart," he said. "Early thirties. French. Do you know him?"

She looked past Poincaré to the Lincoln Town Car parked at the curb. "Lost a child to Christ, have you? Either that or you're FBI. We've been raided every other week by G-men hunting for bomb-making materials. I'm afraid we disappoint them every time."

"Please," he said.

"Are you Mr. Ackart?"

"A family friend."

"In that case, why don't you try joining Alain in Christ instead of assuming he's lost his mind."

"That's why I've come," said Poincaré.

The woman's features softened. "To join him in Christ? You look more like you're from Tobacco and Firearms."

"No, Madame. An address."

"Do you see that twenty-seven on the wall over there?" she said. "Tomorrow it will be replaced with twenty-six and twenty-five the day after. Time is short, and the God who cares about you and me as well as Alain asks for your return."

"So I'm told."

"But you're not convinced."

Poincaré confessed that he wasn't.

"Good," she said. "Honesty helps. Make believe for a moment that one can believe in Christ and still be sane. There are two billion Christians in the world, you know. Do you think we're all insane—or is it that too much belief is the problem? Perhaps Alain's too fervent for your tastes?"

"An address, Madame."

"In a minute. But first you've got to listen to *me*. If you've come to rescue him, stop and consider rescuing yourself. You might ask, for instance, *who* has the real problem."

"The problem is that people I care deeply about have lost their son."

"I understand," she said. "But I'm thinking pride or logic is preventing them—and you—from coming home to God. He's not lost.

Take a step. It will be the longest road you'll ever walk but also the shortest. Alain has taken it. It's a golden road."

"Like Dorothy coming through Oz?"

She patted his arm. "No, not really. Do you believe in anything, or is all this a game out here?"

Poincaré did not have time to wait for Alain Ackart to return. The woman might give him nothing if this became an argument, so he answered in all earnestness: "I do have beliefs," he said. "I believe the world is broken. I believe we suffer and don't know why. I believe both we personally and the world are in need of repair." She waited for more, but he was done.

"Well, that would be half the equation."

"Perhaps. Where's Alain?"

She walked around a folding table. Before Poincaré could produce a pen and paper, she sat before a terminal and scribbled an address. "Hand this to your driver," she told him. "He's Prophet 112 today. He's in the northwest quadrant, parcel eight." She led Poincaré to a map and pulled a pin. "Right here. It's a rugged area—but we know Christ will come to the least among us, so we go to the least among us. Tell Alain that the bus will pick him up at seven and that Sister Lucinda is very proud of him. The spirit of God moves this young man. It's a beautiful thing."

"Why collect money?" asked Poincaré, motioning to the phone banks. "After August 15th you won't need any."

"True. But before that we have expenses. Food. Fuel. Dormitory housing."

"And what will happen on August 16th?"

"What do you mean?"

"If Christ doesn't come."

Lucinda smiled. She showed no hint of anger, no suggestion that she had mortgaged her mind like that youngster on the subway platform in Boston. She did not have Charles Manson eyes. And in no event would she blow herself up to promote Christ's return. Her faith was real even if Poincaré did not share it, and in her he glimpsed the earnest heart of a movement he had yet to grasp: a movement of real people who lived in troubled times and longed for a Savior. For her,

August 15th would be a simple, beautiful transition point in human history. "*What if* are the words of a doubter," she said. "Please, if you have just another moment, let me describe an Earth that can be, as it *will* be in twenty-seven days." She closed her eyes, and Poincaré could imagine she saw herself shoulder-to-shoulder with kindred souls traversing a meadow, storm clouds behind and a full, bright sun ahead. A look of peace settled over her as she began a recitation:

> They will build houses and dwell in them;
>> they will plant vineyards and eat their fruit.
>
> No longer will they build houses and others live in them,
>> or plant and others eat.
>> For as the days of a tree,
>> so will be the days of my people;
>> my chosen ones will long enjoy
>> the works of their hands.
>
> They will not toil in vain
>> or bear children doomed to misfortune;
>> for they will be a people blessed by the LORD,
>> they and their descendants with them.
>
> Before they call I will answer;
>> while they are still speaking I will hear.

She opened her eyes. "Isaiah 65: 21-24. What could be more gorgeous, Mr. Friend of Alain Ackart? Who would choose *not* to accept a world of such blessings? You?" She took hold of his hand, the sweetness in her suddenly stern and forceful. "Right now, I want thirty seconds of your time. Then I'll let go and you'll leave and we'll never see each other again. Agreed?"

She had given him the information, and he had thirty seconds. Still holding his hand in both of hers, Lucinda asked: "What pain do you carry? We all carry pain. What's yours? What cuts you so deep you can't even look at it in the daylight? Feel this pain—the worst kind . . . the kind you brought on yourself through sin. *Feel* it! And now let it go. You can because Christ has taken that sin and taken your pain on His shoulders and died for us. If you believe, if you accept Him as your Savior, then you can lose your pain, my friend, now and forever. You can turn your rage to forgiveness just as our Lord has forgiven you. Imagine a pure, sweet Redemption!" She let go and snapped her fingers.

The air did not clear. Only half the formula had worked: the recollection of Claire, stone-faced. Chloe, gone. Amputations and skin grafts and crushed bones. Hatred. A caged man snarling: *you will suffer*. Poincaré could not forgive, and he would never surrender his rage. He blinked and turned away. Sister Lucinda did not need to see his tears.

Prophet 112 had not drawn a promising district for the saving of souls that day. Poincaré's driver pulled into a rough gravel parking lot bounded by a carpet warehouse, a pawn shop, and a pair of single occupancy hotels—some distance from the Los Angeles of thousand dollar suits and Ferraris. These people earned their daily bread pennies at a time, with cans and bottles delivered to a recycling center at the rear of a liquor store. A white-robed Alain Ackart stood at the head of the line, without a hat in the noonday sun. Poincaré thought to rescue him from heatstroke, if nothing else.

"Uncle?" A look of joy greeted Poincaré. "I'm so glad to see you! Why are you here?"

Theirs was no casual embrace. Poincaré held onto Etienne's crib-mate as if letting go risked one of them sliding away. He took a long moment to run his fingers through the young man's hair. He breathed in the scent of him—clean and healthy—and then kissed the curly forehead with relief. Poincaré held him at an arm's length and saw that the eyes were clear, the delight on seeing his Uncle Henri real. "I was coming to LA on business," he said. "Your father told me about you. I needed to see these robes for myself."

Alain smiled. "He wants you to bring me back?"

Poincaré answered in French. "No. You're a grown man, Alain. Your parents can't order you home. They want to know you're well and for you to know they love you. Their door is always open." Two dozen witnesses watched, some pushing all their worldly possessions along with the bottles and cans in their shopping carts. A short woman wearing a bamboo hat hung her bags from a pole slung across her shoulders. Another rode an oversized tricycle at the head of several linked children's wagons. The bags that each carried were so plump that Poincaré scarcely believed an unclaimed bottle or can could be found in that corner of Los Angeles.

"You look well enough," he said.

"For a madman?" Alain laughed. "That's what Father calls me."

Poincaré looked for signs. "What are you doing out here?"

"Talking mostly, if people want to talk. What about you? Forgive me, but you look tired . . . and older than when I saw you last. Is the family well? How's Etienne?"

If anyone could still make a claim on Poincaré's affections, it was this young man. He deserved a proper answer and would get one, but not here. "Let's talk," Poincaré said. "We'll step out of the sun for awhile."

"I can't, Uncle. I'm working."

"Saving souls, Alain?"

"These people have suffered," said Ackart. "They should know that relief is coming soon." He pointed to the number twenty-seven pasted on the side of a dumpster. "They need to accept Christ in their hearts. None of us has long now. My parents are baptized. I know Etienne and Aunt Claire are. But you, Uncle . . . I remember Claire saying—"

"It isn't your concern, Alain."

"But it is! You deserve peace as much as anyone."

Poincaré did not agree. On arriving, he had noticed a man beside them, pushing two carts, each with a mountain of cans and bottles. The graybeard was restless, Poincaré's same age, leathery from living outdoors. The man fidgeted, and then in an eruption of broken but comprehensible French: "S'il vous *fucking* plait! You are seriously out of line, young man." He switched to English. "You come down here in your robes, preaching to the doomed. How do I know you're not going to take us all out with a suicide vest? What do you have under those robes? Show me or I swear I'll call the cops!" He held up a cell phone.

Ackart backed away. "I'm not one of them, friend. They've perverted God's Word. They dress like us but have nothing to do with us. They *are* crazy. All I do is talk—if you'll talk. Help is coming."

"Help? I've been waiting for help all my life, and not once has God or anyone else lifted a finger. So I've given up looking. The State of California couldn't give a damn. The city doesn't. The federal government is worthless. The churches are busy collecting money to pay off the debts of pedophile priests. *No one* cares even when they say they care. What, you think you can quote gospel and make all the shit go away?" He spread his arms and opened his palms. "You are seriously out of your mind, and I *know* what it means to be out of your mind!"

"Wait," said Ackart. "Just a little longer. Take Christ into—"

"Bushwa! Show me you're not wearing a vest under that or I swear I'll kick your skinny butt back to France!" Poincaré stepped forward, but Ackart motioned him off. And then he saw something remarkable: Alain turning his back to the line and to Poincaré and briefly raising his robes.

"OK," said the man. "Now that that's settled, get the hell out of my neighborhood."

Ackart tried again. "I know the world's failed you. But there's News that will change your life. In just twenty-seven days—"

Graybeard heard this and pointed to a sign with the words *All Redemption* and an arrow over a door through which, one at a time, the men and women in line disappeared with their bags. "The only news I need is the kind that puts food on my plate *now*." He patted a plumped trash bag, and Poincaré heard a clink of glass. "I'll tell you what," said the man, "since you're not from around here. Let's take you to school. You're talking redemption? Let's give you some, American style."

Despite the heat, the graybeard wore an overcoat, long pants, and steel-toed shoes. He dug into a trash bag and produced an empty can of Coca-Cola, which he thrust violently toward Alain. "Take it! Step right up. Come on, son! You and your white-robed brothers are trying my nerves!"

Poincaré could see that Ackart had no idea what to do with another man's anger. He stepped between them. "I'll do it," he said.

Graybeard sized him up and tossed the can of Coca-Cola back into his bag. "Hell, you're even more beat up than I am. But for you and that fine suit, only the best." He placed a different can in Poincaré's hand. This one read *Budweiser*. "King of beers, friend. Welcome to LA!"

Poincaré stepped in line to keep the peace. Graybeard promptly ignored him and shuffled to tunes playing through earbuds. One woman in line danced to no music at all. Several rested their heads against their carts in the heat and stumbled forward as the line moved.

"Next!" a man called from inside the opened doorway. Poincaré had been watching the people ahead of him set bulging bags separated into cans, plastics, and glass onto a scale and wait for a man wearing rubber gloves and a heavy apron to tear a receipt from a machine, bark off a number, then swing each bag onto a conveyor belt. Behind the building Poincaré had seen trash compactors and several tractor-trailer containers. When the man with the apron turned to Poincaré, he found a single beer can sitting on the scale.

"What the hell?"

Graybeard spoke before Poincaré had the chance: "Marvin, he's on a field trip. Weigh the can."

"Get him out of here."

"It's the law, Marv. He came with something to redeem. Weigh it and write him up. I don't care how much it weighs. He's got something."

"It's a single fucking unit, Jimmy." The worker grabbed the can and tossed it over his shoulder without looking, then walked to a machine calibrated to weigh empties in the tens of pounds. He pulled a receipt and held it out to Poincaré. "See. It says here you've got *nothing*."

"It's the scale's problem, Marv. Let's go. I want to get lunch."

"I'll throw both your asses out!" Grumbling, the man signed a slip of paper and recorded a number. He said: "Don't come back unless you need it. These people depend on this place to survive. You come here with one can, you're wasting my time and flipping them the finger. Move on."

Further down the shed, by the exit, a heavyset woman in a floral muumuu stood behind an old brass cash register. She examined Poincaré's receipt and laughed. "Five cents?"

He nodded.

"OK, then." She dug into the register and handed him a nickel. "Don't spend it all in one place, Hon."

Graybeard emerged from the shack folding several bills into his pocket. "A typical haul," he said. "Thirty bucks. You know how long it takes to collect six hundred cans and bottles? Five hours on a good day. I started four o'clock this morning."

Poincaré held out the nickel. "Here," he said. "It's yours."

The man took the coin and looked up with an expression approaching wonder, his mouth a wreckage of neglect. "An Indian Head! I haven't seen one of these in forty years! Look—the profile of an Indian on one side, an American buffalo on the other. A genuine buffalo nickel! You've got some good luck coming, friend. Think hard before giving it away." Graybeard returned the coin, and Poincaré reached into a pocket, emerging with a twenty-dollar bill. "Not necessary," said the man. "Go spend it on that seriously misguided boy of yours. Better yet, hold onto the money and talk some sense into him."

Poincaré unfolded a second twenty-dollar bill.

"I won't say *no* this time."

"Good," said Poincaré. "Sleep in, tomorrow."

Alain Ackart was gone by the time Poincaré rounded the building. He walked to his driver, who had napped during the wait and could not offer a single useful hint to guide a search; so he returned to his hotel and placed a call to Samuel Ackart: *Your son is fine*, he reported. Poincaré told him that while Alain wore the robes of a cult, he hadn't surrendered his reason and didn't pose a danger to himself or anyone else. The fact remained, however, that the young man believed with all his heart Jesus would come to restore a kingdom that humans could not. *If only*, thought Poincaré. He feared for Alain Ackart and for his bitter awakening at sunrise on August 16th.

After dinner, Poincaré made a second attempt at opening Fenster's hard drive. While still in Cambridge, he computed the possible combinations of a sixty-seven character password—95 x^y 67. That is, 95 times itself 67 times. The calculator reported the result in scientific notation:

3.2172258856130695549449401501748e+132

The number was impressive, and Poincaré wrote it out as a kind of cautionary tale. That way, if he found himself making random stabs at the password, he would look at the mountain of zeros and either stop or call himself a fool.

3217225885613069554944940150174800000000000000000000000000000000000000000000000000000000000000000000000000000000000000000000000000000000

Hurley was right: no language had a word for a number this large; and no computers, save the massive arrays used to simulate nuclear explosions, were powerful enough to crack Fenster's password in a time frame not measured in years. A man who could recite every play in every inning of every baseball game he ever watched or heard *could* have committed a random, sixty-seven character sequence to memory. But as a practical matter, would Fenster have typed sixty-seven unrelated characters each time he sat down to his computer? This would be nuisance enough for him to rely on a known number or a phrase. It was Poincaré's only hope.

For this session, he decided on a single, limited line of attack: numbers that held special meaning to mathematicians. Sixty-seven was a prime, perhaps a clue: so using a generator he found online, he computed every sixty-seven digit prime and ran these through Fenster's log-in sequence. Nothing. He entered the first sixty-seven numbers of the value for Pi. He entered them backwards. He started at the second and third-through- tenth values. Nothing. He found a paper online that calculated the Feigenbaum constant to sixty-seven numbers. Again, nothing. He tried the first sixty-seven numbers of the Fibonacci series. He was hours at it, with the same result. Any of hundreds of mathematical constants or series would have been available to Fenster.

Poincaré's approach was barely a half-step better than brute force. A log-in sequence did not flash the message: *You're close—just a few more tries.* You were either right or wrong, and each new effort started from scratch. Poincaré had to be cleverer than this, and at the moment he was too tired to be clever.

He returned the hard drive to its envelope and went to sleep.

CHAPTER 32

As it happened, of the six JPL employees Poincaré had investigated, Randal Young was the only one who had traveled outside the country—to Munich. The dates were still wrong, but he called Valerie Steinholz to inquire further. Young had been diagnosed at the age of twenty-six. "Altogether tragic," said Steinholz. "The cancer spread to his kidneys, lungs, and affected his eyesight near the end. He underwent several transplant operations to keep him functioning—four major surgeries before he resigned this past February. Everyone he worked with thought the world of him. He was buried just up the road, and easily two hundred JPL staffers attended the funeral. . . . His widow's name is Julie. She and her two children still live in La Cañada." Steinholz handed him an address.

According to the report Poincaré read that morning, Young and his wife traveled to Germany on March 9th, they returned on the 19th, and Young died at JFK on the 20th. Poincaré had read the police report and seen a facsimile of both the death certificate and the notice of burial, so Randal Young could not have set a bomb in Amsterdam on April 12th. But before he died, he might have constructed a device and attached a digital timer, though its placement in a hotel room with multiple occupants before James Fenster would have required an accomplice. But then there was the delicacy of transporting and safely storing a volatile substance, according to Meyer. Poincaré had too many questions to leave Los Angeles without visiting the widow. He placed the call, and Julie Young agreed to meet provided he would forgive a chaos of moving boxes. She and her children were Colorado bound.

A short drive up Highway 210 from Pasadena brought Poincaré to La Cañada, one more community that sprouted in Southern

California like native Cliff-asters. He watched well-established sub-divisions roll by, one after the next with tidy regularity, for the most part mission-style homes reminiscent of the county's Spanish past. The feel was Mediterranean and affluent, with green lawns, palms, screened porches, and European cars in circular drives—a triumph, this coaxing of a naturally scrubby habitat into perennial suburban bloom. The driver slowed, made a U-turn, and pulled over to a curbside.

The door was open and Poincaré heard two children calling one another, their voices strangely muffled. Before he could ring the doorbell, one of the voices addressed him from inside a large, over-turned moving box with a spy hole cut out. He knelt and could see a patch of freckles and red hair.

"Identify yourself, Earthling. Mom, a man's here!"

He rang the bell and Julie Young turned a corner, red hair held back in a bandana, shirt sleeves rolled. "I promised chaos, Inspector. We won't disappoint. Carl, Sam—say hello." A second overturned box, connected with a string to the first, shuffled towards him.

"Good morning, Earthling."

"I surrender!" Poincaré raised his hands. From the size of the boxes, he guessed they were the age of his grandsons. In a different home, on a different continent, he would have been on his knees beneath his own box.

"I'd offer coffee, Inspector—but I wouldn't be able to find a mug to pour it in." Young's widow invited him into the kitchen, where she held out a plastic cup. "How about water? There's an open bag of chips somewhere."

The cupboards were thrown wide, half the dishes wrapped in newspaper; canned goods and paper goods rose in precarious piles along the counter, and partially packed boxes reduced passage through the kitchen to a narrow lane. The dozens of already sealed and labeled boxes lined walls at the rear of the house, yet the job did not look nearly done. Beyond the kitchen, a large room with an attached porch and a hot tub opened onto a sweeping view of the San Gabriel Mountains.

"Thank you for making time," said Poincaré.

She retied her bandanna and began wrapping dishes. "We move Monday. We'll manage . . . as long as the boys hold up. We'll have to get on with this, Inspector. You had some questions concerning Randal?"

He was taken at once with how ordinary and solidly suburban Young's life had been: the competent, appealing wife; healthy sons; fine neighborhood; steady employment at NASA. How did a man who lived here cross an ocean to plant a bomb beneath a hotel sink? He saw a photograph. "Ah . . . I saw a passport photo in the personnel file, but this does him real justice. A handsome man!"

"You read his personnel file?"

He moved closer for a better look, but Julie Young set her wrapping paper aside and beat him to the photograph. "Lake Tahoe, five years ago. I was very pregnant with our second son. Randal was healthy then." She held the photo for Poincaré to see; she did not let him touch it.

"Better days," he said.

Randal Young was tall and athletic with sandy hair and an appealing face: lean, thin lips, strong cheekbones, cleft chin. His widow was nearly as tall and powerful with red curls that had passed to the child he had seen. Poincaré heard a shout in the next room; and calmly, he thought, for a woman recently widowed amidst the chaos of a half-packed home, she called for them to talk on their orange juice cans. "Secret spy stuff so no one else can hear!" Julie Young turned to him. "Some days I'd come home from work, and they'd all be in boxes having three-way orange juice can conversations. Randy was planning an upgrade to walkie-talkies before he died."

She cleared a stack of magazines from a chair. "The only hospitality I can offer, I'm afraid. . . . So—your questions, Inspector. I've got only so many hours before the movers arrive Monday morning."

"Mrs. Young," Poincaré began. "I'm investigating a murder. A bombing. It was an unusual crime because not many people could have made and set that particular bomb. Your husband was one of them."

Julie Young sat in the chair she had cleared for Poincaré.

"Your husband had worked with these chemicals at JPL. For three summers, as a student, he worked with a mining company setting charges. And I've checked. The two of you traveled to Europe this past March. So, at present, I have no option but to consider your husband a suspect."

"You're wrong," she said. "We were in Europe, but Randal was dying. What was the date of your bombing?"

"April 12th."

"You're certain?"

"I was there."

"Then you've wasted a trip. We traveled in mid-March to try one last treatment for his cancer. There's a clinic in Garmisch-Partenkirchen that had had some success with an extract of tree bark from South America. The treatment didn't work, and we returned to the States in time for him to collapse in the airport before we ever caught our connecting flight home. He didn't make it out of JFK. But you're Interpol. You knew this."

Poincaré regretted what he was about to do.

"The man could barely lift his head off a pillow," she said. She leaned heavily against a pile of boxes marked *Pots and Counter Stuff*. "We've met, Inspector. The dates don't work. I've got work to do."

"Where did you go besides Garmisch?"

"We landed in Munich, we took the train to Garmisch, we stayed the week for the infusions, and when the blood profile didn't change we returned home."

"You were gone for ten days."

"*Three* weeks before your bombing. After the infusions, we stayed nearby and waited to see if the medicine would help. Two days later, the clinic gave us bad news. We came home."

As he looked through a window to the San Gabriel Mountains, Poincaré recalled Garmisch-Partenkirchen. "The Alps would have reminded you of home, I suppose. And the air would certainly have restored your spirits, if nothing else. Where did you spend those two days, Mrs. Young? Perhaps one of the nearby villages?" Two days would have been enough time to travel to Amsterdam and back.

She studied the kitchen floor, lost in thought. "He loved the mountains," she said. "We would have taken a last-ditch chance on a clinic anywhere. But the fact that it was in the Alps? Randal wanted to see them before he died. We stayed in a village near the clinic."

"In Garmisch?"

"It could hardly matter."

Sometimes, Poincaré felt like a butcher surgeon paid to remove shrapnel without anesthesia. "In fact, it matters," he said. "If you want to remove your husband from a working list of suspects, you'll tell me where you stayed. If you don't, I'll call the clinic and discover that for myself—and assume you have something to hide. If you do, I'll call the clinic and also the inn and speak with everyone he spoke with—to the extent possible. If he was as weak as you say, and there's no reason to doubt that, we'll be able to settle this and I'll leave you alone. I'll extend my apologies and cross him off my list. So, please: where did you stay between his release from the clinic and the final blood tests?"

She was shaking.

Poincaré waited; he needed answers.

"Scharnitz," she said.

"Just over the border in Austria? I know it—on the rail line between Munich and Innsbruck. You stayed at an inn?"

"Yes."

"What's the name of the inn?"

"I don't remember."

"Please," said Poincaré. "It's a small village, and there can't be many inns. I'll call them all, if need be. I could also e-mail your photo and Randal's."

She looked at him, disbelieving. "You would do that?"

"What was the name of the inn, Mrs. Young?"

"We didn't stay at an inn."

"Where, then?"

"With Randal's parents. I took him to say goodbye."

Reasonable, he thought, but odd. "Your husband was an American citizen. His parents lived in Austria?"

"His father was a career diplomat for the State Department. He was stationed in Munich for about eight years from the time Randal was nine or so. The parts of his childhood he remembered most fondly were there. He skied, climbed, hiked—they loved the mountains enough to buy a cottage, which was a kind of base camp to get to the Alps. Lewis and Francine retired in Scharnitz, and Randy visited when he could. It was more his home than Pasadena. If you move six times in your first eighteen years, you can't really point to a place on the map and say, *This is where I belong.* Randy came out here for school—he wanted to work in mining, anything to be around the mountains. We met at Cal Tech, when he was finishing a Masters degree."

"And you were doing what at the time?"

"Also studying chemistry. We met as teaching assistants in an Organics lab."

"I see. And is there much work for chemists in Colorado?"

"No, not where I'm moving."

"And you're going there to—"

"To concentrate on my boys for a few years. My family has a ranch, and I thought it might be good for the children to have cousins and uncles around—if that's alright with you."

"Why didn't you say so at first—about his parents?"

"Because I respect my husband's privacy—and his parents' grief. And now you'll be calling them." Her eyes watered.

"I will call them," he said. "There's a chemical mix in circulation that could do a great deal of harm in the wrong hands—that's already done harm. A man died."

"*My* man died!"

"I know that, and I'm very—"

"Don't you *dare.*"

She was folding in on herself, but he pushed harder: "One more thing." He reached into a pocket and produced James Fenster's passport photo. "Have you seen this man?"

"Go away."

"Or these women?" He placed the photographs of Dana Chambi and Madeleine Rainier before her and watched closely. Her eyes were already red, her chest heaving. It would be difficult to catch a change in expression. She stared in the direction of the photos but did not appear to focus.

"Forgive my intrusion," he said, collecting his things. "I know your husband had no criminal record. He didn't even have parking tickets. I'm sure he was the man you and others say he was. But I've brought a potential bomber and a bombing this close." He showed a thin space between his thumb and forefinger. "There's something I'm not understanding, Mrs. Young. Was your husband a religious man—a devout Christian by any chance?"

"*What?*"

"The End Times—did he believe the world was about to end?"

"Are you *mad*?"

Poincaré took a half-step toward the door. "Last night," he said, "I ran a credit report on your husband and you. This is a fine home, with a grand view. In any event, I saw that the mortgage on the house—some $1,250,000—was paid off on the 24th of March. *Life insurance*, I thought. But Mrs. Young, you didn't return to the United States and your husband didn't die until March 20th. You couldn't have gotten a certificate of death to the insurance company that quickly, and in any event these companies don't pay claims of this size in three or four days. On large payouts, they routinely check for fraud. These things usually take—"

"*Get out!*" she screamed. She grabbed a dinner plate, and Poincaré prepared to duck. But instead of throwing the plate, Julie Young set it on a square of newspaper. Eyes glazed, she wrapped it and began humming a tune.

CHAPTER 33

Suitcase in hand, standing before the Paris Hotel and Casino, Poincaré heard a familiar baritone and felt the clap of Serge Laurent's bear paw on his shoulder. "And you thought nothing could beat the Old World for charm. Viva Las Vegas, Henri!" Poincaré turned to embrace a friend but instead found a ghost. Laurent sipped from a cup of green liquid that smelled of rubbing alcohol and raised a finger. "Shh," he said. "If we don't talk about it, it goes away."

Poincaré dropped his bag. "Have you seen a doctor?" Laurent coughed, and Poincaré realized that no further medical opinions would be needed. "I'm leaving for France tomorrow," he said. "Come home with me."

"Sorry," said Laurent. "I'm submitting my reports on schedule, and the stuffed shirts think I'm functioning at an acceptable level. What they don't know isn't hurting them."

"But it's killing you. How much weight have you lost?"

"Enough. And the work's keeping me alive, if anything. Relax."

Poincaré handed his bag to an attendant. "Find us a bar, for pity's sake."

He followed Laurent through the casino—a windowless, Parisian-themed playground designed, Poincaré supposed, to evoke memories of a stroll along the Seine for those who had never visited. Gaming tables sat beneath verdigris grillwork reminiscent of Paris Métro stations. On the ceiling stretched a painted summer sky. And poking through the room like some robotic Godzilla were two massive, girdered legs of a half-scale Eiffel Tower—the casino's signature landmark. The total effect was in turns preposterous and mesmerizing. It was a movie set with actual people spending actual money, laughing and drinking, enjoying themselves thoroughly. Management had to be pleased if what Poincaré saw at a blackjack table was any indication. A bored-looking woman in a midnight blue dress and diamonds lost thousands when the dealer flipped a jack instead of a long-shot deuce. Gone in an instant, the equivalent of four overdue mortgage payments on his vineyard. Was it possible? She casually slipped another tall stack of chips into three betting lanes. The dealer scooped spent cards and chips in one practiced motion and dealt again. Above the din of slot machines and craps players hollering for sevens floated the music of Édith Piaf.

Laurent found an elevator. When the doors opened into a second floor lounge, Poincaré read the marquis and said: "You're joking."

"*Risqué*," said Laurent. "It's a perfectly good name for a bar. Just shut up long enough for me to buy us a beverage. They have a surprisingly good wine list." They spoke in French, and a young woman showing a good deal of cleavage approached with a hearty "Bonjour!"

Poincaré checked his watch. "Bon soir," he said. "Est-ce qu'on peut s'asseoir sur le divan près de la fenêtre?"

The woman stared, helpless.

"The windows," said Laurent, grinning. "May we sit there?"

They crossed the lounge to a panoramic view of the Las Vegas Strip as salsa music pulsed at a volume that was nearly visible. Poincaré reached for a laminated card that promised patrons *a convergence of elegance and energy . . . for a myriad of appetites.* "What does this even mean?" he yelled over the music. Laurent—winded, his eyes closed—hadn't heard a word. Poincaré shook his arm. "Why are you still here?"

"Two guesses."

"Serge, I'm not playing."

"Neither am I. My assignment was to report on the Soldiers of Rapture. In case you hadn't noticed, there are more souls in need of saving in Las Vegas than anywhere in the world—except, possibly, Los Angeles. Las Vegas is Rapturian central, Henri." He began to cough. "Wait until you see the rest of this place. They've got La Boutique for your shopping pleasure, La Cave for overpriced wines, La Vogue to accessorize the ladies. Only in America—it's a highlights reel, Henri, a comic book. But I'll tell you this, you won't get your pocket picked on Le Boulevard. The security in this casino is unbelievable." He perused the wine list. "You should sell them a few dozen cases. They'll go for anything French, no matter how awful."

All the joy was gone from the insult. Poincaré stared across the boulevard to the Bellagio, where the fountain display had just come on. Addressing the colored jets of water, he recounted for Laurent the present state of chaos in his life: Claire was lost, with one foot in this world and the other in a place he could not enter; Etienne had recently walked a whole thirty paces before collapsing in pain; Lucille's latest skin graft had left her with an infection; Georges, making progress with his new leg, continued to cry for his brother; and Émile, in and out of a now lighter coma, had squeezed his mother's hand before drifting away once more. "And the doctors are calling this progress," said Poincaré. "Etienne won't speak to me or let me near the children." He put a hand to his forehead, checking for a fever.

"You did your job," said Laurent. "It's not reasonable to expect a demented fuck like Banović to sic his dogs on you. . . . Henri, you'd already left for the States when I heard about Chloe. I'm so—"

Poincaré stopped him. "We're not discussing your cancer, and we're not discussing my granddaughter."

Laurent nodded. "Waitress! A bottle of Lynch Bages, 1982."

"What the hell, Serge! That's six hundred U.S."

Laurent smiled as the woman retreated.

"What's so funny?"

"What's so funny is that after thirty years you still can't stand to lose yourself in a bottle of good wine. Really, in the last quarter-century how many times have I seen you just sit back and *stop* for one goddamned minute?" Laurent stretched and leaned into the couch. "I remember your father predicting you wouldn't last in this job. Or that if you did, the work wouldn't put your God-given talents to use. He was a tough nut, I'll grant you. What was the man thinking, naming you Henri?"

"He wanted a mathematician," said Poincaré. "Someone to keep the family business alive since he didn't get the gene. But I was no Jules Henri either. I'm sure I disappointed him."

"Like hell! I may be the one living person who paid attention to the 'Heroes of France' lesson when we were kids. Tell me when I misremember: your great-grandfather began as a mining engineer who investigated an accident that baffled everyone else. He walked straight into a collapsed mine, deduced causes, wrote a report—and later became the Inspector General of the Corps de Mines *while* he was the world's mathematical darling. Chaos theory. Relativity. Topology. Henri: the man dug for a living. You dig. Different mines is all. You *are* in the family business. Your father didn't see it—but Jules Henri would have been proud."

Serge was vanishing. How thin life would be without him.

They listened to music until the wine arrived. After a second glass, Poincaré imagined sitting beside his old friend at the stern rail of a ship, watching the wake churn in the moonlight.

"Lyon wants me out," he said.

"You got that memo, too? I suppose we're now men of a certain age. . . . You know," said Laurent, staring out the window, "not one of my wives could compete with the adrenaline rush I got from being out in the field. All four of them needed me to come home. I needed to be out here, and I got exactly what I asked for. Now I'll be cared for by strangers in the end. To hell with that. I'm going to die on top of a woman, not in a hospital."

The DJ switched from salsa to merengue, and Serge began tapping out the rhythm with the silver nugget on his finger. "I don't care if Las Vegas is a fantasy. I love the place!" A fresh fit of coughing bent him over, and this time Poincaré saw a red stain on his handkerchief. Laurent noted the change in Poincaré's face and said: "Do not fuck me up by getting sentimental. This is hard enough."

Poincaré closed his eyes.

"I'll tell you about my work—it will be a diversion."

"Go ahead. But we'll need another bottle, which I can't afford."

Laurent held up the empty and motioned to a waitress. "You already know how much I detest the Soldiers of Rapture. But give credit where it's due: their marketing, if you can call it that, has been nothing short of brilliant. How many people could you find who won't be looking to the sky on August 15th?"

Poincaré was staring through the arch of his steepled fingers, watching the fountains. "The countdown calendar I saw at the airport this evening read twenty-five. I've been in five cities in as many days. The calendars are everywhere."

"Exactly my point," said Laurent. "There are three strains of Rapturians, best I can tell. The harmless ones you see preaching on street corners in robes wouldn't understand Christian theology if they stubbed their toes on Saint Augustine's grave. The earnest ones, also on street corners, actually know their gospels and are spreading the Good News best they can. These are the original Soldiers. I think of them as Jehovah's Witnesses in robes. Finally we have the schismatics, in two delicious flavors: the ones killing doers of good works to hasten the Second Coming. They scare the shit out of me."

"But not as much as the suicide bombers for Christ?"

"They're total lone wolves, Henri. The schismatics meet in groups to work up their hit lists. The bombers have absolutely no connection to the Rapturians. They've got no religious or political agenda, and at the moment they're putting on robes and shouting *Jesus* because it gives their pathology a higher calling. What amazes me is the countdown to August 15th. Everyone knows the date—it's spread like a flu pandemic. Same model."

Poincaré sat up.

"Don't look so surprised. Mathematicians study rumor the way epidemiologists study disease. They use computer models to simulate spread and discover ways to block it. In one case you've got a virus and in the other, a rumor of the Second Coming. Both leave markers: people with a fever or the appearance of countdown calendars. The dynamics are remarkably similar. When you map these data points, something interesting emerges. You could be looking at the plot of a rumor infiltrating a workplace, a city, a county, a region—and even a nation or continent. Set the graphs side by side, and you can't distinguish the spread at one level from the spread at others. Ditto for flu. Do you remember, in Amsterdam, how Quito told us about the coastline of Christchurch, New Zealand? How—if he enlarged one section of the coast—we couldn't tell which was the one-kilometer slice and which, the forty kilometer? Same thing with influenza and rumors. When you look at a part—"

Poincaré knew the rest.

Deep in his pocket, he found himself working the contours of the buffalo nickel as he might a polished stone. He rubbed the coin thinking a genie might appear, rubbed it for all the luck that had turned bad and—in this casino, why not—rubbed it for new luck, better luck. For that's what the world turned on, he decided. He had tried goodness and right behavior, and where had that gotten him or the ones he loved? He released the coin and allowed that something he had resisted for a long time was demanding a name.

Across the boulevard, reflected in the waters, Poincaré saw gold atoms measured in microns and galaxies measured in light years. He saw rivers in mountains and mountains in trees and lightning strikes in the lungs of a friend who would never again draw a full breath. For weeks, the deepest of deep structures had sung to Poincaré like an angelic host, and he could resist no more. Had this casino been a church, he would have uttered a name. But Poincaré could not—not yet—because across the ocean his family was broken and in the seat beside him his friend was dying. Would that Name have permitted the murder of a child? The suffering of innocents? For thirty years he had watched good men and women stricken, raising their hands to Heaven. He uttered a cry that Laurent mistook for a question.

"I'll tell you why a rumor spreads, Henri: because we demand a path through chaos. I'm dying. Don't you think it would be pleasant for me to accept the Rapture and the prospect of sitting at our Lord's right hand?"

"You don't believe?" said Poincaré.

"I don't believe."

"You think there's nothing after this?"

"Nothing at all," said Laurent. "And along come the Rapturians who offer eternal peace. You grab hold and you're happy. I could but I won't. Was it ever different?"

"I don't know," said Poincaré.

"Do you believe there was a Golden Age? An Eden—a world without suffering?"

"I don't know a thing anymore."

"Well, it's *never* been different. This world's been about to end forever, and I could bore you with a catalogue of the Doomsday cults who thought so because I've researched them all. When we wake up on August 16th, the Rapturians will become one more fringe sect in a long line. The Bombers-for-Christ will stop bombing, the schismatics will stop their assassinations, and life will return to normal—whatever that is—until the expiration of the Mayan calendar. That will launch a new hallucination with contours all its own that will look, if I live to see it, just like the contours of this Rapturian madness. Round it goes, Henri. Different names, the same thing."

Poincaré walked two fingers down his arm. "A path through chaos. I like that. . . . I could use a path straight through the Fenster case. If everyone's telling the truth, I've got nothing. I've got a hard drive with secrets and one in a couple of billion billion chances of cracking it. I haven't found my granddaughter's killer. I believe everyone is lying to me, Serge."

"Well, *that* is progress. You must be getting close!" Laurent raised a glass. "To my dean of Inspectors, Henri Poincaré. My Inspector General of the Corps de Mines, Keeper of the family flame. A miner! To Henri, to digging!!"

They clinked glasses.

Poincaré could stand it no longer and grabbed Laurent's boney arm. "Come stay with Claire and me. We'll set up a room. Better yet, we'll put you in one of the horse stalls where you belong. Don't die alone, Serge."

Laurent shook Poincaré loose and reached for a cigarette. He struck a match and took a drag, deep as his ruined lungs would allow. "Just how stupid are you?" he said.

"You're still smoking—and asking me this?"

"I'll tell you how stupid you are. You're stupid enough to pull yourself along with what's left of your family down into my hole—not that I'm going to occupy it much longer. Last I checked, your hole was deep enough." He looked over Poincaré's shoulder to the lounge entrance and waved at two women. "Ah! My 11 PM appointment. Ladies!" He motioned them across the dance floor. "Come meet my friend, Henri. He's quite famous in policing circles. Also French."

The women were showpieces, real enough but as much a part of the Las Vegas cartoon as the half-sized Eiffel Tower. The one who looked like Marilyn Monroe slid her arm around Laurent's waist. The other one said: "Come party, Hank. Serge needs us both tonight, but we've got friends."

"No, my dears. He's got important work to do. Big questions to settle." Laurent kissed one on the top of the head and whispered: "If you can keep a secret, he's digging. Don't tell." He peeled fifteen one-hundred-dollar bills onto the table. Looking directly at Poincaré, he said: "Goodbye, Henri. I don't suppose we'll be seeing each other again." He turned from the lounge, a woman on each arm, and was gone.

CHAPTER 34

In the corridor that evening, a woman giggled: "Bobby, stop! I'll unsnap it when we get to the room!"

Lit by the glow of his computer screen, Poincaré had once again laid everything he owned on the Fenster case across a hotel bed: folders each for Roy, Bell, Quito, Rainier, Chambi, Family Services of Minnesota, JPL, Randal Young, the Ambassade bombing, Günther's autopsy report, and Agent Johnson's fingerprint and DNA analysis. He sat in the middle of it all with his laptop and Fenster's hard drive. The key to the password if not the password itself would be found in some combination of these folders—or nowhere. Sixty-seven nonrandom characters, ninety-five possibilities for each: if it was a number known to mathematicians, a constant or a series, he would never find it. This much he had already demonstrated. A phrase, then, or nothing.

How would Jules Henri have approached this puzzle, he wondered. His great-grandfather had been calling to him this entire case, so why not invoke his ghost once and for all. *Grand-père—you who were blessed with a gift for pointing to large truths hiding in plain sight . . . take a look.* Poincaré placed his hands on the files. *What is it? What am I missing?*

Poincaré opened the folder marked: *Fenster, Apartment* and, within that, Agent Johnson's report. One by one, he worked through the images from the gallery. This time he forced himself to look beyond the beauty of surfaces and see what Fenster had assembled. An impact crater on Mars, recorded through an orbiting telescope, resembled the cells of a leaf on Earth and also city streets. He turned to his notes and reread his summary of the captions: River delta + cauliflower leaf. Common lichen + Ireland (imaged from space).

Lightning + veins of eye + sidewalk crack + tree + mountain ridge. He read fifty such groupings and forced himself to state as directly as he could Fenster's conclusion: that what was radically and irreducibly its own in this world was, at the same instant, not. Both different and not. Singular and plural. The same.

Poincaré had seen it in the fountains of the Bellagio. He turned to another page of notes, where he had recorded the phrasings Fenster had posted above his captions. *The same name. Difference? Mathematics is an art.* He turned to the inside of yet another folder, where in a careful hand he had copied what Jules Henri had observed a century before and what Fenster had taken on as his own life's work. Guiding the tip of his pencil, he counted words. Twelve. He counted the characters in the words. Fifty-five. He counted the characters plus the spaces between the words: sixty-six. He added the period: sixty-seven.

Taped to the computer for all to see, hiding in plain sight like every other mystery Jules Henri and Fenster had plumbed, a declaration deeper than biology, older than this world or any: *Mathematics is the art of giving the same name to different things.* This time when Poincaré typed the password, his computer screen blinked and a file opened like a rose at its appointed hour.

Chapter 35

The dream was vivid enough that he felt the sun full on his face—except it wasn't his face or possibly his but also his mother's or his father's, he couldn't tell. The emotions were his own, then theirs, then his again. The three of them had spent a morning hiking the lower elevations of Mt. Blanc, climbing meadow trails that with each turn presented another stunning view of the mountain. The air was bright and clear; the wind blew a steady plume off the peak, the edelweiss was in bloom. Twelve years old, Poincaré climbed steadily, happily. At one switchback he paused to check on his parents and found they had stopped—to look at him. It was at this point in the dream he became one of them, or both, and saw himself ahead, waving. Then he was himself once more, wondering why his mother on so magnificent a day would appear to be crying, yet happy, as she held his father's hand and waved. Then he was below once more, holding hands, looking up at himself framed against the meadow and mountain with the broad sky behind, and he felt a terrible ache that was also beautiful and sweet, and he woke in Claire's studio knowing exactly what his parents knew: that what we love most in this world, we lose.

He had taken a late dinner and climbed to the studio and collapsed, waking at first light with his strange dream. He planned to stay in Lyon long enough to renew the lease, meet with the new director at Interpol, and catch a train to Fonroque. After the attacks, he could not bring himself to visit the studio or conduct any business on his wife's behalf. But the lease was now up and he would need to inspect the premises and come to terms with the landlord. Claire would not be painting here anytime soon, and it made no sense to renew now that they lived in the south—especially given the costs. Just the same.

She kept a single bed and a hot plate for the manic, productive times when she refused to interrupt work by returning home for meals or sleep. Poincaré had learned the hard way not to disturb her. Her creative bursts would begin with a note that she was contemplating a new piece and would be spending some time alone at the studio. Once, after a four-day absence, he made the mistake of climbing to the garret and knocking on the door. She answered, saw him looking past her to the work on the easel, and then marched directly to the canvas and slashed it with a palette knife. "Not ready!" she yelled. "Not ready!!" They agreed during a more reasoned moment, when she was not painting, that she would leave a message each day on their answering machine. If he found it, he would not interrupt her; no message meant she was dead and he should come to collect the body. She apologized for the Jekyll and Hyde in her and explained that she had tried to shield him but that, in any event, he knew what he was signing on for.

That was true. They met at a juried exhibition in Paris in which she had exhibited and won a first prize. She was nowhere in sight when he approached her work—a wood-panel miniature that suggested a female nude or, possibly, a coconut palm downed in a storm. "What do you think?" a voice inquired from behind.

"I'm not sure," he answered, eyes still on the miniature. "I believe I like it, though I couldn't tell you why. Is it for sale?" He turned and was startled by the directness of her gaze. Her hair was rolled into a tight bun through which she had stuck a brush. Her hands were smudged with that morning's palette, and she smelled of turpentine.

"It's not for sale," she said. "But I'll give it to you."

Which led to dinner, which in time led to her apartment.

It was this history of Claire's leaving him and returning that gave Poincaré hope she would emerge from her present sorrows. When he woke, he found the workspace as she had left it months before: on an easel sat an unfinished urban scene, though he could not be sure. He thought he recognized city lights in a swath of reds and yellows. If he did not understand her art, exactly, he appreciated that others did. Claire had secured gallery representation in Paris, Milan, New

York, Los Angeles, and Buenos Aires. She crated and sent off what she finished, and her agents sold what she sent. He came to regard her canvases as a series of moods made visual, much in the way melodies can evoke feeling.

All these years later, Poincaré marveled at how Etienne had gotten the best of Claire: her fearlessness, for one, and her genius for thinking both spatially and in colors. He sat on the corner of the bed and pulled her pillow close, but the scent of her was gone. He circled the loft, trailing his hands across rolled tubes of paint and the contraption she used to stretch her canvases. He sorted through the junk she used as props. But try as he might, Poincaré could not summon Claire from any of it. The studio was no longer a living space.

As he prepared to leave, he noticed leaning against a wall by the door a single crate addressed to her agent in New York. Poincaré knew what it was, the portrait she had teased him about months ago—the very idea of which he found mortifying. In the weeks he had spent in Lyon getting on her nerves by securing the house, she had asked several times if he would visit the studio and offer an opinion. "Aren't you curious to know how I see you?" she asked.

"I am," he said. "But I also know that I'll see the piece and ask you not to sell it. You'll accuse me of meddling, which would be true, and we'll fight. So, no, I'd rather not."

She had crated the painting, and he took a hammer claw and pulled the nails along the top edge, then turned the crate upside down, careful to keep his eyes averted. When Poincaré stepped to the middle of the room and looked, he grabbed a chair to steady himself; for Claire, who had said, "Believe me—it's abstract enough that no one will recognize you," had lied spectacularly. She had long disparaged art as photograph. He had never known her to render a close likeness of a bowl of fruit or a country lane, let alone a person. Yet here he was looking at his wiser, more generous self, wearing work clothes with a pruning shears in hand, seated on an upended box on the terrace at Fonroque, the oak tree behind and beyond that the vineyards. The hair was thin and graying; the musculature of his face was yielding to gravity. She was a faithful, pitiless recorder, which was precisely what plucked his heart: for though she showed a man who had climbed a steep hill in life and was easily a stride or two over its crest, she also showed someone who had gained by that effort. About the eyes and the mouth he saw a kindness at odds with the demands of brutalizing work. In the tilt of the head and the not-quite-resolute set of the jaw he recognized a dismay at how cruel the world could be. And in the strong hand that gripped the shears, he saw respect for someone who would answer that cruelty. Mostly what Poincaré saw was the artist's affection for her subject. He came upon the canvas like a widower who discovers the tenderest of letters from his beloved, never sent. The portrait desolated him.

CHAPTER 36

Poincaré placed the Tyvek envelope on a desk before Hubert Levenger, who lifted the package to feel its heft. "Smaller than a breadbox, larger than a Rolex. A present—you shouldn't have."

"A hard drive, Hubert—from an IBM laptop. There's a cable in there, too."

"What's on it?"

"A wall of numbers: eight million, give or take, single-spaced at five columns per screen. I'm hoping you can make some sense of it— tell me what I have. There's no other information on the drive that I could see, but maybe you can confirm that, too."

"You have paperwork for this, I assume."

He was an ascetic-looking man who neither wore nor consumed animal-derived products—the expression of a politics that Poincaré had learned early on not to discuss; for a single question usually led to long discourses and pamphlets delivered to the home. Otherwise, Poincaré had found Levenger to be an affable, dependable colleague. "In fact, the drive came into my possession without paperwork. Sorry."

"I should know where this came from, Henri."

"From an ongoing investigation."

Levenger screwed up an eye. "Ludovici's bad habits rubbing off on you? Next you're going to say that if anyone asks, I never saw this."

"Suit yourself." Poincaré handed him a slip of paper. "The password. Remember to type the uppercase *M* and the period. . . . Nice," he said, straightening one of Levenger's photos. "How many grandchildren now?"

"Eight. The little one—with the curls—just turned five. You should hear her sing 'La Marseillaise.' She could melt the Wilkins Ice Shelf if global warming doesn't do it first." Levenger read the password aloud, more as a question than a statement: "There must be fifty characters here. The national treasury doesn't use passwords this long."

Poincaré shrugged. "What do I know?"

"More than you're saying. But we'll keep that between you and your Confessor. Do you suppose it's true?"

"What's that?"

"About mathematics and different things."

Poincaré glanced at his watch. "Got to run, Hubert—to a meeting with the new director. I believe I'm about to retire. . . . And yes," he said, halfway out the door. "I do, for what it's worth."

"I'M *VERY* glad to meet you, Inspector!"

An American this time, he thought, appraising his eighth Executive Director of Police Services. After the first was sacked for insubordination—having moved too aggressively to catch an art thief who turned out to be the press attaché at the Czech Embassy, which caused considerable embarrassment—Poincaré learned not to grow too fond of his bosses. The job was at least half political, and directors spent their days on phones and along corridors fighting two ends against a largely unsatisfying middle. There were the politically cautious who, out of deference to Interpol's international charter, squelched inquiries for fear of upsetting member nations. These were the know-nothings who bowed to autocrats crying 'internal affairs' whenever an inquiry threatened to expose corruption or abuses of power. Then there were the law enforcement professionals, the cops, who pushed hard for results in the field. There could be no serving both masters, so directors came and went. On occasion some were fired for cause, as Monforte had been, not politics; and it was in response to Monforte's perceived incompetence that Felix Robinson was hired: a former bureau head in Washington, famous for taking a statistical approach to crime—setting priorities in the field as if he were playing Sudoku.

Poincaré expected an automaton but, on crossing the freshly laid carpet of what he continued to think of as Albert Monforte's office, found the director's desk to be reassuringly messy. Robinson apparently cared little for appearances, an impression strengthened by the coffee stain on his tie and a shirt that had been laundered well beyond its useful life. Poincaré extended a hand. "Sir, I've read the secretary general's letter on your qualifications. We're all impressed. Welcome to Interpol."

"Felix, please."

"Well, then. It's my pleasure. Henri."

They sat on either side of Monforte's old desk.

"I've read your file, Inspector. Bravo! Most agents burn out after fifteen or twenty years. What's your secret?"

Poincaré observed him observing the courtesies. "I'm surrounded by good people, Felix—they keep me sharp."

"Like Serge Laurent?"

"Yes, like Serge."

The director folded his hands and leaned forward. "You'll find me to be very direct, Henri. I'm aware that you and he are close. As you know, I'm sure, he's been investigating the Soldiers of Rapture—who'd be nothing but a boil on our collective ass if it weren't for what he's calling their schismatic cells. I have reason to believe Laurent is not healthy. Do you have an opinion?"

It was a simple question with a thousand trapdoor answers. Poincaré was careful not to deny having just seen Serge. "I do have an opinion," he said. "Laurent is the finest agent I know. He'll pull himself from the field when he thinks he can't do the work."

Robinson nodded. "We can add loyalty to your list of virtues. I know you were with him in Las Vegas."

"He reported this?"

"No."

Robinson let that settle in for a moment as Poincaré formed a clearer picture of the man before him. "The Soldiers of Rapture," continued the director, "with their al Qaeda-like network are so decentralized that the best we're able to do is disrupt single actions. Which we've done. Just this past week there was a person slated for execution in Lucerne. Inspector Laurent got this information to us in a timely fashion—the target was a woman working in the clean energy field, and we eliminated the cell. Which is well and good, of course, but operations designed to save individuals drain our limited resources. I've been hired to move Interpol in a more focused, cost-efficient direction with bigger results. You've been around for nearly three decades. I don't believe we can afford any longer to rescue individuals. What do you think?"

Again, Robinson folded his hands and waited.

What Poincaré thought was that the new director likely earned his stripes setting landmines and watching how others reacted when they stepped on one. What he said was, "It's always worth saving a life. I don't envy anyone in your position having to make those calls."

The director nodded. "In Texas we have an expression, *Cut the crap*. In your new role, I'll be counting on you to speak plainly. Straight talk, please."

"My new role," said Poincaré. "Ludovici mentioned something about this."

"That's right. I want you to become supervising agent for all field operations, a post I'm just creating. A large responsibility. The position is strategic, not operational. I want you to upgrade the general quality of thinking in the field, the investigative IQ if you will. You're to be a mentor and sounding board to our agents. Beyond that, you'll get to define the job. There's no one who knows strategy better or who has better instincts, and I want you out of the field, effective immediately, to take on this work."

"I'm flattered," said Poincaré.

"I don't flatter people," said the director. "I need help."

"I suppose I'd be sitting behind a desk here in Lyon?"

"Correct. But there's no reason you couldn't do this work from Fonroque. I understand you own a vineyard. You can send me some wine—though I've been advised to have it tested for arsenic."

Poincaré smiled. "Straight talk, Felix. What if I decline?"

"It will play out as follows," said Robinson. "By the end of the day, you're to submit your Interpol credentials and firearms to the clerk on the first floor. They have a list downstairs of everything in your locker, so I'm sure you'll be scrupulous. If you accept the position, which I hope you will, we'll issue an amended credential giving you the highest security clearance in this building, equivalent to my own. But beyond Interpol headquarters, your authority ends. You are no longer a field agent, Henri. If you decline, then we'll have a watch for you and a pension. Maybe a farewell party with stale cake. You know the drill."

Poincaré knew the drill.

"I've asked Paolo Ludovici to stand by. You'll debrief him on the ammonium perchlorate investigation and turn over all your case notes. Do you understand?"

"And you're taking this action now because—"

"Because as far as work in the field is concerned, I believe you've lost your perspective. That business in The Hague, when you attended the trial of the Bosnian . . . *that* was a mistake. The sergeant-at-arms reported admitting you to the courtroom wearing a firearm. To the trial of a man who had assaulted your family? I don't believe you were exercising optimal judgment at that moment, and an error on your part would have reflected badly on Interpol. The report took a few weeks to find my desk, but had I known I would have pulled you from the field immediately. So you've been living on borrowed time, though neither of us knew it."

Poincaré liked Robinson. Nothing he said had struck a false note, and the man would do Interpol a world of good. He said: "I'm moved by your confidence in me, Felix."

"Inspector, I'm trying to give you a soft landing here. I need the help, and I will fill this position with or without you. Believe me, if I wanted you gone, I'd simply force your retirement. So take it or leave it, as we say in America. Think this over. In the meantime, your Interpol privileges are suspended as of five o'clock. We'll maintain your computer access to our servers as a courtesy—so you can monitor Ludovici's progress on the case. He's in his office, waiting for your files." Robinson walked around his desk. "From what I've read and all I've heard, Henri, you're too valuable for us to let you get killed out there because you're distracted. Whether or not you accept the new position, you're done with field work. And it's not that I don't understand the distraction. What happened to your family is unspeakable. And to whatever extent Interpol failed you in its protection, we are reviewing and correcting procedures—an effort I am personally overseeing. But in the meantime, I will not add to the misery by seeing you killed. Good day, Inspector."

On his way to Ludovici's office, Poincaré placed a call to Fonroque. Claire was napping, Eva told him. She had had a quiet day, sitting on the terrace. "Would you like me to wake her, Monsieur?"

"No," he said. "Tell me. Did she speak at all while I've been gone? In her sleep, has she made sounds?"

Levenger passed him in the corridor, holding the Tyvek envelope and offering a thumbs-up sign. "Handing it off now, Henri. I'll contact you when I have something."

Poincaré waved his thanks.

"No, Monsieur. Nothing."

"Has Etienne called?" On his way to Lyon, Poincaré had stopped in Paris to inquire after Etienne and his family, and to visit Chloe at the Montparnasse Cemetery. He stayed for a time, sweeping the granite slab, and turned at a sound to see his son in a wheelchair, pushed by an attendant. Etienne met his father's eyes. Poincaré moved to speak, but his son made a motion and the attendant rolled him away.

"Yes, Etienne called and asked about Madame."

"And she said nothing?"

"That's right, Monsieur."

"Did he ask for me?"

"It was a brief call," said the girl. "Try in an hour if you want me to put the phone to Madame's ear."

Ludovici sat in his office, reading a case file—propped back in his chair, snakeskin cowboy boots on his desk. "Do you like them?" he asked after Poincaré knocked and let himself in. "The Italians kicked ass, Henri. And yours truly took first honors."

"You shot the fuzz off your peach?"

"I goddamned shot the fuzz *off* the fuzz!"

"Congratulations, Paolo." He set his briefcase on the desk, opened it, and handed over a tall stack of files. Everything I own on the Fenster—the ammonium perchlorate case," he said, which was not quite true. The hard drive Poincaré was holding for himself and Eric Hurley. "I've prepared an executive summary with an index to the files. You know the highlights, in any event, and should have no trouble." He emptied the contents of his pockets onto the desk in a show of full disclosure. There were paperclips, gum wrappers, loose change, and a jeweler's loupe. "For you," he said, handing Ludovici the loupe. "So that you don't overlook any details. And the coins . . . your first cup of coffee and beignet are on me." Poincaré counted out several euros and smiled when he came across an American buffalo nickel, which he returned to his pocket.

"Henri, this is no easier for me than—"

"It's all fine, Paolo. Really."

"Will you take the position?"

"I'm not sure," he said.

"I don't know if I hope you do or don't. You'll need to stay busy, in any event. Maybe you should, so your mind doesn't rot."

"That's thoughtful advice for a retiree. Thanks."

"Go to hell . . . and keep your phone on. I may need you."

WHETHER POINCARÉ did or did not take the position, he was gone from the field—a long chapter closed for him by executive order, a decision made without sentiment. Perhaps Robinson had done him a favor by preempting a slide into caricature. The last thing he or any agent wanted was to become the prize fighter who lacked the grace and good sense to leave.

He walked to his office. In his four hours remaining as a credentialed Interpol agent, he studied the surveillance loop of Dana Chambi yet again. The loop lasted just over two minutes, and he replayed it another hundred times—bringing his total well into the thousands. With digital zoom, he had identified the handbag she carried, a lead that produced nothing useful. He could read the physician's name on the white jacket she had stolen. He could even see that the stocking on her left leg was torn. Hundreds of details were known to him; but no matter how many times he watched the loop, he could not square what he saw with what those who knew Chambi said of the woman: accomplished researcher, teacher with a sense of theater and humor, volunteer at the Math League, dedicated keeper of James Fenster's flame.

She must be all one thing or all the other, he decided. The world of the assassin did not overlap the world of the scholar. And yet here she was on the surveillance loop, setting the diversionary fire and proceeding off-screen to murder a child. And there she was in Amsterdam in the days and hours preceding the explosion. Poincaré could not puzzle it through. At 4:29, thirty-one minutes left in a career that spanned three decades, he played the tape once more.

> Frames 000-025: Subject enters from bottom of screen.
> Frames 026-058: Subject looks right, looks left, opens bag.
> Frames 059-102: Subject drops paper into can, pours accelerant.
> Frames 103-114: Subject looks right, looks left.
> Frames 115-120: Subject lights match, sets fire.
> Frames 121-136: Flames. Subject exits.

Poincaré enhanced the image at Frame 107. It showed Chambi checking the corridor to confirm no one would see her striking a match, her face and neck clearer here than in other frames. Allowing for the distortions of a pixilated enhancement, it was Dana Chambi. He had compared every photograph found of her with the images on the screen. Interpol's own facial recognition software confirmed the match, and yet Poincaré felt compelled to devote his final minutes to a fresh analysis. Again, an indisputable likeness—save for a detail too obvious even for comment: in the video Chambi wore no scarf to hide the angry-looking, amoeba-shaped island of purple on her otherwise unblemished neck. In the twelve photographs Poincaré had collected, she wore a scarf. Add to this the time they met in person outside the lecture hall, where she nervously adjusted the scarf when the discussion turned to Fenster, and the contrast was clear. Scarf, no scarf.

Look harder, he told himself. What he saw this time was an assassin taking care to avoid detection. No assassin intends to be caught in the act, and none intends to be caught after. The rhythm of such a life was to kill, escape, collect payment, and kill again. Yet the woman in the video made no effort to hide the port-wine stain, the single marker that functioned, in effect, as a name-tag that read: "Hi—my name is Dana Chambi!" She checked the corridor—twice—because she did not want to be caught. She let her port-wine stain show precisely because she wanted to be seen.

Poincaré looked across his desk to a photo of Claire and the children. Once again, the answer had been hiding in plain sight. It was not Chambi. It could not have been Chambi. Ludovici swore that Banović, with his reliance on ex-Stasi types, did not order this final brutality. Someone else, then—someone who wanted to annihilate *him* by crushing what he loved best. The mistake had been in not killing Poincaré. For now he would find this person and render a severe justice. This time he would be working alone.

⇢⇒ PART IV ⇐⇠

Who endowed the heart with wisdom
or gave understanding to the mind?

— JOB 38:36

CHAPTER 37

Poincaré composed a brief e-mail: *Ms. Chambi. I know you didn't kill my granddaughter. We need to meet. Contact me.* He pressed *send* and walked to the terrace.

The storms that rumbled through the valley the previous week had scrubbed the air clean. The harvest was coming; and without money to pay the migrant workers, Poincaré would watch the year's fruit rot on the vine. But he did not worry about that now. In a few hours, when the sun rose, he would kiss Claire and open a safe in the cellar, where he kept a gun. He would pack that and, before leaving, would kiss her again—this woman without whom he had no wish to live. Yet one day he would live without her or she without him because that was the way of this world: we love, if we can, and lose what we love.

From Munich, Poincaré took the first train to Innsbruck and stepped off at the village of Scharnitz, in Austria. Julie Young had not wanted him to go, yet here he was with just enough daylight to call on Father Ulrich at Pfarrkirche Maria Hilf. Poincaré hoped he might learn about his parishioners Lewis and Francine Young before meeting them himself. He arrived with little more than an address and the name of the parish priest copied off an Internet directory.

Scharnitz was an idyll of meadows and pastures ringed by the Tyrolean Alps. At that hour, the peaks blazed with a westering sun that left the valley deep in shadow. There was snow at the higher elevations, and already Poincaré had seen promotions for ski lodges hoping for an early season. Evergreens prickled from the humps of the lower slopes. Heavy-beamed houses with steep roofs and large woodpiles huddled on the valley floor. It was the Tyrol Poincaré knew from his youth, where Randal Young, according to his wife, had spent happy years.

He entered the simple church and found a basement office where a man in shirtsleeves sat with his back to the door. When Poincaré knocked, without turning the man said: "Confessions will be heard in fifteen minutes."

"It's not that sort of visit, Father."

The priest rose. "Ah—a visitor! Forgive me."

Poincaré introduced himself and explained his business, omitting the detail that he was no longer a credentialed agent. When he finished, Ulrich said: "Please, Inspector, spare Lewis and Francine further trauma. It's a terrible thing to lose a child."

Poincaré said nothing. At the priest's back, a window opened to a cemetery.

"A sad case," Ulrich continued. "Randal, in the prime of life— married, two children. They arrived in early March, I believe. One look and you knew the end was near. He had spent a good deal of his youth skiing in Karwendel Park. I came to Scharnitz only two years ago, fresh from seminary. When I learned that he was returning to visit his parents, I wrote to my predecessor. Apparently, Randal was a well-regarded skier. I understand several of his records still stand in the youth division. At the time, his father was posted in Munich with the U.S. Department of State. The family purchased a home here. They visited in all seasons, Inspector, but it was winter they loved best. When Lewis was posted to the Far East, they kept the house and returned when they could. They've retired here.

"I never met Randal until his final illness," said the priest. "Lovely people, his parents—but thoroughly broken. They hadn't given up hope when Randal arrived. He and his wife had come with the name of a spa near Garmisch-Partenkirchen that offered unorthodox therapies for his type of cancer. Nothing sanctioned by the medical community apparently, but by this point they had exhausted all other treatments. They went to the spa and returned within a week or so—then left for the States. Very sad. But it's not ours to understand why a young person dies. One trusts there's some good that comes of it."

"I doubt that," said Poincaré.

"Surely we don't know, Inspector. A child dies. Perhaps a sibling or parent devotes years to finding a cure—and tens of thousands are saved. The single loss is real. One does not minimize that. But the good that may come of loss can also be real. These are ebbs and flows beyond our understanding."

"WHO IS IT?" Her German was correct, but the accent was American.

Poincaré answered through the closed door, in English. "Mrs. Young? I work for Interpol," which was true until he decided to reject Robinson's offer. "I've come with some questions concerning Randal." He heard footsteps, then whispering.

The door opened: "Our son died months ago," the man said.

"I know," said Poincaré, "and I'm sorry for your loss. But he may have been connected with a case I'm investigating, so if you wouldn't mind . . . But perhaps this is a bad time. I could return in the morning."

"A case? What case?"

The loss of Randal Young had not been kind to his father. Aside from a pallid face, grief had colored the man gray. The light in his eyes had dulled, and Poincaré wondered which was worse: to be father to a son who pronounced you dead or to have a son who had, in fact, died.

The Youngs had organized their simple living room around a wood stove and what could only be called a shrine to Randal, consisting of photographs from his toddler years through to adulthood. Every combination of the boy and his parents smiled in these photos. Randal, a tiny package bundled against the cold, on skis. Randal making a precarious turn in the giant slalom. Randal with his mother on horseback in an alpine meadow. An underage Randal hoisting beer steins with his parents. And then, leaping years, Randal in a gown-and-mortarboard and Randal with a young, red-haired woman at his side. Then one red-haired child, and two. Poincaré drank tea as Mrs. Young worked him through the chronology.

"You know, he got up on skis the first try and aimed himself straight down the training slope into the hay bales. He jumped up, saying, 'More! More!' In winter, it was all he wanted to do. When Lewis got posted to Japan, Randal was twelve and wanted to stay on here, with neighbors. We brought him with us but promised to keep this house."

"Why," said Lewis Young, "are you here?"

Poincaré prepared himself to gouge an already disfigured man. He respected Young's loss enough to speak directly. "I understand that your son was a propulsions expert."

"That's right."

"And also expert at setting explosives."

"He worked summers for a mining company in Wyoming. What of it?"

"When he returned to Scharnitz in March, Mr. Young, did Randal bring with him any materials from his job in Pasadena? Chemicals, perhaps. In particular, a white crystalline substance that looked like table salt?"

"He could barely stand," said the woman. "No, there was nothing like that. He brought one small suitcase. He had a book on birding, which he left for me. Do you want to see it?"

"He doesn't want *that*, Francine!"

"Did he ever speak of going to Amsterdam?" said Poincaré.

Lewis Young began to work his hands as if he were washing them. "He went to the treatment center just north of here, over the border. He came back for a day or two, then returned to the States where he died. He didn't even make it home."

Poincaré had stirred their grief enough. He apologized for the intrusion and returned to his hotel room, wondering if the trip to Scharnitz had been worth the effort, when an e-mail message arrived from the insurance company that held a $2 million policy on the life of Randal Young. Poincaré had requested payout information, and the brief response surprised him:

```
The policyholder paid no premiums
for the fourth quarter last year and
```

the first quarter this year, after
remaining current with premiums for
five years. Policyholder wrote on 12
February to cancel policy. No claim
made subsequently. No death benefit paid.
Do not hesitate to write with further
questions. Yours, S. Thompson.

Poincaré woke to a brilliant sky, the village still in shadow. The tallest peaks had caught the sun's first light, and the blaze off the snow cast him back to winter holidays in the Alps with his own parents and, later, with Claire and Etienne. Cows wandered the pastures, bells clanging. The day promised to be a glory, so it was with real sadness that Poincaré returned to the home of Lewis and Francine Young to drive a final stake through their hearts. When the door opened this time, he apologized.

"I often work this way, I'm afraid. Questions come to me after an interview, and then I can't sleep. Two brief questions, if I may."

This time there was no offer of tea. Lewis Young, his wife behind him, stood in the doorway. "Get on with it."

"The name of the spa that Randal visited." Poincaré knew the name and, in fact, had come with only one question.

"I told you this last night!"

The man repeated the name, and Poincaré asked for the correct spelling. Then he said: "Your photographs of Randal . . . I noticed there were none before he was two years old or so. Might I see some pictures of him when he was younger?"

Lewis Young slammed the door in his face.

CHAPTER 38

Poincaré stepped off the Munich-bound train at Garmisch-Parten-kirchen. On the wall of a building beyond the station, he saw a red number 8! papered over what looked to be a 9! *Even in the Tyrol*, he marveled. Serge was right to give the Rapturians their due. Before he could hail a driver, a call came through from Levenger.

"Henri!"

"I hope you have something, Hubert."

"You were right. Numbers—nothing but. There were sub-files you didn't see, and the final count is some 27 million numbers, ranging from 47.56 to 13,164.53 with more rises than dips overall. They also segment nicely, with large blocks of about 400-to-800 thousand tending to run in relatively narrow ranges. Still, within a range, I can't discern a pattern. So I'm afraid you still have a puzzle on your hands."

Poincaré instructed Levenger to send the hard drive to Fonroque. He found a taxi and within fifteen minutes was standing before a villa set on a hillside that opened to a lake and, beyond that, the mountains. Franz Meister founded his institute a decade earlier to pursue plant-derived cancer treatments. Though the institute litera-ture could not have been clearer about the experimental nature of its treatments, Poincaré found enough testimonials on the Web site to give a dying man hope. On occasion, infusions derived from Bra-zilian tree bark or aromatics from South Asia extended or improved a cancer patient's quality of life. More often they did not, and the institute made no effort to hide that fact. Still, patients came by the hundreds—among them, Randal Young.

Poincaré waited for an aide to close tall oak doors before approaching the windows in the villa's library. Herr Director, he was informed, was completing rounds and would join his visitor soon. Poincaré did not mind the wait. He took his morning medication, surprised and pleased that it had continued to suppress his arrhythmia. He could not deny feeling stronger, and he would need that strength; for whoever made Dana Chambi run was the person who had hired her double to kill Chloe. Trouble was coming and his body, for once, felt up to the task.

"Welcome!"

He was older than Poincaré by at least fifteen years and reminded him at once of the doctor his parents used to call when he was ill—a man who could improve his spirits simply by sitting at his bedside. Meister was both a physician and a biochemist. He had founded a pharmaceutical firm in the 1970s that, in time, was bought by AstraZeneca. With his millions, he launched a research program that pursued pharmaceutical exotics in rain forests throughout the world. The villa in Garmische served as the institute's administrative center and as a clinic and final refuge for the desperately ill.

Poincaré recounted the bombing in Amsterdam and the discoveries made at the Jet Propulsion Laboratory. He reviewed Randal Young's skill set and explained how the particulars of timing worked against his involvement. "What I can tell you," said Poincaré, "is that many people have vouched for the character of this man, yet certain facts implicate him. Given the timing of his death, I can neither prove a connection nor clear his name."

"You must know," said Meister, who sat opposite Poincaré behind an ornate desk, "the people I see are gravely ill. I don't ask about their lives before arriving because, once diagnosed, my patients tend not to think of themselves as insurance agents or teachers or bankers. They're simply people who want more life, and I do my best to help. Our clinic can do two things. We can restore some order to a patient's body, enabling him to beat the chaos of metastatic cancer—or fight it to a truce. When we can't do that, we try restoring a sense of order to the patient's soul. Randal was of the second sort. I analyzed his blood and knew he wouldn't last long. I told him so. We tried an infusion, but the prospects were not good. Still, he was willing. I must say I was touched by the devotion of his family."

Poincaré cleared his throat. "His sister, Dr. Meister?"

"Yes, his fraternal twin. And his wife."

Poincaré rose. "Dr. Meister, how long could Randal Young have lived after you discharged him?"

"He died within a few days, I understand. At an airport."

"I know that. I mean how long might one live?"

"There's no predicting, Inspector. I've seen a man with end-stage kidney cancer will himself to live until his son flew halfway around the world to his bedside. One observes the phenomenon even among coma patients. So *how long*—there's no objective way of telling. I can say I was a surprised by how rapidly he declined. I thought he'd have a little longer."

Poincaré opened his briefcase and produced photographs of Julie Young, Dana Chambi, and Madeleine Rainier. "These two," said Meister, pointing. "Randal's wife and his sister. Did you know that in the sixteen months prior to his admission, his sister donated a lobe of her liver, bone marrow, a vein in her leg, and a cornea—all in separate surgeries? It's a tremendously affecting story, her devotion. One sees so much pain in my profession. But it's also true that in the months and days leading up to a death, one sees profound acts of love."

The interview with Dr. Meister left Poincaré pensive as he sat on the rail platform in Garmische, waiting for a return train to Scharnitz. For an hour he tried to sleep, and when he finally managed to doze his phone startled him awake. He answered reflexively, a poor choice: for it was Felix Robinson, whose calls Poincaré had been avoiding.

"Henri!"

"Hello, Felix."

"You're a hard one to reach. Where are you?"

"Taking a holiday in the Alps." Poincaré did not put it past Robinson to trace the call. He figured he may as well tell the truth.

"A personal trip?"

"That's right. The weather's fine this time of year."

"Your attendant in Fonroque said you'd be away for awhile. I'll make this brief. You can be on holiday provided you are not acting in your investigative capacity as a field agent."

"Felix, you know I'd never do that."

"If it gets back to me that you're exacting some sort of vigilante justice for your granddaughter, do not make the mistake of thinking you'll find a friend in Lyon. We are investigating that case ourselves. It's a priority for me. But you have *no* role to play. None. I advise you to spend time where you're needed. Home."

"Thank you for that."

"I will not permit a rogue agent to—"

"The line, Felix. There's static on the line. I can't quite—"

He flipped his phone shut and it buzzed again. He was about to kill the power altogether when he saw an incoming message. He flipped open the phone and read this:

```
Insp Poincaré. I'm frightened. Meet me in
Gletsch on morning of Aug 8. D. Chambi.
```

CHAPTER 39

Poincaré understood.

When Madeleine Scott disowned her adoptive parents at the age of eighteen, she began a search that ended eight years later in Pasadena where she found Randal Young, already diagnosed with cancer, living with his wife and two children. Poincaré imagined the reunion: joy in knowing that Randal and she completed each other as only twins can, and despair. She had tried saving him with one part of herself at a time.

Poincaré had now linked Randal Young and his expertise with explosives to James Fenster, through Rainier. Eighteen months before the Amsterdam bombing, Rainier and Fenster were still engaged to be married, which meant that Rainier would have spoken of her brother to her fiancé or introduced them directly. But then she and Fenster split. What monumental betrayal, he wondered, could have prompted her to turn on the man she loved and coax her brother into building a bomb—or, perhaps, teaching her to build one?

Returning to Scharnitz just before sunset, Poincaré approached Pfarrkirche Maria Hilf, hoping Father Ulrich would be available for a franker discussion. Possibly Rainier had avoided Scharnitz altogether, unwilling to meet her brother's adoptive parents. Poincaré would soon find out. When he arrived at the church, he found the lights off and the windows shuttered. He walked to the rear of the building, by the cemetery, and looked in the window of the office where he had found Ulrich the day before. The church was deserted. As Poincaré considered how he might find an address for the priest, who couldn't be far, he noticed a man and a woman kneeling by a grave.

He watched them. The man rose and offered a hand to the woman. They stood for a moment, arms around each other, heads bowed. When they stepped up a path, Poincaré recognized Lewis and Francine Young. He crouched behind a bush and followed their progress out of the cemetery, waiting until they were well out of sight before trying an old iron gate. The valley by this point was deep in shadow, but above there was light enough to find his way. He turned left off the center aisle, aligning himself with the spot where he had stood by the church. He walked several paces more and discovered a fresh bouquet. The stone read: RANDAL YOUNG BELOVED SON, HUSBAND, FATHER.

In Poincaré's experience, one body was not typically buried in two places, whatever the claims on the deceased. Either Young was buried at the Mountain View Cemetery in Pasadena, or he was buried here. If Poincaré were still a field agent, he would have ordered both graves opened; but with his credentials canceled and no time for a request that would be bitterly contested, he sought permission to do a terrible thing from the only court that mattered to him now: his own conscience. He forced the lock of a garden shed, found a shovel, and waited for nightfall.

At the hour when every light in Scharnitz went dark, Poincaré began to dig. The moon was up, providing nearly too much light; for he was certain to be seen in silhouette if anyone approached. But then who walks by a graveyard in a sleepy village in the dead of night?

The work was difficult for all the obvious reasons: his back and legs hurt; and then there was the natural aversion to decomposed flesh. But Poincaré had seen corpses in all manner of decay. The greater trouble was how, the deeper he dug, the less this became the grave of Randal Young and the more it became a grave in a corner of the Montparnasse Cemetery. He dug to ankle level, then to his shins—the work slow and tiring. His clothes were filthy; his hands, blistered. Foot on shovel. Step. Grunt. Scoop. Heave. A hundred times, another hundred. He lost count, but each time his thoughts turned to Chloe, he counted again from zero to clear his mind. *I will find you.* One. Step. Grunt. Scoop. Heave. Two. *You need air and I will find you and give you air. It's only a sleep, my dear. A big sleep. You'll wake, I know it. Wait a little longer.* One. Step. Grunt. Scoop. Heave. Two. Three. Four. *Because how could you die? Not a child.*

The night was still, the mountains spectral in the moonglow. Bats flew, but no ghosts troubled Poincaré save the ones he brought with him. He continued digging, and sooner than he would have guessed, the hole at knee level, the head of the shovel broke what sounded like a ceramic jar. *No casket?* he wondered. He reached into the jar and rubbed grit between his fingers. He grabbed for a handful and switched on a pocket light. Realizing what he had found, he returned what was in his hand to the jar and climbed from the grave. Decency demanded that he fill the hole; so he set to work, an easier job. The top level of sod he had peeled back in sections, and he laid these carefully in place before returning the shovel to the shed. Behind the church, he found a spigot.

With time to spare, Poincaré stood washed and changed on the rail platform in Scharnitz, waiting for the 6:10 to Munich. He would be gone well before Father Ulrich or anyone else could confront him with the desecration of a grave—albeit not a typical interment. For these remains had been charred. Cremated. Lewis and Francine Young had, in fact, stood over the grave of their son.

Poincaré placed a call.

"Paolo."

"Is that you, Henri? Do you know what time it is?"

"Tell me—the evidence bags from the Hotel Ravensplein, the toothbrush and the hair samples I had you throw away by the canal. Madeleine Rainier's. Do you still have them?"

"Of course. We went to our rooms that night, and I circled back to the trash can."

"Do me a favor. Run a DNA analysis on them and fax the results to Annette Günther at the medical examiner's office in Amsterdam. Ask her to compare your results to the ones she took off the remains at the Ambassade—along with the DNA profiles faxed from Boston. And in my notes, you'll find a DNA analysis of some baby teeth from Fenster's apartment. Fax that, too."

"Henri . . . what's all this about?"

In the distance, he could see the headlight of the approaching train. A custodian pushed a cart with mail sacks up the platform and lit a cigarette. A whistle blew. "Paolo," he said. "James Fenster is alive and in grave danger."

CHAPTER 40

Driving the Grimsel Pass is not for the faint of heart. Poincaré geared down at a hairpin curve on an outside lane, the mountain hard to his left, nothing but a rumble strip between him and a thousand-meter free fall to eternity. The Germans have a word for these places: *der Abgrund*. Poincaré knew of no word in any language that quite expressed its mix of terror and fascination. A misstep at the abysm meant certain death; yet one fought an urge to walk the edge, to creep on hands and knees if need be, and stare. This time Poincaré did not stop or stare. He was driving hard, to Gletsch, for a meeting with Dana Chambi.

He traveled a route through mountains well known to Char-lemagne, the Romans before him, and earlier still Paleolithic hunters who tracked game up these glacial valleys and over mountain passes. It was at just such a passage, at the head of the Rhône River and the ancient glacier that fed it, that they would meet. Poincaré knew the place. As a boy standing alongside a quay in Lyon, he once asked his father: "Where does it come from—all the water?" His father pointed east and said, "I'll show you." That weekend they set out, following the river northeast to Geneva and on to Lausanne and Montreux before dipping south to follow the Rhône to Mar-tigny, where the river turned sharply east and north to Oberwald and finally Gletsch.

Gletsch could not properly be called a village. Abandoned in the winter because of deep snows, it consisted of a hotel, a stone chapel, and a few buildings set in a narrow corridor pressed hard against the mountains. He walked with his father to the glacier. To his young eyes the dirty ice had the wrinkled, living skin of an elephant. Peaks with broken teeth rimmed the ice, and clouds scuttled just beyond reach. They rolled their trousers and stuck their feet in the glacier melt and hollered with the cold. "The Rhône," his father said, "starts here, runs to Lyon—past where we were standing—then south to the sea." The young Poincaré could hardly believe it. They ate schnitzel that evening at the hotel, and his father offered him a sip of beer. Cresting the Grimsel Pass, the Rhône valley opening below him, Poincaré recalled these things and remembered what it was like to be happy.

He found her beside the glacier, throwing stones into the chasm. Chambi rose at his approach and said: "I hardly know you, but I think my life depends on you." Over her shoulder, the river roared itself into existence. The sky, like the glacier, was dirty white and the air at that hour snapping cold. She wore a scarf.

"Where is James Fenster?" he said.

"Moving. Like I am."

"You helped stage his death?"

"Yes."

"Quito's after him or Bell. Or both?"

"Quito. It started back in Cambridge."

"He planted you there to spy on Fenster?"

"I'm not proud of that. But yes, Inspector. I sent Eduardo information for a few months. But I couldn't continue. I wrote to tell him, and he grew furious. He threatened me and James. Then Charles Bell started pushing for the same information."

For a moment words failed her. She pulled at her scarf. "James proved that there is a definite, deep connection underlying everything we can see and name. Everything, Inspector. A deep structure to reality itself . . . a mathematical unity across every dynamic system that exists. Storms, the movement of nutrients through cell walls, the wobble of planets in their orbits, the ideas that come out of your head or mine—it's all one system. He proved it. And the only thing Quito could think to do with that knowledge was make money. James *was* modeling the markets—minute-by-minute stock averages for more than fifty years."

That's what was on Fenster's hard drive," Poincaré realized. The raw data.

"It was a small thing for him to find a pattern and predict the price of stocks. The behavior of the markets merely confirmed the larger truth. Quito couldn't see past the money or the advantage it would give the ILF. We really are going to hell."

That may be the case, thought Poincaré; but before he did he needed certain questions answered. "Randal Young," he said. "Madeleine Rainier found him—her brother—and brought him to the Ambassade. He took Fenster's place in the explosion. You snuck him into the room somehow. You were there."

Again, Chambi tugged at her scarf. "Dr. Meister's treatments kept Randal alive long enough for us to move him to Amsterdam. He and I rented a suite at the Ambassade for a week before the explosion, under assumed names. That's where he built the bomb. For safety's sake, I rented another room and stayed several blocks away. Two days before the explosion, I checked us out of the hotel and left; Randal moved to James's room. Before bringing him to Europe, Madeleine took Randal to James's apartment in Cambridge after it had been cleaned. She stayed outside while he left prints and DNA. James slept in hotels after that and hacked the dental clinic's computers to swap Randal's x-rays for his own. After the explosion, Madeleine had the remains cremated and sent to Randal's parents."

"His adoptive parents."

"That's right."

"Then who posed as Randal Young at JFK? Who *died* there, Ms. Chambi?"

She was stricken. "You've got to understand we didn't want any of this," she said. "We were put into a situation. . . . The man was another patient at the clinic, Ricardo Goren. He and Randal became friends and reached an understanding. They were both dying and wanted some good to come of it. In exchange for taking Randal's identity, Ricardo secured his family's future. He was twenty-eight, with three daughters. James used his equations and computers to anticipate movements in the market and within a few days generated a great deal of money. We had documents forged and Ricardo, posing as Randal, returned to the States with Julie. He was in such pain from pancreatic cancer that he said swallowing pills in the airport would be a relief. The man was too obviously sick for the authorities to have bothered with an autopsy. They took Julie's word for the cause of death, and she had his remains cremated and returned to Ricardo's family in Vienna."

"Two bodies. Two false IDs," said Poincaré. He turned toward the glacier and recalled how, as a child, he had watched the sun play with the mist above the chasm, creating rainbows that shifted like curtains in the breeze. There was no sun this morning, only ice and stone. "Someone or something got buried in California," he said. "I saw a certificate."

"Mostly sand," said Chambi. "To weigh down the casket. Also a skiing medal and a photo."

"His wife paid off the funeral director?"

Chambi closed her eyes.

"Dr. Fenster retired Julie Young's mortgage, I suppose."

"And then some, yes."

Chambi squared herself to him, and Poincaré once more saw the person who held the attention of a packed lecture hall at Harvard. "Julie Young has needs," she said. "Her children will be able to attend college now. She'll have a home. She'll have food, a new life. This was never about wealth, Inspector—James's or anyone's. Listen carefully. The whole idea of the deception was Randal's. James was willing to face Quito alone, but Randal and Madeleine talked him out of it because he's no fighter. Anything but—if you only knew him!" Her voice broke. "What he discovered had to be protected. Madeleine had found Randal by then and explained what was happening to James, how something large and beautiful was being threatened. You have to understand about James and his gifts. It felt like we were rescuing Newton or Galileo, Inspector. He *had* to be saved. When Julie agreed, James agreed. Randal and Julie both wanted something positive to come of his death."

"All of you . . . did this for him." He had never heard of such a sacrifice.

"Too much was at stake. James never wanted to hurt anyone. Randal technically committed suicide, which would have voided his life insurance. James wouldn't defraud the insurance company and insisted Randal cancel the policy. In Amsterdam, he sent an anonymous gift to the insurers who paid for the renovation of the hotel. And because the city spent time and money cleaning up the site, some months later an anonymous donor underwrote the cost of canal maintenance for years. James believed in making people whole. He wouldn't let anyone lose—except himself. There would be no James Fenster after Amsterdam."

From what Poincaré knew, the man was never much in the world to begin with. "People could have been hurt in that bombing," he said.

"Randal knew exactly what he was doing," she said. "Madeleine knocked on every door in that section of the hotel to make sure everyone was out. We knew the blast would be going up, not down or sideways. After three days of checking, when she finally called to tell him *all* clear, he walked to the sink and detonated the bomb."

Poincaré recalled Annette Günther poking at what was left of the torso with a telescoping wand: *Notice the splinters of porcelain on the front, not the sides, of the victim. This man didn't know what was coming, Henri. Otherwise, he would have turned. He didn't suffer.*

"Quito's rage," said Chambi, "was like a storm. He was determined to use James's work to make billions for the ILF and finance indigenous reclamation projects around the world. Indigenous schools. Industry. Elder care. Then he was going to convert all the ILF money to gold and publish James's equations. What do you suppose would happen when brokers in New York and Hong Kong realized they could make 5,000 percent returns on their investments in a week? Money would be worthless, Inspector. It was Eduardo's dream to punish the West by collapsing its monetary system—and he was gifted enough to know exactly how to do it. When James realized why Eduardo had sought him out—the real reason for their collaboration—he broke it off. That's when Eduardo found me. Harvard had already accepted my application as a doctoral student in mathematics—but with another professor. Eduardo offered to pay my way if I would switch to James as my advisor. I was to report back on any work that might touch on the financial markets.

"After a few months, after I got to know him, I couldn't betray James any longer. A week after I quit, my car was burned. James received threatening calls—people saying they'd kill him. He couldn't go to the authorities with his discovery. The equation was too dangerous because, in the wrong hands, it *could* be used to generate destabilizing wealth. Some agency would have buried his work on national security grounds, and what James discovered—his breakthrough, his gorgeous insight—would have been lost. For my protection, he wouldn't even show the equation to *me*.

"A month after the bombing, Quito visited Cambridge and insisted that no one could havve wanted James Fenster dead. He claimed the assassination was faked and that James was alive. He demanded the equation. I told him he was crazy, but my reaction gave it away. He swore he'd find James himself—and crush anyone who tried to stop him. I got scared and ran. That's when he must have hired the woman who looked like me and sent her to the hospital. . . . I am so sorry, Inspector."

"A name," said Poincaré. "Who was she?"

"I don't *know*. They painted a stain on her neck to look like mine. Eduardo wanted us both out of the way so he could pursue James without any problems."

He could have killed me in Québec, thought Poincaré. Quito must have considered it. An Interpol agent killed on assignment, in a riot started by the Indigenous Liberation Front? *No*, Poincaré reasoned. The man was smarter than that.

"Inspector, he knew that if every police department in the world was hunting me I'd disappear, because if I were caught I'd have to tell someone that James was alive—and he would find out that way. So I disappeared. And you needed to go away, too. He said something about your never quitting, how you could make problems for him. So he had your granddaughter killed. He wanted to crush both of us. Two birds, one stone—it's how Eduardo thinks.

"He was a good man once," she said. "He did good things for the Indigene. But something happened, Inspector. He got tired of fighting. He got tired of seeing the winners always win."

CHAPTER 41

A light rain had begun to fall, and they left the glacier to sit in a stone chapel by the river, in the valley. "Help me to understand," he said to Chambi. "I want to know what Dr. Fenster saw."

She sat facing a rough altar, lost in contemplation. Her scarf had shifted, exposing the port-wine stain across her neck. "It would be a relief," she told him. "If you're going to help James, you deserve that much. What do you know about computational research?"

Poincaré shook his head. He had never heard the term.

"It's a method of doing science by beginning with data," said Chambi, "not with hypotheses and experiments that generate data. James worked with the raw numbers of Nature—with tens of millions of temperature readings, for example. Weather is a good case, because it's complex enough to produce unexpected behavior. It turns out that millions of similarly complex systems interact around us and in us at every moment. Each of these systems can become violently unstable. You've heard of the butterfly effect, how a puff of air in the Amazon can cause tornadoes in North America? No one can predict which puff, but in theory it can happen in any complex system."

"Chaos," said Poincaré.

"Exactly. Computational researchers write programs with certain rules like addition and subtraction and calculus. Then they set their computers loose on the data of Nature—say, the movements of glaciers or populations of salmons."

"Fenster's hard drive," said Poincaré. "That was nothing but data. Millions of numbers."

"Stock prices, Inspector. Quito and Bell were right. James was studying the markets, among other systems. Given the Dow Jones Averages over decades, or the data from other systems, he would calculate backwards to a simple equation that, if operated forward millions of times, could generate similar data. The computer generates candidate equations, which we test rigorously with new data. Most equations fail under stressing; but every so often we find one that begins to look like a fundamental law that took scientists centuries to discover through experimentation. None of this was possible before computers.

"Other researchers studied data sets according to their interests—maybe cardiac rhythms or the spread of cholera. James was interested in everything he saw. He did not stick to one field or set of complex systems. That was the first difference between him and the others. I believe you saw his apartment—the photographs?"

"I did," said Poincaré.

"His photos were the visible evidence of the mathematics underlying each of the systems he studied. In programming his computers, he assumed that lightning bolts looked like the ridge line of mountains because they *are* alike—mathematically. This was the second difference between James and the others. He investigated similarities, whereas others looked for differences. Once his computer program was in place, he studied data of all sorts: wind flow, elk migrations, mating patterns of dung beetles, war dead. What he found was monumental—or would have been, had he published. Every data set of every system he ever studied, thousands of them, reduced to a variant of a *single* equation. He could not find a disconfirming example. He discovered a law, Inspector—and Quito and Bell wanted to keep that to themselves and exploit it."

"How?" said Poincaré. "They would have needed to predict the markets. Is that remotely possible?"

"It's an easy problem," said Chambi, "given James's approach. He fed his computers current market data and ran the equation repeatedly—faster than real time. The equation held."

Poincaré was confused. "You told me he investigated systems in Nature. Stock values are not in Nature. The global financial markets are not in Nature—not like the meadow outside this chapel. Not like this." He plucked a weed growing from a crack in the window well.

"I can explain," said Chambi. "Are you in Nature, Inspector, like the meadow? Like this weed?"

"I am."

"And would you agree there are thousands of complex systems operating in your body this very moment, systems that will continue to operate until you die? Insulin regulation, digestion, blood pressure? And would you agree that systems will be in place after you die to break down your flesh and bones?"

"Yes," he said. "I know this is true."

"Well, then. James took this understanding a step further and showed how humans, both individually and in groups, are complex systems. That's to say, you, Inspector, are as complex as a storm, and the outputs of your life, just as the outputs of a storm, can be recorded and analyzed. A storm generates measureable rainfall and wind. We humans generate language, wars, economies, art, social welfare systems. The products of our hands and minds are *in* Nature every bit as much as the rain, Inspector Poincaré. James studied the distribution of notes in Mahler's Ninth Symphony and the behavior of the Dow Jones Average and found they were indistinguishable, at a deep level, from temperature variations in a low pressure system over the eastern United States. The equation he discovered enabled him to make predictions about stocks with the same degree of certainty you'd expect from a forecaster predicting how hot it will be tomorrow. The markets behaved like every other system he studied."

Is it possible, Poincaré wondered. He pointed to a floorboard. "That ant," he said. "If I made a grid and mapped the ant's movements—"

"I know what you're thinking, and the answer is *yes*. Assuming you run the data through James's program, the map of the ant's movements would look a great deal like a map of the stock market or any other complex system. *Which* system doesn't matter because order and disorder are operating in all of them. It's the tension between order and disorder that matters, the *dance*, as James called it. On a good day, the system is orderly, and we can make reasonably accurate predictions. But there's no predicting what will tip a system into chaos—or when. Quito tried to tip your life into chaos by ordering the death of your granddaughter. That was a hammerblow, not a puff.

"When Eduardo and I first met, he told me that one day fifty years ago he decided to leave his alpaca herd—something his parents instructed him never to do—and walk to the village for candy. He turned a corner and saw his father begging so their family could eat. The puff, Inspector, was not the trauma of seeing his father beg but the harmless decision of an eight-year-old who thinks the herd is fine, the village is only a kilometer away, and he'd like something sweet. That started the chain that led to Quito's ordering your granddaughter killed a half-century later. Avalanches begin the same way, with a puff—the tiniest hint of a change, nothing consequential in its own right. But the system is tipped and madness reigns. Prediction becomes impossible. In time, the system resets and order is restored."

"Not my system," said Poincaré. "Not yet. Not ever."

"I am so sorry for your pain, Inspector. From inside a system in chaos, you can't know what the new order will look like or when it will come. But in time, disorder *will* yield to order. It always does. The new, ordered state will differ from the previous one. Sometimes, it may even be adaptive as in the case of evolution. A new, more resilient species can emerge from chaotic episodes."

Poincaré heard this and something savage in him rose. "There's a man sitting in The Hague who hired assassins to destroy my family! Before that he massacred half a village. You're calling his rampages *adaptive?*"

"I'm saying it's possible. I'm saying there was a puff in this man's life just as there was in Quito's. That excuses nothing. But any complex system, including any one of us or any group of us, can be turned to madness. There was a shirt factory fire in New York in the early 1900s, and nearly 150 people burned to death. That localized chaos could not have been worse for the victims or their families. But laws protecting workers followed. Nothing like that happened again. The system state changed between employees and employers."

The past months had cast him into the very pit of blackness. But if Chambi was right, that pit had a false bottom. One could fall further, to indifference. "Are you saying there's no forward motion without destruction?"

"Who knows if the motion is even forward, Inspector. The beauty James saw is a terrible beauty. His equation is neutral on the death of the workers in the factory. Neutral on the death of your granddaughter. The equation is neither moral nor immoral, I'm afraid. These are human categories, not Nature's."

He turned away and more to himself than to Chambi said: "I don't know a soul who'd willingly choose such a world."

She rose from the bench. "Don't you see, it's beside the point whether you would choose it or not because this *is* our world, which happens to be held together by a rule. At first, I thought the news would change everything. We wouldn't have to talk about *believing* anymore. There would be no more religion without evidence. No more debate about Jesus or Buddha, who merely saw what James did without the mathematics. This is replicable science, Inspector, and it could have marked a new direction in the human story, a fresh start because no sane person could regard James's work and still think the Universe random.

"Do you recall my student's question in the class you attended? The inference was correct: if there are rules, there must be a rule maker. I can draw no other conclusion. Believe me, I've tried resisting it, and I have colleagues who insist that complex systems order themselves. But my colleagues have no concept . . . they have no language to explain how all systems could spontaneously create the *same* order, could arise from a *single* equation. It was James's shattering insight. It changes everything. But the world isn't nearly ready. . . ."

When she stopped, he listened to the rain and to the wind. He looked across the valley to the mountains, where water bound up in ice for millennia leapt from the glacier with a roar. Downstream there would be farms and barge traffic, cities and people. Here the world was simpler, though hardly simple. In the line where the mountains met the sky he saw a boundary as jagged and cruelly beautiful as his own life. The world ended at that jagged line. *Ended.* Where was Chloe? He wanted her back. He wanted Claire to whisper his name.

He said: "When Fenster dies—when he dies for real—what becomes of his work?"

"There's a box in Zurich with instructions," said Chambi.

"Could Quito do this himself—what Bell's trying to do: pay others to discover the equation? What are the chances of another scientist replicating Fenster's achievement?"

Chambi laughed bitterly. "It would be like your great-grandfather at the height of his powers competing with children in a math contest. It will be centuries before someone replicates James's work—at which point, unless people are a great deal better than they are now, we really will be talking about the End Times. The Quitos and Bells will tear each other apart grasping for money and power. James's insight even allows for this, for humans destroying themselves. It would be as natural as my niece choosing to skip, not walk, down the street. James's equation is indifferent as to whether we do or do not survive as a species."

"And this is how your Rule Maker provides, Ms. Chambi?"

She adjusted her scarf. "James saw God. He never claimed God cared."

Poincaré was silent for a time. Even if he lacked the knowledge to understand all she said, he had seen enough to know it was true. In two hundred years, he would not be around to stop the machinations of a future Eduardo Quito. He could stop this one, however, both for James Fenster's sake and his own. He could, at least one more time, for one more dance, be an instrument of order. "We'll end this," he said.

"How?"

A career distilled to a single act. He spoke without thinking, certain of what must come. "You and I will meet on the morning of August 15th," he said. "In Amsterdam. You will have a life again. The equation will be safe, and James Fenster can finally live in peace with Madeleine Rainier. He deserves that. I suppose they've married by this point."

She looked at him, bewildered.

"What?" he said.

"I thought you knew, Inspector. James is Madeleine's older brother."

CHAPTER 42

August 15th. The Lord's Day.

The thousands who gathered in Dam Square for the 11:38 AM arrival of Christ milled about in the carnival of a lifetime. Poincaré arrived just after sunrise to a sea of tents and sleeping bags, and—no surprise—to a maximum security zone. One at a time, both those who came to be Raptured and those looking for lunchtime entertainment passed through metal detectors, then chemical residue detectors. Random body searches followed; all bags were x-rayed. When Poincaré's turn came, he identified himself as an Interpol agent. He placed a brown paper bag on a table and declared his weapon, a 9mm Beretta wrapped in its holster. Because he could provide no credentials, having returned those to Felix Robinson three weeks earlier, he expected what followed: the officer at the checkpoint confiscated the weapon and detained him.

"Gisele De Vries," said Poincaré, as he was being cuffed to a metal bar in a van.

"What did you say?"

"Lieutenant De Vries will vouch for me. I've lost my credentials. I'm here on assignment. She and I worked together earlier this year at the World Trade Organization meetings. Call her."

"The lieutenant is in charge of security for Dam Square, today," said the young man. "Wait here." Poincaré knew this, having devoted the week to preparing for his encounter with Charles Bell and Eduardo Quito. Aside from studying maps of Dam Square and surrounding buildings, he scoured the Dutch National Police database for details of the security arrangements for August 15th. He assumed De Vries would be involved since she had worked the WTO meetings; he thanked his good fortune that she would be directing the show. Perhaps the buffalo nickel was changing his luck after all.

When the officer left to find her, Poincaré figured he might as well get used to the view from inside the police van, given his plans for that morning. He sat on a metal bench within metal walls; metal fencing bolted from the outside covered a ventilation hole. *Austere*, he thought, like Peter Roy's office. If it came to that, he would contact Roy for legal advice. Minutes later, the door swung wide and De Vries, looking surprised, said: "Release this man and return his weapon. . . . Inspector Poincaré, why are you here? You should have called ahead for clearance. I apologize."

As planned. Rubbing his wrists where the cuffs had pinched him, he said: "I only just determined that I had to come. I'm still on the Fenster case . . . and have reason to believe the Soldiers of Rapture who were involved in that bombing will be in Dam Square today."

"The bombers—*here?*" The alarm was real. "At all costs we're working to avoid violence. Who can understand these people? According to their own logic, there should be no trouble today of all days."

"Well, then," he said. "It would seem we're partners once more."

That Poincaré was using her distressed him. But the morning was all about crossing inviolable lines, and this one in the scheme of things was minor. He followed her into the command center and spun a fiction about losing his credentials, ending with details of the supposed threat. She issued a badge that he clipped to his jacket. "My people will leave you alone," she said. "Good luck."

Why not, he thought. *For once.*

Already, vendors selling breakfast fare were hard at work, and the smell of fried dough and sausages was pleasant on this fine morning in high summer. The pilgrims who had camped in the square were soon packed and tending to the serious business of Rapture. Some had set up portable baptismal fonts—kiddie wading pools filled with water from public spigots. Many were dressed in tailored white robes, some in improvised bed sheets. One man called to Poincaré: "Brother! Come for holy water and a chance at Eternity!" One splash would cost five euros. In front of the De Bijenkorf department store, a competing Baptist was selling salvation at twice the cost, claiming her water came from Lourdes. A girls' chorus sang hymns before the Royal Palace. The bells of the cathedral rang. He saw jugglers and street musicians and vendors selling shades to protect people's eyes from the Lord's fiery descent. Poincaré declined invitations to have his portrait painted alongside a radiant likeness of Christ. Only ten euros. Like anxious tourists searching for a lost watch, some Rapturians walked the square on their knees in a final show of humility. *Come one, come all*, thought Poincaré: the penitent and the huckster, the policeman and the pickpocket—and, in time, the financier and the killer. The sun around which this chaos lurched was an enormous digital clock counting down the minutes and seconds to Redemption: 5:12:13. 5:12:12. 5:12:11.

"Hallelujah! Hallelujah Halleluuuujah!" a man in a business suit shouted. Poincaré declined his offer to clasp hands and wait for Glory. Having made several tours of the square, he walked to the northwest corner, where he would meet Quito and Bell. Snaring them had been easy. Poincaré contacted Eric Hurley in Cambridge and asked that he call Charles Bell with a proposition. Given that public servants in the city were underpaid and that he, Hurley, was set to retire on a less than adequate pension, funds contributed to a policeman's benevolent association might go a long way to securing a certain hard drive. Hurley wired himself for the occasion. When a large sum was transferred to the charity in question, he arranged a second meeting and passed Bell a note: *Dam Square, August 15th, 11:00 AM. Corner of Royal Palace and Nieuwe Kerk*. As for Quito, Dana Chambi merely sent an e-mail in which she expressed exhaustion and regret: *I can't run anymore. I have what you need. You were right. Our cause means everything.* Same date, same place. 11:30.

According to close readings of Scripture, the Rapture would occur at 11:38, local time, around the world. That is, it was to be a rolling Rapture that would not inconvenience people in Los Angeles by asking them to stay awake until 2:38 on the morning of the 15th. For reasons Poincaré never understood, Christ was to appear first in the Central European Time Zone, which meant that those in a band extending from Riksgransen in Swedish Lapland all the way to Lubango in southern Angola would have the honor of standing first in line for Redemption. He was not surprised to learn that travel agencies in every time zone outside CET had arranged special Rapture packages to ferry the especially fervent into what they were calling the "first tier" Rapture—on the theoretical possibility that the sky would fill and there would be no spots left at Christ's right hand. Deluxe packages included hotels, meals, linen robes, airport transfers, and bronze name tags to be worn around the neck. Inevitably, protesters gathered to advertise their causes in the event the world and its troubles survived until the 16th. Poincaré read signs denouncing the occupation of Tibet and the junta in Myanmar. Pro-choice activists shouting slogans competed with soapbox prophets decrying everything from the diminished nutrient value of irradiated foods to the U.S. invasion of Afghanistan. A child tethered to her mother wore a sign that read: "God doesn't fix the World. We do!"

The media caught it all: the penitents, the vendors selling Stroopwafels and herring, the orderly queues at the portable toilets, the singers and the dance troupes, the baptismal pools. Major networks sent reporters and cameramen into the crush, their images projected onto large screens above the platforms that rimmed the square. Several of the faithful who granted interviews showed off what they called "bloodied knees for Christ" and declared how good it would be to meet their Maker. On the news platforms, anchors carefully balanced the opinions of fundamentalists who took time out of their preparations for Rapture with the views of secular experts who tried, as one put it, "to situate this hysteria in its proper historical context." In a word, Dam Square was the circus Poincaré hoped it would be.

At 10:38, the Countdown Clock at 01:00:00, a robed woman climbed the largest of the platforms and stood at a lectern flanked by enormous speakers, below the De Bijenkorf sign. "Sisters and Brothers in Christ," she began, her voice silencing all competitors. "Let us be comforted in this hour by the words of Paul to the Corinthians:

> Behold, I tell you a mystery: We shall not all sleep, but we shall all be changed—in a moment, in the twinkling of an eye, at the last trumpet. For the trumpet will sound,

and the dead will be raised incorruptible, and we shall be changed. For this corruptible must put on incorruption, and this mortal *must* put on immortality.

Thousands turned as if obeying a summons. The woman's voice had the quality of one's earliest church service, when what flowed from the pulpit to young ears was the voice of Heaven itself. She worked the scale of human possibility, and one hardly needed to understand the words to know that Doom and Salvation hung in the balance. Up until this point, the mood had been festive. When she began, however, Poincaré felt a change as if, in unison, the multitude recalled the seriousness of the moment. Believers bowed their heads. The equivocal, hedging bets, maintained a respectful silence. Even those determined to sneer and watch the supposed end of the world come and go looked on with something approaching dread. For if the woman's call to Rapture were true, where, exactly, would they and all their cynicism be then?

The speaker moved on to Acts 2:38: "Peter said to them 'Repent, and let every one of you be baptized in the name of Jesus Christ for the remission of sins, and you shall receive the gift of the Holy Spirit.'"

Chambi arrived on schedule. She turned a corner at Mozes en Aaronstraat and met Poincaré by the Royal Palace, beside the cathedral.

"Are you ready?" he asked.

"For Charles, yes. He's a bully and he's greedy. But he's no Eduardo. I don't think he'd actually hurt anyone—even though he makes so much noise."

A man holding a camera interrupted them. "Would you mind? My wife and I want proof we were here when the world ended." He pointed to a shopping bag filled with hats and gloves. "Just in case we don't get called to the sky and have to deal with next winter!"

Poincaré snapped the picture. A teenager on a unicycle, juggling bowling pins, wheeled by. "All you need to do is what we rehearsed," said Poincaré. "Walk off, across the square—there." He pointed to the far side of the Royal Palace. "I'll be standing here, and Bell will approach. When you see us talking, cross the square and stand at my side. He will be surprised. I will say something to him in your presence. If he responds as I expect, you'll never hear from Charles Bell again. Then it will be Quito's turn. He'll find you, where I'm standing now. Then I'll join you, and you will walk away. I'll handle the rest."

"What do you mean *handle the rest*?"

"The problem will go away, Ms. Chambi."

"How?"

"Trust me."

"I do, but I'm scared."

"Good. People without fear tend to die, and I don't expect to die today. I'm quite sure you won't."

"You mean you're scared, too?"

"Let's say that I'm alert, Ms. Chambi."

"But Quito. He's—"

"I know *exactly* what Quito is. You'll do what we rehearsed. I'll take care of him. Now get to your position." Poincaré checked his watch. "We've got a few minutes. Why don't you try one of those Stroopwafels. They're very good."

"But my stomach—" She started off to find a vendor then paused, looking back over her shoulder. "Are you baptized, Inspector?" A clown with orange hair and a red putty nose walked by, banging a drum and singing *The Lord's day, the Lord's day, elders weep while children play*. Poincaré smelled madness in the air, desperation posing as devotion. From the platform, the woman's voice rose: *If you abide in Me, and My words abide in you. . . .*

He smiled, shaking his head. "My wife's been trying for decades."

"I think I'll buy some holy water from that man over there," she said. "A little sprinkle couldn't hurt."

"I thought you were a scientist," he laughed.

"I'm a good Catholic *and* a good scientist, Inspector. I never understood why people call it a contradiction. The water's for you!" She adjusted her scarf. "Did I dress properly for the end of the world?"

CHAPTER 43

Poincaré knew that whatever was about to come, despite his careful planning, would unfold according to its own logic, not his. This did not keep him from shifting his left foot to verify, for a third time, that he stood directly on an **X** taped to a cobblestone earlier that morning in the presence of Paolo Ludovici. "Do you see me?" he whispered.

He looked to the east end of the square, past the Dutch National Monument to the top floor of the Hotel Krasnapolsky, where the sun glinted off an open window. Ludovici was in place. "You're directly on spot, Henri. I can count the number of whiskers you missed shaving this morning." The voice came through a tiny earpiece. "Shall I shoot them off for you?"

"Maybe next time, Paolo."

"Gisele looks to be running a good operation, don't you think? I've been watching through the scope."

"She knows you're up there. It's all fine."

Charles Bell was late. Poincaré looked about the square for him and noted that the security presence, both uniformed and plainclothes, was substantial—though not so strong, he supposed, to prevent him from executing Eduardo Quito. To do that, someone would have to be monitoring him at every moment through a scope—someone like Ludovici. He recalled Felix Robinson's warning. *Paolo?* he wondered. *Not possible.* But, in fact, it *was* possible that Robinson had ordered Ludovici to shadow Poincaré and prevent whatever he was about to do in the name of vigilante justice. But not Paolo. He had agreed to this last favor—just his sort of favor, working outside the rules. Still, the square was teeming with security any one of whom, seen or not, could be monitoring Poincaré. A complication, then. He had not planned for it, but there was nothing to be done. He felt Ludovici's scope on him.

Charles Bell arrived with 00:18:14 showing on the clock. "I should have figured you for a dirty cop," he said, entering the square through the Eggertstraat checkpoint. "Fine French accent, same old shit. I paid my money, now give me the hard drive."

"You look tired," said Poincaré.

"Go to hell."

Poincaré checked the clock. "You know, before the hour is out I actually may. You were right to be worried, Charles—about losing your advantage if a competitor got hold of Fenster's work." Poincaré carried no briefcase and showed no obvious bulge in his jacket. No envelope for Bell. "Just so you know, the hard drive is in the state's evidence locker in Massachusetts. Hurley set you up, I'm afraid. I believe you Americans call this a sting."

"You sonuvabitch. I paid a quarter-million—"

Bell stepped closer, and Poincaré held up his hand.

"Don't." By this point Chambi should have been at his side. Poincaré did not risk turning away from Bell, and Bell showed no sign of recognizing anyone in the square behind him. "Two hundred meters away, in that building over there—you can see the open window—I have a friend with a rifle and a scope. He will put a bullet behind your ear if you touch me."

Where's Chambi?

"*I* don't have to touch you," Bell snarled. "But someone else may. The world can be a dangerous place for people like you and that fat-assed Hurley."

"No, you won't hire anyone either," said Poincaré, reaching into his jacket and producing a digital recorder. "Technology is a wonderful thing, Charles. The deal you made with Hurley is captured on videotape. Here's the audio portion." Poincaré clicked a button.

> *You're telling me that if I pay the money, you can get the hard drive?*
>
> *That's right. But you wouldn't be paying me, Mr. Bell. We'll be less direct than that. The money would go to the Police Benevolent Association of Massachusetts. That way it's philanthropy, not a bribe.*

Ha! And tax deductible! I love it.

A little money now, a show of good faith—what we discussed on the phone. I hope you brought an envelope. . . . Very good. Let's see . . . the full ten thousand's here. We're in business. I'll wait for the rest by wire transfer.

The ten comes out of that.

Sorry. The ten's a handling fee. Agreed? When you wire the funds, I'll have your information.

"You bastard, Poincaré!"

"It gets better, Charles. Listen. This came from your second meeting."

Well done, Mr. Bell. The association thanks you. And here's my card of appreciation. You'll find instructions that involve a bit of travel, but I think you'll be pleased.

Government should always be this efficient. See you around.

No, Mr. Bell. You won't.

"Here's how this will work," said Poincaré. As Bell listened to the audio, Poincaré chanced looking around quickly for Chambi. He saw no sign of her. "I will give you some information, which you can choose to believe or not. And then you will remain silent. If you contact me or Dana Chambi or Eric Hurley in any way, precautions are in place that would deliver this tape—and there are many copies—to the federal prosecutor in Massachusetts. If our comfort is disturbed in any way, if you send anyone to knock on our door, the prosecutor gets the tape. If any of us happens to die prematurely, the prosecutor gets the tape—so, in fact, you'd do well to pray for our continued good health and happiness. But cheer up, Charles. I wouldn't leave you emptyhanded."

The ever-confident Bell was ashen-faced. He was also a quarter-million poorer, though Poincaré figured he could afford many times that as a contribution to the policeman's fund. "I've been around long enough to know bad people when I see them," said Poincaré. "Charles, you don't have it in you to be truly bad. You're merely repulsive, and you're completely out of your league. Here's my information for you. First, I've established that you did not kill James Fenster. If it's worth anything to you, you are now off my list of suspects. Second, as you suspected, Dr. Fenster was researching patterns in the stock market. I found evidence that he was studying trading patterns, but whatever he knew died with him. I am certain no other competing fund acquired his techniques, so you will retain whatever advantage you currently have. If you fight Harvard for the hard drive and win the case, you will find a sixty-seven character password that is impossible to crack. I've been assured that not even government computers can unravel this. So it's a fool's errand. Do yourself a favor and give it up."

Poincaré handed him the digital recorder. "Now, I think, would be a good time to leave. You're lucky enough to own even a fragment of Fenster's work. Your business is flourishing. You're wealthy. So stop this, Charles. Go live your life. It would give me no pleasure to ruin you, but I will. Now I've got to go."

The clock read 00:14:12.

CHAPTER 44

As Bell walked away, Poincaré wheeled around, scanning the crowd for Dana Chambi. He had asked her to walk just thirty meters off; but between his spot and hers hundreds of people stood fixed in their places, watching the Countdown Clock and waiting for the zero moment.

He sensed movement in the crowd, and he saw her, panicked—a prisoner. Quito had Chambi by the arm. He looked directly at Poincaré and pointed at him, as if in warning. Then he pointed to a backpack unattended on the cobblestones and yelled: "Bomb!"

In the screaming and scrambling that followed, Poincaré lost them. Security personnel tackled three robed men and a woman standing near the pack. "It's mine!" yelled one of them, his face pressed to the stones. "There's no bomb! I took it through security!"

Poincaré yelled into his lapel. "Paolo!"

"They're moving toward the monument, Henri. Quito's half-dragging her. She's not happy."

He took off in a dead sprint but a uniformed policeman, a much younger man who saw him fleeing the location of the backpack, tackled him from behind. "Down! Now!" first in Dutch, then English.

Poincaré twisted from his grasp and held up his security badge. "No time," he gasped. "No time!" Which was true, for if Quito dragged Chambi beyond Ludovici's line of sight and beyond a security checkpoint, Poincaré would lose them.

"Henri, to the right of the monument, approaching the hotel."

Poincaré was up, his chest a wheezing bellows. He knocked people aside. He stumbled across folding chairs. Penitents grabbed at him. A man shouted: "Stop! Repent!" But he did not stop and, far from repenting, he was determined to kill. Circling the monument, he yelled: "Paolo—where!" The clock read 00:02:12.

"To your right, Henri! Right! I'm losing my angle!"

Poincaré looked and leapt in a single motion, tackling them both before Quito had seen him. "Run!" he called to Chambi, his hands at Quito's throat.

She scrambled away on her knees.

"*You!*" Quito roared, the words half-choked.

The man's strength was immense. He lifted Poincaré directly off his chest, then flailed his arms. He caught Poincaré's cheek with a fingernail; he gouged his eyes. Poincaré lost his grip and staggered back, drawing a gun. People screamed as the voice on the platform rose with a last promise of Redemption: *If you abide in My word . . .*

The clock read 00:01:03.

You are My disciples indeed.

Quito lay on his back gasping as Poincaré aimed. "She was a *child!*"

The instant before he pulled the trigger, the gun jumped from his hand and he heard a pop. The force of the bullet rocked him backwards into a wading pool. He was hit, his hand on fire, the water turning red. He looked right and left but saw no shooter. All eyes, now, were on the clock as the numbers slipped towards Doom. *Enough*, he groaned as he lay in the water, staring at the sky. He saw no chariot, no fire. No Savior.

At the zero moment, the voice boomed: WE COMMEND OUR LIVES TO YOUR CARE!

Nothing in this world, not even a shooting, could distract the assembled from their appointment with Eternity. As thousands looked up, Poincaré heard a second shot and a third and fourth. Clutching his wrist, soaking wet, he stumbled to his knees to find Eduardo Quito dead on the cobblestones, three red stains on his chest. Chambi stood over him trembling as his gun dropped from her hand. Seconds later, Ludovici was at his side—having stopped first to retrieve the gun and slip it into his pocket. "Henri, goddamnit, you're a civilian. If I let you kill him, it would have been murder."

Poincaré stared. "You?"

"Who else is going to protect you from yourself, you fool? I should have put a bullet through that thick skull of yours."

"Robinson sent you?"

Ludovici nodded.

"You were working with *me*." He was soaking wet and felt a chill coming on.

"Well, I'd hoped not to have to say anything. Felix was worried for your health as much as I was. I told him that I'd be here watching your back. He's a better man than I thought. Look, we were worried about what you were going to do, and we agreed that you should not be the shooter. I can assure you Quito was not leaving the square."

"You were prepared to—"

"I was prepared to intercept a known terrorist, whatever that required. As it happened, events outpaced us and I only had to shoot you. I'm sorry for that; but really, after thirty years you should have known the agency would never sanction this. And don't think it's about saving you from prosecution. Felix didn't want the bad press. . . ." Ludovici pulled a handkerchief from his pocket. "Here, wrap your hand."

The president of the Indigenous Liberation Army lay as he fell, eyes open, legs bent at an angle that would have hurt were he still breathing. Chambi had not moved. Hundreds now formed a broad circle around them and watched in silence, for something had happened below while all their attention was trained above. Poincaré tightened the linen at his wound.

Accompanied by two officers, De Vries broke through the circle just as the voice from the platform, with more urgency, called: OH LORD, TAKE US!

Nothing happened.

Now, LORD! *Now!*

But it was the wrong formula or the wrong date, and the digital clock in the window of De Bijenkorf's blinked 11:39. Someone from the crowd yelled at the podium: "Phony! Go home!" A vendor near the monument called: "Waffles! Stroopwafels!" Poincaré heard sirens in the distance.

Ludovici said: "Well, everyone. It appears we've got ourselves a body."

"Only one," said De Vries. "Which I can tell you is a relief. Is this Eduardo Quito? He was the one who shouted *bomb*. There was no bomb. The backpack was a backpack. Who shot him?"

"I can tell you who *wanted* to shoot him," said Ludovici, pointing to Poincaré. "But he didn't get the chance because I shot him first. I don't know who killed Quito. I used a small caliber bullet, which won't match what you find in the victim. Here—for your ballistics team." Ludovici handed her his rifle as a pair of police vehicles pulled up to the Hotel Krasnapolsky, lights flashing. De Vries and her officers left to meet them.

"Don't go anywhere," she said.

"I can promise he won't," said Ludovici. "And I want that gun back." When she left, he pointed toward the monument. Poincaré turned, and not ten meters away he saw Madeleine Rainier standing beside a slender man her same height, his back turned, his hair a halo of blond curls. *The child in the photos . . .*

With a halting wave, Rainier mouthed the words: *Thank you.*

"I picked them up in the scope," said Ludovici, offering a quick assessment. "Imagine my surprise on seeing Rainier—wanted in connection with the death of a man who's still alive. So I can cancel out her Interpol notice—she was never charged with a crime, in any event. And as it happens, yesterday the border police in Portugal detained the woman they thought was Dana Chambi. At the hospital she made the mistake of cutting herself when she sliced Chloe's respirator. The DNA match was perfect and she made a full confession about her role and Quito's, so *this* Dana Chambi is no longer a person of interest. I can also remove her from the Interpol listing. Henri, Gisele will return with the others very soon, and you and I had better decide what happened here. Quito did not shoot himself."

Poincaré nodded.

"Here's what I see," said Ludovici. "I see the body of the man who ordered your granddaughter killed. I have a strong suspicion that the bullets in his chest were fired from a gun that will never be found." He patted his pocket. "So Gisele's forensics investigation will turn up very little. I, personally, didn't see who shot Quito because I was running down the stairs of the hotel to check on you. And all our potential witnesses were looking at the sky at the moment of the shooting. No one saw a thing, Henri. For all we know, the shooter is long gone. We'll make our inquiries, of course. Gisele and I will interview a few people, but I don't anticipate detaining anyone. That's what I see." Ludovici crossed his arms. "What do you see?"

Poincaré looked across Quito's body to the circle of disappointed penitents. At the monument, Rainier was leaning against the man beside her. Poincaré motioned to her, and she crossed the circle. With his good hand, he emptied his pockets. Coins fell to the cobble stones and he dropped to his knees, searching.

"Dr. Fenster?" he said. "Your brother?"

Rainier nodded.

Swaying from pain, Poincaré found what he was looking for. "Take this. You both deserve better luck . . . a new life. Tell him I'm sorry. . . . I'm sorry we're not ready."

She accepted the buffalo nickel, smeared with Poincaré's blood, and said nothing. But she spoke in her way, as she had at the Ambassade with those gray, almond eyes. *Do you understand*, she asked him. *Do you understand the good you've done?* Behind the glasses, the right lens thicker to correct for the cornea she had given her brother Marcus, Poincaré saw gratitude. De Vries was returning and would recognize her. Rainier left him.

"Here's what I see," said Poincaré, still on his knees. "A man died. I agree that in all this confusion we would be unlikely to find the shooter. The papers will report that a known terrorist was killed. There will be an investigation, and we'll all go home." He would not have said it a lifetime ago, in April, but the world had changed.

"Are you sure?" asked Ludovici.

Dana Chambi crossed the circle to stand by Madeleine Rainier, who placed an arm around her. Poincaré looked once more at Fenster—at his back and at the young woman who finished what he had not. What he saw was a family of two who had once been five, a cup no longer full because life, and death, had intervened. Yet someone new had entered their circle, and their reunion was that much sweeter. He watched the three of them dissolve into the crowd, and he longed for a reunion of his own.

"Yes," said Poincaré. "I'm sure."

Afterword

O what authority gives
Existence its surprise?

— W. H. Auden

O_n August 16th, the sun rose over a world no more or less redeemed than it ever was. That Poincaré knew, Jesus had not called the faithful to His side in the sky; but then many believed the Lord would appear only to deserving hearts who could see, without trumpets or fanfare, that the time was at hand—and, in fact, had always been at hand. For them, the Rapture was to be a poetical rising of the spirit; and though their bodies remained in Glasgow or Bangalore or Amsterdam, they would walk with one foot in Paradise and see what others did not: that their God was everywhere, hiding in plain sight, present simply for the asking. And those who could not see? They were condemned to living as they always had: in what some called Hell, this work in progress we call the world.

Poincaré's medical leave delayed the necessity of deciding on his future at Interpol. The damage to his hand had been considerable and the surgery, extensive. His main business at the farmhouse was to heal and, for a few months, forget about algorithms and the Soldiers of Rapture—who, in their disappointment, had stopped murdering innocents just as the profilers had predicted. Even they, with their tortured logic, allowed that murder had not hastened His arrival. For the most part talk of the End Times receded and, with it, the appearance of robed prophets calling on sinners to get right with the Lord. As if a switch had flipped, the psychopaths who set bombs for Christ found other outlets for their demons. Gradually, a more predictable mayhem took hold.

Summer yielded to autumn rains that prepared the fields for another year's bounty, and Poincaré tended his wife with patience and a gentle hand. He fed and bathed her. He smoothed her hair and, daily, invited her return. And though Claire continued to say nothing and for many more weeks closed her eyes to him, she did return.

It happened this way.

Poincaré's finances were in ruins. Etienne and his family were well enough to resume their lives in Paris, but the hospital bills generated by their prolonged care in a private clinic and the continuing fees of consulting physicians had wiped clean Poincaré's savings and virtually all his equity in the farm. On a Tuesday in mid-October, he traveled to Lyon to visit with his banker and renegotiate the mortgage, again.

"You have no case to make," said the woman reviewing the papers.

"I have my good name," he answered.

"Monsieur, we're looking for more tangible collateral."

"Of course. How about this?" He had taken up Serge's habit of spinning that monstrosity of a silver ring in times of stress. The lung cancer had finally claimed Laurent, who got his wish and died in one piece—albeit a considerably diminished piece—buried beside his first wife on a hillside in Bordeaux. He willed Poincaré the ring along with a considerable wine cellar as a grand, final joke. In honor of Serge, Poincaré met the banker head-on. "Reduce the loan-to-equity ratio to three percent," he said. "You'll own ninety-seven percent of a prosperous vineyard. You know, the almanacs are predicting an excellent vintage next year. And apparently, having let my crop rot on the vine this season prepares the soil for an excellent harvest in the future."

"We deal in present value, Monsieur Poincaré. We don't want your wine."

Doesn't anyone? he wondered. "Alright, then. Let's refinance to five percent, and I'll figure something out."

There was not much to figure. He had only his salary left from a job he might quit. The bank president, a former neighbor in Lyon, asked that he step into his office: "Henri," he said, "we can refinance a final time—to six percent equity at market rates for forty years. But if you default again, we'll sell the property. You're a good soul and your difficulties have been, well, epic. But there are limits to—"

"I appreciate your position," he said, rising to excuse himself. "Please draw up the papers."

After a long and uncomfortable return trip to Fonroque, his arm still in a sling, he turned up the gravel drive to the farmhouse and saw smoke rising from the chimney. A car was parked in the drive, and he did not recognize the plates. He walked to the front door, ajar slightly—which annoyed him because heating costs had soared of late, and he had made a point of conserving. But then, through the open door, he heard a sound that lifted him just as surely as Ludovici's bullet in Dam Square had laid him down. Laughter. He nudged the door open and saw Georges and Émile dodging before a blindfolded Claire. Georges ran and spun, and while Poincaré could plainly see the child wore a prosthetic leg, it did not seem to slow him or otherwise reduce his pleasure at grazing Claire's skirts and pushing his brother forward.

"You go this time," he said to Émile.

"No! It's *your* turn." At both ears, Émile wore hearing aids.

So Georges edged toward his grandmother, blindfolded as in their old game, and Poincaré watched as she extended her fingers to feel the child's face. She pulled him onto her lap and kissed his cheeks and then inhaled the scent of him. "Ah," she said. "You are delicious, Monsieur Strawberry! I require two hugs and a kiss on the tip of my nose."

Georges squealed: "I'm your *cream*, Mamie! Émile's your strawberries!"

Claire removed her blindfold and pulled the children close. Notwithstanding their months in the hospital, the boys had grown. Both angled onto a lap that was now too small to accommodate a pair of healthy seven-year-olds. Poincaré pushed the door further ajar, and when she noticed the movement and saw him across the room, actually saw her husband for the first time in a half-year, Poincaré prayed she would accept the penitent standing before her. No words passed between them. The clock on the mantle ticked. Ticked. Ticked. To the children she said: "Émile, Georges. I feel a draft. Please close the door."

They turned and they were on him.

"My hand, watch my hand!" he cried as the young life tumbled over Poincaré to shouts of *Papi! Papi!*

Stipo Banović, convicted of crimes against humanity, managed to hang himself in his cell the morning after his verdict was read, despite a suicide watch. Felix Robinson called with the news. "Finally, this business with Banović is over, Henri." And so it was. If Poincaré faced threats again in his life, they would not come from this man who, so brutalized, had himself turned brute. When Poincaré heard what had happened, he turned in silence to his own family, occupied with the little motions that constitute a life: Claire was finishing *Les Misérables*; Etienne, who had approached him one day and said *I'll try . . . if you help*, was building a moon colony with the boys, using every pot in the kitchen; Lucille was practicing her viola. Peaceful days passed. Late one afternoon, he was sorting mail and opened a letter postmarked Cambridge, Massachusetts.

Henri,

I hope this finds you well. I have received new correspondence from Madeleine Rainier—who, I am relieved to learn, is no longer a fugitive from justice. Miss Rainier has come into some money, quite a lot. She has opened an unrestricted account in your name at the Bank of Geneva with 12 million euros. French taxes have been paid on the original amount of 19 million, so the money is yours *in toto*. She asked that I send along the paperwork and relay the following message: "One buffalo nickel, redeemed in full. Thank you, MR—and, by the way, my father sends his regards."

I look forward to our correspondence, Henri.

Yours sincerely,

Peter Roy

Life, thought Poincaré, *is so very strange*. He neither jumped for joy nor called Claire into the room to pronounce their money troubles over. She knew nothing of them in any event, having only just returned from a fearful journey. Poincaré reread the letter and walked to the terrace, where he looked across the vineyards to the hills winking in the sunset. He thought of Banović and of a ravine in Bosnia; he thought of Eduardo Quito and of a man who drank whiskey for breakfast, mourning a wife dead and a daughter lost; he thought of these rolling hills, of grape arbors and trees in winter and of the cold, cobalt sky; and he thought of Claire, when she finally spoke his name. Each its own, each a facet of the jewel James Fenster had discovered but kept, with good reason, from an undeserving world. It was enough for Poincaré to acknowledge that at every instant he no less than the mighty oak on this terrace was branching and reaching. He returned to the house, to his desk, and wrote two letters, the first to a physician in Boston:

> My dear Dr. Beck,
>
> After careful consideration, I have elected not to have the surgery you recommended. My heart, such as it is, will have to do. Thank you for wise counsel just the same.
>
> Yours,
> Henri Poincaré

The second letter he addressed to Peter Roy.

> My friend,
>
> You have delivered extraordinary news. There is much to discuss, and perhaps we'll do so soon, in person. But foremost in my mind is this: I ask that you establish and become administrator of a Trust account for the benefit of a certain widow and her two children. I enclose their present address in The Hague and ask that my name never be associated with their care. The widow is to receive a monthly stipend of 8,000 euros for her family's maintenance. All expenses for the education of her children through to university are to

be paid directly by the Trust, with application made to you or to your agent in The Hague. Payment of her monthly stipend is to continue throughout her life. Thank you in advance for discretion.

Yours,

HP

He sealed the envelopes and set them on the corner of the table. Hearing a first call to dinner, he squared the blotter on his desk and dusted a picture frame, which held three images: two, from Fenster's apartment, via the collection Jorge Silva had managed to save; one that his doctor had presented after surgery.

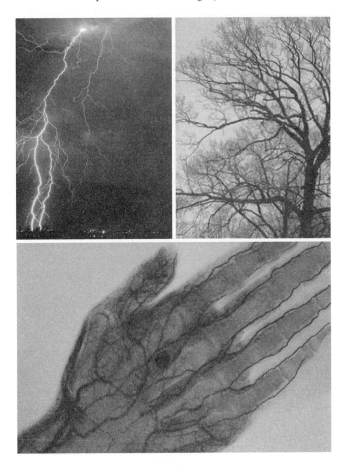

Poincaré would have preferred straight lines. He would have chosen love without loss and goodness without pain. But then no one asked for his opinion when the foundations of the earth were laid. What Jules Henri had glimpsed and Fenster proved settled everything and nothing in ways that moved him to tremble at the sweep of wind through tall grass and the cry of a child in the night for his sister. For he, too, had seen the Aurora, both above and below; and he, too, had named the dance from which this world springs into being at every instant. He once thought retirement would bring an end to the words *why* and *who* and *where*—words that had served him well over a long career. But this could never be. Indeed, his investigations had just begun.

Henri Poincaré rose and adjusted his sling. His hand ached, and he knew that the strength he was regaining would not restore the strength he once had. He thought of Chloe and choked back a sob. From the kitchen, laughter rose like music through a house of mourning, breaking a spell that had settled for too, too long.

Etienne leaned into the room. "Papa, dinner."

"Yes," said the father to his boy.

Poincaré closed his eyes; when he opened them, Etienne was still there.

ll

CREDITS

TEXT

Opening epigraph. Rami Shapiro, translation of Psalm 29. Used by permission.

Parts I–IV epigraphs. Job 38: 17, 19, 25, 36. NIV. Matthew 24:24, Revelation 14: 6–11, Isaiah 65: 21–24: Scripture taken from the HOLY BIBLE, NEW INTERNATIONAL VERSION®, as presented on biblegateway.com. Copyright © 1973, 1978, 1984 Biblica. Used by permission of Zondervan. All rights reserved. The "NIV" and "New International Version" trademarks are registered in the United States Patent and Trademark Office by Biblica.

Afterword epigraph. W. H. Auden, Preface to "The Sea and the Mirror." In *Collected Poems*. New York: Modern Library-Random House, 2007. 403.

Mark 13: 24–27. Scripture taken from the NEW AMERICAN STANDARD BIBLE®, as presented on biblegateway.com. Copyright © 1960,1962,1963,1968,1971,1972,1973,1975,1977,1995 by The Lockman Foundation. Used by permission.

1 Corinthians 15: 51–53, Acts 2:38, John 15:7, John 8:31. Scripture taken from the New King James Version, Bible, as presented on biblegateway.com. Copyright © 1982 by Thomas Nelson, Inc. Used by permission. All rights reserved.

Hotel Paris (Las Vegas). "A convergence of elegance and energy . . ." Online ad copy.

Jules Henri Poincaré. "Mathematics is the art . . ." *The Future of Mathematics*.

Text on ammonium perchlorate and explosives. By Graham Orr. Used by permission.

Thornton Wilder. "Money is like manure . . ." *The Matchmaker: A Farce in Four Acts*.

IMAGES

Lightning, negative image. © Stasys Eidiejus - Fotolia.com

Epitaxial growth. Image courtesy of F. Gutheim, H. Müller-Krumbhaar, E. Brener; IFF, Forschungszentrum Jülich, Germany.

Christchurch, New Zealand. NASA. "Image of the Day Gallery." http://www.nasa.gov/multimedia/imagegallery/image_feature_678.html

Bacterial growth, Petri dish. Fig 1(d) in the paper "Cooperative strategies in formation of complex bacterial patterns," by E. Ben-Jacob, O. Shochet, I. Cohen, A. Tenenbaum, A. Cziruk, and T. Vicsek, in the journal *Fractals*, 3 (1995), 849–868.

Maidenhair fern. Image courtesy of George Yatskievych, Missouri Botanical Garden.

Fern. Image courtesy of Henry Domke, Nature Art for Healthcare. http://www.henrydomke.com/

"Stiff" fern and "Schizoid" fern. By Lon Kirschner, Kirschner Caroff Design, Inc.

Mathematically generated fern and accompanying equation. Image courtesy of Larry Bradley.

France [maps]. Stella Maris, "Cartes vectorielles." http://www.stellamaris-edu.net/cartotheque/europe/france/france.htm

France [maps]. "Communes of Metropolitan France." Godefroy. Wikipedia Creative Commons License. http://creativecommons.org/licenses/by-sa/3.0/

Metal alloy (Al-Mg-Mn) crystal grains and equation. Created by Slinky Puppet on 20th Dec 2005 for use in Recrystallization (metallurgical) article. Wikipedia Creative Commons License. http://creativecommons.org/licenses/by-sa/3.0/

Cracked sidewalk: Courtesy of Kari Cates.

Electrocardiograms. Reprinted from *The Lancet* 347.9011, A. L. Goldberger, "Non-linear dynamics for clinicians: chaos theory, fractals, and complexity at the bedside." (11 May 1996): 1312–1314, with permission from Elsevier.

Leaf. Progressive Gardens: Knowledge tree/plant physiology. www.ProgressiveGardens.com

Québec [map]. By Lon Kirschner, Kirschner Caroff Design, Inc.

Lightning over Tucson, AZ. Fotolia/valdezrl.

Tree branches. Author photograph.

Hand with arteries. Courtesy of Ashley Davidoff, MD [Image altered to show darkened circle].